I0741081

LELAND
Jimmy Sutton's Summer

—

a novel

Gene Warner

BoysMind Books

Grand Haven, Michigan USA

The locations of this story are real. However, the story is purely fictional. Except for certain well-known historical facts, the events and persons appearing in this novel are purely fictitious. Any resemblance to actual events, or real people, living or dead, is unintended and entirely coincidental.

Published in the United States by

BoysMind Books
www.boysmindbooks.com

Book Description: Leland is a tale about ordinary people living amidst the extraordinary beauty of the storied National Lakeshore; about the not-so-good side of good people, and the good side of the not-so-good; about the young and the old, and how they become enmeshed in circumstances that conspire to destroy the beauty in their lives and the character of their personal histories.

Publishers Cataloging in Publication Data
Warner, Gene L.

 Leland – Jimmy Sutton's Summer
 First Edition – September 2011 (Rev Sept 2017)
   5 7 9 0 8 6 4
 p. cm.
 ISBN: 978-0-9797896-5-6
 1. Leland, Michigan - Fiction. 2. Lake Michigan - Fiction. 3. Manitou Islands - Fiction

F813.W376   2011   FIC043000
PS229-231   FIC025000
LCCN: 2011915929   FIC030000

Author Website Address: www.boysmindbooks.com
Cover Photo: Andrea ("*Andee*") Tate

For
"Little Willie"
... an erstwhile spirit

LELAND
Jimmy Sutton's Summer

1

Leland was a summer place. From Memorial Day to Labor Day it was a good-time town, thriving with activity from first light to midnight. It was dead now, but all sorts of people would be in town then; old timers who'd come up to their family's summer place ever since they were kids, and who would pass it on to their children just as it had been passed on to them; scouts and religious youth groups headed for adventures on the Manitou Islands; the yuppies and beautiful people aiming to create storied weekends they'd be able to embellish and brag about back at the office; artists, wannabe artists and aficionados who came to what they considered to be an art colony in hopes of picking up some pseudo-credentials and the latest art-speak; and just the curious who came to find out why everyone else came.

Now, in mid-April, Leland seemed nearly deserted, almost like a ghost town. There were people here, of course, because people lived here all year around. But they were rarely seen on the street. Off season, there usually wasn't much going on, and not much available by way of goods and services. If you lived in Leland and needed something, you had to drive to Traverse City to get it. The main street was actually a highway, state road M-22. But there wasn't any through traffic to speak of because it really didn't go anywhere.

Going north, M-22 went up to the tip of the Leelanau Peninsula, around to Northport, then back down to Suttons Bay and Traverse City. Northport was also mostly another summer place, so there wasn't any reason for anyone to be going up there, and if you wanted to go to Suttons Bay or Traverse, that was the long way. Going the opposite direction, M-22 went south to Glen Arbor and Empire; more out-of-the-way summer places. So, the only traffic on Leland's main street was the very occasional indigenous Lelander heading out to, or returning from, a trip to Traverse.

Yet there was something about the deathly pre-season quiet that Jimmy liked. His grandfather, now going on seventy-one, was one of those old farts who'd been coming up to the family's summer place every summer since he was a boy. Gramps was also rich, having climbed the corporate ladder to CEO, and then elected Chairman of the Board before ultimately being put out to pasture as *emeritus*. But he still had affairs to attend to now and then in Leland; "the Foundation," he called it. Jimmy didn't know exactly what that meant, but enjoyed coming along for the ride and wandering around the deserted town while Gramps attended to whatever it was that he needed to attend to.

People in town generally knew him, or at least knew who he was. He was *Lee Smith's grandson* to most of them, and for most of them, that's all they needed to know about him, or cared to know. It was enough for a wave or a nod, and sometimes even a "Hello, Jimmy. Your grandpa in town again?" All this worked to cultivate his fourteen-year-old imagination, producing a feeling of belonging and being somebody.

Back home in Indianapolis, he was just another kid ... a *divorcee kid* at that ... and his grandpa was just another corporate *wheel.* Nothing special in either case.

On these quick weekend business trips with Grandpa Smith, they flew from Indy to Traverse City in the corporate jet, driving up to Leland in a Hertz rent-a-car. He'd usually get to play co-pilot for a while after leaving the Indianapolis area and before contacting the Traverse City air traffic controller, and he liked to notice how people, especially other kids, looked at him as he stepped down from the sleek white jet and walked across the tarmac to the transient aircraft terminal at the Cherry Capital Airport, being pretty sure they were enviously wondering who he was.

Since he had turned twelve, when the weather was good, which it usually was, and the traffic was light between Suttons Bay and Leland, which it almost always was during the off season, Gramps usually let him do the driving, with an agreement that neither would ever tell anyone else about it, especially not his mother, who was Lee Smith's daughter and only child. With that in mind, Gramps would usually let him choose what sort of vehicle they'd get from Hertz, so by now, at fourteen, he'd driven just about everything with four wheels that Hertz in Traverse City had to offer.

All this was also a great ego-booster.

His mother was quite aware of the positive influence her son's relationship with his grandfather had, and was therefore always eager to have him go. Besides, it gave her a free weekend, with space to do whatever she might wish to do. She was still young and attractive, and rarely wanted for opportunities.

Jimmy was the result of too much fun during her first year at college, and her hurriedly arranged marriage hadn't lasted long enough for him to ever come to know his father, or at least, his father of record. The divorce had been uncontested. Needing no financial support, and daunted by the prospect of a paternity test, the unusual decree included no ongoing financial obligations, and the college boy whom she had married had disappeared, never to be heard from again. By virtue of that, Jimmy had figured out that the name on his birth certificate was probably not his real father, and after that he never had any more interest in knowing anything about his mother's ex-husband. Nor was he ever curious about whom his real father might have been.

For her part, *Julie,* as he called his mother, had never done anything to cultivate or encourage such an interest. Unlike many young divorcees, she accepted her complicity in the unhappy affair, and never engaged in blaming or male-bashing. Between her and her son, it was what it was. She never pretended that he was anything other than an accident, but a *happy accident,* as she always put it, who was loved deeply and unconditionally in spite of the somewhat dubious circumstances of his birth. As a result, he accepted the family he had, in which he and Julie were more like partners than mother and son. He also understood that his young mother still had a life, with a right to have friends of her own, and without every male companion needing to feel that he was being sized up as a prospective father figure. With this in mind, he was happy to spend some weekends away with Grandpa, thus giving her some space.

* * *

2

"We'll be meeting over at Jerry's office again. I'll be over there most all afternoon; probably 'til dinner time."

"Okay, Grandpa."

"What will you be doing then ... all afternoon?"

"Nothing. I'll just hang out around here. Maybe at the marina, or maybe I'll go down to the docks and see if the Robinson's are doing anything down there. Else I'll go back to the cottage and do something."

"So, you'll be at the cottage by six, then? Maybe we'll go over to Joe's in Empire for dinner?"

"Yes, that'll be good."

With that, they parted company for the rest of the afternoon. Jimmy decided to head down the River Street hill and see if anything was going on at *Fishtown*.

The park guys were there, with their little boat on a trailer, apparently getting ready to put it in the water for the first time this season. The boss man acted cool and aloof, as usual, pointedly ignoring him as he approached. The others followed suit, leaving him standing there, totally ignored, as if he was invisible, or irrelevant. Jimmy understood. Harley, the head Marine Division ranger, was never nice, and he'd never seen any evidence that he was liked by anyone. On the contrary, he'd sometimes caught Harley's men flashing expressions of exasperation and feigned insubordination behind their boss' back; sneakily sending friendlier little signals that said, 'don't worry about him boy – we all know he's a jerk.'

The Marine Division was close to being a joke anyway, at least around the docks in Leland. The little boat, the "M.V. Burton," was a smallish 28-foot Munson aluminum crew boat; twenty-five years old. It looked like a small, tinny cabin cruiser which might have been intended for conservation officers, or maybe marine construction foremen. It wasn't big enough for anything other than transporting a few passengers, or a little light express freight, like mail or groceries. So, they next bought the barge, otherwise known as the "Nahma." It too was a light-duty aluminum affair, but built like a little landing craft with a blunt bow that dropped down to provide an easy-on, easy-off ramp. The Nahma, was a 34-foot Munson *Packman LC,* and was actually capable of carrying some freight – something as big as a pickup truck, for example. But most of the time it was out of commission. Harley was the one who had picked her out after the Park Service finally acknowledged that the Burton was a mistake, but he didn't know much about how to keep its fuel-injected Volvo diesels working. So, most of the time they didn't.

Harley wasn't really very imaginative, but he was practical. The barge didn't really ever have a name. It came used from the Upper Peninsula's Big Bay De Noc, having been owned by Nahma Township until they decided they didn't need it and shouldn't have afforded it. When the park received it, it had "Nahma Township" hand-painted on its stern, proudly done at some point by a professional sign painter. Harley finally had to resort to methylene chloride to remove the "Township" part, which also

6

took off all the gray paint right down to shiny bare aluminum. But with a little careful touch-up work with a spray can of gray primer, the boat became the "Nahma." That meant *salmon* in Ojibwa, so was a rather dumb name for the barge. But nobody knew that anyway or, at least, Harley figured that few would know.

Since nobody ever seemed to have anything good to say about Harley, Jimmy wondered how come they never fired him. But Gramps just said, "It's the park service ... it's a government outfit. Competence is optional." He wasn't sure what that meant, but it sounded like something everyone else probably understood, so not wanting to appear dumb, he just accepted it as an answer with a slightly vague "Oh," and an affirming nod.

Being deliberately ignored as usual by the park men, he twisted his mouth to the right, thought to himself, "Yeah, government!" and moved on towards the ferry dock.

The *Keche-Chéemann* was there, and the *Ningwis*. An old Panasonic canister vacuum cleaner lay in the middle of the narrow dock, with a long orange heavy-duty extension cord running all the way back up to the gift shack, and its flexible hose draped over the side of the Ningwis. So, something was no doubt going on, and he fully expected to find the Robinsons working on their smaller boat. But as he stepped over the vacuum cleaner, he still couldn't see anyone aboard.

The Ningwis was an open boat, except for the cabin under its forward deck, and bending down to have a look, he didn't see anyone up front. He therefore guessed they must be aboard the big boat, and stepped over the open gangway, and on-board the Keche-Chéemann. But there didn't appear to be anyone aboard her either; not on the forward deck, the aft or topside passenger areas, or in the pilot house up top.

Going back down to the main deck, he jumped off onto the dock, and then boarded the Ningwis, thinking again that they must be working in her forward cabin.

Both boats had blue, silver and white Busch beer cans all over the place; not really as litter, but more like someone was intentionally accumulating a collection, maybe to show how many six-packs it would take to get the boats readied for another visitor season. There were a lot more of them on the Ningwis, than on the bigger boat.

The Robinsons ran the boats as a ferry service to North and South Manitou islands, which were part of the Sleeping Bear Dunes National Park ... actually a *National Lakeshore.* The smaller boat, the Ningwis, usually made the shorter run to North Manitou, transporting back-country campers and their equipment. The bigger Keche-Chéemann took day-trippers and campground campers to South Manitou and back. Both boats were ancient, each having provided over a half-century of service here and there. But they were still both seaworthy and reliable.

The Robinsons had always had the ferry service concession, simply because nobody else ever bid on it when it came up for renewal every ten years. Besides, the Robinson family had run boats back and forth between Leland and the islands for as long as anyone could remember, which was long before the park came. They were mainly connected to North Manitou. The connection to South Manitou had always been from the dock at Glen Haven on Sleeping Bear Bay, a seven-mile trip. From Leland to South it was a seventeen-mile trip. But after most of the South Manitou islanders had left to seek an easier life on the mainland, the only transportation available was the Coast Guard boat, and opportunities to make the crossing with them arose only when they had some official reason to go to Glen Haven, and then they'd take only passengers. Anyone who had any freight to haul – personal effects, farm equipment, supplies, livestock, or whatever – was usually obliged to call Rollie Robinson. After even the Coast Guard left South Manitou, Rollie's boat became the only alternative, and he became the connection between both islands and the mainland.

Rollie's real name was Rolland Redstone Robinson. It was easy to tell those who really knew him from those who didn't. The former pronounced his name as *Rahl-lund*; those who really didn't always mispronounced it as *Rho-land*. He was not a religious man. At his funeral the borrowed minister disingenuously claimed "Although he was not a religious man, before his passing I came to know *Rho-land* very well." and, of course, the funeral-goers understood that he really hadn't known him at all.

Rollie was of British ancestry, which was slightly unusual, because most of the Manitou Passage people were German or Scandinavian. But they were the more recent immigrants. The Robinsons' namesake in America came over more than a century before them, and somewhere along the line one of the ancestors, a fur trader at Redstone Old Fort on the Monongahela River, had taken up with an Iroquois Indian squaw. Honoring that aspect of their American ancestry, every Robinson male born since then had been given the middle name *Redstone,* the name of the squaw's father, who was supposedly an important Indian chief.

The Robinsons had originally been North Manitou islanders, having come as wood choppers working for the Pickard brothers towards the end of the steamboat era. The Pickards were in the business of providing steamboats with four-foot cord wood to fuel their boilers. After the wooding station's business petered out, the Robinsons moved over to the mainland and took up farming east of Leland.

But Rollie wasn't cut out for farming. He got himself a boat and made a living carrying passengers and freight to the north island. Back in the day, some wealthy families and their rich friends from Chicago came and turned the east side of the island into their own luxury summer resort. They weren't averse to spending money, so he was able to make a go of it providing transportation and delivery services for them, as well as the few farmers and fishermen left on North Manitou. That era was followed by even better times when a war profiteering tycoon bought up most of the island, using it as his own personal retreat and game preserve, and Rollie was easily able to make good money carrying Mr. Angell's freight and friends back and forth during the summer seasons. That enabled him to buy a succession of bigger and better boats; ultimately ending up with the one he named *Ningwis,* which was Ojibwa for 'My Son.'

When Rollie finally died, his son Clayton Redstone Robinson took over. His close acquaintances all called him *Clancy,* for reasons nobody could remember. He was a man of few words; the quiet type, but was very well liked and respected. He was liked and respected because everyone knew that he was honest and reliable. He always ran a regular schedule and, in cases of emergency, neither high winds nor dirty water would prevent his answering a call to help someone in need.

About the time that the Angell syndicate was winding down, the government came. The National Park Service didn't get its hands on North Manitou right away, because old man Angell had died, and his interests had been taken over by a foundation. The Angell Foundation spent a few years haggling with the government, hoping to get top dollar for the land it held in trust on North Manitou, which included most of the island.

After the government finally took over, the Park Service surprised most locals by deciding that North Manitou would be treated as *wilderness*, which at first seemed like the end of Clancy's career, since *wilderness* in the NPS vernacular generally meant *no traces of human habitation*. But eventually the government was forced to relent, permitting back-country camping on North, which meant that someone would have to provide regular ferry service to carry the backpackers back and forth. Clancy wasn't up to handling the bureaucratic details of working with the federal government, but his loyal friends in Leland came to his support, and helped him win the original ten-year concessionaire contract.

Meanwhile, the Park Service had also acquired most of South Manitou Island and, once again being forced to bow to public pressure, decided to compromise the integrity of that island's wilderness designation by setting up three campgrounds and providing for day-use visitation. That's when Clancy, again with the help of his friends and neighbors in Leland, got the big boat. She was actually an old Mackinaw Island passenger ferry from the straits that had been decommissioned by Arnold Transit. But she was still serviceable, and plenty good enough for service to South Manitou. Having a thing for Indian names, but not that much imagination, he named her the *Keche-Chéemann,* which in Ojibwa, as he understood it, meant 'the big boat.'

By then Clancy's son, Jacob Redstone Robinson, had come of age, so they operated as partners, with Clancy usually making the runs to North in his old boat, and Jake running the Keche-Chéemann to South.

Jimmy figured that if the Park Service was to see these beer cans all over the place, some eyebrows would be raised. The Park Service was always really big on political correctness. But, in fact, the Robinsons weren't on the Park Service's dime at the moment. Their contract involved only the five months between the middle of May and the middle of October. Outside that season, they were quite within their rights to do as they pleased.

Jake Robinson was not *his father's son,* as it were. While nobody ever had a bad word for Clancy, they weren't so generous with their feelings about his only son. He, and Jake's sisters, all older, had spoiled the boy. As a child, he became known to most as spoiled, impudent, and annoying, but he was tolerated out of regard for, and deference to, his respected father. After he'd grown up, he seemed to have the idea that pleasantness was an option. He was nice when he felt like it, which was perhaps somewhat less than half the time. He was otherwise surly, snippy, and occasionally, when irritated by some little thing, became quite rude.

He was not a big man, so many jokingly attributed his neurotic behavior to *short man syndrome.* Not long after Clancy retired and Jake took over the business, he began wearing a khaki uniform

12

with a Captain's cap while on duty, which only served to reinforce that diagnosis. The Keche-Chéemann was not so bad looking as old passenger ferries go, but other than that, she was a slow and inefficient old tub that hardly justified having a uniformed Captain at the helm. When run by one of the younger Robinsons, the uniform-of-the-day was usually, weather permitting, Bermuda shorts, a company tee shirt, and summer sandals or flip-flops.

The Robinsons were evidently all quite loyal to their favorite brand of beer. Surveying all the empties, Jimmy wondered whether it was *they* or *he*; whether this collection accumulated over the winter months from one guy's offseason consumption of the brew, which his grandma sometimes disgustedly called *horse pee*, or just one or two days with the boys working together down here. At any rate, there were nothing other than Busch cans all over the place, and they were all empties.

He absently picked one up and, pivoting his wrist back and forth, lightly shook it. Well, not quite all empty; at least not that one – and the can was cool, so maybe not too stale, he thought. With nobody apparently watching, he decided to have a little taste of its remaining contents.

"Yuck! ... Pthew!"

Along with the remaining ounce or so of beer came a cigarette butt and ashes.

"Hahahah! What a stupid ass!"

His shoulders tightened and his back straightened as he unexpectedly discovered that he wasn't alone. He could feel the blood rushing away from his face, and the hair prickling up on the back of his neck.

"What the hell 'ya doin' on my boat boy!" the voice behind him demanded.

"… and what's yer grampa gonna say, 'ya goddamned little thief, when I tell 'em you were down here sneaking other peoples' beer and getting yourself all schnockered up."

Jimmy didn't turn around. He couldn't. He just stood there wondering who it was, afraid if he turned around the fear would show, and he might start crying. He knew he shouldn't have boarded the vacant boats. And probably they really did think he'd been drinking their beer, although he hadn't seen anything but empties.

The voice didn't sound like any of the Robinsons. Maybe it was the Harbor Master. No; he wouldn't be on duty this early in the season. Maybe it was the Leelanau County Sheriff or one of his deputies. Yes, they knew his grandfather that well. He felt like he was in trouble. There was also a feeling of urgency in his loins, like maybe he was going to pee, and he tried tightening up to keep that further embarrassment from happening.

"Oh, turn around you little shit-head. It's only me."

Slowly turning, head still bowed but with eyes peering up from under his eyebrows, *only me* turned out to be Eddie Gunderson, the Indian fishermen's hired boy. Their work boat, a crudely homemade steel thing that looked more like a long, narrow scow with a plywood fore cabin, was docked on the river just a way up from the shanty where fresh fish and smoked chubs were sold; a boat or two ahead of the Keche-Chéemann. He'd probably been back there and saw him wandering around atop the big boat.

He didn't really know Eddie Gunderson, because he was older; about eighteen he thought. He knew who he was because he'd seen him around. But Eddie wasn't his type. Working with his dad and the others on the fish tug, Eddie was muscular and, by the time summer arrived, was always darkly tanned. He really didn't have any Indian in him, but by mid-summer, by virtue of his buff build and deeply tanned skin, he sure looked like he did. And most people thought he probably did, because of the fact that he and his dad worked with the Indian fishermen on their boat.

He was also handsome in an unusual way, with facial features that gave just a hint of some savage background. It was mainly his eyes; a little narrower than most – somewhat like the Mongols or Eskimos. Gramps said that was because he was really Scandinavian, to which he also attributed the older boy's enthusiasm about sex and his attractiveness to females. Gramps had muttered something about Eddie having *hot pants* and something else about ancient times when the Scandinavian's were all seagoing rapists, especially the damned Norwegians.

That much was apparently a fact; Eddie Gunderson had shown great prowess with females from the time he passed through puberty – females of all ages! Even when he was Jimmy's age, only fourteen, Eddie hung around the docks all summer, flirting, and probably more, with girls who were usually in their late teens and early twenties, but sometimes even older. He had an ability to wrap them around his little finger, which seemed quite uncanny, but also comical. In a weaker moment, Gramps once muttered disgustedly and under his breath that one day that boy was going to get his tied in a knot.

That was another thing Jimmy didn't have in common with the older boy. He had never been confident about girls. It wasn't because of his looks. He wasn't the angular, dark and handsome type like Eddie, but he wasn't unattractive either. He was slim, trim and cute, but cute in a way that preteens and adults find pleasing; not girls his age. In their case, his problem was that he was also a nice boy; polite and well-behaved to the extent that most girls found him uncomfortable to be with, and not very interesting.

From his grandpa's attitude towards Eddie Gunderson and Eddie's father, he understood that Gramps didn't approve of the Gundersons, so he had always avoided him. That wasn't difficult, since it seemed like Eddie Gunderson had no interest in him either. He assumed that Eddie probably thought he was just another one of the little snots that came up to Leland with their stuck-up resorter families every summer.

"So what ya doin' down here on my private dock, dickhead?"

"Your dock?" answered Jimmy.

"Fuckin-A my dock! My dad owns this dock, all the way up there to the dam!" … expansively gesturing from where the Keche-Chéemann was tied up near the end of the dock, back up-stream past the Indians' boat, to the waterfall where the damned-up Leland River ran over the spillway on its way out to the big lake.

Jimmy knew better than that, because Gramps had told him all about Fishtown, and who owned what. Most of the place, including the marina docks, was owned by Leland Township. The dock immediately along the river and all its rustic little shanties belonged to the people who owned the smoked fish place. That family had owned the property right along the north side of the river forever, passing it along from one generation to the next. They rented some of the shacks and shanties, now considered to be rustically interesting and attractive, to others, usually with some dock space thrown in. *Others* included the Robinsons and the Indians. Raising his head, now looking at Eddie more directly, he somewhat tentatively shook his head back and forth a little, left and right, indicating his unbelief.

"Okay, smart ass. So, fuck you! You really want a beer?"

"No, I wasn't really ..."

"Oh, sure you wasn't. That's really lame; going around suckin' on empties. What's up with that ... grandpa too cheap to keep beer up at the cottage? Or won't he let you have any."

"He doesn't drink beer."

"Well, pin a rose on grandpa's nose!" He doesn't drink beer! Your people got something against beer drinking?"

"Not really."

"Damned straight; because my dad already told me about yer mother."

That comment took Jimmy by surprise. What could these unsavory characters know about his family? He didn't answer, because something inside was suggesting that he didn't want to get that personally familiar with Eddie Gunderson. Instead, he just dropped his head a little, and bit the left side of his lower lip, as if he was thinking of something to say next.

"So, if I were you I'd get my ass off Jake's boat before he comes back down here and catches you. He's in one of his shitty moods today. He catches you vandalizing his boat, and yer ass'll be grass."

"I wasn't vanda ..."

"Oh, sure you wasn't. You were just waiting around ... Oh, never mind all that bullshit. So, how about it ... you got enough balls to have a beer with me?"

Climbing back off the little boat, it was only just going on one o'clock, so it would be a long time before Gramps' conference or meeting was over. But they were both underage.

"Where are you going to get any beer?"

"I'm gonna steal it off the Robinsons, just like you, stupid! ... Nah, don't worry about it. We got beer on our boat. And it ain't that Busch Lite horse-piss either. That's women's beer. We get the good stuff ... PBR."

He caught the *horse-piss* comment; the same thing Grandma sometimes said.

"What's *PBR?*"

"Pabst of course! What else!"

Jimmy wasn't sure what *Pabst* was, but not wanting to appear stupidly naive, just said, "Oh, yeah. Pabst." as the two boys climbed aboard the *Tarnobitch*, as the ugly Indian fish tug was familiarly called by Lelanders.

The name painted on its transom was actually the *J.R. Tarnovitch*, which was the name of its owner-operator. It was not a pretty sight, having been built by the Tarnovitch brothers, who were obviously more into function than form. She was made using steel plates salvaged from Leland's old water tower when it was torn down. Her engine came out of an old Bainbridge-type wooden fish tug, which had caught fire, burned and sunk over in Green Bay, Wisconsin. The pilot house, built using three-quarter inch plywood, didn't match the look of the rest of the boat at all, and appeared to perhaps have been an afterthought; as if they'd forgotten about a providing a place for the helm. That sat atop a short steel top deck that covered the front quarter of the long, narrow boat, with the engine apparently somewhere under that.

The aft three-quarters was an open well; a work area. The boat was panted dark green and navy gray, obviously without any real scheme. The hull and pilot house were green; the gray was used on her top deck, work well, and the inside of the pilot house. All and all, not a very attractive boat, even as fish tugs go.

Going forward, they entered the plywood pilot house, and then went below into what turned out to be a surprisingly spacious compartment under the forward deck. It was also surprisingly neat, set up almost like a little day room or lounge, albeit somewhat Spartan. Not what one might expect to find on this sort of work boat.

"What's this all about?" Jimmy asked.

"What's what all about?"

"This room. What's up with this. It looks like a bunk room or cabin or something."

"Yeah? ... No shit, Miss. Molly!"

"I mean ... looking at the boat from the outside, you wouldn't expect to find this inside. It's kind of nice down here ... roomy, daylight, and all ..."

Jimmy also noticed that the boat was clean smelling, not fishy. It had an odor that was sort of a mixture of engine room and enamel paint ... like a real boat should smell he thought.

"What's through there?" he asked, pointing to a hatchway on the aft side of the compartment.

"That's the engine room. Wan'na see it?"

Passing through the hatchway, he was surprised again. The engine compartment was also very clean, with the engine itself painted glossy gray, its exposed brass and stainless-steel parts brightly polished. It almost looked like it was hardly ever used.

"Who does all this?" he asked.

"My ol' man. Besides workin' at the church, he helps out part-time down here. He was in the Coast Guard ... knows all about scraping, painting and polishing. Scraping, painting, polishing, and drinking."

Oscar Gunderson had been a Coast Guard Chief, until they kicked him out of the service for being drunk on duty too much of the time. But he was eligible for retirement, so the government was charitable enough to let him retire, rather than subject him to a court-martial and strip him of the benefits he'd earned during his twenty-four years of service. The best he'd done since then was to work part-time as the custodian at the Congregational Church. He was a good fit there since he needed the position more than the money and the church wasn't able to pay much. Moreover, he knew how to fix things, and was a stickler for neatness. But to most people around Leland he was seen as an errant drunk, always amiable, but lit most days by nightfall. It was he who spent much of his time down here in the bottom of the Tarnobitch, mostly by himself.

"So what kind of brew do you like Dude ... PBR, Pabst, or Blue Ribbon?"

"I don't really care. Whatever you've got will be fine."

"Sheesh, what a dumbass! You sure you can handle a beer? You ever had a whole beer before?"

"Of course ... well, no, not really. This will be a first." Jimmy confessed with a sheepish little laugh, beginning to lighten up a little.

"Well, I hope yer not going to get all funny on me ... pass out or somethin'!"

Twisting off two caps at the same time with one hand, he handed Jimmy one of the Pabst Blue Ribbon bottles.

"Here's to ya' Dude. And don't chug-a-lug it; I got a limited supply down here!"

Grandma was right. It did taste like horse pee, or at least like he thought horse pee might taste were he to have a cold bottle of it. But he swallowed down a slug, raised the bottle a little and nodded in approval, as if he was really liking it.

"Yer Grandpa would shit a brick right now if he knew you were down here slummin' and getting beered up, wouldn't he?"

"Well, he probably wouldn't approve of it. But he wouldn't be real mad about it. He hasn't forgotten that boys will be boys. He lets me do stuff that other people would never permit, and don't need to know about."

"Other people ... like your Momma?" Eddie asked in a curiously surly way, but then quickly switched gears, "Like what kind of stuff?"

"They usually let me fly the jet for a while on the way up here and back, and he sometimes lets me drive between Traverse City and here. Maybe have a glass of wine at dinner when we're alone at the cottage ... that sort of stuff."

"You're shittin' me ... they let you fly the jet?"

"Well, I really just sit in the co-pilot seat. It's on autopilot most of the time then. I just watch the instruments. Sometimes the pilot disengages the autopilot and lets me handle the controls while we're out over farm country. I've learned a little about flying that way."

"You never use any cuss words, do ya'? Probably wouldn't say *shit* if you had a mouthful!" ... then almost musing and to himself as he looked down at the bottle of beer and rolling it back and forth between his two open palms ... "A genuine goodie two-shoes."

Jimmy wasn't sure that was a compliment.

Having said that, Eddie looked up at him. The expression on his face had changed. The cocky, self-assured look had suddenly been replaced by something else – maybe wondering, maybe melancholy – as if perhaps he had been struck with a feeling that maybe he didn't really have life by the ass after all. Then he dropped his head, looking at the beer bottle rolling back and forth again.

In that brief moment, for Jimmy, a bond of friendship with this unlikely older boy began to form. For a moment the cock hound he shouldn't be seen with and the hot shot that he wasn't very comfortable being with was revealed as a boy who had feelings and value as a real person. In that brief look he suspected that Eddie had betrayed himself, revealing who and what he really was – tough, and laughing on the outside, but vulnerable, and crying on the inside.

* * *

<u>3</u>

"Well, okay." said Eddie after a moment. And looking up again, now as his former self, and raising his bottle, "Drink up, Jimmy-boy, yer beer's getting warm."

He was surprised when Eddie used his name. He wasn't aware that Eddie knew his name. It hadn't been brought up, and he'd been calling him everything else but, as if he really didn't know it. *Dude ... Shit-for-brains ... Dumbass.*

When he said *Jimmy-boy,* it seemed like a gesture of newly found respect and acceptance. And there was something in the tone of his voice that seemed to underscore that; as if perhaps he'd been struck with the same feeling as Jimmy at that same moment – the feeling that Jimmy was a real person, and someone he could maybe trust and like.

"What's you and yer grandpa gonna be doing tonight?"

"I have to be up at the cottage by six. Then we're going over to Empire to have dinner at the Friendly."

"Grandpa got something against the Bird or the Lodge?" asked Eddie, referring to the Blue Bird restaurant and the Leland Lodge ... and sounding as if he probably already knew the answer.

"Nah, it's too early in the season, and those places are not very busy. I don't like them when they're that way. It feels like we're in the way; like if we weren't there, they wouldn't have to bother. They're okay later on, in the summer after they come to life again.

Gramps and I like Joe's Friendly Tavern. They're more like regular people over there. Sometimes they even sit down and talk if they're not that busy, especially in the morning – if we go over there for breakfast. Sometimes we go to Art's in Glen Arbor."

"Grandpa ever take you to the Side Traxx in Traverse?"

"The side tracks? No, where's that?"

"Nah, never mind."

"In Traverse City we sometimes go to the Park Place ... Minerva's ... and sometimes Mabel's ... and sometimes ..."

"Never mind. I get it."

"Get what?"

"Nothing. Forget it."

Eddie cracked open two more brews and handed him another. He hadn't finished his first, so gulped down what was left of it, which created a momentarily painful gas bubble in his gullet, causing him to puff out his cheeks as he handed the empty bottle back to Eddie.

Jimmy still felt like he had to pee. The feeling of urgency at the base of his belly had never really gone away, and the beer only made the feeling more acute. About half way through the first bottle, he began having to make a conscious effort to hold it. After a couple swigs on the second bottle, he began to feel cramps.

Bending forward a little, he asked Eddie "Is there a bathroom here?"

"Why – you thinking about takin' a bath?"

"I've got to pee."

Grinning, Eddie nodded.

"Yeah, right! The bathroom. Me too. I gotta' race like a piss-horse! Right this way, Pal."

They went up, and out of the green plywood shack that served as a pilot house, then off the boat and across the dock, squeezing between the Tarnovitch shanty, and pair of net reels, into a secluded space behind. With both of the big windmill-like reels still loaded with drying gill nets, and junk piled high all around the back of the space ... fish boxes, old oak-stave barrels, some fish boxes with corks and leads, and an assortment of net buoys ... the space seemed secure enough from the eyes of passersby.

Jimmy was modest and used to complete privacy when eliminating wastes. He worried that Eddie didn't look like he intended to provide it. Instead, and without any hesitation, Eddie unzipped the fly on the front of his jeans, immodestly hauled it out and began watering down the side of one of the barrels, calling out "Wan'na cross swords, Dude?"

Jimmy didn't know what that meant, and decided not to ask. Biting his lower lip and turning his back to Eddie, he tried to conceal his exposed private part and his embarrassment by bellying up into a small space between stacks of fish boxes. He hoped that maybe the rather strong odor of urine back here in *the bathroom* might be suggestive. But it didn't help. Neither did the sound of Eddie's strong stream as it splattered against the empty barrel.

He'd been in this embarrassing predicament before. Unlike all the other boys he knew, he just wasn't able to stand and *piss like a man* when anyone else was present. So, he did what he always did in such circumstances; he pretended he'd went, shook it off, put it back in his pants, and zipped up his fly. For the moment, the familiar feelings of humiliation and shame were, once again, overpowering the feelings of urgency at the bottom of his gut. But he knew it would soon be back, and that he'd have to come up with some excuse for going again so soon – and for coming back here alone.

Back they went, across the dock, onto the Tarnovitch, into her green plywood pilot shack with the battleship gray interior, and down below. Eddie cracked open another beer for himself, but holding Jimmy's second bottle up to the light and seeing it was still more than half full, didn't offer him another.

"C'mon Jimmy-boy; you're falling behind!"

"I'm not much of a drinker, I guess."

"Bull pussy! You're yer grandpa's boy, ain't ya?"

Then after a healthy, tonsil-rattling belch, which also sounded a little foamy ...

"Well, maybe you take after yer Dad's side. Yer grandpa always said he was a ..."

But then, realizing that his tongue had gotten a little too loose, Eddie abruptly cut himself off. Once again, Jimmy had the feeling that this older boy, whom his grandpa had always seemed to shun, somehow knew a lot more than he should about his grandpa and his family.

"Always said what – about my father?"

"Nuthin' Forget it. I mighta' been thinkin' 'bout somebody else. What about your dad, anyway. How come he never comes up here with you?"

Jimmy wasn't much of a judge of body language, but was pretty sure Eddie had just lied to him and was trying to fake a change of subject. He knew it was true that his grandpa never had anything good to say about his mother's first husband, and he figured Eddie had probably heard some talk. Grandpa was a good late-night customer at the tavern end of the Blue Bird and up the hill at the Lodge, and did sometimes get a little too conversational after having a few *Scotch highballs*, as he insisted on calling a short glass of Johnny Walker and soda.

"Well ... I don't have a dad. I mean ..." shrugging, and tilting his head a little towards his right shoulder, "... I never had a dad."

Realizing that didn't sound right either, he started over, as Eddie leaned back a little and pretended that he wasn't as keenly interested as he actually was in what Jimmy might have to say about this.

"What I mean is that my mother's husband left her right after I was born. I don't really know exactly why they got divorced, but he has never been seen or heard from since."

The *'my mother's husband'* comment had apparently slipped right over Eddie's head.

"Well that's definitely a kick in the ass. What a prick!

Guess he didn't care much about you, huh?"

That was a remark that Eddie regretted as soon as it spilled out of his mouth, and Jimmy knew it.

"It's okay. I never knew him, so I don't wonder about him."

"Well, my mother ran off too, and I don't miss her either ... the cunt."

Jimmy could see that wasn't true either. They had obviously blundered into a conversation that was dredging up some bad feelings, especially on Eddies end. So, he didn't offer any sort of response that would encourage more talk on that subject.

"You better git fer home, boy. You look half-drunk to me. You better git home and sleep it off before yer grandpa takes you over to Joe's. He finds out you been drinking and where you got it, my ass'll be grass."

Jimmy checked his watch. It was going on three. He'd been messing around for almost two hours since having had lunch and parting company with Gramps. Eddie was good company. He enjoyed the new acquaintance, having found that the time flew by while they kept each other company. Eddie certainly wasn't like any of his other friends. He was fairly presentable on the outside, but unusually unpolished on the inside to say the least – no, actually outspoken and profane ... even vulgar ... Jimmy admitted to himself.

He remembered the slogan ... about profanity being the attempt of a weak mind to express itself forcibly. But he reasoned that didn't apply to Eddie, since he surely couldn't be accused of having a weak mind. He seemed really smart; not in the scholastic sense, but in a worldly way. But then, he really didn't know if Eddie was or wasn't smart in school subjects. Maybe he was that too. But he was, for sure, not naive when it came to real-life things, like Jimmy knew that he, himself, was.

"I need to go up and pee again first. If it's alright with you ... I'll be right back. You can finish your beer while ..."

"Aww, just go ahead. Don't worry 'bout it."

He had the ambivalent feeling that Eddie had figured him out – that he didn't want to be watched while peeing. He was, on the one hand, glad of it, and on the other, shamed by it. But at any rate, he really needed to go, so quickly got up and left. By now his bladder was aching so badly under the pressure that he couldn't stand up straight.

Assuming the same position at the same place in *the bathroom*, it was still hard to get started. He'd held it back for so long that the muscles seemed to be locked up, and he wasn't sure that Eddie was going to stay put. But after a minute or two, he hadn't heard anything, so began to trust that he was being left alone. He had learned that the more he thought about it, the less likely it would be that he'd be able to go, and therefore to divert his thoughts to something else. So, he began to count the nail-heads in the fish boxes in front of him, and to think about how many there might be in total, and within a few moments a stream finally issued forth. Once started, it seemed to go on and on, without any feeling of relief, to the extent that he began to wonder just how much water his bladder was capable of storing up. He leaned forward against the boxes, just letting it happen and waiting, and eventually the stream diminished to a dribble and finally stopped. After a couple of contractions and squirts, it was over.

Relief at last! He felt much better as he came back to the boat.

Eddie was sitting on its gunwale, waiting for him.

"You, ahh ... best go on up alone. It's probably better for you if yer not seen with me."

"Why would you think thaa ..."

Eddie raised his hand to hush him up ... "Just do it, Dude. I gotta watch my image, ya know!" ... then dropped his head, looking down at his shoes. There was nothing more to be said.

Jimmy left him.

* * *

4

The River Street hill seemed steeper than he ever remembered it. As he walked up the road and out of Fishtown, his forelegs felt weak, and he leaned a little forward, into his footsteps, which seemed to create a better balance, making the up-hill walk easier. He wondered if he was a little under the influence, but then dismissed that. With only two beers? No, that wasn't enough to impair anyone, at least not physically. He decided it was probably just the sitting for two hours.

He didn't need to go up the steepest part of the road anyway, and his forelegs quit complaining soon after he'd turned left at Lake Street. The cottage wasn't far; just a little over three blocks north of River. It sat atop the low bluff, overlooking the beach, Lake Michigan and the islands. It was a fine view. Although it was in town, it was also quite private, a dense growth of forest on either side creating a feeling of seclusion. Lake Street, from the Fishtown end, actually looked more like a private drive, so nobody ever wandered down that way into what most outsiders assumed to be a private cottage area.

The cottage was chilly inside. He and Gramps had been here, but only to park the car and drop off their overnight things. They hadn't turned up the heat, which Gramps like to leave at 55 when nobody was here. It was only 3:30, so it would probably be a while before Gramps got back. He fell onto the couch in the front sun room, pulled Grandma's quilt off its back and cuddled up under it, drawing his legs up to his stomach like a small child.

He thought about the difference between himself and Eddie Gunderson; between Gramps and Eddie's father; about his mother, and what it would feel like were she to suddenly leave him like Eddie's mother had him.

He thought about the dark red car out in the driveway and remembered, with a touch of poignancy, the strangely cute looking "zoom-zoom boy," who they used to show in their commercials. That was the only reason he wanted Gramps to get the Mazda from Hertz, which turned out to be not very cute at all, and not that much fun to drive either – not like the cars they had when Micah Kanters was in their commercials – yes, he had researched the cute *zoom-zoom boy* on the Internet; even downloaded his short *Sailorman* movie and watched it many times. He knew he'd be grown up by now, but he was attached to the image of that 10-year old, all dressed in black, with the impish look, who only said "zoom-zoom."

He had begun breathing deeply.

He had fallen asleep.

———

In his dream he was out in a boat with Gramps, and things were not going well. The sky had turned black, and the fearsome waves were testing grandpa's sailing skills. A queen wave was sneaking up from the northeast, behind Gramps' back. He didn't know it! They were going over ...!!!

"Hey, wake up boy!"

He opened his frightened eyes, grabbing the sides of the couch to brace himself as she capsized. He heard Gramps again calling from a distance, barely audible over the roar of the winds and waves.

"Jamie ... wake up!"

But it was too late. He could feel himself being tossed overboard and the swells tossing him up onto their foamy white crests. Then instantly the storm ended. Strangely, he was suddenly in the cottage ... in the sun room ... looking into his grandfather's face with a blank, bewildered expression.

"What'cha say Jamie ... ready for dinner?"

The sun had dropped low into the west, with its bright orangish light streaming into the windows, creating long shadows. He was wet from sweat. The sun room had warmed up.

"What time is it?"

"It's a little past 6:30. Sorry I'm a little tardy. Things went on a little longer than I expected. How long have you been passed out here on the couch?"

The *passed-out* part of that momentarily raised an alarm. Jimmy could suddenly sense the smell of beer on his breath and looked away now as he replied.

"Since about 3:30, I guess."

"Well that figures. How many did you have?" asked Lee, trying to strike a firm expression, which was betrayed by his smiling eyes.

"A couple."

"Do you want to tell me where you got it?"

"No."

"No, I'd guess not." And speaking over his shoulder as he turned away his grandpa warned, "Better never let your mother or grandma catch you with *horse pee* on your breath, boy!"

Then he turned back towards his grandson again, smiling...

32

"They'll fear that you're picking up your grandpa's bad habits, and our little trips together will be history."

"Get off that couch boy, let's go to Joe's."

For the next thirty minutes, driving from Leland to Empire, hardly a word was exchanged between Jimmy and his grandfather. Lee did the driving; Jimmy rode shotgun, with his elbow on the open window. Propping his head up with the palm of his right hand, the breeze of this unusually warm early Spring weather messing up the front of his feathery light brown hair, he absently gazed at the panorama as it hurried by, one scene seeming to blur into the next – glimpses of the big lake flashing through the trees along with shafts of sunlight, the long shadows, the fallow farm fields, the Kelderhouse swamp with its ashen dead trees, the old house on the hill as they approached Port Oneida with its next-door cemetery beside the road, the pastured slopes rising picturesquely up to wooded hills, the shallow little river that meandered along on the left for a ways, the narrows that separated big and little Glen Lakes and the monumental face of the Sleeping Bear dune at the far end of Little Glen ... and finally the big sweeping curve as they came into Empire, the blinker light at the junction M-22 and M-72 always seeming like a drumbeat that stopped the ever-changing scenic flow at journey's end.

Out of habit, and without any reason, Jimmy usually began counting in his head in cadence with the blinker ... *one, one-thousand; two, one-thousand; three, one-thousand; four, one-thousand; five* ... The orderly and reliable one-second timing of the blinker light always drew his mind's attention. He had developed some sort of emotional connection with it. It was always there; caring, dependable; night or day, rain or shine, in the freezing sleet of winter storms or the sweltering humidity of hot midsummer days ... *blink, one-thousand; blink, one-thousand; blink* ... every one second exactly; yellow on the M-22 sides, red for travelers arriving here at the end of M-72.

Lee turned right at that intersection, towards Joe's Friendly Tavern, leaving the blinker behind. Joe's was on the corner across from the little U.S. Post Office at the end of this short street, which the little village called West Front Street for reasons nobody understood. It wasn't really in front of anything, and there was no East Front Street. By the same token, West Front Street ended at Lake Street, which didn't go to or by any lake either. The street that went out to the city beach at the big lake was Niagara Street. Jimmy figured that might have been named after a ship, as was the town itself; *Empire* being the name of the first ship to visit its new dock back in the old days. Maybe a *Niagara* was the second.

A small hand-painted wooden sign swinging above the front door said *Joe's Friendly Tavern* but nobody ever called it that. Everybody called it either *Joe's* or *the Friendly*. Back in the day it was just the Empire tavern; a real tavern, where men went to drink – mostly beer – and to brag, and cuss.

"Grandpa, what's a foundation?"

Jimmy really didn't want to know that, but dinner had been unusually non-conversational so far. He thought that it might be because his grandfather was actually somewhat peeved about his beer-drinking episode. This was his rather feeble attempt at changing the subject.

Lee was, in fact, in somewhat of a mood, but it wasn't about that. He had something else on his mind. He didn't feel like cooperating.

"The bottom of a building, of course. You should know that."

"Come on Gramps; you know what I mean. I'm talking about the meetings with Mr. Maguire and the others. What does that kind of foundation do?"

Gramps just grunted "Humph!" and continued cutting up his salad with his table knife and fork. He did seem disgusted about something. His attitude was unusual, and made Jimmy uncomfortable. He had really been thinking about a way to steer the conversation towards questions about his missing father, but it began to look more and more like this wasn't going to be a good time for that.

"Well, I'll tell you boy ..." Gramps finally offered. "A foundation is a scheme where a chunk of money is carefully invested and the yield ... the dividends or interest it earns ... is doled out to worthy causes."

"A foundation is for just *giving away* money?"

"Yes, that's about the size of it."

"Why would it want to do that? What does it get for the money?"

"Well, let me put it a different way, kid. A foundation is a deal where some old bastard who has become filthy rich by screwing over other people all his life, tries to bury his guilt by pretending to be generous with all his ill-gotten wealth."

With that, Lee pushed his plate away, placing the knife and fork on top. He had decided that his dinner was over.

"I'm sorry grandpa. I didn't mean to make you angry. I shouldn't have taken the beer from ..." He almost leaked the name. "I mean I didn't *take it*, it was given to me, but I shouldn't have accepted it. I knew I was doing the wrong thing. But I didn't want to feel like a ..."

"Never mind, Jamie. It's not about the beer. And I'm not mad at you. It's just a mood. I'm a little disgusted with myself at the moment. It'll pass. The sun's about down. Let's go down to the beach and see if you can catch the green flash."

"The green flash? What's that?"

"You'll see." and tossing the keys to Jimmy, "You drive."

The City Park at the Lake Michigan beach in Empire was only around the corner from Joe's, and down the gentle slope at the end of Niagara Street. What looked like the park's entrance and parking lot was actually another street, called Lake Michigan Drive. This time the name was appropriate, since the street passed through the park, and out of its north end, continuing on along Lake Michigan until turning eastward at the end of Big Bar Lake, which was only about a mile long, and just 300-feet, or so, inland from the big lake. Jimmy nosed the Mazda up to a big log which served as a barrier between the parking area and the sandy beach, being careful not to bump it. The two got out and sat down, joining three elderly folks, two women and a fairly large man with a can of beer in his hand, who were already sitting on the far end of the same big log, and another couple who had brought folding lawn chairs. They and one of the women on the log held paper cups. The shorter woman, the one sitting closest to them, called out ...

"Well, hello Lee ... Welcome to the Green Flash Club!"

"Hello Margaret. Henry; good to see you." responded Gramps.

His grandpa had been around Leelanau County for a long time, and seemed to know just about all the other old timers. It

36

wasn't unusual for them to be recognized by people Jimmy had never seen before. Henry and Margaret looked at him and nodded a silent hello, but otherwise said nothing and didn't ask to be introduced. That wasn't unusual either. Once in a while one would ask about him, but usually they didn't.

The sun was nearly on the water, way out in the big lake. It seemed to grow larger and larger as it fell from the sky, and at this very low angle painted a wavering golden path atop the water, from far out in the lake right up to the sandy shoreline. A fleet of clouds lay motionless along the shoreline, extending out over the lake, and were being painted various shades rose and orange on their undersides with shadows in shades of gray in between, and gilded in gold trim along their westward edges. The painting overhead changed, moment by moment, as the sun dropped lower and lower, and got larger and larger. Finally beginning to change from an orb to a semicircle as it dipped into the lake, its fall seemed to be speeding up.

"Now keep your eyes on the sun as it goes down, Jamie. It'll get smaller and smaller, until its last little speck finally seems to *pop* into the lake and disappear – then you will see a quick green flash all across the horizon, just along the surface of the lake way out there."

* * *

5

Lee made four or five more trips up to Leland and back between that April and the time school was dismissed for the summer. He hadn't asked Jimmy to come along on any of them. Except for one, all the trips up were made on weekdays, and the one that wasn't lasted into the next week, giving Lee an excuse for not taking Jimmy along, since he was still at school. So, Jimmy spent the rest of the spring at Indianapolis. He felt it was his own fault, surmising that Gramps had figured out where he'd gotten the beer, and didn't want him hanging around with boys like Eddie Gunderson.

Lee and his wife Joanne had always spent much of the summertime in the cottage at Leland, "Josie" and Julie remaining there full time, with Lee commuting back and forth, usually every weekend. After Lee's retirement six years ago, they'd been spending the entire summer in Leland together, coming up in late May to open the cottage, and staying until the first week of September. Julie usually brought Jimmy up after school was out. He'd then stay all summer, coming back to Indy with his grandparents just before school started again.

Last summer had started off differently, and unhappily. Josie had called Julie on the first Sunday in June, and during the conversation mentioned ...

"Your father feels it would be better for you to keep Jamie with you this summer ..." then hedging, "... at least for a little while."

"What for? There's nothing for him to do here!" Julie had retorted.

She had gotten her back up almost instantly, jumping to the conclusion that Lee was angry with her again for something. That was always the way with her father. He'd feel offended by something, or become angry over some little thing, and she'd never hear a peep out of him about it. He'd just let it fester, becoming increasing annoyed as the time went by until he was downright unpleasant. Then he'd pull some pay back stunt like this.

"What's Daddy's problem ... what did I do this time?" she asked, the annoyance and frustration clearly intoned in her voice.

"I don't really know dear ... and you shouldn't always take things so personally. I don't think it's about you. Your father has just been in sort of funk the past few weeks. He'll get over it ... he always does."

"So fine; he's in a bad mood! So, take it out on me and Jimmy! Spoil our vacation!"

"*Your vacation?* And just what exactly is *your vacation* dear? You bring the boy up here and dump him off every summer. We hear nothing from you all summer long. Then you don't even come back to pick him up in the fall! Just what exactly do you do all summer Julie, and how do you think it makes Jamie feel ... to know that you don't care for him to be a part of whatever it is ... don't want to share your time with him? He's not a child anymore Julie. He has questions. He has feelings."

Josie was almost in tears.

"Oh, brothers! Here we go again with all that. Shit happens, Mother. It is what it is. I'm sorry I wasn't perfect. Are you going to keep blaming forever? Maybe it's time for you and Dad to move on."

Josie had felt the familiar hollow feeling developing somewhere near the top of her chest; the hopeless feeling that usually came whenever she had a serious conversation with her daughter. Julie was thirty-three years old, still had the self-centered attitudes of a child, and behaved like a spoiled brat. She was sorry she'd been drawn into this sort of conversation again. Trying to have a rational, heart-to-heart conversation with Julie was always a waste of time. The results were always the same; she'd come away from it feeling sick at heart, and would feel awful for the next several days. But that didn't mean she had to give in. Julie's level of emotional intelligence was low. She wasn't quick about considering *what ifs* before blurting out things she didn't need to say. That time she would be *hoist with her own petard*, as it were.

"Yes, dear. You're probably right. Time for Dad and me to move on. So, that's exactly what we'll do. We'll see you next fall then. Good-bye dear."

As she abruptly snapped her little cell phone closed she caught just a snippet of Julie's come-back; something like

"What's that supposed to ..."

So that summer, the summer when Jimmy was thirteen, was the first that he had not spent in Leland with his grandparents.

Now history was repeating itself, except this time there was no call from Josie. As was her way, Julie was not able to take the hint, and decided to call her mother in Leland to find out if the jet was going to be available for a quick round-trip to Traverse.

Jimmy, riding in the car at the time with his mother, had heard her side of the conversation, and had heard enough of these sorts of conversations that he was able to pretty much fill in his grandma's side. He also knew his grandma; knew that she was a lot smarter under these circumstances than his mother, and was always likely to come out on top.

"I guess that means I'm not going to Leland again?" he asked quietly, after several minutes of silence – more of a statement actually, than a question.

Julie also knew her mother, at least good enough to know that she had just blown it again. It wouldn't do any good to call her back now. Her mother had outsmarted her once again, and wasn't one to change her mind. She'd talk to Daddy later.

"Oh, just shut up! I don't want to deal with it right now. Josie's just an annoying bitch; why would you want to be with them anyway! Maybe you can still get into Culver."

That did indeed shut him up. She had done that last summer after Josie had put her foot down. She used her influence as Winston L. Smith's daughter to have him enrolled in successive summer programs, stranding him at the Culver Academy with a bunch of other unwanted kids from early June through most of August. That had cost her upwards of $20,000. Most of the other boys were like him, with a single parent, and wealthy grandparents. He and one other, a boy who was two years younger, were the only ones who stayed all summer; the others all being enrolled in programs that lasted only six weeks. Most of the parents and grandparents were good about visiting on weekends, at least a couple of times during the six weeks, others weren't. Julie never did. Nor did his grandparents, since Julie had never told them that he was there.

During that summer at Culver he learned how to ride horses, fly flight simulators and sail. He also learned that a lot of rich people have inconvenient children, and were willing to spend whatever it took to get rid of them for a while in the summer. Many of them were regularly enrolled in boarding schools ... many at Culver ... so weren't around during most of the school year either.

He and the other boy were called *the orphans* by some of the other kids. The eleven-year-old cried a lot in his bed at night and grew dependent on him for companionship and support. They were both unhappy, but for the other boy's sake, Jimmy tried to look and act upbeat whenever they were together, which eventually became almost all the time. Sometimes he crawled into the other boy's bed beside him at night and held him tight until the crying stopped and he fell asleep.

The other boy's grandparents finally came to get him a couple days before Julie came for Jimmy, and as his summer companion walked away hand-in-hand with his grandmother, he didn't cry. He never looked back. Jimmy had never seen or heard from him again. For his part, Jimmy did cry as the boy walked away. But he hid the tears.

All those miserable memories came flooding back when Julie mentioned Culver. He said nothing, but in his mind, he thought very emphatically, *No way!*

He was never going to go there again – ever.

Julie was just as sure that he wasn't going to spend the summer at Indianapolis doing who knows what with who knew whom, and when her appeals to *Daddy* fell on deaf ears later that evening, she decided to call a friend at Culver first thing in the morning.

When she made that call, she had the unhappy experience of being turned down because, they claimed, all the summer sessions were totally enrolled. Being a person who was not used to taking no for an answer, she climbed through the chain of command during the conversation; finally raising hell with the *Administrative Assistant to the Head of Schools* herself. At that level she was politely, but firmly dismissed, and the call was terminated.

So, she thought about calling Howe instead.

She didn't notice that Jimmy wasn't there as she left for the office the next morning, nor when she rushed back in that afternoon. There wasn't anything unusual about that. He never got up early when he didn't have to, and when she came home in the afternoons, he was usually downstairs in the family room playing video games or something. After quickly showering and changing, she was off again, calling down the stairs …

"I didn't have time to pick up anything honey, so just call Chan's or Jet's for delivery tonight, okay? You know where the card is … and don't forget the tip … 15%, and no more, okay?"

She didn't hear a reply, but that wasn't unusual either, since Jimmy usually had his ears plugged with ear buds.

"Okay, honey. Bye."

And with that she left.

She also didn't notice that Jimmy was gone when she returned that evening. She did look down the stairs, and seeing only darkness, assumed that he was in bed, even though it was only going on ten. Being somewhat stressed and tired from a night out with a new acquaintance, who had turned out to be much less interesting than expected, she went to her own bedroom, and quickly entered dreamland.

When she awoke the next morning, she remembered the unhappy episode on the phone with the people at Culver, and that she had forgotten about calling Howe the morning before. It was too early to call the Academy right then, so she resolved to remember to make the call first thing when she got to the office downtown. She thought she'd better tell Jimmy to stick around today, just in case.

That was when she finally looked in on his room, only then discovering that his bed was still neatly made, and he wasn't anywhere in the house, or outside. That was annoying! Where could he be at six-fifty in the morning?

Unfortunately, she didn't have time to find out, having to leave for the drive downtown at seven.

Several times during the day she attempted to call home, and Jimmy's cell phone, receiving answers at neither. She came back home early that afternoon, and called his cell number again from the kitchen. She was much relieved when she heard his ring tone coming from his room, then her anger flared and she hurried in that direction with the intention of berating him for not taking her calls all day.

But his room had remained as it was that morning, when she hadn't noticed the iPhone laying atop his dresser. She realized then that he had gone, and didn't want her to know where.

Hurrying back to the kitchen, she grabbed her cell phone and punched in "911." The answer came even before she heard a ring ...

"Marion County 911, what is the exact location of your emergency?"

That caused immediate second thoughts. Trouble! She didn't need that! She could just see herself featured on the six o'clock news as the distraught mother in an AMBER alert. When Lee and Josie got wind of that up in Leland, they'd be back in a flash, and angry as all hell.

"Oh, I am sorry. I thought my boy was ... Oh, never mind. My mistake."

... and she flipped the cell phone closed, ending the call.

* * *

6

Josie was gardening on the side of the cottage when she sensed a presence behind her. Turning slightly while still bent over, she saw him standing there. He looked more forlorn than she had ever seen him look before, his clothes rumpled, hair mussed and dirty, and his sandals muddied.

Straightening up, with hands on her hips, she exclaimed ...

"Jamie! For the love of Mike, what are you *doing* here?"

He went tentatively to her, put his arms around her, with his face buried on her left shoulder. She felt the spasms, and realized that he was sobbing, so held him tight as the tears welled up in her own eyes. After a few moments she pushed him away, lifting his chin with her soiled garden-gloved hand so she could look him in the eyes.

"Whatever it is, Jamie, you're here now. You're safe. You're welcome."

And then, beginning to imagine what might have prompted this scene, her tears came again, flowing more freely this time as she tried to wipe them away with her other hand, the soiled glove leaving streaks as the tears turned earth to mud.

"Goddammit!" Lee blurted out as he came around the corner from the cottage's front yard.

"I told that girl that she ...!" he began to say until being abruptly shushed by his wife, who had raised both open palms and was wagging them and her head back and forth in a *No – not now!* gesture.

He looked at her questioningly and she shook her head *no* once again, this time with a forlorn look that he clearly understood. With that, he realized there was a situation again, shrugged, wagged his own head *no* with an expression of frustration, and said ...

"Okay. Well, you're here, and you look like hell. Go on inside and get cleaned up."

"I don't have any clothes with me, Grandpa."

Josie intervened ...

"Take those sandals off out here, and then go into the bathroom and throw out what you've got on. I'll wash them up quick. You can wrap up in a towel while they dry."

Besides feeling sweaty and dirty, he was tired, having not slept much, if at all, the night before. The warm water of the shower was a great pleasure, splashing over his head and running down his bare body, gradually washing bad feelings down the drain along with the dust from his hair and day-old perspiration from his still boyishly fair skin. He stood there relishing that sensation for a long time, with his hands on the wall in front of him to prop himself up.

As the water rained down, massaging his head and shoulders, then drizzling down over his body in tickling little rivulet's, down his legs to his feet, then onto the tiled floor where it rushed toward the drain, he could feel muscles begin to relax, not gradually, but seeming releasing their tension in some logical sequence. His eyelids grew heavy ... drooping ... drooping ... and as they finally closed he marked that he could still see daylight through the skin.

His world seemed to be growing smaller and smaller as his span of consciousness contracted. Finally, it disappeared altogether and he was in darkness.

Magically the light faded back in, brightening up the scenes in his mind as he dreamed about warm things in pastel colors, about being taken to faraway places, where he felt new, free and joyful. He would not remember any of it; the details being erased as the warm places began to turn dark and cold.

He awoke standing in the same position. The reserve of hot water had been depleted, and a cold rain now chilled him. He quickly turned the faucets closed, then resumed his position. As the water dripped off his body, its natural heat began to recover, and began drying his skin. He wasn't actually aware of having fallen asleep and dreamt, but the good feelings from the dreams lingered, dissolving most of the unhappiness accumulated over the past thirty hours, or so.

Josie had taken his soiled things away, and thrown in two towels, a regular bath towel, and his own beach towel. It was one of his favorite things, this humongous black and blue striped beach towel, which was big enough to use as a robe, which he often had after a refreshing swim in the chilly waters of the big lake on a summer evening. She knew that, of course – that he would be comfortable wrapped up in this familiarly cozy thing, and then he'd feel better about his situation.

He found his grandparents having a late breakfast of coffee and toast at the picnic table out on the front lawn, overlooking the lake. Josie had also brought out a bowl of dry cereal, a small pitcher of milk and a banana for him. When she saw him coming, she began slicing the banana into coins atop the wheat flakes, as he had always liked it. He sat down opposite the two of them, and without being asked about it, began to share the details of his adventure between spoonfuls.

"Yesterday morning, I got up early and took the IndyGo buses from home to the bus station downtown on Illinois Street. I bought a ticket to Traverse City on an adult fare, using my own money. I thought somebody might ask about my age and stop me, but nobody did. I rode the buses for ten and a half hours ... I had to change buses twice; once at South Bend and then in Grand Rapids ... and finally I got dropped off in Traverse at Hall Street, on the bay."

"I got to know an Indian kid on the bus from Grand Rapids. His dad was there to pick him up. He works at the casino in Peshawbestown. They live there. His dad gave me a ride to Suttons Bay, and I walked the rest of the way from there."

"You walked? That's almost ten miles!" interjected his grandpa.

"Yes, so by the time I got here it was way after dark and I didn't see any lights on, so I went over to Fishtown, and spent the night on the Tarnovitch."

"Jamie! Why didn't you just come in? You know the door is never locked while we're here." said his grandma.

"I wasn't sure if you wanted me anymore." Jimmy replied, the tears beginning to blur the contents of his cereal bowl.

It was too much for Lee. He turned away, looking at the lake and said, mostly to himself, "Goddammit!"

Josie got up and hurriedly came around the table to the back of the boy, hugging him from behind and warning ...

"Don't you *ever* think that, Jamie. Don't you *EVER* think that!"

She sat down beside him, turned towards him with her left elbow on the table, propping up her head with that hand and lovingly petting the feathery light brown hair on the back of Jimmy's head with her other. With the tears gently dropping onto her cheeks, her lips pressed tightly together, there was nothing to say. She just wagged her head a little, back and forth from left to right, as if not knowing what to think of this whole affair. Lee's back was still turned towards them. He sat bent over, with his elbows on his knees and chin in his hands.

"I didn't wake up until the ferries left at ten. Their horns woke me up when they left. I didn't mean to sleep that long. I was afraid they'd catch me, so I quick got off their boat. Then I came here."

Straightening up and turning around, Lee offered a little reassurance on that point.

"They wouldn't have caught you. They're not here right now; they're all up at the Soo ... at a powwow over on the Canadian side. What made you think that old tub was a good place to hole up anyway?"

"There's a little cabin down below up front, with a bunk. And it's neat and clean in there." replied Jimmy, not thinking about them wondering how he would have known that.

"I assume that means you've been there before?" suggested Lee, turning his head slightly to the right and raising his eyebrows slightly in an inquisitive gesture.

"That's where I had the beer that day." Jimmy confessed.

"Beer?" exclaimed Josie.

"Yeah, he's a real sot now." answered Lee, trying to lighten up the mood a little. But then he continued,

"I don't suppose you stole it?"

"No. Eddie Gunderson caught me on the Ningwis, which was full of empty beer cans. I was checking some of them ... to see if they were really empty ... when he caught me. I was scared. I thought he was Jake, or maybe the Sheriff. But it was just Eddie, and he asked me if I wanted to have a real beer with him. Then we went over to their boat, where he had some. He said it was his."

"Uh-huh. So, thus far in life you've had two beers ... two bottles of horse pee." said Lee, flashing a quick little smile at his frowning wife. Then he continued ...

"Well, okay. We've heard the *what, when, where and how,* but we haven't heard the *why.* What made you decide to run off from your mother?"

"Julie was going to send me to Culver's again for the summer. I didn't want to go back there."

"That wouldn't have happened again, Jamie. I've seen to that!" assured his grandmother.

After having previously heard Jimmy's report about his experience at the summer camps, and agreeing that Julie had just dumped him there to get him out of her hair for the summer, she had called her friend Wilma, half of the couple who ran the schools at Culver, to see to it that Julie wouldn't be able to use them in that way again. She wasn't yet aware that her friend had been as good as her word. Jimmy had left without knowing that his mother had already been turned down at Culver.

All in all, he'd only been gone for a little over twenty-four hours, so Lee and Josie weren't surprised that they'd heard nothing from Julie. They were well aware of her sprightly lifestyle, and that Jimmy was actually neglected much of the time. But as time went on with no call from a distressed mother, they decided to just sit tight, to see how long that situation would continue ... how long it would take Julie to discover that her fourteen-year-old son was missing ... or to acknowledge it.

They would be waiting for a long time.

* * *

7

"Well, then; I'm going to go in and get your things out of the dryer. While you're changing back into your clothes Jamie, I'll fix the three of us a light lunch. Then, later on, after we've had our lunch, Grandpa will drive us into Traverse so we can get you a toothbrush ..." Josie said with a wink in Jimmy's direction, "... and fit you out with a summer wardrobe. You're most likely going to be here for the duration, and we're just thrilled and happy about that! Isn't that right Lee?"

Lee thought to himself that *thrilled* did not really describe his feelings, but he was happy about Jimmy's coming, and that he'd probably be around all summer. Other than that, what he was really feeling inside was a muddle of anger and remorse.

He was angry about the way things had turned out for Julie — about her being the way she was. At the same time, he felt responsible; that it was largely his having failed her that had resulted in her self-centered ways and inability to cultivate a successful long-term relationship with anyone. He felt that Jimmy was also his fault — the result of their only child's having been permitted to grow up as a spoiled brat. He was also sorry that in his recent futile attempts to teach Julie a lesson he had succeeded only in hurting the boy.

He felt especially sorry about that. Regardless of the dubious circumstances of Jamie's birth, he dearly and deeply loved his grandson. And that gave rise to even more bad feelings, since in a secret place within his heart lay the hurtful truth that he had never really felt that sort of affection for his own daughter.

"Yes, Jamie, that's right. We're glad you're here. We're always glad to have you around."

Gramps was sitting with his back to the table again, elbows on his knees, head propped up by the thumbs of his folded hands under his chin. He was speaking at the ground, almost in a mumble. He did not look up.

Josie ducked into the cottage and brought back an armload of cleanly laundered boy's things ... briefs, tee shirt, no socks, carpenter pants and a well-worn long-sleeved chambray shirt. Handing Jimmy his trousers ...

"Here Jamie, slip these on, roll up the legs a bit, then take your muddy sandals down to the beach and rinse them off in the lake."

"They're leather." Jamie cautioned.

"That's alright." suggested Lee. "Just slosh them around in the water a little — don't soak them. And wait 'til we're in the car before you put them on. They'll be dry enough by the time we get to town."

On the thirty-minute trip to Traverse City, the mood seemed to steadily become more cheerful.

"I have my own money." offered Jimmy.

"Well, good!" answered Lee. "How much you got?"

"Let's see. I started with 843-dollars and 56-cents. The bus ticket was $130, so that leaves ... seven hundred and thirteen dollars and ... No, wait. The IndyGos were both 75cents, so that's another dollar-fifty. And I had a couple cans of pop ... another two bucks. So, what does that make ... a hundred thirty-two fifty? So, I should have seven-hundred eleven and some change."

"$710.06." corrected Lee.

"Is that going to be enough, Grandma?"

"Lee, maybe you'd better take us to Goodwill instead of Front Street!" kidded Josie.

"Yes, let's." added Jimmy, having not caught the joke.

"Have you two lost some of your marbles?" asked his grandfather. "We're not going to be seen shopping in Goodwill for any kid of mine."

Jimmy caught the last few words of that comment. They expressed a sentiment that he was not used to, raising feelings within him of being wanted, and of belonging. They also renewed his feelings of love and admiration for his grandparents.

"And who do you suppose might see you shopping there?" asked Josie. "What fun it might be to find some of our neighbors, or some of your colleagues, shopping Goodwill. Yes, now I'm insisting on it. We must go to Goodwill!"

"We'll go to the Captain's Quarters!" insisted Lee.

"Oh, for goodness sake Lee! That's a men's store. They don't have anything for boys!"

"He's not a boy; haven't you noticed? He's become a young man. Came all the way up from home all by himself and with his own money, didn't he?"

"Goodwill is on Airport Road, by the railroad tracks." answered Josie, still intending to have her way.

"How would you know that?" wondered her husband. "Have you been shopping there behind my back?"

"Never mind. I know a lot more about a lot more than you might think."

"Yes, I'm sure you do. Which railroad tracks?"

"The tracks by Cass."

"Well, that's not very conveniently located. Let's just go to the mall."

"Goodwill, mister! Just drive. I'll show you how to get there."

And so, Mr. W. Lee Smith was treated to a new experience; shopping a second-hand store. He was surprised to find that the Goodwill store was not so much different than a regular department store, with an assortment of merchandise neatly arranged – mostly apparel for women, men, girls, boys, and toddlers, but also jewelry, furniture, and towards the back of the store an assortment of all sorts of miscellaneous, but interesting, *junque*, as he put it, neatly arranged on several rows of shelves, but without any logical system of order. While Josie and Jimmy searched through the racks of boy's clothes, Lee wandered off towards these shelves, and was soon engrossed with inspecting their contents, often wondering what the heck this item was or what that gizmo might be used for.

He even found a couple of treasures; things he really wanted to take home, yet was quite reluctant to buy, not wishing to become a *Goodwill shopper*. On a shelf loaded with old 33-1/3 RPM LP record albums, he discovered the old Columbia Record Club recordings of Civil War songs, with songs of the north and south in separate blue and gray cloth-bound albums entitled *The Union* and *The Confederacy*, which were actually books with glossy pages of historical essays and photos. He had owned just such a set as a boy, and could still remember the tunes and words of some of the songs on these old vinyl platters, which had been prized among his favorite possessions, but which had somehow been lost. In his head, one of his old favorites came playing back ...

> *Oh, I wanted much to go to war,*
> *so, went to be examined.*
> *The doctor looked me o'er and o'er,*
> *my back and chest he hammered.*
> *Said he, 'You're not the man for me.*
> *Your lungs are much affected.*
> *And likewise, both your eyes are cocked,*
> *or otherwise directed.'*
> *So now I'm in the "Invalids."*
> *I cannot go and fight, Sir.*
> *The doctor told me so, you know ...*
> *Of course, he must be right, Sir.*

He also found a very nice model of a little sailboat. He wasn't really aware of any reason that should have caught his eye, except for the fact that it was, in his opinion, quite a nice model, and would look good somewhere in the cottage. He also wasn't aware that it was actually a cheap import from China that someone had previously purchased at Hobby Lobby for only $9.95.

He rather sheepishly carried his two record albums and his sailboat through the store to deposit them in Josie's shopping cart.

"The albums are 75-cents each, and the boat's a buck and a quarter." he advised her.

"Umm ... I see." said she, "And do we know anyone with a record player?"

He hadn't actually thought about that.

"No, but I can have someone take the songs off there and put them on a CD, or something." ... although he wasn't sure of that. "Isn't that right Jamie?"

"Sure Gramps. I know how to do that. We did that once in school. We converted the records to audio CD's, and it's easy to convert those to MP3's."

"Right. Em-pee-three." ... said Lee, nodding in agreement, although not really knowing what Jimmy was talking about.

"And what's with the sailboat, Lee?" wondered his wife.

"Nothing. I just like it. It's a very nice model. Somebody obviously put a lot of work into that, and I'd be willing to bet it probably once cost somebody a whole lot more than a dollar, twenty-five."

She felt like telling him about Hobby Lobby, but decided not to spoil his moment.

Josie and Jimmy were, in fact, able to find several good quality shirts and pants, all seeming to be nearly new, and others actually new, with stickers and tags still attached. They couldn't know it, of course, but many of the items they selected had just come into the Goodwill, having belonged to a boy of Jimmy's same age and physical stature who had been tragically lost under the ice in the Boardman River six months before. They were a dead boy's clothes. Ironically, or perhaps merely coincidentally, his name had also been James.

They had picked out four good pairs of pants, plus two shorts, and a nice pair of pleated slacks for Sunday or other dress-up occasions – seven sport shirts and two belts, one of leather and one an army-type web belt – all for only $29.15 plus sales tax, or

$30.90 total. Josie paid $2.92 for Lee's treasures while he waited outside.

"Are we done now?" hoped an impatient Lee as they exited the Goodwill parking lot.

"No, we're not done." scolded Josie. "Turn right and drive over to the mall. We need to go to Penny's next."

"What for? You had a whole cart load of things. What more does he need?"

"Underwear. Socks. Shoes." Josie passively answered.

"And maybe a swim suit?" Jimmy added.

At J.C. Penny's Josie had picked up six-packs of regular white cotton briefs and matching tee shirts, when Lee intervened.

"He doesn't want those. They look like *Depends* for cripes sake! Get these." he suggested, handing her two packs of a lower-rise version.

"And you had better get a dozen, not just six. There are seven days in a week, you know."

"And we have a washer and drier at the cottage, Lee."

"Well ..." objected Lee, "Get two packs anyway. Just in case."

"Are you buying?"

"No, I'm not! The boy has his own money."

"Fine, then six will be enough."

"How much is that Grandma?" wondered Jimmy.

"Well it's ... Oh, my! These are both twenty-six dollars ... $52? That's crazy!" exclaimed Josie.

"That's okay, Grandma. I have that much."

"Oh no, no, my dear boy! I see you have some things to learn about wealth and stewardship. Remember what it says in the Bible: *A fool and his money are soon parted!*"

"Umm, I think that was Benjamin Franklin, Josie." corrected Lee.

"Well, nevertheless. Take us over to Walmart. It's just back there a block or two."

On the way out of the mall, Jimmy spotted a cool-looking bathing suit in one of the windows of Macy's. It was a trim, *Sea Pants* boxer style, in a light blue and white Kona Coast print, not one of those ugly knee-length things that looked like basketball shorts.

"That's what I want, Grandma." he declared rather excitedly pointing to the window. "Right there. Can we stop in here first?"

Josie approached the window, squinting to inspect the style and price. To her delight, it was on sale ... marked down from $44.00 to $19.99 and for today only, an additional 25% off.

"Okay, now you're talking, Jamie. If they have that in your size, it will be a real steal."

Unfortunately, there were no underwear bargains to be found in Macy's either, so they moved on to Walmart. At Walmart, Jimmy was able to buy the same things they had selected at Penny's, but for about a quarter of the price. He also bought a package of white cotton socks, a couple pairs of black cotton socks for dress, and a neat-looking pair of wheat-colored casual shoes, also for dress. At check-out, the whole bill came to less than fifty dollars.

Jimmy's wardrobe was complete.

"Well, let's see. I spent $46.47 here, $15.89 at Macy's and at Goodwill ..." reaching for the sales slip in that bag ... "at Goodwill we spent $30.90. Umm ... about how much did that add up to

Gramps?" knowing that Lee was good with figures and probably already had the total in his head.

"It's not *about,* it's *exactly* $93.26." answered Lee. "You done good, boy! ... And in only ..." looking at his watch "... only a little over four hours."

Ignoring Lee's complaint about the time, Josie looked back at Jimmy with a smile, feeling perfectly gratified as they headed back to the cottage.

* * *

8

"Am I going to be upstairs again, Grandma?" asked Jimmy as he gathered up his bags of newly purchased clothing from the back of the car.

"You can if you want." she answered. "But you don't have to. You can use the back bedroom if you'd rather be downstairs. It's much cooler downstairs, you know."

Upstairs was really just the cottage's attic. It had been finished off to some extent, with drywall and a hardwood floor, but had never been partitioned, so was a great open space the size of the whole house. The ceiling followed the shape of the cottage's simple single-gable roof until meeting the walls, which were only about four-feet high on either side. There were dormers with simple twelve-light double-hung windows on either side of the roof, and matching sixteen-light windows fore and aft, in the end facing the lake, and the opposite end over the driveway, so there was always plenty of light during the daylight hours. Although most of the roof was shaded by nearby birches and beech trees, it did sometimes become rather warm upstairs during fine summer days, but open windows after sundown invited the fresh, cooling breezes from off the lake. In the quiet of the night Jimmy could lay in his bed under the cover of a single sheet, or often no cover at all, and listen to the gentle wavelets pester the assortment of pebbles that lay all along the shoreline down on the beach, while gazing up to a sky so full of stars it looked foggy, or *milky*; an impossible sight back home in the city. During all the times in his life that he had been at the cottage, the attic had almost always been his assigned accommodations – *Jamie's room,* as it were. He had come to love its familiar spaciousness, and the feeling of it's being his personal domain.

"No, that's alright, Grandma. I like it upstairs."

"Well, then take your things up there and put them away, and I'll be up in a minute with clean sheets. And we got rid of those old pillows up there, so I'll need to bring you up some pillows too."

Jimmy took all his newly purchased things upstairs, and sorted them all out neatly on the pillow-less bed. When laid out in that way, all the things he had picked out really didn't look like much of a wardrobe, he thought. But then he shrugged as he thought, 'Oh, well ... this is plenty enough for summertime here.'

Of all the things he had bought that afternoon, the coolest and most eye-catching was the Macy's swim suit. Forgetting momentarily that Josie was likely to be coming up with the bedding, he decided to try it on again and see how it looked in the dressing mirror down at the far end of the attic. He liked what he saw. The trunks fit perfectly all around, snug, but not skin tight, and squared off from the top of the low-rise waist band to the bottoms of the legs, which were only about an inch below the crotch. As he admired his reflected image he decided the only thing that could use some improvement was his color - he looked a little white, even anemic perhaps. But then a couple of days on the beach would change that. He always tanned readily.

As he continued to examine the boy in the looking glass, that inexplicable emotional feeling began to arise from somewhere deep within.

"Well, it looks like someone is eager to get down to the lake!" said Josie from the top of the stairway.

"I was just trying things on again ... to make sure everything fits." attempted Jimmy.

"Yes. Well, here are your pillows, and clean sheets and pillow cases. I also have a clean mattress cover, so come over here and help me with that, will you please."

Josie was, meanwhile, folding his things and stowing them neatly away in the drawers built into the wall on the north side of the room. Still in his swim suit, he came back to the bed and helped her wrestle the stubborn fitted cover onto the mattress, then the two of them partnered up to make the bed with sheets and comforter, with the two new pillows propped neatly up against the headboard.

"Thanks grandma. I love this bed. I always feel ... sort of ... *at home* up here."

"I'm glad you do. That's as it should be. I suppose most kids feel safe and secure when they stay at their grandma's house. I know I always did."

"Now, if you're going to go down and jump in the lake, you'd better get to it. It's now going on five, and we'll be having dinner pretty soon."

He didn't need to be coaxed, swinging down the stars on the handrails, taking four and five steps at a time, then out of the cottage and across the grass lawn to the weathered outdoor stairs that went down the bluff from the end of the lawn to the beach below. Exuberantly swinging down these stairs in the same manner, he hadn't noticed the boy sitting on the bottom step until almost kicking him in the back of the head.

"Oh! Sorry ..." he offered.

"That's okay." said the boy. "Do you live here? Am I allowed to sit on your steps?"

"It's my grandparent's cottage. I'm just visiting."

"Oh."

"But you can sit here. They won't care."

"Okay."

"I'm James. Who are you?"

"Kenny ... er, I mean Kenneth Grant Jennings. My dad is the new minister at the church up there." motioning towards the town.

"Which one?"

"Congregational."

"Oh. We're Catholic ... or, I mean, my grandparents are. I'm not really anything."

"Where do you go to church, then?"

"They usually go to St. Francis' in Traverse. I have to go with them. At home, I don't go anywhere."

"We're really Presbyterian. My dad is really just the interim minister up here."

"What does that mean ... *interim* minister?"

"It means he just fills in until they can hire somebody else."

"Where are you from then?"

"Kalamazoo. He worked at Presbytery there."

Jimmy didn't know what *Presbytery* meant, so just said, "Oh."

"What does your dad do?" asked Kenny.

"I don't have a dad … only a mother. She doesn't like to have me hanging around in the summertime, so I came up here to stay with my grandparents."

That was something Kenny didn't understand, so it was his turn to just answer, "Oh."

"How old are you Kenny?"

"Twelve. How old are you?"

"Fourteen – but maybe we can be friends anyway?"

Kenny had stood up, and was leaning on the railing at the bottom of the stairs. As he talked, Jimmy looked him up and down. He thought he looked rather small for twelve, but he was slight, still with boyish features. He wore only blue jeans and sandals, the elastic band of his white underpants rising above the belt-less waistband of his jeans. Their blue and gold strips suggested they were the same kind of boy's briefs that he had just bought at Walmart. His hair was coarse and very dark brown, almost black, and was cut short, but still long enough to comb. His ears stuck out a little, but only enough to be cute. He seemed kind of skinny, his rib cage clearly visible on the sides, and even above the middle of his chest, below his prominent clavicles. His skin was very fair, with traces of bluish blood veins showing randomly from beneath the surface on his chest and stomach. Like himself, Kenny could use a little sun, he thought. But most eye-catching of all was his face, or perhaps the expression on it, which didn't seem to give away what was going on underneath. There was a hint of a smile, but yet a serious look, sometimes almost plaintive. He didn't know what to make of it. But he did know that Kenny was a beautiful boy, and he was happy for the possibility that they might become friends.

"Jamieeee! Come up; dinner!" called Josie from atop the bluff.

"I have to go up. Do you have a swim suit Kenny? Can you come back after dinner – maybe about seven?"

"Maybe. I'll ask." answered Kenny, but not sounding very confident.

Jimmy bounded back up the stairway, but taking only two stairs at a time on the way up, as Kenny headed back down the beach towards Fishtown, climbing around the end of the fence with the sign that said *No Trespassing – Private Beachfront Beyond this Point.*

Jimmy didn't change back into his clothes for dinner, but rather just ran upstairs to slip on one of his new tee shirts, then came back down in swim trunks and tee shirt.

"Who's the black-haired boy?" asked Lee.

The question surprised him somewhat, since he wasn't aware that Gramps had been watching them.

"He's Kenny. His dad is a minister here."

"Hmm ... the new Congregational preacher, I suppose." mused Lee. "How old?"

"Twelve."

"What was he doing on our steps?" wondered Lee.

"I don't know ... just sitting I guess. I told him you wouldn't care."

"Good." grunted Lee.

"He might be back after dinner." Jimmy hoped.

"Uh-huh." nodded Lee, no longer seeming to be paying much attention.

"Well if he does, bring him up so we can meet him." chirped Josie, always quick to make the acquaintance of new summer people. "I heard they were from Kalamazoo."

"Hopefully not the nut-house." suggested Lee, with mock sarcasm.

"There's a nut-house in Kalamazoo?" asked Jimmy with some concern.

"Oh, yes. It's been there for years! It's for the sexually depraved." answered Lee, hiding his appreciation for his little attempt at humor.

"Lee! Stop that! What's gotten into you?" scolded Josie.

Jimmy was somewhat more concerned now.

"Do they call it the *Presbytery*?"

With that, Lee couldn't hold back anymore and busted out laughing.

"Yes, something like that, I think." ... which brought even more laughter up from his belly.

"Lee! That's not nice at all!" said his wife.

"No, Jamie. The nut house ... um ..." shaking her head to correct herself ... "I mean the *State Hospital*, is not called ... Oh, just forget it. Lee, sometimes I wonder about you!"

"Just don't worry Jamie. I'm sure they're very nice people." reassured his grandmother.

Jimmy was always quick to help clear the table and do the dishes. It wasn't because he wanted to be seen as a *goody-two-shoes*; it was because he understood that his grandmother took that gesture as an expression of respect and affection, and he enjoyed being able to please her in that way with so little effort. There was usually little to do, anyway – mostly just the tableware, because she had always been in the habit of cleaning up things as she went, having all the pots, pans, measuring cups, and other food preparation things washed and drying in the dish rack before the meal was served. Afterwards, she and Jimmy would clear together, and then he'd begin washing the dishes while she put away the things that had dried themselves while they were eating. Their teamwork had become a developed habit. He couldn't remember when it started.

After the dishes were done, he ran back down to the beach. A small gaggle of gulls got up from their perches on the sand with a little annoyance, and padded up the beach several yards as he came bounding down the stairway, then stood there, alert, but feigning nonchalance as they looked back over their backs to ensure that he was keeping his distance. Other than that, the beach was vacant.

The sand had been hot earlier in the day, almost too hot to walk on with bare feet, but it was now just cozily warm. He walked more gingerly as he approached the water, and its apron of pebbles. They came in all sorts of sizes and shapes and colors. Some granite, some limestone, and the occasional *Petoskey Stone*, a kind of ancient coral with a strange-looking hexagonal pattern that could be made into jewelry for tourists. The pebbles were mostly all smooth and polished, after having been rolled around for eons in the sandy wash at the water's edge, as if in a giant tumbler, giving the feel of walking barefoot on a fine terrazzo surface, except for the occasional blow-in whose still-pointy edges were available to stab the sole of the unwary foot.

The evening had come, the breeze had subsided, and the big lake had calmed. For unmeasured moments he stood on the wet pebbly surface at the water's edge, feeling the refreshing coolness as little wavelets lapped at his toes. Every now and then a more aggressive little comber rushed in over the others, swamping his feet, then rolling pebbles gently back against their Achilles connections and around his ankles, rendering a pleasant feeling that fell just short of tickling ... perhaps more like a very gentle massage ... and with each such episode, his feet sank a little bit deeper into the slurry. Was it really every seventh wave, he wondered, as he began to count the intervals between the occasional rogues? His mind wandered and he lost track of the count, but it seemed so. Or maybe it just seemed so because his grandfather had told him so long ago that it was, and that's what his mind had come to believe.

The Lake Michigan waters off the Leland beaches were clean and fresh, so much so that one might, without much reservation, dip a cup full for drinking. From the shoreline out into the increasing depths the pebbles rapidly increased in size until becoming larger stones, mostly flat, but placed haphazardly enough as to be uncomfortable under foot and therefore unsteadying to the wader. As Jimmy ventured out into the water, its comforting coolness quickly became chilling. But he was used to that phenomenon, giving his body time to gradually become adjusted as he slowly, but deliberately waded out into deeper and deeper water. The moment of truth always came just as the gently rolling surface reached the bottoms of his swim trunks, and as, by going up on tip-toes he would always unsuccessfully attempt to avoid, the inevitable shock as the next wave brought the chilly surface up to his crotch.

Once that part of his body was immersed, the chill water seemed to warm up significantly, and within another few steps he worked up the courage to plunge the rest of it in, taking a jumping pike dive forward and doing the breast stroke with frog kicks under water for as long as his breath would allow. By the time he came up, he was standing on the sand which lay out beyond the stony apron. Shaking the water from his hair and squeegeeing it from his face with his hands, from forehead to chin, he saw that the gulls were still alone on the beach, so knowing that once in, one must stay in, he rolled out onto his back, cruising lazily along on the surface, doing his improvised back stroke.

Looking up as he gently rowed himself along, the evening sky was beginning to paint a nighttime display. Although it was not yet dusk, the moon had appeared just over the bluffs to the east, and a couple of bright stars. No, he thought, they couldn't be stars, they must be planets ... one Venus, no doubt, but what could the other one be? But wait; that one is moving across the sky from southwest to east ... maybe it's a jet ... no, maybe a satellite. What he was actually seeing was the setting sun reflecting off the orbiting International Space Station as it passed overhead.

Jimmy wasn't a strong swimmer, and was always cautious about wandering out into depths that were over his head. During the daytime hours, when the sun was high, he had learned to keep away from deep water, even while swimming on his back, by noticing the brightness on either side of him, as the light-colored sand on the bottom reflected the sun's beams. When the water began to darken, he'd know that he was drifting out too far, and would turn a little towards shore. In the absence of the overhead sun, he frequently touched down carefully, to assure himself that the bottom was still within reach in water that was not more than chin deep. If the bottom wasn't there, the panicky feelings would instantly begin to bubble up from deep within his gut as he began to thrash shoreward. He couldn't help it.

He had tried to train himself to keep his head by wading out into chin-deep water, then launching himself ahead a few yards with breast strokes and frog kicks, keeping his face above the water, and then trying the touch down to confirm that he was then indeed out over his head, but with the consolation of knowing that safety was only a few yards back.

That only worked for those sorts of exercises. Whenever he found that he had inadvertently strayed into deep water, panic would instantly take over his mind and body. During the summer when he was only four, he had nearly drowned after falling into a little river, little more than a creek actually, and was able to save himself only by encountering a providential tree root growing out of the bank below the surface. That scary experience had apparently burned an indelible fear of the water into his mind, which he was ashamed of ... and admitted to nobody.

As he floated along on his back, looking at the one star that remained not far from the moon, it seemed like the two were a pair, the star perhaps swinging from an invisible line attached to the lower tip of the crescent. He thought about Kenny, and strangely relished the vacant feeling that arose in his chest as he imagined how nice it would have been had he been able to come back, and how disappointing it was that he hadn't.

"Tweee-u-weeeet! Jamie!"

His woolgathering was suddenly broken off by the sound of his grandpa hailing him from the water's edge on the beach with his two-fingered whistle, and he swooped his arms widely backwards to right himself, touch down on the sandy bottom, and wave back with both arms raised high.

"Your grandma says it's getting dark ... time for you to come up!"

Jimmy began running shoreward, at least to the extent that a person who is mostly under water can run against its weight, simultaneously flailing his arms like the side wheels of a steamboat to help provide more forward thrust. As the water became more and more shallow, his speed increased until he finally came splashing wildly over the rocks, then onto the pebbles towards his grandpa.

Lee backed off quickly to avoid getting sprinkled. The gulls remained unperturbed by this commotion and hadn't moved. Lee had brought down the warm black and blue striped beach towel, which he draped over Jimmy's shoulders as his grandson bent over to wipe the drizzling water down off his abdomen and legs.

"Come on, boy ... let's go up before you get a chill."

As they turned toward the stairway, Jimmy noticed a small form with dark hair, hanging on the fence with the sign that separated Fishtown from the cottage row along Lake Street. He waved, and his heart sunk a little as the small form with the dark hair waved back, then turned and ran back up the grassy slope towards Main Street. He wondered how long Kenny had been there, and why he didn't come back over? Maybe he had seen Gramps coming down the stairs, and was just shy, or maybe just thought it was too late. But he had a feeling that Kenny had actually been lingering there on the other side of the fence for longer than that.

Maybe he had said or done something wrong the first time they met. He tried to remember – to figure out what that might have been. He couldn't think of anything other than the possibility of his being too eager to be friends. That sometimes turned kids off. It had happened before.

But Kenny had waved back and then run off, like he was trying to send some sort of message – like he was trying to signal that his not coming back over didn't mean that he didn't want to be friends.

* * *

<u>9</u>

As Jimmy lay in his bed that evening, looking out his window at the starry canopy over Leland, his mind ran back over the history of his recent escape from his mother's house in Indianapolis, and her devious Culver intentions for him. He had been here with her parents, Lee and Josie Smith, for only one day, yet he felt perfectly cozy in this bed ... *his bed* ... in this cottage, and at this place. The day, which had started off with fear and uncertainly, had turned out to be eventful, and fun – and even *special* by virtue of his having met, and instantly hit it off with a really nice boy who seemed sure to become a very good friend. With his mind ruminating over these peaceful and loving feelings, the pictures in his head gradually dissolved into the mist of dreams as he drifted off to sleep.

———

Josie loved starting her day by weeding and watering her little flower gardens in the morning before the sun got too high. She'd had coffee and toast with Lee, and was busy on the street side of the cottage, hose in hand and quietly singing to herself ...

> *"The farmer and the cowman should be friends.*
> *Oh, the farmer and the cowman should be friends.*
> *One man likes to push a plow,*
> *the other likes to chase a cow,*
> *But that's no reason why they cain't be ..."*

... when she noticed the shadow of someone standing behind her. Turing her head and shoulders slightly to the left while continuing to spray her hostas and impatiens ...

"Yes?" she asked.

"Does a boy live here?" the visitor inquired in a rather weak, treble voice.

She turned, still holding the hose on the garden. It was a youngster ... a rather slight boy with dark hair, dressed in shorts, tee shirt and flip-flops. Very cute ... actually darling, she thought.

"Well, let's see. Yes, we have two. Which one could it be ... Winston Leon Smith, or James Winston Sutton?"

The boy drew his chin in and back a little, with a look of uncertainty, not recognizing either name she had offered, and as if wondering if, perhaps, she might be a little *strange.*

"Hum ... from the look on your face, I'm guessing it is probably not Lee that you're looking for, but probably Jamie. I'm afraid he's not here."

She was teasing, and when the boy's look turned to one of disappointment as he began to turn away, she quickly continued ...

"Jamie is already down on the beach this morning. Just go around this side of the house, across the lawn and down the stairway, and you'll probably find him there."

"And by the way, whom have I had the pleasure of meeting this fine morning?"

He looked confused.

"That means; what's your name ... who are you?" she clarified the question.

76

"Oh. My name is Kenneth Grant Jennings. I'm the minister's boy."

"I'm pleased to meet you Kenneth Grant Jennings. I am Joanne Marie Smith, wife of Lee Smith. You may call me ..." she was about to say *Josie*, but, considering the possibilities of his parents' preferences, changed her mind ... "*Mrs. Smith* ... or if you are a very close friend of Jamie's, perhaps just *Grandma*. That's what he calls me. May I call you Kenneth?"

"Everybody just calls me *Kenny*."

"Good. *Kenny* it will be."

Having finished with the introductions, she motioned to the side of the cottage with a sort of pointing wave to indicate he should go as directed to find her grandson. He smiled and nodded, and began walking purposefully in the direction she had indicated. She watched him go, leaning slightly to the left to see around the corner of the cottage, hose still trained on the hostas and impatiens. When he thought he was around the corner and out of her sight he broke into a run, hurrying across the grassy lawn to the stairway and quickly sinking down over the edge of the bluff.

She smiled, pleased that Jamie had apparently already found a new friend, and one who was adorable in both looks and behavior. She also thought she would have to inquire as to who the *minister* was. As it occurred to her then that perhaps they were just visiting, or tourists – that this might not be a very long friendship, her smile faded, and she went back about her business of watering the flowers.

Kenny found Jimmy in his Kona print swimsuit, ponderously strolling along the pebbled apron of the beach, hesitating now and then for a closer look at something, sometimes picking it up, and then underhandedly casting it out into the water. Whatever Jimmy was doing, he was concentrating on it so intently that he hadn't noticed Kenny's approach.

"Hi." Kenny announced.

Jimmy turned and raised has gaze from the boy's flipflopped feet to his face, acknowledging the salutation with an involuntary grin.

"What are you looking for ... did you lose something?"

"Petoskeys."

"What's *petoskeys*?"

"Like these." replied Jimmy, handing Kenny two small pebbles.

The pebbles didn't look much different than many of the others. In fact, they were sort of brownish-gray, and not as pretty as many of the others. Kenny shrugged, having no clue as to why Jimmy had picked up these two particular stones.

"Lick them." said Jimmy.

"Huh?"

"Lick them ... make them wet."

Kenny rolled his tongue around in his mouth to generate some saliva, and then licked the larger of the two stones. It turned dark brown, and a sort of honeycomb pattern appeared.

"What is it?" he asked.

"They're Petoskey stones. You can only find them along the beach around here ... mostly over there by Pyramid Point ..." pointing southward across the water. "There usually aren't many around here, but sometimes there are some. I just happened to see those two and thought maybe there would be more."

"What do you do with them?" asked Kenny.

"Nothing. I give them to my Grandma. She mostly gives them away."

Jimmy could see that Kenny's inquisitive expression had still not been satisfied, so continued ...

"Some people polish them up and make jewelry out of them. They're sort of like turquoise."

"Oh." said Kenny.

His curiosity about that satisfied, he began to stroll slowly alongside Jimmy, with head down, peering at the wet pebbles along the shoreline, looking for a stone with the honeycomb pattern.

"You can't usually find big ones in the water, because the tourists have already picked everything all over." continued Jimmy. "Gramps told me a secret they don't know ... to look for dry Petoskeys on the beach with the sun ahead of you, watching for rocks that sparkle a little."

"Like that one over there?" asked Kenny, pointing towards a light gray rock that did, indeed, seem to sparkle a little in the sun, which had by then risen high enough to be beaming down from atop the bluff.

"Maybe. Go get it and dunk it in the lake to see."

Kenny went over and picked up a stone about the size of a flattened baseball, brought it back to the water's edge and dipped it into the lake. It wasn't a great specimen, being part Petoskey and part something else, but it was indeed partly Petoskey, and that part of it had a very pretty rendition of the honeycomb pattern.

"Well, I'll be!" congratulated Jimmy. "You must be a natural when it comes to Petoskey stones!"

"Here ... you can have it." offered Kenny somewhat proudly.

"No, you keep it. It's yours ... your first Petoskey stone."

"I saw you by the fence last night."

"I know. I saw you wave." replied Kenny.

"How come you didn't come over?"

"My Dad was mad at me ... he said I had no business going beyond the fence ... that I was bad for disobeying the sign, and not to do it again."

"Awe, that sign is just for the tourists. Gramps said they used to come down and have parties on the beach all day and all night, right in front of the cottages. So, he and some other neighbors had the fence put up ... and the sign."

"Oh."

"I was sorry you didn't come back. I thought maybe you didn't want to, but then I saw you up there by the fence. How long were you there?"

"A little while ... maybe a half-hour ... I don't know. I saw you when you came down and while you were swimming, and I wanted to come over. But my Dad ..."

"I wish I would have seen you there before. I would have run down there and got you."

"It's okay, Jimmy. How come your Grandma calls you *Jamie*?"

"Only her and Gramps call me that ... because my name is *James*. James – Jamie, Jim – Jimmy. Everybody else says *Jimmy*."

"Is the water warm?" wondered Kenny.

"Jump in and find out." chided Jimmy. "How come you didn't bring a suit ... can you go in with those shorts."

"I did." said Kenny while dropping his shorts and peeling off his tee shirt. "But I forgot to bring a towel."

80

"My Grandma has lots of beach towels. ... Wow — a real *Speedo!*"

Under his shorts Kenny was wearing a dark brown formfitting brief, with *Speedo* printed on the left hip. It matched the color of his hair almost perfectly, and very attractively complimented his slim boyish figure. He looked ... well ... *sexy*, Jimmy thought.

"I swam races back home." Kenny explained.

"Really? Are you a good swimmer?" wondered Jimmy.

"Pretty good. I sometimes won."

Jimmy suddenly felt a sinking feeling. If he went into the water with Kenny, his new friend was sure to soon find out that he was not a good swimmer, and panic prone. He hated the thought of having to admit that to this younger boy, whom he had suddenly taken a great liking to. Trying to put the best face on it, he admitted ...

"Well, that makes you and me different. I'm no good in the water."

"You can't be good at swimming if you're afraid to get your face wet." answered Kenny to his friend's surprise and embarrassment.

Jimmy couldn't immediately think of a way to respond to that remark. Understanding that he had probably said the wrong thing, Kenny apologetically footnoted it ...

"Sorry. I just noticed that you usually kept your head up, that's all."

The two sat down on the dry sand, just above the high-water line the waves were leaving that morning ... cross-legged and facing each other.

"Well, you might as well know it. You'll find out soon enough anyway. I'm afraid of the water. I panic if anything goes wrong."

"Why?"

"I don't know. I think it was because I almost drowned when I was little. I don't remember being so scared then, but I must have been, because I ..."

"It's okay." interrupted Kenny. He wasn't comfortable seeing Jimmy berate himself that way. "Swimming isn't important. Who cares if you're not a good swimmer!"

"I care." answered Jimmy. "I love being in the water. I hate being such a baby ... afraid of drowning all the time. I wish I could just swim, swim, swim ... so good that I'd never have to worry about it."

"Even a good swimmer has to worry about drowning." Kenny advised. "Even good swimmers never swim alone in deep water."

"Really?" Jimmy doubted.

"Really. That's one of the first rules in swimming class. Never swim alone. Things can happen even to good swimmers."

"Like what ... shark attacks?" joked Jimmy.

"Yeah. C'mon. Let's jump in the lake!"

And with that Kenny suddenly leaned forward, rising without the use of his hands, ran down into the water up to his knees, and then dove in. Jimmy duplicated the maneuver, the two boys momentarily disappearing, swimming almost side-by-side beneath the water. Kenny very considerately remained close to shore, in water that was almost over his head, but not Jimmy's. After romping around for a while, the two wound up swimming lazily on their backs ... Kenny with the more polished form, Jimmy with his improvised version of a back-stroke ... but together

82

looking somewhat like a pair of pike cruising slowly and effortlessly along side-by-side.

Coming out of the cold water into the warm late morning sun raised goose bumps on the shivering boys, with Kenny, the slighter one, shaking quite visibly, his teeth chattering as he tried to talk.

"Let's run, Kenny. It'll warm you up."

And they took off together, running up the beach towards the little point to the north. As they rounded the point, Kenny gave up, purposely falling on his face into the warm sand. Jimmy stopped abruptly, backed up, and sat cross legged beside his panting friend.

"You really can swim, you know ..." said Kenny "... under water, on your back, and stuff. With a little instruction like I had, I bet you could be a really good swimmer."

"Thanks." answered Jimmy, thinking that Kenny was just saying that to make him feel better.

"I used to be really afraid." continued Kenny. "Now I'm only a little scared ... or maybe *cautious*."

"Awe, c'mon Kenny. You don't need to say that. I'm okay with it ... now ... between me and you. Maybe someday I'll get over it."

Kenny sat up, now more earnest.

"But it's true! Even really good swimmers respect the water. My instructor always said that people are not fish. When people are in the water, they need to remember that they are in the fish's world, and are only a little better off than a fish would be in theirs."

"I hardly know you Kenny, but already you feel like a best friend."

Kenny looked down at his bare legs and the clean golden sand. He felt like telling Jimmy something like that too, but couldn't think of anything that didn't sound like he was parroting, so said nothing.

Looking up, and feeling he wanted to change the subject, he noticed a small sailboat laying on the beach a hundred or more yards from where they'd crashed. It lay at the bottom of the bluff, tipped on its left side with the mast at an angle, some of its lines seemingly broken and dangling a little in the gentle morning breeze.

"What's that?" he asked, suddenly jumping up and continuing the run in that direction. Jimmy more deliberately rose to his feet, then followed on the run. He caught up as they reached the little boat.

"It's a Mackinaw boat. It's been here for a while. It was here the last time I came ... not last summer, but the year before."

"Oh. At first, I thought it was a shipwreck." admitted Kenny, with all earnestness.

"Well, it is kind of a wreck ... but not a *shipwreck*."

"Maybe it's abandoned. Look it has a name ... *SEA SCOUT*"

"No, it's probably theirs ..." pointing up to the cottage above the bluff ... and then noticing a man watching them from up there with hands on hips.

"Someone's watching ... we better not monkey with it." warned Jimmy, waving tentatively to the man on the bluff.

He did not wave back.

"We'd better go." advised Jimmy, and headed back towards the water on the run.

Kenny followed, and the two ran splashing into the water, and dove, as they had before. They swam as far back as the little point, and then walked the rest of the way back to the stairway, kicking up a splash with upturned toes as they strolled playfully along the water's edge. Sitting on the bottom step and drip-drying together, Jimmy wondered ...

"How long will you be staying?"

"I have to be home by lunch time."

"No, I mean how long will you be staying here in Leland."

"Oh. I don't know. Until they find a new minister, I guess. My dad is just temporary."

"Will it be for the summer?"

"I guess. Are you going to be here all summer too?"

"Unless my mother comes up here to get me ... which she probably won't."

"How come you don't have a dad?"

"He left ... and he never came back." answered Jimmy, pushing his toes under the warm sand.

"Oh." was Kenny's only response, sensing that the subject might make his friend feel uncomfortable.

"What's it like to have a dad?" asked Jimmy.

"I don't know ... nice, I guess."

"What's your mother like?"

"She's okay. Sometimes she yells a lot ... but she's okay. What's yours like?"

"She's like ... uh, she is like a ... Oh, I don't know. I ran away." confessed Jimmy.

"You ran away? From where? Why?"

"We live in Indianapolis ... Indiana. Speedway, actually ... it's all the same. It's where the race track is on the west side. She was going to dump me for the summer at the same dumb military school where she dumped me last summer. I did her a favor and ran off."

"Did her a favor? My mother would probably go crazy if I ran away. How could running away be doing your mom a favor?"

"Because she would have gotten rid of me one way or the other anyway, and Culver ... uh, the summer school ... would have cost her a lot of money. Now I'm gone, and it didn't cost her anything."

"Why do you think that? My mom would never want to get rid of me ... or my dad. Why would they?"

Then, on thinking about *why would they*, Kenny continued ...

"Is there something wrong with you? Did you do something bad?"

"Nah, she just wants to have her own life. She just doesn't want any kids in the way."

"Then why did she want to have you?"

Jimmy thought that the conversation might be getting too close to things that Kenny wasn't supposed to know about, being a minister's kid, and all. He knew a lot of things about a lot of things because he was a latch-key kid with Internet and cable and lots of time alone. But he suspected that Kenny, being younger and from a nice family, probably didn't know about such things. He decided to continue anyway ...

"She didn't ... it was an accident. I'm not supposed to know that. The guy who ran off wasn't really my dad. She *did it* with other guys and when I came out, I didn't look like him ... I looked like one of the other guys. That's why he beat her up and ran off.

I'm not supposed to know that either." To that he sardonically added ...

"I'm just supposed to think that everybody wants me and everybody loves me, and we're all just one big happy family ... Gramps, grandma, Julie and me."

"*Julie* is your mother?"

"Yes, *Julie* is *officially* my mother. But I call her Julie because she doesn't like to be called *mother* or *mom*. Her real name is Julia."

"Maybe it wasn't her fault. She probably got knocked up because she's Catholic, and they aren't allowed to use birth control. My dad says that just dumb."

"Knocked up!?!" exclaimed Jimmy with a grin, having suddenly realized that his puritan evaluation of Kenny was obviously a bit wide of the mark. "Knocked up!?! ..." he laughed.

Kenny shrugged, and sheepishly answered ...

"You know what I mean."

"Yes, I know. I wasn't sure you knew about *doing it* and all that. You're only twelve."

"So what? Everybody I know knows about screwing and babies, and all that. How old were you when you found out?"

Jimmy rolled off the bottom step into the sand, giggling with some embarrassment ...

"Eight, I think!" ... continuing to laugh with his head turned away.

"So ...? Why should I be any different?"

"Because you're a nice boy. Your parents are nice. Your dad is a minister."

"You're nice too. Your grandparents are nice ... at least your grandmother ... I haven't met your grandpa."

"Gramps is okay too. I guess I was just being stupid. Your parents must do it, because ..." the laughter was coming again, Jimmy was starting to get silly. "... because they had you ... or were you hatched from an egg!"

That struck Jimmy as really funny, and his sides were beginning to ache.

"You talk about doing it like it's bad." observed Kenny.

"It is, isn't it? That's why they call it *doing the nasty, getting down and dirty*, and stuff like that, and don't talk about it in public ... like in church and stuff."

"My dad says that it's a natural way of expressing love. He says it's only wrong when you do it with somebody you don't love, because that's like lying." explained Kenny.

"Well then I must just take after my mother ... a bad boy ... because I see girls I don't even know and think about doing it with them. Don't you ever?"

"Sometimes, but my dad says that thinking about it isn't the same as doing it."

Jimmy was beginning to understand that Kenny was more advanced in this area that he was, and sensed that it was because Kenny had a real dad who had apparently spent time with his son and willingly answered questions. He couldn't help feeling somewhat slighted by his own circumstances, and sorry for himself.

"What time is it?" wondered Kenny.

"I don't know ... maybe noon. Here; let's see." said Jimmy, pushing a stick into the sand, straight up.

"Umm ... the shadow is still on this side ..." indicating the side towards the lake ... "but not by far. So, it must be just a little before noon."

"I better go. I have to be home by lunch time. Then we're taking my sister to the airport. Maybe I can come back over tonight, after we get back."

Kenny went down to the water to grab his shorts, shirt and flip-flops, while Jimmy remained sitting in the sand at the bottom of the stairs.

"You have a sister?"

Coming back up, carrying his things in his arms, Kenny answered ...

"Yes, but don't worry. She's too old for you ... she's twenty-one. Besides, she already has a boyfriend."

"Do you have any other brothers or sisters?"

"No, she's the only one."

When they got to the top of the stairway, Josie was there setting out lunch on the picnic table at the edge of the lawn.

"You may invite your friend to lunch." she suggested.

Jimmy turned to Kenny, who was putting on his shorts, tee shirt and sandals ...

"Kenny, would you stay for lunch?"

Then without waiting for an answer, he turned immediately back to his grandmother, answering with feigned politeness ...

"No, I'm sorry Grandmother. Kenneth won't be having lunch with us today. He has to take his sister to the airport in Traverse."

Kenny looked up at Josie with a smile.

"Thank you, Mrs. Smith. I do have to go. Bye Jimmy."

And with that he took off across the lawn on a trot towards Lake Street.

Gramps came out of the cottage just as he left, and followed him with what appeared to be an interested gaze.

"Harrumph ... that one again." said Gramps, but with no special tone of voice. Jimmy understood, and was glad that Gramps approved of his new friend.

————

During their lunch, Jimmy asked Lee about the sailboat on the beach. Josie answered first ...

"Oh, that's the *Sea Scout*. She belongs to Tommy Thomassen. Tommy and his wife used to go out sailing in her almost every day, or every day when the weather was decent. Now she just lays there, the poor old boat."

"Why don't they go out anymore, Grandma?"

Lee answered ...

"Because his wife died four years ago. Sailing around here with Tommy was one of her favorite things. After she passed away, Tommy beached the boat, and it has never been moved since."

"I think we saw him up on the bluff, standing there like this ..." Jimmy got out of the picnic table for a moment to demonstrate the stance ... legs apart, hands on hips. "... and watching us."

"For gosh sakes, don't mess with his boat." warned Lee, "He might shoot you!"

"Oh, Lee ... Tommy isn't going to shoot anybody."

"Do you think he'd sell it?" asked Jimmy.

"That wreck ... who'd want it now!" muttered Lee.

"I would." answered Jimmy earnestly.

His grandfather looked at him with a frown, and shaking he head.

"You must be mad!"

"Wouldn't cost anything to ask." offered Josie in support.

* * *

10

With his grandmother's encouragement, Jimmy decided to go up the road and see Mr. Thomassen. After lunch he changed into his best Goodwill jeans, the new ones, and a short-sleeved sport shirt, put on his old sandals, combed his hair, and headed up the street.

It didn't appear that Tommy Thomassen was very prosperous. His cottage was a small, rectangular single-story place with green shingled siding and a weather-beaten hip roof. What had probably once been a lawn around the place was mowed, but had turned mostly to weeds, as had what was left of the little flower gardens either side of the deteriorating wood platform that served as a back porch on the street side. There was no door bell, but there was a knocker on the door – a brass anchor with a hinged ring and striker plate.

He had been reluctant to come here by himself, but had worked up the courage to make the effort. Now he was beginning to feel uncomfortable again. He looked to the left and to the right, then half turning with the thought of calling it off. But on second thought he asked himself what was the worst that could happen ... Mr. Thomassen would kick him in the pants and tell him to get off his property and never come back? Nah, he thought, he could survive that. So, taking a breath, he lifted the anchor's ring, tapped it lightly against the striker plate a few times, and then waited.

There was no response. He felt a little bit relieved. He thought about quickly deciding that Mr. Thomassen wasn't home and hurrying away before being proven wrong. But he tried the knocker again anyway.

There was still no answer, and no sign of anyone around the place. Again, he breathed a little easier, but thinking that he probably wasn't going to get an answer so might as well prove to himself that he wasn't lacking in courage, he picked up the brass ring again, this time tapping much more forcefully.

"Okay!" he said to himself, but out loud. "Three strikes and you're out!" and he turned to leave, stepping down off the wooden platform onto the partly overgrown steppingstone walk that led back out to the street.

"On the contrary, boy!" a voice behind him said. "The third time's the charm. What'd ya want."

"Are you Mr. Thomassen?" Jimmy asked.

"Who's asking ... and why?"

"I'm Jimmy ... er, I mean James Sutton ... Lee and Josie Smith's boy ... I mean grandson."

"Yeah? That old bird send ya over here? Or was it her?" the man asked suspiciously, his head slightly cocked to the side and eyeing Jimmy out of the corners of his eyes.

"No, I came on my own." He assumed this must indeed be Tommy Thomassen.

"Well, well! ... I bet Winston told you I was an old sonofabitch, didn't he?"

Not very many people around Leland, if any, ever called his grandfather by his real first name. That was different ... suggesting that Tommy Thomassen probably wasn't included among the regular people around Leland. He came off as pretty coarse and gruff, but remembering his grandma's admonition ... that Tommy's bark was much worse than his bite ... Jimmy bit the side of his lower lip and continued on the chance that she might be right.

"He said you might shoot me." he admitted, still nibbling on the side of his lower lip.

"Well, by Jesus, I might just do that too! So, why are you here? You got a death wish, or what?"

"I wondered if you might be willing to sell your sailboat."

"Yeah, I saw you and the other little brat down there messing around with my boat this morning. Lucky for you, you ran off before I could get my shotgun. You'd a' been picking rock salt out of each other's asses."

He wasn't comfortable having Kenny referred to as a brat. It struck a hurtful chord, and he felt he should stand up for his younger friend.

"That was Kenny. He's the new minister's boy."

"Worse yet! Preacher's kids are always bad apples."

"They are?" asked Jimmy.

"Damned right they are ... always the worst! You'd be smart to steer clear of that kid. Nothing but trouble. Big trouble."

Jimmy didn't like this conversation. He knew that wasn't true about Kenny. But he didn't dare argue with Mr. Thomassen, so just kept his opinion to himself.

"Do you think you might be interested in selling your sailboat."

"It ain't no damned *sailboat!* Didn't yer grandpaw teach you nothing? *Sailboats* are for candy asses. She's a Mackinaw boat ... a real boat. I built her myself ... er, actually me and yer grandpaw. A

94

Huron type Mackinaw boat, to be more exact. And no, you can't have it! Go on home and tell your grandpaw to stick it up his ... ah, to stick that in his pipe and smoke it."

"Gramps doesn't have anything to do with it. I know how to sail. I earned a certificate last summer. I thought maybe I could fix it up and ..."

"Oh?" said Mr. Thomassen mockingly. "You earned a *certificate*! Well, well. Where is it? Let's see it."

"It's not here; it's home in Indianapolis."

"Oh, yes. Indianapolis ... a well-known port city. All sorts of sailing going on down there in Speedway. You're yer grandpaw's boy all right; that much's for sure. Yer as full if it as he is."

Jimmy sighed and shrugged his shoulders. This was going nowhere. And he wondered how Mr. Thomassen knew that he lived in Speedway.

Noticing the boy's impatience, and suspecting he might be close to losing him, Thomassen changed tacks ... "What do you know about fixin' boats anyway?"

"Nothing right now, but I can learn."

"Well, the *Sea Scout* is real nail sick. She'll need a lot of fixin'."

Jimmy caught the quick change in the conversation's mood ... as if Mr. Thomassen was beginning to mull over the possibility of selling.

"How much would you want for her?"

"How much you got?"

"Six hundred and sixteen dollars ... and eighty cents."

"Done! Gimme yer money, then get down there and haul yer damned *sailboat* off my beach!"

"I don't have it with me. I can quick go get it."

"No, sir! By the time you got back, I would have changed my mind. The deal's off. You gotta learn to strike while the iron's hot, boy. Should'a come prepared. You can go now."

So that was Jimmy's introduction to Tommy Thomassen. He was a strange old coot ... but interesting, and in an odd way, even likable.

———

"So, how'd it go with the Chief?" Josie asked when Jimmy got back to the cottage. She really didn't need to ask. She could tell from Jimmy's lack of exuberance how it had gone.

"He almost let me buy his boat, but just because I didn't have my money with me right then and there, he changed his mind."

"How much was he asking for it?" wondered Josie.

"What I have ... $616.80."

"Heavens, Jamie! That old canoe isn't worth that ... it's been sitting there rotting away on the beach, summer and winter, for three or four years now, and it was over fifty years old before that! Didn't you try at all to dicker with him on the price?"

"Well, no." answered Jimmy sheepishly. He had wanted the boat so badly that the possibility of bargaining didn't even occur to him.

"Why not, for goodness sakes?" chided Josie.

"I guess I hadn't thought about what it might actually be worth. I just wanted it, and I guess I thought it was probably worth more than I had."

Lee had walked into the kitchen from the sun porch and, on hearing Jimmy's explanation, chimed in ... "That's called *thinking with your balls*, boy."

"Honestly, Lee!" Josie scolded.

96

"Well, it's true. Young guys only think about how much they want something ... how *cool* it would be to have it. They never give a thought to how badly the other side might want to sell it, or *need* to sell it. They never do their homework ... just trot off in a big hurry to get separated from their money."

"Oh, Tommy wouldn't have taken his money, Lee. You know that."

"Oh, I do, do I?"

"Yes, you do."

"Why did you call Mr. Thomassen *the Chief,* grandma?" wondered Jimmy.

"He's retired from the Coast Guard." answered Lee. "He was a Chief Boatswain's Mate, and was the Chief at various Stations all around the Lakes, and on a couple of ice breakers, and even some patrol boats off the Atlantic coast. Everybody in the service or sailing on the Lakes knew him."

"He kept thinking that you put me up to something, Gramps. I told him you didn't even know I was going over there. But he said stuff like you were *full of it* and could *stick it in your pipe,* and stuff like that."

"Oh, he did, did he?" said Lee with a rather impish looking smile.

"You don't get along?" Jimmy suspected.

"Pshaw ... they've been friends for over fifty years." interjected Josie.

"Fifty-seven." corrected Lee.

"They just love to tease each other ... they're just like a couple of little boys ... maybe both going into their second childhood. You just put yourself in the middle of it. Tommy was pulling your leg just to get your grandfather's goat."

"He said that Kenny and I were brats ... that Kenny was bad because he's a minister's boy, and that I should keep away from him."

Lee laughed out loud, and Josie broke into a smile as she explained ...

"Tommy is a minister's boy himself! He came here just like Kenny ... when his father accepted a call to the Congregational Church. Reverend Thomassen was the minister there for over twenty years before he finally retired. That's why he was saying that ... he was just teasing again. I'm sure he really doesn't think you and your friend are brats."

"So, do you think he might sell me his boat, Gramps ... I mean, after he gets done pulling your leg?"

"Tommy and I built that boat together, back when we were your age. He was actually two years older ... sixteen. I was fourteen that summer. It was a scout project ... we were in *Sea Scouts.*"

"Sea Scouts?" asked Jimmy.

"Yes. It was part of the Boy Scouts ... you know ... Cub Scouts, Boy Scouts, Eagle Scouts, Sea Scouts, and all that. Scouting used to be a popular pastime for boys. When Tommy came here with his family he was already a Scout ... a Cub Scout. Leland didn't have any scouting until his dad came and talked the church into starting up a troop. So, I joined up that summer too. I was only seven, I think."

"What did Sea Scouts do?"

"Oh, you learned about boating and sailing and safety on the water, the law of the sea, how to take care of boats and all that ...

98

it was sort of like a junior Coast Guard thing. *Women and children first!* That use to be our motto."

"How come you built the boat?"

"Sea Scout groups were called *ships* back then. We figured that meant an actual boat. There was only the two of us ... just Tommy and me. We *were* the Leland Sea Scouts ship. Nobody was going to provide a boat for just two boys, so we got the idea we would build one for ourselves."

"How did you and Tommy know about how to build a boat?" wondered Jimmy.

"We didn't know anything about boat building, but that wasn't the plan to begin with. There was an old Mackinaw boat out on North Manitou that had belonged to the light keeper, and had just sat there for years after the government closed down that light. We heard that the Coast Guard over there was going to burn it to get rid of it, so Tommy's dad asked if Tommy and I could have it for a Sea Scout project. They towed it over here for us. It was in such bad shape that they made Tommy's dad ride in it and bail with a hand pump all the way across to keep it from sinking. When we looked it over, it was plain to see that she wasn't worth fixing up. The Coast Guard hadn't been able to find any sails, her lines were all either rotted or missing, some of her wood was dry-rotted; it was a big disappointment. The only part that was salvageable at all was her mast, which had apparently been replaced just before the Light Station was decommissioned."

"Boy, you and Tommy must have felt really bad about that. You probably had really high hopes, just like Kenny and me."

"We all felt a little foolish too. The Coast Guard told us that she wasn't worth towing over to the mainland. But we thought we knew better. Tommy's dad was the laughingstock of Leland for a while, since he was the one who talked them into it."

"If you two gentlemen will excuse me ..." interrupted Josie, "... I've already heard the story about the famous *Sea Scout,* so I'll leave the floor to you. I'd rather be outside with my book, enjoying the cool breeze off the lake, than sitting in here listening to all this *hot air.*"

Lee turned up his nose at her, and wagged his head and hand towards the kitchen door. His expression was one that said without saying it that women cannot, by nature, appreciate the significance of *man talk,* so she might just as well go. Jimmy had become so wrapped up in the story, he hardly noted the interruption.

"So, what happened to it Gramps ... to the boat?"

"We took the only good thing she had ... her mast ... stood it up, and built a new boat under it."

"Aww, come on, Gramps!"

"It's true! Actually, Tommy's dad got his back up because of everyone's ribbing him, and it was he that decided that we'd build a new boat. None of us knew anything about boatbuilding, but he came up with the idea of tearing the old boat apart and using the pieces as patterns. So, that's what we did. We actually created a kit, you might say, and then we put it together just like we had taken the old boat apart. It took the better part of two summers, but in the end, it was worth it. We had a fine new Mackinaw boat, and nobody was laughing then."

"Weren't you here only for the summertime when you were a boy?"

"Yes, but Tommy and his dad were permanent residents. I worked right alongside them during the summer, but they worked on the boat all year round. Come September, I always had to go back to Speedway. But while they continued to do the physical work, I had a little part-time job at home, and earned the money that bought most of the materials and supplies, including new sails and lines."

"You did? When you were only fourteen or fifteen?"

"I was old man Pottier's *fair-haired boy*, so to speak ... had been since I was ten or eleven. He owned the company my dad worked for. He just liked to have me around, and was willing to pay for the privilege."

"What was your job?"

"Well ..." Lee hesitated, seeming to be grasping for an acceptable answer ... or perhaps drifting back in his memory to earlier times ... "Well ..." he began again. "Ah ... odd jobs, this and that ... whatever he wanted. I was good to him, and he was very good to me, let's just say."

"What did your dad do at the company?"

"He was Vice President of Sales ... on the road most of the time, even overseas. Not around home much. Your great-grandmother always thought we were so lucky that François Pottier had taken a liking to me that way ... *like the son he never had*, she'd say."

"She was right, wasn't she? After you grew up, you wound up running the company and making *a lot* of money."

"Yes, well she never really knew what ..."

Lee quickly stopped short, having forgotten himself for a moment. He had strayed into an area he'd always been careful to avoid, almost revealing things that others didn't need to know about his past, least of all his grandson. His head dropped slowly, as if he was drifting off into the depths of memories from long ago, or had perhaps noticed something on the floor that diverted his attention from the story he was sharing. After several moments, he suddenly looked up asking ...

"Ah ... what was it we were talking about?"

"You and Mr. Pottier in Speedway." suggested Jimmy.

"No, I mean before that?"

"We were talking about how you and Mr. Thomassen and his dad rebuilt the boat."

"Yes. Well, so that's how it was done. And we wound up with a much finer boat than the light station had, because ours was mostly all teak wood, brought over from Africa by old man Pottier."

"What's *teak wood*?"

"Ah, it a fine hardwood from India and Africa and places like that, that's the best wood for boats because it's impervious to bugs, doesn't rot, and just gets nicer and nicer looking, the older it gets. That's why the Sea Scout is still here after all these years. Had she been rebuilt out of pine, she's have rotted away years ago."

"Mr. Pottier got it for you?"

"He came up to Leland now and then during the summers. Sometimes he'd come up to see my dad on business, and other times he'd go over to North Manitou to hobnob with other business tycoons and celebrities. When he found out about our boat project, he insisted it had to be built of teak wood, so had what we needed sent over by air. It came clear from Africa."

102

Josie came back in right then with Tommy Thomassen in tow, whom she introduced by saying ...

"Look who I found snooping around our back yard!"

"Hello Winston. Joanne says you've been busy filling this little con man's head with lies about the Sea Scout ... is that true boy?"

Jimmy shrugged.

"Well did you find yer money yet? Or did you just make that up?"

"No, I have the money. But Gramps said I was dumb to offer that much and I should have tried to get a better deal."

"Yeah, well that's Winston for ya ... always was a party pooper, even when he was your age."

Jimmy looked at his grandpa and smiled.

"So, do you think you'll ever be willing to part with the Sea Scout, Mr. Thomassen?"

"Well I'd have to consult with your grandpaw here, but I think we might be able to come up with some sort of a deal. Why don't you make yourself scarce? Winston and me will talk it over, and then we'll let you know what we decide."

————

Jimmy went outside, crossed the lawn to the stairway leading down to the beach, and sat down on the top step. The afternoon was waning, and the sun was beginning its descent into the lake, where it would eventually fall behind the bluffs on South Manitou's far side.

"Hi" said Kenny, as he sat down on the step beside him.

"Back from the airport already? Did your sister get off okay?"

"Yes, exactly on time. So, what's going on? Your grandma said you were out here waiting for your grandpa and his friend to decide about the boat."

"The boat belongs to Mr. Thomassen ... the guy who was up on the ridge. He and Gramps built it together when they were our age. I didn't know anything about that, and went over to ask Mr. Thomassen if he might be willing to sell it to us and ... well, it's kind of a long story."

"And so ...?"

"And so, Gramps and his friend Tommy are talking it over ... whether they want to sell it to us, or not."

"How much do you think it might cost. I don't have much ... only what's in my savings account. My dad doesn't have much either ... ministers don't make much."

"Mr. Thomassen said we were brats ... and you especially because you're a minister's kid." shared Jimmy impishly.

"Aww, that's okay. Lots of people think that ... especially other kids. Do you think that?"

Jimmy turned towards his younger friend, held Kenny's head with his hands on either side of his face while gazing intently into his eyes.

"Hmm ... I do sometimes wonder what evil lurks beyond those two beady little windows to your mind! Yes, I think Tommy was right. I'd best keep away from you!"

And with that he jumped up and went swinging down the stairway, balancing on the handrails, jumping down four steps at a time. Kenny chased him down to the beach, and then along the water's edge until he fell into the sand, totally winded. Making a wide sweeping turn, Jimmy came trotting back and plopped down, huffing and puffing, beside him.

"No, Kenny. Mr. Thomassen was only teasing. He was you about sixty years ago, when his dad came here just like yours ... to be the minister at the Congregational Church."

———

Back at the cottage, Lee and Tommy were enjoying each other's company just as much as the two young boys on the beach. Their affection and admiration for each other had been equally strong, and had not faded much over the years, in spite of their having gone their separate ways into careers that were as different as night and day.

"Are you really serious Tommy? I know how much the Sea Scout meant to you and Susanna. She would have never been able to part with it; I'm pretty sure of that."

"Yeah, Susie loved to sail around in that old boat, didn't she? She was an old *Norsky* too, you know. That's why." answered Tommy jokingly. "Those were the days."

"Yes, those were the days. The four of us had some good times together back then!"

"Yep! ... Well, that was then; this is now. Ya know, Winston, when I saw those two boys down there by the boat, for a moment it was like you and me all over again."

"And we were just as handsome and cute, were we not?"

"Well, I'm not so sure about that ... at least not in your case." teased Tommy. "But your grandson is a looker, and seems to be such a nice boy ... must'a taken after Joanne!"

"He took after her for looks, and me for brains." retorted Lee.

"The other boy's a nice one too ... a preacher's son, no less! I'll be damned if it ain't me and you all over again." swore Tommy. "Anyway, when I saw them down there, I knew the one was your boy, and I got the idea right off ... how nice it would be to watch history repeat itself ... two boys and a boat ... just like you and me a half-century ago."

"Fifty-six years, actually." corrected Lee.

Tommy scowled at him affectionately. "Once a bean counter, always a bean counter!"

"I wasn't no damned bean-counter!

"Yeah, I know. You were a "chief," just like me ... you a *CEO* and me a *CBM*." Tommy sighed. "Two *Big Chiefs!* And look at us now ... just two fat, ugly old farts with piss stains on the front of our pants and balls hanging down to our knees. What the hell happened, Winston?"

"You can speak for yourself ... or for your own balls, Tommy. Mine are just fine." laughed Lee. "But I agree ... beauty is wasted on the young. I look in the mirror and see the same thing you do. I don't like growing old. I don't recommend it. Now that you've mentioned it, I see the same thing in those two boys that you do. And I'm like you ... sentimental, I guess. Yes, it would be nice to see them working together on the old Sea Scout. It would be nice to see her out on the water again."

"Then it's done, and done!" concluded Tommy, rapping the heal of his hand on the table like a gavel. "The boat is theirs, if they want it."

"But not without some strings." cautioned Lee. "People don't value things that don't cost them anything."

————

"Oh, oh. Here they come." warned Kenny.

Jimmy turned to see. Gramps and Tommy Thomassen coming down the stairway.

"Ahh ... so this is the preacher's brat, I presume?" was Tommy's salutation as they approached the two boys.

Kenny stood up and, with his feet spread and his hands on his hips, looked Tommy Thomassen directly in the eyes and replied ...

"Likewise, I presume?"

Tommy, having busted out laughing at Kenny's feigned impudence, came over to muss his hair and say "Well, looks like that cat's out of the bag!"

"Okay, boys ..." said Lee, getting right to the point. "Here's our proposition. If you want to do all the work it'll take to restore the Sea Scout and make her seaworthy again, you can have the boat."

"How much are you asking, then?" wondered Kenny.

"I said that if you're willing to do all the work, *you can have the boat*. Tommy ... er, Mr. Thomassen ... is going to give it to you. We will help you out by showing you what needs to be done and how to do it. But you'll have to do all the work, and then whatever it takes, money wise, to fix her up will be up to you to pay for yourselves. Tommy says the sails are in his garage and are still good. But you'll have to have new lines. Other than that, we don't think you'll need much more than some cleaning supplies, some nails and roves and varnish, and such ... shouldn't cost very much."

Jimmy was smiling so broadly his face almost hurt, and he was so happy that he was having a hard time keeping his happiness from bubbling over into a silly fit of laughter.

"It's a deal!" he exclaimed.

"Uh, I'll have to ask my dad." said Kenny, much less
enthusiastically.

* * *

11

Kenny did ask his dad, and his dad wasn't all that excited about the proposed project.

"Why not, Dad?" Kenny pleaded.

"Off hand, I can think of at least three reasons." answered his father, the Rev. Grant Jennings.

"First, I have no way of knowing how long we might be here. It could be a month, or it could be a year. I'm working on a month-to-month basis. There are no *Terms of Call* because this congregation didn't want that sort of commitment. Some of them have the idea that they'll be able to come up with a good candidate sooner, rather than later. In view of what they're able to offer by way of a compensation package, they're probably mistaken. But, nevertheless, that's the deal. I'm just a *rent-a-preacher.*"

"Secondly, you're thinking about partnering up with people who are quite wealthy, and who have no problem dumping a few hundred, or a few thousand, dollars into a project like that. We don't have that kind of money, so how much of a *partner* would you be, really?"

"Finally, whether we leave in a month, or in a year, we will be leaving. And when we leave, your share of the boat, whatever it might be, will have to remain here. It'll all fall to your friend by default, so all the work you put into the project, and whatever you might spend out of your savings and allowance, will fall to your friend as a gift. Would that seem fair to you?"

"Beyond that, boats have to be registered, and licensed, and insured ... and none of that can be done by minors. So, who's going to be the adult silent partner for your project? How do we know that Mr. Thomassen isn't just fishing a couple of young boys into rebuilding his boat for him for free?"

"These people aren't like that, Dad. They're nice people."

"How could you know that? You've known them less than a week ... even less than a day!"

Realizing that he had just cast aspersions on his son's ability to form valid opinions of others, he revisited that unfortunate comment ...

"Well, I mean maybe they are. But there's an old saying ... *nice guys finish last.* In other words, people don't usually become successful and rich by being fair minded and thoughtful of others. Quite to the contrary, I'm sorry to say."

"So, then the answer is *No*?"

"I'm afraid so, son."

Kenny dropped his head and turned away before the tears of disappointment began to drip from his eyes. It didn't seem fair ... his father taking that decision when he didn't really know when they might have to leave Leland ... what if it turned out to be never? And he didn't even know Mr. and Mrs. Smith, or Mr. Thomassen.

Having turned away, he replied respectfully, merely saying "Okay, Dad. I understand." as he waked slowly out of his dad's office, the tears still dripping.

Jimmy was waiting patiently on the steps of the church. His friend lingered inside the narthex before coming out with the bad news. He didn't want Jimmy to see him crying about it, or to suspect that he had been crying, so he tried to dry his eyes and take some deep breaths. When he finally opened the church's big front door, Jimmy had only to take one look at him to see what the answer had been. Kenny's face was still reddened and stressed, and he sat down beside him without saying anything. After taking another deep breath, Kenny confirmed it ...

"He said *No.*"

He was relieved that he had been able to get that out without tearing up again. "Why?" asked Jimmy.

"Because he thinks we might not be able to stay here very long."

"So what? We can work on the boat while you're here. It would be something to do ... something fun. Better than just sitting around doing nothing all summer. If you have to leave, well ..."

"It's not only that. He had some other reasons."

"Like what?" wondered Jimmy.

"Like ..."

Kenny stopped himself when it suddenly occurred to him that some of what his dad said might sound offensive if repeated to Jimmy.

"... Oh, never mind. It doesn't make any difference. He just said *No,* so it's *no.* I can't help on the boat."

Kenny was struggling with his composure again. As yet, he wasn't quite sure why. It wasn't really about the boat. It was about his new friend. He and Jimmy, in spite of their two-year age difference, had clicked on first sight. For whatever reason, they were very strongly attracted to each other, and instantly liked one another. The boat project would have provided a reason for them to be together all day, every day, all summer long. Now Jimmy would probably decide to go ahead without him, and would maybe find somebody else to help. He'd be left out, and alone.

"Maybe he'll change his mind." Jimmy tried to be encouraging.

"He never changes his mind."

"Really ... well, there's a first time for everything. Maybe if I talk to him, he might ..."

"No! Don't." Kenny blurted out.

He knew that would only serve to harden his father's attitude, and he didn't want Jimmy to hear his dad's other reasons.

"Why not?"

"Because he would think I put you up to it. When he says *no*, it's no. Period. He expects me to take *no* for an answer when that's what the answer is. If I don't, he thinks that's disrespectful, and I get punished."

The big church door opened again behind them, and Eddie Gunderson warned ...

"Move it, or lose it Dudes!"

"Hi, Eddie. What are you doing here?" wondered Jimmy.

"That's for me to know, and you to find out."

Noticing Kenny, he continued ...

"What's up with you kid ... yer dog die, or something?"

Kenny, a little embarrassed that his emotional state was still so easily recognizable, dropped his head and looked at a spot on the step between his feet.

"Kenny's the minister's son. They just got here." offered Jimmy.

"Kenny, this is Eddie Gunderson. He lives here with his dad. His dad's the custodian here, and they work with the Indian fishing boat too."

"Uh-huh … cute." answered Eddie. "Yer grandpa met him yet?"

Jimmy assumed Eddie was referring to the minister.

"Not yet."

"Uh-huh." responded Eddie, eyeing Kenny carefully.

"So, what's your problem, little dude? What you been cryin' about?" asked Eddie.

Jimmy answered.

"We wanted to fix up Mr. Thomassen's Mackinaw boat. He said we could, but Kenny's dad says no. So, it looks like the deal is off."

That struck Kenny as being encouraging … that Jimmy didn't intend to go ahead without him. His mood quickly brightened a little, and a feeling of admiration and affection arose somewhere deep under his breast bone.

"Bullshit! Tommy Thomassen isn't going to let you two dorks fuck with the famous *Sea Scout* … never happen! No way!" said Eddie.

"Yes, way!" replied Jimmy. "He and Gramps decided we could have it, provided we were willing to fix it up with our own money."

"What's your grandpa got to do with it?" wondered Eddie.

"Him and Mr. Thomassen built it together … when they were boys like us." said Jimmy.

"No Shit? I never knew that." was Eddie's response.

"I offered to buy that from the old fart last year, and he told me to go fuck myself … that he'd sooner burn it. So, now he's giving it to you two? Let me see if I can figure this out. Hmm …"

Eddie stood there, assuming the pose of *the thinker*, his chin in his right palm, the elbow of that arm being supported by his left hand.

"Hmmm ..." he repeated, with a mischievous looking grin beginning to form.

Neither boy had the slightest idea what Eddie was thinking.

"So, what's the matter with your old man, Kenny? He got a fart crossways today, or is he just always a tight ass." continued Eddie.

Kenny decided he wasn't going to like Eddie Gunderson, and had no reason to ignore his vulgar and disrespectful behavior any further.

"No, he doesn't ... and no, he isn't. And he's not my *old man*; he's my *father*." Kenny shot back.

"Arghh!" replied Eddie. "Like father, like son!"

"Are you always so crude?" Kenny retaliated.

Eddie was being bested by a twelve-year old, and he didn't like it. It didn't show on the outside, but he was feeling hurt on the inside, because he knew it was true ... he was not a decent person. He knew how to put on the charm for older people when need be; the crass and vulgar boy could instantly vanish, magically replaced by a gentlemanly young man. But in casual situations like this, he was just himself, and nobody ever thought anything of it or, at least, never said anything about it if they did. In fact, younger boys, however *nice* they might be, were always apt to emulate his behavior when around him, which he took as an expression of their admiration and respect, and that made him feel good. Not so with Kenny.

"Fuck you; you impudent little shit! I was gonna go back in and talk your *old man* into letting you have the boat, but now you can eat me! It'll be fun watching you do without, you little prick."

With that Eddie turned and walked off towards River Street, probably headed down to the Tarnovitch.

Jimmy suppressed an urge to bust out laughing. Maybe it was nervousness, but the situation was also funny. Kenny was actually such a gentle kid, and there seemed to be something really humorous about his getting his back up, especially to a much older kid. At the same time, Eddie had, for once, been put in his place ... and by a little twelve-year old! That seemed funny too, even if with some ambivalence. On the one hand, Eddie had it coming, but on the other hand, he rather liked Eddie so was willing to make allowances, understanding that he was a product of his rather troubled upbringing. He was also sensitive to Eddie's feelings, and knew that his feelings had been hurt.

"Well, you and Eddie didn't hit it off, I'd say." chuckled Jimmy.

"I don't like him. Who is he, anyway?" asked Kenny, wondering how Jimmy could have a friend like Eddie.

"That's a long story ... probably longer than I know." answered Jimmy. "I've seen him around forever ... I mean, for as long as I've been coming here ... but I only got to know him a little this spring. If you knew him better, you might change your mind. Eddie's maybe like a diamond in the rough."

"Or maybe like a diamond in the dirt!" scowled Kenny.

"Gramps says his motto is to always presume that a man is honest and worthy of respect until he proves himself otherwise. Maybe we should give Eddie a pass until we know him better."

"I'm not sure I want to know him better." admitted Kenny.

"What's going on boys?"

Kenny's father, the minister, had come outside. He was tall, slim and looked significantly younger than his age. In fact, he was still rather boyish looking. Jimmy was used to Priests ... dressed in black with white collars. Kenny's dad was wearing casual clothes, even while apparently on duty.

"We were just talking to someone, Mr. Jennings ... or, I mean, Reverend Jennings ... Eddie Gunderson. He lives here in town." answered Jimmy.

"I'm guessing that you're the Smith boy ... Jimmy?" asked Kenny's dad.

"My name is really Sutton ... James Sutton ... but I am Lee and Josie Smith's grandson."

"You're a friend of Eddie's?" asked Rev. Jennings.

"No, we just recently got acquainted ... only this spring. He's a lot older than I am."

"And how old is that?"

"He's eighteen, I think."

"No, I meant how old are you?"

"I'm fourteen, sir."

"I'm pretty sure I'm not going to like him. Why was he here?" asked Kenny.

"What's the matter with him, son? He seemed like a very nice young man to me."

Jimmy looked at his friend, hoping that he would remember his grandpa's motto about men. Kenny answered ...

"Well, maybe I should keep my opinions to myself then ... maybe it's like Mom says ... *If you don't have anything good to say, don't say anything.*"

116

"Yes, that's good advice. Your mother's right about that. Eddie was here talking to Mrs. Cooper and the CE Committee. She thinks he might make a good leader for our Youth Ministries ... our twelve and ups."

Jimmy and Kenny looked at each other ... Kenny incredulous and Jimmy totally surprised and perplexed.

* * *

12

When he got back to the cottage that afternoon, Jimmy found his grandfather sitting at the little kitchen table by himself, playing Klondike solitaire.

"We won't be able to do the Sea Scout project, Gramps. Kenny's dad won't let him."

"Did he say why not?"

"Not really. Kenny said his dad thought they might not be staying here very long, so he shouldn't get involved. There was more to it than that, I think, but whatever the rest was, he didn't want to tell me."

"So, get somebody else." Lee suggested.

"I don't want anybody else. I like Kenny. We get along with each other really good. And besides, I don't really know anybody else."

"You didn't know Kenny a couple of days ago. Maybe you'll meet up with some other boy you'll like just as much."

"Nah. When Kenny's dad said no, that just suddenly took all the fun out of it. It just wouldn't be the same with somebody else. I'd be thinking about ... well, it just wouldn't be the same."

Lee recalled his previous conversation with Tommy, remembering how Tommy felt when first observing the two boys from the top of the bluff as they were looking over the boat ... and how it turned out that the boys' circumstances were so similar to theirs when they were about the same age. He had to agree.

"Yeah, I guess not. It wouldn't be the same. Tommy might not agree to the deal anyway if some other boy was involved. He's sort of taken a shine to your young friend ... feels connected in a way ... since he was also a preacher's boy."

"The church might hire Eddie Gunderson." Lee put down the cards.

"What?"

"Eddie was there too, and Kenny's dad says they might hire him as a youth director."

"Jeeesus-Key'ryst! Who told you that?"

"Kenny's dad. He said some lady in the church came up with the idea. So, Eddie was there ... applying for the job, I guess."

"Good Gawd!"

"Before that, Kenny lit into Eddie for being such a foul mouth and talking about his dad in a disrespectful way, and he told him off. It was funny; I could hardly keep from busting out laughing ... little Kenny going up against that big, tough, older kid."

"He's no *kid* anymore. He just turned nineteen a while ago. He's been legal for more than a year now."

It didn't occur to Jimmy to wonder how his grandfather happened to know that Eddie had just had a birthday, or to wonder what he meant by *legal.*

"I didn't laugh, because I knew Eddie felt bad. He knew that what Kenny was saying was right, and I think it hurt his feelings to hear it. I think he just talks like that because he's trying to look like he's a big wheel, or something. Inside he's really not so bad."

"You're a fine boy, Jamie. It's a good thing that you look for the best in people. But sometimes what you see is what you get. The best of us are not without our faults, and even the worst people have some good in them. A little bad doesn't make a good man evil, but a little good doesn't compensate for a whole lot of bad in a man who is."

"I'm not going to tell you to keep away from Eddie, but I can tell you that he's carrying a lot of baggage ... stuff you don't know about, and probably never will. People who own pit bulls all say the same thing: they're such nice dogs ... until they chew some baby's face off. I'd suggest you keep that in the back of your mind whenever you're around Eddie Gunderson."

Jimmy was completely nonplussed. Lee had just told him, in so many words and with earnest seriousness, that Eddie Gunderson was dangerous ... even *evil*. That didn't seem like the Eddie Gunderson he had become acquainted with. But he knew that Gramps was never one to exaggerate.

"How do you know that, Gramps? I mean I'm not trying to ... I mean, I believe you. But I wonder how you know about Eddie. Does everybody know?"

Lee was grateful for the opportunity to skip the first question by going right on to the second ...

"Evidently not. He's got some people in the Congregational church totally fooled, hasn't he!"

"And Kenny's dad?" added Jimmy.

"Oh, he doesn't know anything about anything. He just got here. Eddie wrapped him right around his little finger, I'm sure. He's really good at that. He's like a *social chameleon*."

Jimmy didn't know exactly what that meant.

"It means he can quickly adjust his personality as needed to take advantage of whatever situation he's in." Lee explained.

Jimmy felt like asking again how his grandfather knew so much about Eddie, but he couldn't think of a way to form the question such that it wouldn't sound like a challenge. So, he dropped it.

"Oh. I guess I've never met anyone like that before." he admitted, thereby affirming his grandpa, without actually signaling acceptance of everything he was saying.

"I can tell you one thing for sure." continued Lee. "If Kenny's dad persists in that foolishness, they'll be packing up and leaving for Kalamazoo much sooner that he thinks. Nobody's going to sit still for that. For Christ's sake don't say anything about that in front of Tommy ... he gets wind of that, and he'll be the next man on the moon!"

Tommy Thomassen did, in fact, soon get wind of that, and it wasn't from Jimmy or his grandpa.

"Good morning!" a tall young man offered from the street end of Tommy's stepping stone walkway. "GOOD MORNING!"

Tommy stopped, looked toward the road, and then shut down his mower.

"Good morning." said the young man again. "Am I correct in assuming that you're Mr. Thomassen?"

"You are." answered Tommy formally and noncommittally, assuming the visitor was a peddler, or something of the sort.

Having received that much encouragement, the visitor stepped forward, offering his right hand ...

"I'm Grant Jennings, your new interim minister."

"Oh, yes. I've met your son. Nice boy." Then squinting slightly to more closely examine Rev. Jennings, he added ... "Must take after his mother for looks."

"Well, yes, Others have suggested that there is a stronger resemblance to Mary." he agreed.

Grant Jennings didn't catch the joke. Tommy made note of it.

"How come you quashed the boat project?" he got right to his main concern.

"What? Oh, yes. The sailboat." Tommy made note of that too ... *the sailboat.* "We just felt that might not be the best thing for him right now."

"We? You and your wife?"

"Well, no. Just me."

"Why not?"

Grant was becoming impatient with this line of conversation. It wasn't what he'd come for, and he really thought it was none of Mr. Thomassen's business.

"Well ... with respect, Mr. Thomassen, I guess that's really between Kenneth and me."

"I guess that's probably right ... between you and your boy. Nice meeting you ... drop by again sometime."

And with that, Tommy reached down and yanked on the starter cord, starting the lawnmower up again.

"I'M SORRY ... I GUESS THAT MAY HAVE SOUNDED A LITTLE RUDE. I DIDN'T MEAN TO BE SHORT WITH YOU." Jennings called over the noise of the mower.

Tommy turned back towards him a little, looking back over his shoulder inquisitively, with the old mower still running loudly ...

"WHAT'S THAT?"

"I SAID I DIDN'T MEAN TO BE SHO ..."

Tommy shut the engine down again, and pushed the mower to the side. Grant suspected that Tommy Thomassen was not a person who could easily be dismissed with an evasive answer.

"About the boat project ... I just felt that we will probably not be here long enough for him to see that through, and he'd wind up disappointed ... having to just walk away from whatever he'd put into it."

"I see. I guess you don't really understand what it's all about then. After those two boys get all done, there'll be an old Mackinaw boat layin' on the beach, just like it was when they found it. They may go their two separate ways, and what they'll take with them ain't gonna be haffers in some old boat, but the friendship that grew out of the blood, sweat and tears they put into fixing it up one summer. That might very well last forever, and if it does, it'll sure be worth a lot more than a half of a boat."

"Well, Mr. Thomassen, when you put it ..."

"Call me Tommy."

"Oh, thank you. I was going to say ..."

"Right. You've seen the light and changed you mind. Yer boy'll be glad to hear it. Now what did you come here to talk about?"

"Nothing, specifically. I'm aware, of course, that you've traditionally been more than generous towards the church, and ..."

"Of course." interrupted Tommy, inferring, somewhat cynically that the church's finances would be among a preacher's first concerns.

"... and I've been told a little bit about you ..." continued Grant "... and just thought it might be nice to meet you."

"Yeah, they all talk, I suppose. Don't believe any of it!"

"Actually, it was Kenneth who filled me in. I daresay he has quickly taken quite a liking to you."

Tommy smiled. He was glad to hear it. He had also taken a quick liking to this man's son, but didn't say so. He was not one to share his feeling about such things. He changed the subject.

"Well, don't thank me. It's my father's money; not mine. He was one of your predecessors, you know. He was smart enough to know that he was never going to get rich as a preacher, so he got himself involved in several other interests, most of which panned out quite good. It all fell to me when he passed on."

"But I'm just a simple person ... I get my Coast Guard retirement check every month, and that's enough. I don't need my pa's money, so the better part of it went into the foundation ... Winston's and mine ... and the rest I'm divvying up to the church he built up here ... your church now."

"Oh, so you were in the Coast Guard! Then I expect you and Oscar Gunderson are well acquainted with each other?"

"Yes. I know ... er, I mean I used to know Oscar. He was a helluva good man once. Still is a good man, in some ways ... as you'll probably discover."

"I guess he has a drinking problem?" said Grant, sounding somewhat as if he was fishing for information.

Tommy couldn't resist the straight line ... "Oh, he ain't got no problem drinking!" he laughed. Then more seriously he added ...

"He may have drank a lot, but it never really interfered with his work. He always showed up, and could perform his duties just as good, whether he was tight or stone sober. That's how *real men* were back in the day. But after the war years the Coast Guard got full of candy asses who couldn't accept that a man like Oscar was better'n them, so they mustered men like him out of the service."

Sensing Tommy's seemingly very charitable attitude towards his former colleague, Grant announced "We're considering his son Edward for a position as Youth Director."

"The hell you are!?!" Tommy responded incredulously.

"Yes, he comes highly recommended by Lucy Cooper. She thought Edward could balance Bible College in Grand Rapids with his Sunday duties for a couple of years, and also put together some summer ..."

Tommy's face hardened and eyes narrowed as he looked directly into the minister's ...

"I'd belay that, if I were you mister!"

"I beg your pardon?" wondered Grant.

"Talk about puttin' the goddamned fox in charge of the henhouse!" exclaimed Tommy. "Lucy Cooper knows better'n that. He *must be* fucking her!"

"I beg your pardon!!!" sputtered Grant, not really repeating himself.

"Pardon my French, Jennings. But that young woman knows full well that nobody's gonna sit still for that, and if she doesn't, she's either gone nuts, or he's got her dick whipped."

"She has shared with me that Edward's background is somewhat checkered, but she thought he deserved a chance to better himself, and if given that chance, he very likely would."

"Now you listen to me, mister. Some bad things have happened around here in Leland, and so far, nobody knows for sure why. But I'm telling you, there's a snake in the grass here somewhere, and Eddie Gunderson's it."

"There ain't going to be no course-changing for him. He's either going to die young, thanks to some pissed off father or husband with a twelve gauge, else he's gonna wind up wiling away the rest of his life down in Jackson." referring to the state prison.

"You come up here out of the blue, with all kinds of good intentions, no doubt, and there's no reason why you would suspect any of what I've told you about that boy. Maybe you know a little bit about Oscar, but I'm telling you, the only thing that boy inherited from his dad was his last name. If there is such'a thing as the Devil, he's it!"

Grant made one more attempt ...

"I have spoken to the boy, and I must say I found nothing in his words, appearance or demeanor that would hint that any of what you are saying is true."

"Oh, yes. I'm sure you didn't." replied Tommy. "Devil ... as in *D-evil one*. He's got that nice act perfected. Look at it this way ... just like Jesus in the desert, you just had a face-to-face with Satan himself, and lived to tell about it."

"Hmm ..." was Grant's only response to that.

"What you're talking about is a good way to bust up your church ... and to get yourself run out of town on a rail."

"Hmm ..." replied Grant again. "I'll certainly take all this under advisement. I was going to propose that to the Church Board when we meet this week."

"Oh, yes. I'd forgotten there's a Board now. Well they would have quashed that idea right off the bat ... all of them but Lucy Cooper anyway. You might better talk to her and find out what's going on in her head. That little bastard must have her over a barrel somehow ... maybe blackmailing her. She's got some skeletons in her closet too, or at least that's what she thinks. Actually, everybody knows all about *her* secrets ... Leland's a small town."

The Reverend Grant Jennings let his hands limply fall to the front of his thighs like a man suffering of Asperger's Syndrome and dropped his head, wagging it back and forth as if incredulously wondering how in the name of God could all that he had just heard be going on in this beautiful place and seemingly placid little community. Tommy noticed.

"People are people, Jennings. It doesn't matter where in the world you go. The only thing that changes is the scenery."

"I guess so." agreed the minister resignedly. "I guess so."

Once again Tommy bent over and pulled the starter rope on his lawnmower. The old engine started right up with a puff of light gray smoke, and Tommy resumed mowing his weedy lawn parallel to the previously cut strip.

Grant Jennings walked back to the church with his head down and hands in his pockets, thinking about how he might go about peaceably turning off the Eddie Gunderson plan.

* * *

<u>13</u>

"Wahoo!!!" was Kenny's elated and excited response to the news when his father announced and explained his change of heart. His son wasn't usually given to such outbursts, so Grant then understood how badly he had wanted to be involved, and how disappointed he must have been upon hearing his original decision.

"Can I go tell Jimmy, Dad?"

"Yes, by all means ... please do!"

When he got to the Smith's cottage, he knocked, but nobody came to the door, so he walked around the side of the house, finding Jimmy's grandparents at their picnic table on the lawn by the bluff, with Mr. Thomassen. Without waiting for the obvious question, Lee raised his arm and pointed over the back of his head towards the stairway, indicating that Jimmy was down on the beach.

He was so eager to get down to the beach that he attempted Jimmy's method of taking four or five steps at a time by swinging down the handrails, almost stumbling twice, but quickly arriving at the sandy bottom. Seeing Jimmy a ways up the beach, he took off on the run towards the little point. As soon as he was within shouting range of his friend, he began yelling ...

"He changed his mind! He said I could help! We can do it!"

And on reaching Jimmy, the two boys joined arms, facing each other and jumping excitedly and happily up and down.

"See, I told you he might change his mind!" kidded Jimmy.

"Yeah you did!" laughed Kenny, as they continued hopping up and down and around in a circle.

The jumping stopped momentarily. "I wonder what happened?" pondered Jimmy.

"I don't know. He went over to talk to Tommy ... I mean, Mr. Thomassen, and when he got back he said he had changed his mind."

"Good old Mr. Thomassen!" exclaimed Jimmy, with his arms raised high. And resuming their dance, the boys chanted, "Tom-me! Tom-me! Tom-me! ..."

Then breaking apart, they charged towards the stairway whence Kenny had come in a headlong dash. Arriving breathless at the picnic table, Jimmy asked ...

"When can we start?"

"Start what?" ask Tommy, passively, winking at Josie with the eye the boys couldn't see.

"On the boat!" replied Kenny, almost in a girlish squeal.

"Hmm ..." contemplated Tommy, tweaking a lower front tooth with the fingernail of his index finger "How 'bout first thing in the morning?"

The arm-in-arm jig resumed again on the grass, "First thing in the mor-ning ... first thing in the mor-ning ..." until Kenny seemed to suddenly remember himself. But too giddy to be serious, he snapped to attention facing the old Chief, said ... "Aye, Sir. First thing in the morning. Very good Sir." then spun around on his heels and walked deliberately away with Jimmy, almost as if marching.

"Bring yer shovels!" Tommy yelled behind them. "... seven o'clock sharp!"

When out of sight beyond the corner of the cottage, they fell to the ground, both possessed of a laughing jag.

————

Things were not so joyous in Reverend Jennings' office. Having decided to bite the bullet, and face up to a bad situation immediately, rather than permitting the inevitable crisis to grow until the music was finally faced, he had called Lucy Cooper and the boy Edward with an invitation to meet immediately at the church. Both arrived expecting a favorable outcome, although knowing that the Church Board had yet to meet.

Laying his folded hands on the desk in front of him, Grant began with the hope of avoiding as much of the pain as possible for all concerned.

"I have concluded, with regret, that what we previously discussed will not be possible at this time."

Eddie gulped, with surprise. Lucy's head dropped.

"That's it?" asked Eddie, inferring that more detail was needed.

"I'm afraid so, Edward."

"That's not fair." suggested Eddie, struggling to maintain his composure. "Can't you give me a reason?"

"No ... I'm afraid we'd best leave it there."

"Reverend Jennings ... Grant ..." Lucy attempted to intervene on Eddie's behalf.

130

Grant merely held up his arm, palm out towards her and shaking his head; the gesture signaling that an appeal would be futile.

"Somebody got to you, didn't they!" Eddie muttered. "Who was it?"

"I'm not at liberty to share any of that Edward. Suffice it to say that there seems to be several members of the congregation that have issues with your serving in that role. Were I to go ahead anyway, it seems likely that most of them would be highly displeased, to say the least. In the end, it's their church. I serve at their pleasure, and am obliged to conform to their wishes in such matters."

"But you don't even know me! It's not fair ... you're taking their word for everything, and you don't know them any better than me."

Eddie was right about that, of course. And he could see that the boy was hurting ... and probably on the verge of tears. This wasn't going well at all, as he expected it wouldn't.

"Grant, I told you that Eddie has sometimes been no angel; that his mother's escapades have been fodder for the gossips, and you already know about Oscar. But, dammit, Grant ... he's right. It's not fair. Everybody deserves a chance ... at least once in their life!"

"Lucy ... I *am* sorry. I wish my decision could be different, but ..."

"It's about the fuckin' money, isn't it!" blurted Lucy. "Who pulled the rug out? Was it that goddamned Tommy Thomassen? ... Lee Smith and their damned *foundation?* Who was it Grant?

I've got money. Whatever they think they can pull out, I'll make up for ... and two times over."

"No Lucy. It's not about money. Nobody has threatened to leave the church or withhold their financial support."

Standing up with feet spread and hands on hips, Lucy demanded to know more ...

"Well, then what, dammit? I demand to know!"

Eddie intervened ... "Forget it, Luce. Just forget it." And with that he got up and left the office.

Once outside the front door of the church, Eddie rushed down and around the steps, crouching in the corner of the building and the steps. Then he broke down, his broad shoulders heaving with the sobs.

Kenny and Jimmy were on the way to the Jennings garage in search of another shovel when they spotted him there, alone and crying, almost secluded in his corner. As they cautiously approached, Jimmy asked quietly ...

"What's wrong, Eddie?"

"Oh, nothing. They just stuck it to me again!" sobbed Eddie. "I could'a had a chance to be somebody ... just one chance. But no ... that was too much to ask for! Some fucker shot me down!"

"Who?" wondered Kenny.

"Who knows! Maybe you, you little bastard. What did you tell your old man about me? Did you tell 'im I cussed a lot? ... that I said *fuck* a lot? I don't like you. I bet *you* told him not to take me on, didn't you?"

"No, I didn't ... honestly!" assured Kenny. "He said you couldn't have the job?"

"Yeah; well I'll find out who. It'll come out. And when I do, there'll be hell to pay for them. Whoever they are, they're dead!"

Eddie had stopped crying. The hurt in his face had dissolved into hate. The redness, to gray.

————

That evening at the supper table in the Jennings home, Kenny told his father …

"Eddie Gunderson felt really bad about not getting the job, Dad."

"I know, son."

"How come he didn't get it?"

"It's complicated, Kenny."

"He said somebody *stuck it to him again.*"

"Language, Kenny." cautioned his mother.

"I was just repeating what he said … that's how he said it, Mom."

"I understood that, Kenny. It's okay." said his father.

"He said he would find out who it was, and they were going to wind up dead."

Grant, startled at that, sat up straight, and put down his knife and fork.

"Don't ever repeat that to anyone else, Kenneth. Do you hear me!" cautioned his father.

"Well that's what he said, Dad."

"People say things they don't mean when they're upset."

"Yes, Dad. I understand. He was crying at first. It sounded funny to hear a big guy cry … I don't mean *funny*, I mean …"

"Pathetic." his mother offered.

"I'm not sure what that means."

"It's a feeling ... like when you feel bad for someone ... or you wish you could do something to help ... that sort of thing." instructed his father.

"Yes, I guess that's what I mean. Eddie's almost a man, and it seemed much sadder to see a man crying like that. Kids cry all the time ... it's not the same."

"Well I'm genuinely sorry that Edward felt that badly. I wouldn't have thought it would be that important to him. The job was only part-time, and didn't pay much." explained Grant.

"Anyway, after he stopped crying, that's when he got mad and said that. He thought it was probably my fault ... that I probably told you that he used bad language and said the *f-word* a lot."

"Okay, Kenny! That's enough!" demanded Mary.

"I told him it wasn't me ... I didn't say that."

"I said *enough!*" demanded his mother again.

In spite of his admonition to his son, Grant wondered if he needed to pass that threat on to Tommy Thomassen. He decided to take his own advice.

* * *

14

There were two young boys in Leland who hardly slept at all that night. The eastern sky finally began to brighten with the sun still below the horizon at 5:30 the next morning, but it was enough to coax both boys, in their separate households, out of bed.

Kenny dressed himself in the same shorts and tee shirts he'd worn before, but put on white socks and his hiking boots instead of the flip-flops. The boots and socks made him feel like a *working man*. He carefully and quietly crept downstairs, through the house, and out the back door, cringing a little as its hinges squeaked, and closing the screen door carefully so it wouldn't slam. He grabbed the shovel that he and Jimmy had found in the garage and had stashed next to the back porch, and was off to Jimmy's house. He walked. He didn't run or hurry because it was still very early, and he thought that by walking slowly he could kill some of the time. When he got to the Smith's cottage, he planned to just sit down at their picnic table and wait for Jimmy to come out.

When he did get to the cottage, it was still only just a little after six o'clock, and Jimmy was already out ... sitting on the top step of the stairway at the edge of the bluff, holding his shovel between his legs, with its business end between his feet. Kenny sat down beside him, holding his shovel the same way.

"Hi." said Kenny.

"What you doing here so early?" asked Jimmy.

"What are *you* doing here so early?" responded Kenny with a little grin.

"Couldn't sleep."

"Neither could I."

"You look cool ... with the working boots, and all. All you need is a hard hat and you'd look like a real construction guy."

"They're really hiking boots." said Kenny.

"All I've got is these sandals. My shoes are for Sunday. Maybe I can get Gramps to take me back to Goodwill when we go to church Sunday; they have boots something like that there. Then we can both look like working men."

"Goodwill?" asked Kenny. "What's that?"

"Used stuff. A store where you can buy used stuff for really cheap."

"Do they have hard hats?" laughed Kenny.

"I don't know. I don't think so. Well, maybe." Jimmy smiled.

"What in the world are the two of you doing out here this time of the morning?"

Josie had gotten up at dawn, as was her habit, and had spotted the two boys from her kitchen window as she was getting the coffee started.

"We're going to start working on the boat today." answered Jimmy.

"I thought I heard Mr. Thomassen say seven."

"Yes, he said seven o'clock sharp. We're just waiting here to make sure we won't be late." explained Kenny.

"Oh, I see." said Josie indulgently. "And I'll bet neither one of you have had any breakfast?"

Both boys just shrugged, not wanting to admit that they were so eager about getting started that they hadn't thought about breakfast, and were now just sitting here on the top step wasting time while they waited for seven o'clock to come.

"No time this morning, grandma." attempted Jimmy.

"Oh foot, no time! It's only just a quarter past six. Why don't you two get up and wipe the dew off the picnic table, and I'll go inside and make you some breakfast."

Josie was gone about fifteen minutes before returning with a tray, bringing out three breakfast plates, two glasses of orange juice for the boys, and coffee for herself. Their dishes featured generous portions of scrambled eggs and bacon, and two slices of toast with butter and strawberry jelly. The boys, who had been prepared to skip breakfast, gobbled it up as though they hadn't been fed for days. About every five minutes or so, one would wonder ...

"What time is it now?"

As Josie finished her first piece of toast, she finally said "It's just a little past ten of seven ... time for you two to get. Get going now."

Jimmy began to clear the table, as usual.

"Just leave that, Jamie. I can take care of it this morning.

You and Kenny better get for Tommy's place."

He and Kenny were happy to obey. Grabbing their shovels, they hurried down the steps to the beach with Josie affectionately watching them go as they ran off down the shoreline and around the little point towards the boat.

Tommy wasn't there yet, so they sat down on the bottom step of his stairway and waited. At precisely seven o'clock, they heard his heavy footsteps as he descended the stairway.

"Well, well, well!" exclaimed Tommy. "I figured you two lubbers for nine o'clock scholars! And here you are at six bells bearing shovels and ready for action!"

Kenny's face flushed. Having not heard the word before, he understood the old Chief to have referred to him and Jimmy as *lovers*.

"Here's your first step, boys. You'll have to dig her out of the sand a bit, and then we'll pull her down that way some ..." pointing towards the water.

"She's sitting on a wood cradle, but that's got fully covered over with blow sand, so it's gonna be a bitch to dig that out." Looking all around the sides of the boat he added ... "Can't even see the damned thing!"

The boat was listing quite a bit to its port side, with the bow towards the bluff. The winds had drifted the sand all the way up to her gunwales on that side, and built up a little mound aft, burying the bottom half of her rudder. The starboard side was mostly clear all the way underneath to her keel.

"Where should we start?" wondered Jimmy.

"Start right back here at the stern. Clear out all this sand around her rudder, and we'll try to rock her up and out of the sand on this side ..." referring to the boat's port side.

"Maybe your grandpa will be down here by then. The four of us can probably handle that ... then drag her off the cradle."

"Can't even see her cradle anymore! It's probably not too far down under the sand. She's just sittin' on the sand now ... the snow drifts in under her and freezes up ... must'a lifted her right off her perch during the past couple of winters. I'll be damned if it didn't!" exclaimed Tommy with some amazement.

"Be careful not to scrape or gouge her when you're digging close in boys."

By nine o'clock the two boys had cleared the transom and rudder, but Lee had not yet shown up.

"Well, I suppose the three of us can right her and drag her off the cradle." Tommy decided. "My Susie and I used to do it ourselves ... you two squirts are probably the equal of her."

"Come around this side and we'll see if we can heist her up to even keel."

Jimmy and Kenny joined the old man on the port side of the boat, putting their backs into it with their heels planted firmly in the sand while he pushed up under the gunwale with all his considerable strength. The hull was planted more firmly in the sand than was apparent, and it took all their combined strength to budge her. But she was slowly righted, and when the mast was close to straight up, Tommy instructed ...

"Keep going boys! We need to pitch her over to starboard a little ... say to about one o'clock."

"Okay, that's good. I'll hold her here now. You two go grab your shovels and fill in under this side so she can't settle back into the hole."

With Tommy propped against the port side to keep it up, Jimmy and Kenny furiously shoveled sand into the depression left after they lifted that side out. That took a lot of shoveling. Tommy had turned himself around to serve as a prop. With his shoulders against the side of the boat, his legs stiff and his feet planted firmly in the sand, it really wasn't much work for him. The boys, already tired from the previous work of removing the drifted sand from the back of the boat, were getting pooped out, each shovelful of sand seeming to become heavier and heavier, and the space where the port side of the boat had rested was still less than half filled.

"C'mon boys ... put yer backs into it. You're about half way there." encouraged Tommy.

But that wasn't encouraging at all. Both hoped that they were just about done, and Tommy's attempt at encouragement proved totally deflating. They had to stop for a rest, leaning on their shovels, huffing and puffing.

"Guess I was wrong." Tommy teased. "The two of you wouldn't be the equal of my ol' lady, God rest her!"

"Well this is a pretty sight!" said Lee, having appeared from behind the boat's other side. "These two leaning on their shovels, leaving it to an old man to do all the heavy lifting."

"You got out of bed already, Winston? And here it's only ..." looking at an imaginary wrist watch ... "Well it ain't even noon yet! That's the difference, boys, between bankers and sailors. By the time yer grandpa usually gets out of bed, us sailors'll have a half-day's work done!"

"Rave on, you old fool. Anyone can see who's been doing all the work here. Look at them – red faces, sweaty foreheads, huffing and puffing. And look at you."

"Well, somebody's gotta hold her up. They can do the shoveling. I don't do that kind of women's work."

"You two get under her, just like Tommy ... one on either side of him." ordered Lee. "He and I will spell you for a while."

The two boys took Tommy's place, while he and Lee finished the task of filling in, burying them up to their knees in the process as they heaped sand in under that side, so that when the boat settled back into it, she'd sit approximately level and plumb. Before they finished, they heaped a lot of extra sand around the boys' legs just for fun, burying them almost up to their hips.

"Okay, let her settle back and crawl out of there if you can." said Lee.

As the two boys bent forward, the boat settled back towards her port side, and back against their backs, making it almost impossible for them to wiggle themselves loose out of the sand.

Looking at his real wrist watch, Lee said ... "Well, Tommy; looks like it's just about lunch time. Shall we go up and see if Josie has fixed us anything?"

"Sounds right to me." answered Tommy.

And the two men propped the shovels against the side of the boat, and walked off around the stern, towards the little point, leaving Jimmy and Kenny still squished under the side of the boat and stuck in the sand. After a lot of wasted wiggling, Kenny suggested that Jimmy help pull him out by leaning forward and hugging him, then leaning back as far as he could. That ended with Jimmy bent way backward, over the mound of sand that he was stuck in, with Kenny laying on top of him. But Kenny was freed. He then rolled off Jimmy, helped him straighten back up, grabbed his arms and pulled as hard as he could. With Jimmy thrashing like a hooked trout, and Kenny pulling on him, he was finally able to escape his sandy trap.

After brushing themselves and each other off a little, they started off for the cottage, but upon rounding the back of the boat, found Lee and Tommy leaning against her other side, chuckling to each other.

"Sorry boys, you missed lunch while you were playin' in the sand." teased Tommy.

"What took you so long?" asked Lee, still smiling.

"Oh, you two are real funny!" said a third voice. Josie had come down to see how things were going. "Just like a couple of silly little boys!" I have to wonder who the real men are on this job. The ones as are doing all the work will be the ones that get the lunches ... not the clowns."

"Well we'd better get with it then." said Lee. Let's get this old canoe pulled off her cradle."

With Josie, Jimmy and Kenny on one side, Tommy and Lee on the other, moving the boat a length or two toward the water was an easy task. There was still no sign of the cradle.

"So ... start diggin' boys." said Tommy.

Jimmy and his young friend each took a deep breath, and with a pained, but resigned look on their faces, retrieved their shovels, returned to where the boat had been, and began digging. They'd only been on the job for a little over three hours, and it seemed to have already turned into a lot more work than they'd bargained for. But as Jimmy stepped his shovel deep into the sand just ahead of where the rudder had been, it struck something solid.

"I think we've found it, Mr. Thomassen!" he yelled back to the three adults standing next to the boat.

The three came back up to the dig, as Jimmy and Kenny scraped the sand back to expose a two-inch thick piece of wood with something like carpet tacked to its upper edge.

"Yes, that's it." agree Tommy.

142

"That's the back end of the cradle. It'll be about five-feet wide ... this way." as he pointed back and forth to the left and right. "Then it's about twelve feet this way." pointing front and back to indicate the cradle's approximate length.

"It's an open rectangular affair with a couple of cross pieces. So, just dig what you must to expose the front, back, sides and cross beams, then we can just lift her out. No sense in digging up the whole beach."

It turned out that the cradle wasn't very far under the surface, so was fairly easy to uncover. After the boys had cleared the sand away from its shape, Jamie, Kenny, Tommy and Lee ... positioned at its four corners ... lifted the structure up and out of the sand.

"Let's just take her down to the water and let the lake wash her off." suggested Lee.

Kenny removed his boots and socks, and Jimmy kicked off his sandals. Both boys rolled up their shorts as high as they could, then hoisted the lakeward end of the cradle, and the four carried it down to the water. Jimmy and Kenny waded into the water to guide the floating structure into lake. Once it was fully launched, they repeatedly pushed it beneath the surface and let it briskly resurface, washing off the accumulated sand. After repeated immersions, the last of which were mostly for fun, they pushed the cradle back to shore where Lee and Tommy were waiting to retrieve it. Together with the boys they carried it back onto the beach and laid it just aft of the boat. With Tommy and Jimmy on her port side and Lee and Kenny on the other, the boat was wrestled onto the cradle, and things were beginning to look like progress was being made.

"Now we're going to drop the mast. You can take that up to the yard ..." said Tommy, pointing up the stairs to his place. "She's gonna need some work; you can do that up there in the shade, and where the wind won't blow sand and dust into the wet varnish."

The Sea Scout's spar was only a twenty-three-footer, weighing only about seventy pounds, but when leverage was considered, that was enough to get out of hand if not carefully handled.

"Are we using the boom as a gin pole Tommy?" asked Lee, in a tone that suggested that might be a good idea.

"Nah, I think the five of us can handle her." answered Tommy. Looking at Kenny, he continued ... "See that gyve up there Kenny?" pointing to a metal shackle hanging loosely a little over half way up the mast. "You think you can shinny up there like a monkey and pass these lines through, then bring the ends back down with you?"

Kenny looped the loose ends of the lines around his waist a couple of times, then with the ends tucked under the waistband of his shorts, climbed the mast, did as instructed, then wound the loose ends around his waist as before, and came slipping back down.

"Now you and Jimmy each take a pair of lines, you go over there, and Jimmy over there." pointing to opposite sides off the bow of the boat.

"Us other three will drop her; your job will be to keep her coming down true ... don't let her swing this way or that." alternately motioning to port and starboard.

"Josie, if you'll sit right up here ..." indicating a position just forward of the spar ... "I'll unlatch the strap here and pick her up out of the shoe, and you can keep her butt end from slipping forward as Lee and I let her down over the transom."

With those arrangements having been made, the mast was uneventfully removed from the boat.

"Okay!" said Tommy, feeling some satisfaction with that smooth operation and wiping his hands.

"Now all's we need to do is take up her bottom boards and fill 'er up. Then that'll be about it for today. You boys can watch her and keep her full."

The bottom boards were the deck boards inside the boat that provided a flat surface inside the hull. They were lightly attached to trusses with brass screws which removed easily.

"You can take those up top too, along with the spar. They'll need to be cleaned up and recoated too." advised Tommy.

Lee had brought two five-gallon plastic buckets down to the job when he came that morning. Jimmy and Kenny hadn't noticed. They also didn't know what Tommy was talking about when he mentioned filling her up and keeping her full. Full of what? ... they wondered.

"Okay, boys." Lee said. "Take those buckets over there, fill 'em up with water out of the lake and dump it into the boat 'til she's full to the brim. Then keep her filled up."

"What?" asked Jimmy. "Why"?

"She's all dried out and nail sick." answered Tommy. "She'll leak like a sieve until she gets soaked up. Then after that we'll mark the bad spots along her strakes. They'll all have to be re-nailed. Just keep topping her off until she stops spilling her water. That'll probably take a couple of days."

"It's almost noon, men." interrupted Josie. "Better take time out for lunch."

Filling the boat seemed like it would be simple enough, and after lunch Jimmy and Kenny ran back down to the beach to complete that task. But the inside volume of the nineteen-foot boat amounted to over 350 cubic feet, which would require over five hundred full five-gallon buckets to fill, each bucket-full weighing around forty pounds. What made matters even worse: in the beginning the Sea Scout was leaking it out almost as fast as the two boys could pour it in! They carried water for over three and a half hours ... until their backs sorely ached, their legs felt like rubber and their arms felt like they'd been stretched several inches, and at that point, the water level was still over a foot below the gunwales!

Kenny finally plopped down in the sand, his bucket between his legs.

"Maybe I should have listened to my dad. Maybe I should have taken no for an answer."

Jimmy let go a long exhaling sigh. "Look at this tub!" he exclaimed. "... at the water drizzling out of her all over the place!"

"Maybe this is another one of their jokes." suggested Kenny.

That hadn't occurred to Jimmy, but as soon as Kenny suggested it, he could see Mr. Thomassen and his grandpa sitting up atop the bluff giggling to each other with smug self-satisfaction, and waiting for two exhausted boys to come dragging up the stairway.

"You know what would be really funny, Kenny? ... Maybe we should take the boat down to the water and sink it. Then go up there and when they ask, we'd say: *Sure, she's all filled up. See ya later!*"

"That seems like a better idea than this anyway. Why didn't we just do that to begin with?" wondered Kenny.

"Probably because they're pulling our leg." answered Jimmy.

They sat with their backs to the bluff, so didn't see Jake Robinson coming down the stairway.

"Looks like somebody's finally resurrecting the old Sea Scout!" was his salutation. "Boy, she's leakin' badly ... gonna take a lot of soak time, I'd guess. You boys need a fire hose and a pump!"

"Yes, we've already dumped a million buckets of water into her." complained Kenny.

"Well there isn't really any other good way to do it ... not out on the beach, anyway. Up at the marina they'd put her in the hoist and sink her in the well over night, but down here you'll just have to keep on doing what you're doing. She'll begin to tighten up pretty quick."

"We thought maybe Gramps and Mr. Thomassen were playing another trick on us." admitted Jimmy.

Jake laughed at that idea ... "Yes, that would be about their speed, I guess!"

"So, what's up with this project. The Chief going to start sailing her again?" wondered Jake.

Jimmy and Kenny explained what the deal was. Jake grimaced and shook his head.

"Well, by the time she's yours, you will have earned every inch of her! Who's this, Jimmy?" inviting an introduction to his younger friend.

"It's Kenny. He's the new preacher's boy."

Kenny came forward with right hand outstretched ... "Kenneth Grant Jennings." he offered. "I'm very pleased to meet you ... are you Mr. Robinson, the ferry Captain? I saw you leave on the bigger boat yesterday morning."

"Yes, I'm glad to know you too. Our family's been members of the church since it was built ... most of 'em baptized, married and buried there ... so I guess we're going to be family, aren't we ... I mean, *church family.*"

"My dad doesn't think we'll be staying very long." advised Kenny.

"Yeah, that's what they all think. Then they get a real taste for the place, and you can't get rid of 'em." encouraged Jake with a smile.

"Interims can't be hired in." responded Kenny, surprising Jake somewhat with an understanding that seemed advanced for the boy's apparent age."

"How old are you, Kenny?" he wondered.

"I'm twelve."

"Oh, twelve." repeated Jake, realizing that he had underestimated Kenny's age by about two years, and thinking that the boy was somewhat slight for his age ... still boyishly built and complexioned ... that puberty had not yet begun to take its toll.

"I came over to see Tommy, Jimmy. Maybe he's over to your grandpa's?"

That being affirmed by Jimmy, Jake made off down the beach towards the Smith's cottage.

The two boys went back to the chore of carrying water, having been rested somewhat, but now working at a slower, more businesslike pace. And, thanks to Jake Robinson, with the confidence that they were not being played for fools.

There were two young boys in Leland who slept like logs that night after their first day of work on the boat, and they weren't up with the crack of dawn on the second day.

* * *

15

Jimmy woke up slowly the following morning. The aching muscles and sunburn acquired during the previous day's work had taken their toll during the night, resulting in his tossing and turning and fitful dreaming. His mind was awake, but so far, his eyes had been reluctant to open, as if his mind was willing, but his body thought it still needed more recovery time. Clearly, he wasn't used to hard work, he thought. And he thought of the term he'd first heard from Tommy Thomassen on his first visit about the boat. His lips soundlessly formed the words *candy ass.*

With effort, he was able to raise his eyebrows as high as they would go to force his eyelids open a crack. The attic seemed dark, as if dawn was just breaking, yet the light outside the windows was sunny and bright. In a moment, his brain put two and two together ... the sun was high; it must be well past dawn ... probably mid-morning!

His next thought was of Tommy Thomassen waiting impatiently for him and Kenny down by the boat. Again, the words came to mind ... *CANDY ASS!* That served as his wake-up call. He quickly threw off the comforter and sheet, jumped out of bed, and headed for the stairs.

'But wait!' suggested his awakening mind ... he was wearing only his briefs ... the Walmart *whitie-tighties* with the blue and gold strips on their elastic waist band, just like Kenny's. He quickly reversed course, running back up the few stairs he'd descended to find his shorts, tee shirt and sandals.

Bounding into the kitchen, he noticed the electric clock above the sink; it was ten 'til ten! Then he noticed Kenny and his grandma sitting together in the little bay window nook on the kitchen's north side.

"Have you been down to the boat already, Kenny?"

"Yes."

"Was Mr. Thomassen there?"

"He whistled at me from the top of the bluff and waved me to come up. He said there's nothing to do today but keep the boat full."

"Was there any water left in it?"

"Yes,"

"How much?"

"Oh, about three or four buckets full." answered Kenny, concealing a wink towards Josie, who smiled back.

"Crap!!!" exclaimed Jimmy.

"Don't you mean drat, or gee-whiz, or good gosh, or something like that?" scolded Josie.

"Yes ... maybe *DRAT!!!*"

"That's some improvement, I guess." conceded his grandmother.

"I'm sorry grandma. I'm still all tired out from yesterday because I didn't sleep good last night."

"You made some mistakes?" joked Kenny.

"Tee-he-he! Very funny! What about you ... did you get any sleep?" he asked Kenny.

"Sure. I always sleep like a log, and hard work only makes me sleep that much better!" bragged Kenny, exaggerating somewhat, of course.

"Well then I guess maybe I *am* just a candy aaa ..."

"A candy-what?" wondered Kenny.

"Oh, never mind. It was just something Mr. Thomassen said."

He had cut himself off to spare himself from a second language admonition from his grandmother.

"Candy ass." she answered for Kenny's information.

"It means sissy, or limp-wristed, usually referring to someone not accustomed to hard work, or hardened by experience."

"Grandma! Language ..." Jimmy kidded with a grin.

"I was just quoting." Josie offered.

"I was just kidding anyway, Jimmy. The boat still has lots of water in it."

"How much?"

"Maybe, like a foot below the top." Kenny estimated.

"Did you fill it back up?" Jimmy asked hopefully.

"No. I didn't want you to think I was taking over, or anything. I thought I should wait for you." Kenny offered with feigned sincerity."

"Oh, thanks!"

Getting back to the subject of language, Kenny told Josie "Mr. Thomassen also called Jimmy and me lovers."

Josie laughed out loud ... "No! He didn't!" she doubted.

"That's what he said." added Jimmy. "Why would he think that?"

"Are you sure it wasn't *landlubbers?*" Josie laughed.

"Yes ... maybe." Kenny agreed. "So, what does that mean ... land lovers?" he continued with a sheepish smirk.

"It's *luB-Ber*, Kenny; not *luV-Ver*. It means someone who isn't a sailor, and doesn't know anything about the sea."

"Oooooh!" exclaimed Kenny, with obvious relief, and looking toward Jimmy to see what he might have made of it.

"Mr. Thomassen called me up top so he could give us this book ..." pointing to an old, well-worn cloth bound book laying on the table "... not to have, just to borrow. He said to read chapter seven and chapter thirteen ... that reading it in the book would save him from having to tell us everything."

Jimmy reached over, slid the book to his side of the table and opened its cover, the embossed printing on which had lost its gold leaf coloring. The title page inside said ...

BOAT SAILING
IN
FAIR WEATHER AND FOUL

BY
CAPTAIN A. J. KENEALY

1905

"Wow – ancient!" was Jimmy's rather surly assessment.

Lee had come into the kitchen from outside, and seeing the book in his grandson's hands, he joined the conversation ...

"Ah, *très bien!* Captain Neely's book. Tommy give you that?"

"Yes." answered Kenny. "This morning. He said it will take a day or two for the boat to tighten up and quit leaking, and we could read this while we wait."

"So, he's kept that book all this time!" said Lee with admiration for his friend. "He and I went by that book when we built the Sea Scout ... that's how long he's had it."

"So why would we need to read it?" asked Jimmy.

"He didn't say to read the whole thing, just chapters seven and thirteen." corrected Kenny.

"But what for?" persisted Jimmy.

"Just read it, boy!" answered his grandfather.

Jimmy flipped the pages until coming to page 101, then began reading out loud ...

"VII
OVERHAULING THE YACHT"

"Anything in the shape of a boat may be made water-tight, no matter how leaky she may be, if treated with careful ingenuity. I would be the last man to suggest patching and puttying up a ramshackle craft whose frames and planking are rotten. Supposing, however, that the hull is fairly sound, but through exposure to the hot sun her planks are cracked in sundry places, and that in fact she leaks like a sieve, there is no reason why she should be condemned. There is a lot of good fun to be got out of a craft of this kind, if the proper repairs are made ... Here, then, is where a handy man or boy has a capital opportunity to try his hand as a craftsman. I repaired an old 18-foot boat in my younger days, when money was scarce and I had the alternative of giving up my pet diversion of sailing or making the ancient bucket tight."

"This is how I went about it."

"The craft in question was hauled out on the shore above the high-water mark. She had been abandoned by her rightful owner, who had moved inland and left her to the tender mercies of the sun in summer and the snow in winter. For sixteen months she lay on the beach neglected. Every day I cast covetous eyes on her. I will make a clean

154

breast of it now in my old age and confess that I had contemplated stealing her. That sin was, however, spared me, as I found her owner's address and wrote, asking if he would sell her. He replied that he would give her to me and welcome, and thus made me the happiest youth in the land."

Josie, by the kitchen sink, raised a dishtowel to her eyes, and smiled with a pained, pathetic smile at her husband. As she took in the scene at her kitchen table ... Jamie sitting there reading out loud, with Kenny standing behind him, intently looking over his shoulder and following the same lines of text ... her mind slipped back over the years, turning the boys Jimmy and Kenny into the boys Tommy and Winston. She had never been more proud of her husband and his enduring friendship with his boyhood companion, who was now also her neighbor and friend. She loved them all.

"And it goes on from there ..." recalled Lee "... to tell all about how he fixed up that old boat. That's what Tommy wants you to read about. You'll learn all sorts of things from that book, just like we did."

Then nodding as he went back outside ...

"Good book!"

Josie thought a light breakfast at this late hour would be enough to hold the two young shipwrights over until lunch time. A bowl of raisin bran with banana coins sprinkled with a few blackberries and sugar, and with a splash of fresh whole milk would do. After breakfast Jimmy and Kenny cleared the table and did the few dishes, Jimmy washing and Kenny wiping. Then they were off to the boat.

Kenny had been a little too optimistic when he had estimated that the water in the boat was only down a foot, or so. In fact, at least half of it was gone. So, the rest of the morning was consumed with the task of filling her back up. Then they sat down under the hull, on the shady side, and Jimmy continued reading chapter seven of the book out loud, picking up from where he had left off just before breakfast.

After several pages, he blinked and asked ...

"You wanna read for a while now?"

"Sure." answered Kenny, leaning over to take the book without losing the page, then picking up at the place Jimmy pointed to.

Kenny read well, rendering the content of the pages as natural sounding and animated as if he was old Captain Kenealy himself. Jimmy lay back under the boat, his arms raised with his hands under the back of his head to keep it out of the sand. With nothing to look at but the bottom of the weather-beaten hull, he closed his eyes, rationalizing that doing so would improve his concentration. But his mind refused to pay attention to the knowledge and advice Kenny was peeling off Captain Kenealy's pages. It wanted, instead, to listen to the voice itself, a sound it had taken a liking to. As Kenny continued to read, the sound of it seemed to grow misty, as if coming from a distance ... almost like a song.

"Do you ever sing?" he unexpectedly wondered out loud.

"Huh?"

"Do you ever sing ... like in church, or anything?" clarified Jimmy, his eyes opened now, but still staring at the peeling white paint on the bottom of the boat.

"Sometimes." answered Kenny.

"Where?"

Kenny shrugged ... "Anywhere, I guess. Don't you?"

"Nah."

"Everybody sings ... at least in church."

"We don't go that much. And when I go with grandma and Gramps, the Catholics sing these sappy songs that seem ... Oh, I don't know. I just don't like to sing them."

"Oh." Kenny indicated that he understood, although he really didn't.

"I really meant, do you ever sing alone ... just by yourself ... like in front of other people?"

"Sometimes ... sometimes I sing solo parts in church with the choir. Sometimes in the summer, just by myself ... sometimes with my sister, when she's home."

Jimmy sat up suddenly, carelessly bumping his head on the bottom of the boat, but ignoring it ...

"Sing me something!" he requested.

"Here?"

"Yes. I love the sound of your voice ... especially the way you read the book. I'll bet you sing really nice ... I want to hear it."

Kenny acted as if he might do it, but then thought about it for a second and decided to decline.

"Nah, I don't want to ... that would look weird ... me singing to you under the boat, wouldn't it?"

"Who's to care? There's nobody here but you and me." encouraged Jimmy.

"I have to sing in church Sunday. How about you coming and singing with me in church?"

"Alone? In front of people?"

Kenny nodded.

"Forget it. I'd be so scared, I'd probably pee my pants!"

"So? ... You could wear *Depends!*" laughed Kenny. "We've got some ... I've seen where they keep 'em."

"Very funny! Very funny! Maybe I'll just come and watch you ... maybe I'll just come and sit in the front row and see if I can crack you up."

"I won't even look at you."

"Yeah, but you'll know I'm there, and you'll be thinking about cracking up, and you'll crack up anyway." teased Jimmy.

"I'm not worried."

"Really?"

"No, because I like to sing in church ... because people really like it, and I never feel like getting silly when I do that. And I know you'd never do that anyway."

"Yeah, you're right. I'd never do that ... but I *would* love to hear you sing. I bet you're really good. Maybe Gramps will let us go to your church this Sunday."

"Guess what!"

"What?" asked Jimmy, confused by the abrupt change in Kenny's expression.

"We're not getting dripped on!"

It had suddenly occurred to Kenny that they were lying under the leaky boat, but had not suffered even a single drip of water. Crawling out from under their shadowed space, they scrambled all around the boat, noticing a little seepage here and there, with wet spots in the sand below but, by and large, she had tightened up a great deal in what had been only a little less than twenty-four hours. Kenny looked over the gunwale on his side to check the water level inside the boat, wondering how much she had leaked while they were sitting beneath, reading the book.

"Sweet!" he exclaimed with obvious delight. "We haven't lost more than a bucket or two, I think."

"It's only been a couple of hours." Jimmy cautioned, with the intention of throttling Kenny's apparent over enthusiasm. But his enthusiasm wasn't to be throttled.

"So, what? Look at her! I think this old boat is in a lot better shape than we thought. I think this old boat wants to be fixed ... she wants to sail again!"

"Let's fill 'er up again ... right to overflowing this time." said Jimmy.

So, they headed down to the lake again with their five-gallon plastic pails. It actually took nine buckets of water to fill the boat up to the tops of her gunwales with the water then spilling over her sides at the lowest point.

Meanwhile, Tommy Thomassen had come down to see how things were going. He looked at the boat, now full to the brim with water, then at the boys.

"How's she doing?" he asked.

"She already stopped leaking." answered Kenny excitedly "... well, almost stopped, I mean. I think she's eager to go sailing again." he added playfully.

"Well, she might be, at that." agreed Tommy. Appreciating Kenny's excitement and not wishing to dampen it any more than need be, he added ...

"But it's gonna be a while. You two tyros still have a long way to go with her before she'll be ready to try her wings again."

There was another new word ... *tyros*. Kenny wondered if he dared ask what that meant.

"Have you been studying in my book?" Tommy asked accusingly.

"Yes. We've read chapter 7 ... all the way up to ..." Kenny picked up the book and opened it to the place he had marked by inserting the little seagull feather he'd picked up on the beach. "... all the way up to page 110. That's almost half way."

"Well then you know what comes next. Give 'er another day, I'd say, and then you can mark the places she's still dribbling from before you pull the plug."

Walking studiously around the boat, he added ... "Looks like there's damned few! By golly she's tightening up better'n I thought she would."

"After you spill her water, it'll take her a few days to dry out a little so you can work on her ... depending on the weather. If we can get some northerly winds, it'll probably only take her a couple. Did you read about the rivets in the book?"

"Rivets?" Jimmy wondered vaguely.

"See all along here." Tommy was pointing out a row of what looked like nail heads all along the edge of one of the strips that made up the boat's hull.

"These is all copper. They hold the strakes together. They're stuck through from the outside like this, through a rove on the inside and then peened over, like rivets, so to speak."

"Oh." said Jimmy.

"Where she's still leaking, it'll be because her rivets at that point have loosened up, and you'll have to stick a couple more in like the book says; one on either side of the loose one."

160

"Couldn't we just replace the bad one?" wondered Kenny.

"Yeah, you'll have to do that too. First you use the two regular size nails, then you have to use the next bigger nail size to replace the bad one ... and that's really only to just plug up the hole."

"Oh." said Kenny.

"Anyway, after she dries out, you fix the leaks like that. Then you two will have to go all along each one of these strakes with your bucking hammer and your ball peen hammer and your rove set, making sure there ain't no loose ones."

Kenny looked at Jimmy, then at Tommy inquisitively.

"Gosh ... there must be thousands of them?" he exclaimed questioningly, wondering if Tommy really meant every one, along every strake, from keel to gunwale.

"No, there's less than a thousand ..." assured Tommy. "Maybe seven or eight hundred. Don't worry; with the two of you working, it'll go pretty fast. And when yer all done, you'll know you got a boat that ain't gonna open up on you somewheres out there in the middle of the drink."

"Let's just let 'er sit like she is over the weekend. Don't put no more water in 'er, and we'll see what she looks like Monday morning." advised Tommy.

The boys were glad to hear about the *no more water* part.

Jimmy hadn't realized that it was Friday already.

"Can I go to church with you this Sunday, Mr. Thomassen? Kenny's singing this Sunday."

"You better ask your grandma and grandpaw if they'll take you." Tommy suggested.

"They always go to Traverse." Jimmy objected.

"Oh, no ... not always. We ... I mean, they ... they've been to LCC before. Lots of times."

"Well maybe ..." agreed Jimmy tentatively. "But if they don't, and it's alright with them, could I still go with you?"

"You don't really need to *go with* anybody. It's just a church, for Christ's sake, not a private club ... you can just go in and sit down, just like anybody else."

"Oh, I get it ... sorry. You don't want to. It's okay. I understand."

"Oh no you don't. If I were to walk into that place now boy, lightning would probably strike me dead and burn the damned place right down to the ground!"

Kenny laughed out loud.

"That would be something to see!"

"Might not seem so funny were you to find yourself up there on the chancel singing away with the burning timbers crashing down all around you, my young friend!" Tommy kidded. "What are you gonna sing."

"I'm going to sing at the beginning, and during the offering."

"Well, good luck with that." said Tommy. But then not really wishing to discourage or belittle the boy, he patted him on the shoulder, saying ...

"I'm sure you'll do real good sonny."

* * *

16

Saturday mornings were always more hectic and busy around Main Street and River than most other summer mornings. With the Sea Scout still soaking, it would have been a good day to start on her spar, bottom boards and such at Mr. Thomassen's place, but since Kenny had to spend the morning practicing for the Sunday service with his mother, who played the piano, Jimmy didn't feel like starting with that by himself.

He decided instead to go down by the docks to see what was going on, and watch the island ferries leave. The two park boats were in their slips, as expected, since Harley Spence and his men almost never worked on weekends. Jake was standing on the dock leading to the Keche-Chéemann and the Ningwis, in uniform, also as expected. Jake Jr. was also on hand, in jeans and a short-sleeved olive drab work shirt, milling around the crowd of passengers, making sure everyone knew which boat was which.

The passengers were the usual assortment. There were a bunch of kids about his age, boys and girls who all seemed to know each other, so he assumed they were from a summer camp, or maybe from some city's youth recreation program. They all came with backpacks and hiking boots, so he expected they'd be boarding the Ningwis. A group of elderly people who seemed to be together tried to stay on the side and out of everybody's way ... probably a reunion of some sort. They'd be going to South. There were a couple of older ladies in olive colored park maintenance uniforms ... probably volunteers also headed for South. Then there was a group of yuppie types ... guys and gals inappropriately dressed in shorts, tee shirts and sandals. They'd be day-trippers headed for South. They'll be shivering on the way over, and coming back with poison ivy all over their legs and feet, and with fly bites everywhere else, he figured. Finally, a couple assortments of more lightly equipped campers were obviously headed for the campgrounds on South.

He thought he'd give Jake a try. Sometimes he was in a good mood. More often not.

"Good morning, Mr. Robinson."

"Hello Jimmy. Going out to the island?"

"No, I'm just watching."

"Same old show ... pretty much." said Jake, looking over the growing crowd.

"Looks like maybe you'll have a boatload today." said Jimmy, trying to hold his own in an adult-like conversation.

"Pretty much." agreed Jake.

"Who are all those kids?" Jimmy asked, motioning to the group with the backpacks and hiking boots.

"Ah, they're from some church in Traverse. I don't remember which one ... or wait, I take that back. They're from St. Francis' Jr. High School. Catholic kids. Going to North today."

"Oh." said Jimmy, pretending that his interest was casual, and went no further than that.

In fact, there was one particular girl in that group who had caught his eye, which is why he'd wondered about them. He wondered where she might be from and if she might be his age.

164

He was interested in hearing that they were from St. Francis, and wondered if he might be lucky enough to see her again when he went to Mass there on Sunday mornings with his grandparents. He made a mental note of it.

"If you're not doing anything else today, you can ride along up top with me if you want."

Jake was obviously in one of his good moods today. That was a very unusual offer. It was also hard for Jimmy to resist ... riding in the pilot house with the Captain ... an opportunity to boost his ego, as it were ... about like getting off the jet on the Traverse City tarmac.

"Gee, thanks! But I'm waiting for my friend; then we're supposed to go over to Mr. Thomassen's and work on the boat a while."

"How's the boat project coming along?" wondered Jake.

He didn't wait for an answer, grabbing Jimmy's shoulder to signify he'd have to leave it at that, then turning and heading down the dock to the bigger boat. Within another few moments her diesel engines came to life below her deck with a muffled rumble. It was five before ten.

About the same time Jake Jr. boarded the Ningwis, and her engines also started up, she making gurgling sounds as the exhaust tubes at the waterline on her transom occasionally dipped below the surface. At exactly ten o'clock, Jake Jr. pulled the cord and the Ningwis emitted one long blast on her air horn. The dock hands raised her mooring lines off the spiles fore and aft, threw them aboard, and she immediately began pulling out of her slip. The Catholic kids were all riding atop her cabin, eagerly beginning their adventure. The girl looked back at Jimmy as the boat began to leave, or at least he thought she had. The Ningwis was always backed into her slip, so she headed immediately out of the harbor, and into the lake. When well beyond the breakwaters, she would make her usual ninety-degree turn to starboard, and would be on her way to North Manitou.

As the Ningwis cleared the harbor, the air horn on the Keche-Chéemann spoke up ... one long blast, and three shorts ... the standard maritime signal meaning *I am leaving the dock ... getting underway*. The bigger boat was always docked with her bow headed inland, towards the Tarnovitch, because it was easier to back her out, than in. Her lines were thrown on-board, as Jake began slowly backing out. Past the end of the dock, she swung around to port in the harbor basin, lining up with the channel through the breakwaters, and then moved smartly ahead and out into the lake. With a shallower turn to starboard, she was headed to South Manitou.

After the two boats left, the dock area was suddenly vacant and quiet. As he walked back in from the end of the ferry docks, he noticed Eddie Gunderson moving around on the back of the Tarnovitch, so rather than heading back up the hill, he continued along the dock.

"Hi Eddie." he yelled, much louder than his normal tone of voice.

Eddie was cleaning up the work area at the back of the boat with a pressure washer fed by water being pumped out of the river. It was a small electric affair, built like a little cart ... almost cute in a way, but much noisier than one might have expected for such a small machine. Eddie didn't look up.

"Hi Jimmy. What's happening?" he yelled back.

There wasn't any use in answering, or attempting to carry on a conversation above the racket. So, Jimmy just stood there on the dock leaning against a spile, with his arms folded over its top and his chin on his clasped hands, watching Eddie as he finished the job. Eventually Eddie turned the little machine off, and all was very quiet again.

"Were you out this morning?" Jimmy wondered.

"Duh! What'd you think I'm doin' here. Hell yeah, we were out ... went out late last night and pulled nets off South. Got in this morning ... about dawn ... five-thirty, or so."

"You go out there in the dark?"

"Of course, that's the best time ... pretty calm then. And there's almost a full moon now, so it's just about like daylight."

"Oh." said Jimmy.

"We'll be going out again, Monday night. You can come along Dude, if you want to help."

"I'd probably just be in the way. I don't know anything about fishing. I don't know any of the Tarnovitchs either."

"So? ... What difference does that make!"

"Maybe they wouldn't like it."

"What makes you think that? Like you said ... you don't know any of 'em. Why do you always think people might not like you? I'm an asshole, and I like you!" asserted Eddie with a grin before continuing ...

"They wouldn't care. I've taken friends out before ... sometimes even alone. Alls they care about is the fucking nets ... and the fucking fish. They get a good haul, and they're happy. Otherwise they're a couple of pricks, but then I just tell 'em to get pumped. They're okay. Don't worry about it. If you want to come, just be down here around eleven-thirty Monday night."

"I'll have to ask if I can."

"Yeah, right!" said Eddie, already knowing what the answer to that was going to be.

"How'd you like to get some pussy this afternoon?"

That abrupt change of subject struck Jimmy as funny ... pure *Eddie Gunderson,* he thought. But then, in truth, his nervous laugh came more as an involuntary response to embarrassment. Eddie was probably teasing ... pretending to assume that he wasn't innocent ... that a normal boy of fourteen would have a lot of that sort of experience under his belt. In spite of his embarrassment, he knew it would be no good to try and make Eddie think otherwise.

"I probably wouldn't know what to do with that if it hit me right in the face." he admitted.

"HAHAHA!" Eddie laughed. "That's a good way to start, Jimmy boy. Right in the face!" Eddie thought that was really funny coming from him.

"That's not what I meant. It was just an expression."

"Yeah, sure it was ... you filthy-minded little freak!" Eddie continued laughing.

"So, grandpa's fair-haired boy is cherry, huh? We can fix that. I can get you fucked any time you want. Just say the word." added Eddie.

"I don't suffer lust." answered Jimmy, with mock sophistication.

"Oh, sure you don't!" chided Eddie. "I bet you make love to Rosy Palm and her five skinny daughters every night."

Jimmy was now truly embarrassed. He felt his face reddening, and there was no way he was going to admit to that. He needed to change the subject.

"Suppose I *was* interested. What did you have in mind?" he ventured.

"There's some poontang up here ... from Traverse, I think ... staying at one of the cottages on the south side over there ..." motioning to the opposite side of the little river.

"They been jumpin' off the pier there for the past couple of days ..." motioning towards the end of the inner breakwater.

"One of 'em is really *HOT!* I saw her up there yesterday, and decided I'm definitely gonna get me some of that."

"Just like that?" Jimmy scoffed.

"Bet'chur ass, just like that." assured Eddie.

"How old are they?" asked Jimmy, wondering if one of them might have been the girl on the ferry that morning.

"Old enough." answered Eddie.

"I mean are they like ... your age?" Jimmy continued to wonder.

"What the fuck, Dude. Who cares! *Old enough to bleed; old enough to butcher!* That's all you need to know. There's no such thing as bad pussy. Why be so picky about it?"

"I don't know. Just seems like ..." began Jimmy.

"That's why you're still cherry. You think too much. Here ... have one on me."

Eddie had retrieved a couple of PBR's from somewhere on the back of the boat, without Jimmy having noticed. They were wet and very cold, as if perhaps he'd just pulled them up out of the river. It was a quarter before eleven. He'd had no breakfast, so the beer was going down into an empty stomach.

"We better get below." thought Eddie. "... before some do-gooder sees you sucking up the brew and calls the law."

They drank beer and talked, as they had before early in the spring. This time Jimmy did not have to pee quite so bad, even after downing three. As the time wore on, it began to seem as if Eddie was just blabbering irrelevantly and becoming increasingly distant. Jimmy was just sitting there rather dumbly responding by nodding his head and saying ...

"Uh-huh ... uh-huh."

Finally, Eddie looked at his watch and suggested ...

"It's already past noon ... past lunch time. What say we go up to the Bird and have something?"

"Uh-huh."

As he got up, Jimmy seemed to lose his balance and drift into the bunk on the opposite side of the little cabin.

"Whoa!" cautioned Eddie. "Steady there, Dude."

"I've gotta pee now."

Eddie put his hands on Jimmy's shoulders and directed him up the steps to the deck of the boat. Jimmy wobbled over to the side, lifted the pant leg of his walking shorts and began peeing in the river. Eddie laughed.

"Sheesh ... you are drunk, you shit head! Everybody's gonna see you there pissin' in the river! Stick it back in your pants you dope!"

"Fuck it." uttered Jimmy.

"What!?!" laughed Eddie. "You said the F-word!?! ... drunk ... cussin'! I can see I'm a good influence on you. There might be some hope for you after all!"

After getting some food in his stomach and peeing a couple of more times, Jimmy began to feel more like himself again. He

170

hadn't really been drunk; just a little *tight*. Three beers was a new record for him, and he had learned that it wasn't a good idea to drink alcohol on an empty stomach. Eddie paid the check and left the tip.

"C'mon Dude ... let's go out to the pier and have a look at the scenery." coaxed Eddie.

"Maybe I better see if Kenny's done ..."

"Forget Kenny! I'm gonna show you some stuff that'll make you forget all about that dork."

That comment fell on Jimmy's ears with annoyance. He understood that Eddie didn't like Kenny, and that the feelings were mutual. But he did. In fact, he liked Kenny a lot, and those feelings were mutual too. Letting those sorts of comments pass without objection made him feel like he was betraying their friendship. He felt guilty for not speaking up, yet he did not speak up. He felt like he should leave, yet he did not leave. A feeling in his loins strongly suggested that he should go out to the pier to see what Eddie was talking about. Who knows? Maybe something would happen. The beer had made him a little more courageous about perhaps meeting a girl who might be willing to do something with him.

As they crossed the beach, walking towards the inner breakwater, Eddie suddenly grabbed Jimmy's arm, and abruptly stopped in his tracks.

"Shit, man! There she is."

"Where?" Jimmy asked. "Which one."

There were several girls on the end of the breakwater, randomly jumping off into the water on the river side, then climbing back up again, dripping wet.

"Where, my ass!" demanded Eddie. "The hot one ... the one in the yellow."

From a distance, it appeared that Eddie was mostly right. The girl with the dark hair in the yellow bikini was very nicely proportioned, in an athletic sort of way. For a while they remained fixed where they were, Eddie seeming to be awe struck to the point of suddenly having lost his grip on all the bravado and charm he had learned to use to impress unsuspecting females. She looked real nice, but not so much nicer than some of the other girls.

"That *is* choice stuff." exclaimed Eddie.

"So, is this as close as we're gonna get?" pestered Jimmy.

Eddie seemed to snap out of his stupor, or whatever it was, looked at him and said "In a pig's ass. C'mon."

As they climbed up onto the pier, several of the girls, including the yellow bikini, were looking intently over the side and into the water on the river side.

"Lose something?" asked Eddie to nobody in particular.

One of the other girls looked back at him to answer ...

"We just knocked her iPhone over the side." indicating that *her* was the yellow bikini.

"Well, I guess we can kiss that one goodbye." said Eddie, suggesting that the matter was no big deal.

"My dad's gonna kill me!" said the yellow bikini. "Can you get it for me? ... It's that shiny thing right down there."

"Why don't you get it?" asked Eddie, as nonchalantly as before.

"There's huge fish down there on the bottom ... they're creepy!" she responded with a mock shiver.

"They're harmless." encouraged Eddie. "They're just catfish."

172

"Would you please get it for me?" she pleaded again. "There's a twenty in the back of its case ... you can have it if you get it for me. Please ...!"

Eddie sat down on the pier and took off his work boots, then stood up and stripped off his shirt. Jimmy noticed how these stupid girls were instantly enamored by the sex appeal of this barefoot, bronzed, muscular creature in nothing but tight-fitting jeans standing there before them ... especially the yellow bikini girl!

Seeing that, and the way all this had transpired thus far, everything falling right into Eddie's hands like a gift, he was dumbfounded by this boy's uncanny luck with the opposite sex.

Eddie went over to the edge, and then just stepped off, entering the water feet first, and going down like a harpoon launched at the iPhone. He remained perfectly visible in the twelve feet deep, glass clear water, as he flipped over far beneath the surface, dove to the bottom and retrieved the shiny thing. A moment later he popped back up on the surface with the prize in his right hand, held high in the air.

As he climbed back onto the pier, dripping wet, the yellow bikini ran over to hug him, thanking him profusely ...

"Oh, thank you, thank you, thank you!!! He would have killed me ..."

Then thinking further ahead ...

"I suppose it's ruined now. What am I going to tell him? It's a $400 phone!"

"Maybe you won't have to say anything." suggested Eddie.

"Take the case off, shake it out and let it bake here in the sun on the hot cement. Then take it home and stick it in a bag of rice overnight."

"Rice?" she asked.

"Yes, rice." assured Eddie politely. "Rice loves water, and will draw all the moisture out of it. It'll probably work again after that, and if it doesn't you can just say it conked out for some reason. iPhones are famous for that."

"That would be like lying." she supposed.

"I didn't say to lie about it; I said just say *it conked out for some reason*. That wouldn't be a lie." assured Eddie earnestly. "If he asks why, just say that you were swimming, and it was lying on the pier, and next time you went to use it, it didn't work ... like maybe the battery was dead or something."

"Get it? You can choose your words so you don't have to lie, and you don't have say that you dropped it in the drink either." instructed Eddie, tapping the side of his head with his index finger. "My name is Edward."

She put her hand to her mouth in surprise.

"That's my dad's name too! Edward ... Edward Haggard! I'm Keegan."

"Keegan?"

"It's actually Bethany. Keegan is my mother's maiden name, and my middle name. *Bethany* sounds too religious, so I like Keegan. It's Gaelic and means fiery and passionate."

Eddie smiled lecherously ... at least it looked like a lecherous grin to Jimmy.

Keegan smiled back, blushing just a little.

* * *

174

<u>17</u>

Keegan ... the yellow bikini girl ... probably was pretty *hot*, Jimmy agreed. But not so much more than the other girls. After they had gotten to the pier, Jimmy could see that besides having a nice, athletic sort of shape, she also had a pretty face. It wasn't actually what he would have called beautiful, nor would he have described it as cute. It was just, well ... attractive, and in a way, he wasn't quite able to pin down. It looked like the face of a girl who had, perhaps, just been crying he thought. Yet there was something like a hint of a smile behind that. It was unusual. It didn't fit into *a look* that he was familiar with, so it was difficult to classify. But still, she wasn't all that much more sexually attractive than some of the others.

She and *Edward* were now sitting on the edge of the pier with their legs dangling over the water. She was apparently as quickly taken with him as he was with her. Their exchange of light, playfully teasing and good-natured conversation was lively, and apparently came easily. For his part, Eddie was on his best behavior, suddenly speaking much more intelligently, and without even any of the commonly used slang expressions, let alone profanity. She was sitting very close, half facing him with her leg touching his. She seemed intensely absorbed in listening to his every word, and while listening or speaking, she exhibited the cutest mannerisms and facial expressions ... *darling,* might have been a better description, he thought.

He wondered what, exactly, it was that made Eddie Gunderson at once see this particular girl as being so far superior to her companions. Having often heard his grandma say *there's no accounting for taste,* he shrugged a little, and decided to attribute it to that.

He also wondered how old these girls were. They didn't look much older than his friends back home in Indianapolis. He couldn't help feeling a little jealous that Eddie seemed to be getting all of their attention. But then he didn't feel comfortable with the word *jealous,* so replaced it with *envious.* That didn't feel right either, so he change it yet again ... to *desirous* – not desiring to be like Eddie, but desirous of his situation ... older, angular, physically attractive, and easily a center of attention for the opposite sex ... a *chick magnet.*

But then reason set in: Eddie was five years older. In five more years, he would probably be all those things too ... and more, since his family was also rich – something that Eddie would probably never be.

As he stood there feeling awkward and small and irrelevant, it was clear that this was Eddie's scene, not his. Nobody noticed as he quietly turned and began walking back along the route from whence he and Eddie had come.

Or so he thought.

"Wait up!" called a giggling thin voice from behind.

It was apparently one of the other girls from the pier – but not one from among that select group whom he had judged to be equally as attractive as the one Eddie had cut from the herd. In fact, he hadn't noticed her up there at all.

She also wore a yellow bikini, but one with a print of hearts in various shapes, sizes and colors. She was short; probably only five-foot, four, or so – slim, but not skinny – flat and small hipped. She wasn't as tanned as most of the others. Her hair was pulled back in a simple pony tail. It was just regular brown hair. In fact, everything about her seemed to be just regular. She was not *hot*. She was plain ... just a girl.

"What?" Jimmy asked, wondering what she wanted.

"Nothing." she answered, somewhat out of breath. "Where you going?"

"Nowhere, I guess. Just ..."

"Sit down a minute." she interrupted. "I'd like to talk to you?"

"About what?" Jimmy wondered.

Her answer was just a patronizing smile. Then heading towards a massive log that had been beached sometime or another by stormy weather, she called back over her shoulder ...

"Over here!"

He sat down beside her on the log, but at an appropriate distance. The two of them sat there for a moment, saying nothing, looking out at the lake and the two islands way offshore.

"So!" she began. "What shall we talk about?"

Jimmy was immediately uncomfortable. He knew that making conversation with girls had never been one of his strong points.

"Hmm ... I don't know. I thought maybe you had something on your mind. Did you come after me for a reason?"

He was really thinking that it was probably Eddie – that she wanted to ask him about Eddie.

"No, not really." she claimed. "Actually, I don't really know. I just thought it would be nice to talk to you ... maybe?"

She ended the sentence interrogatively – as if it might have suddenly occurred to her that he might not be as interested in talking to her. She looked down, and seemed to blush a little.

"I thought you were probably going to ask me about Eddie." he admitted.

"Eddie?" she wondered. "Oh, you mean *Edward!* No, but he's a hottie, isn't he! Is he your brother?"

"Do we look like brothers?" Jimmy responded in a rather surly sort of way, and was immediately sorry about having blurted that out.

"No ... I guess not."

What she was actually thinking about saying after the *No* was that Jimmy was much cuter, but her courage had immediately abandoned her, so she said she guessed not instead. Then it was she who rued that seemingly poor choice of words. She thought she was pretty sure how he was feeling as he turned and walked off the pier. Then she understood why she had run after him ... it was about empathy.

"I mean ..."

"Never mind." said Jimmy. "It's okay."

"No, it's not!" she objected. "I feel like I've insulted you."

"You didn't. Don't worry about it. Eddie's not my brother ... just a guy who lives around here. He's really smooth with girls and women. I'm not. It's okay. No personality, I guess."

"Do you live here too?" she asked.

"Yes ... and no."

She looked at him blankly ... "Explain?"

178

I live in Indianapolis, Indiana with my mother. Actually, in Speedway. My grandparents, her parents, have a cottage over there." ... pointing to the bluffs on the other side of the little river.

"I'll probably be living here with them all summer."

"I'm Jamie." she said, offering her right hand.

Jimmy smiled broadly.

"What's so funny?" she wondered.

He took her hand and shook it briskly.

"I'm Jamie too. Pleased to meet you!" he laughed.

"You're kidding me!" she suspected.

"It's really James. Most people call me Jimmy, but my grandparents always say Jamie."

"Mine's really Jama, but everybody calls me Jamie. If I write 'Jama' it usually gets pronounced *Jam–uh*, so Jamie is less ambiguous."

"Who's the girl with Eddie?" Jimmy wondered if they were together, and if so, why.

"Keegan. She's my cousin."

"How old is she?"

"Fourteen ... or fifteen now, actually."

"Oh." acknowledged Jimmy. Thinking about what Eddie had said so cavalierly about *butchering*. The term *jail-bait* also came to mind.

"How old is he?" Jama wondered.

"Nineteen now, I guess."

"Are you sure ... he doesn't look it. I was guessing maybe sixteen. How old are you, Jimmy?"

"Fourteen."

"Good! I got that one right, anyway." she happily admitted ... making him aware that she was at least interested in him to the extent of having spent a few moments sizing him up.

"I'm fifteen." she added. "... last month."

It began to dawn on him that he was sitting here on the beach, on a log, talking with a girl, and was comfortable doing it. He was less aware of the fact that the details of her physical appearance were a matter that was silently fading into the background ... that his interest was building as he began to accumulate knowledge about her, and as he became more familiar with her, she seemed to grow increasingly attractive.

"Do you live here?" he asked.

"No, we're mostly all from Fountain Point. We're just all staying in that cottage over there for the week." pointing southward down the beach to a small, not very attractive, house.

"It's a birthday party sort of thing ... not for me. For my cousin ... Keegan. She turned fifteen last week."

"Fountain Point?" inquired Jimmy.

"It's on the lake." this time pointing back over her head towards Lake Leelanau. "... On the east side just a little way south of the narrows. It's not a town ... just a place ... a crossroads with a church. Keegan's dad is the minister there."

"So, she's probably wild then?" suggested Jimmy.

She knew what he meant.

"Oh, that's not true! Minister's kids are not always wild." she smiled. "Actually, Keegan is very nice."

He felt like it would be appropriate to offer some corresponding remark about Eddie, but knew it certainly wouldn't be honest to say anything like that. If her cousin really was nice, he thought he had a duty, of sorts, to warn Jama to caution her about Eddie Gunderson, the lady killer – the cherry buster. But then he also heard the words Kenny had recently uttered to his father with respect to Eddie ... *'If you don't have anything good to say, don't say anything.'* So, he said nothing.

"What about Eddie?" she asked. "He seems very nice too."

"Well, Eddie is Ed ..."

He didn't get a chance to finish. She jabbed him lightly in the ribs with her elbow a couple of times to signal that Eddie was coming towards the log.

"Are you about ready to go, James?" Eddie asked.

That seemed like a providential interruption, since Jimmy knew he'd have otherwise been awkward about breaking off the conversation.

"I guess." he answered as he rose to his feet.

"I would like to see you again." said Jama, with Eddie still just outside hearing range ... at least for her thin little voice. "Can you text me?"

"I don't have my phone up here ... I left it back home. I'll look for you on the pier, okay?"

"Or just come over." she suggested.

Jimmy nodded. As he and Eddie walked away, Eddie resumed the *man talk* again.

"You gonna fuck that?" he teased.

"Is that all you ever think about!"

"Now don't get'chur back up. I'm just teasing you."

"She's your new girlfriend's cousin."

"No shit?"

"She says her cousin's a nice girl." advised Jimmy.

"Meaning …?" asked Eddie.

"Nice … as in pleasant and well-behaved, I suppose."

"Well she's right about that. Keegan is that, for sure. – But that doesn't mean she won't screw. Women love the feel of a big hard dick in 'em … and she's gonna find out what that feels like tonight."

"She's only just turned fifteen."

"Bullshit!"

"That's what her cousin said."

"She's sixteen. That's why they're here … it's a week-long birthday party … her sixteenth birthday. She's legal."

"She told you that?"

"Yup, and she's also gonna sneak out tonight, and we're gonna take the boat out for a nice, romantic moonlight cruise. The moon, the stars, the gentle roll, and a little wine, and she'll be on her back begging for it."

"Then what?"

"What'd ya mean, *then what?*" Eddie laughed. "Then she'll get fucked."

"I meant after that. After you've showed her that's all you cared about." explained Jimmy.

"Wow … what is this; a soap opera? … Poor little thing gets fucked by big dicked badass? I can tell yer growing up without a man around the house!"

"That hurt."

"Well it's true, ain't it? What makes you think maybe it's not the other way around … maybe it's her who figures she's set me up, and gonna fuck my ass?"

It was true. That thought hadn't occurred to him. For a while now he had begun to feel the urges to operate his reproductive

182

apparatus. Along with it came all sorts of weird and nasty thoughts and ideas, but he had never thought of the possibility of that sort of arousal also occurring in girls. Somehow, he had learned that the male was the sexually aggressive side of the species, the female being the passive receptor ... and usually having to be carefully coaxed and cajoled into submission. Where had that idea come from? It wasn't from his mother; she never talked about sex, and he doubted that she ever *did it* anymore, having gotten burned so badly the first time. It was all too much. He shook his head ...

"Oh, I don't know." he finally answered.

"Well, I do know ... *treat a queen like a whore, and a whore like a queen.* And in either case, stick to the 4-F program ... *find 'em; feel 'em; fuck 'em; and forget 'em.* That's my advice to you kid." asserted Eddie.

"Do you ever think about getting married someday, Eddie?"

"Of course, doesn't everybody! Why would you ask that?"

"I like you Eddie. But sometimes the stuff you say about people is hard to ... I mean especially about girls ... women ... well, it's ... disappointing."

"Well I like you too, but sometimes the stuff *you* say makes *me* think ..." Eddie answered, wagging his head back and forth from side to side in mocking him, "... like I'm thinking right now ... *FUCK YOU, ASSHOLE!*"

It grew very quiet then. Jimmy offered no response, and cited no justifications for his critique. Eddie was the one who finally spoke up ...

"I'm sorry. I didn't really mean that ... I mean I really do like you ... but not the other."

"It's okay; I understand. And you're right, of course. I really don't know much about girls."

————

At exactly eleven-thirty that night, Keegan silently left the unattractive little cottage on the beach, hurried north along M-22, across the bridge over the dam in Leland and down the River Street hill, where she found Eddie waiting at the big green boat. He politely helped her board, threw off the lines and jumped aboard, quietly started the engine, and guided the boat slowly and silently out of the Leland harbor, through the breakwaters, and out into a placid, moonlit lake.

The coarse but rhythmic rumbling of the boat's engine and the swishing of the water as the Tarnovitch plowed through little wavelets was almost like music she thought, as she leaned back on the deck just aft of the homely plywood wheelhouse, watching the lights along the shore at Leland become smaller and smaller. Eddie soon sat down beside her, facing her.

"Who's driving the boat?" she wondered.

"She doesn't need anybody now. She knows her way out to the Manitous." he reassured her.

"What if we run into something ... or someone?" she kidded.

"We won't. Not tonight ... not now."

"Where are we going?"

"Nowhere ... just for a cruise. When we get out a ways, we'll shut 'er down, and just let her drift. It'll be quiet, and nice. Look what I've got."

"What is it?" she asked with childlike excitement.

"Lafite Rothschild, 1899." he answered with a feigned class, as he produced two plastic wine goblets, a paper towel draped over the arm holding the bottle.

"Really?"

"Actually, it's Good Harbor, and I don't know the vintage ... maybe last week's. I stole it off their truck."

"Oh, you did not!" she demanded as he poured a little in each plastic glass.

In fact, he had. After sitting the bottle down on the deck, he raised his glass ...

"Here's to us." he proposed.

"Here's to us!" she repeated exuberantly.

"Mmm ... I like it, whatever it is." she reported, pushing her plastic goblet towards him. This time he filled it up.

The boat continued its seaward voyage, ever so gently rocking, the engine now sounding more like a rhythmic drone that sometimes seemed to modulate in cozy tones, almost like a lullaby. She began humming along with it. At some point, Edward got up and turned off the music, then came back and sat beside her as he had before. She leaned forward, to taste his lips, and he bent forward to accommodate her wish.

Having broken the ice, she lurched forward again, this time wrapping her arms around his neck and firmly planting her parted lips on his.

All was still, except for the occasional splash of a little wavelet against the steel bow. The boat still rocked, ever so gently, much like a baby's cradle, and the moon and the stars showed peacefully down on two young lovers, silently adrift the Manitou Passage.

When it was over for the first time, she looked into his eyes, smitten, crying. Then, with her head lying on his shoulder, she pulled him very close, and hugged him very tightly.

* * *

18

At ten minutes before nine the next morning, the bronze bell atop the Congregational Church began its sixty-second ritual of calling the faithful to worship. As the bell completed its part, Rose Myers, who had been the Congregational Church's organist for many years, began playing the prelude, a version of Bach's *In Dulci Jubilo* which she had arranged so it would come out at exactly nine minutes. As she played it, the participants entered the sanctuary in a solemn procession, led by Kenny's father, who carried a large bible resting in the crook of his left arm, an elder, who would serve as the liturgist for this day's service, and finally the choir of thirteen people, in robes of pale blush purple, one of whom was Kenny's mother.

They all marched in solemnly, climbed the three steps up to the chancel, and took their appointed seats.

At exactly nine o'clock, Rose finished her piece, raising her feet from the pedals and her fingers from the keyboards with her usual flourish. Kenny's dad immediately arose, walked purposefully to the center of the chancel, and then stepped down to the sanctuary floor.

"Welcome, in the name of our Lord Jesus Christ! It's wonderful to see so many fresh, smiling faces on this ..." He went on with the usual trite welcoming comments, announcements, the inquiry about visitors and guests – giving anyone who wished to embarrass themselves or someone else an opportunity to do so, and finally with what Kenny referred to as the *Passing the Germs* ritual – the shaking of hands and the greeting of nearby pew-mates. As the commotion began to die down, and the less cordial began to reclaim their seats, Kenny's dad returned to the middle of the chancel, announced, "Let us now prepare our hearts and minds for worship." ... and then returned to his chair.

In the very front pew, on the left just below the pulpit, four worshipers waited silently for what would come next – Lee and Josie Smith, Jimmy Sutton ... and *the Chief,* Tommy Thomassen.

A small treble voice from up in the balcony over the back rows of pews began singing *a cappella* in the stillness ...

> *Oh, the spirit of Jesus is in this place.*
> *I can see the change he's making on each face.*
> *When the pow'r of Heav'n is tapped,*
> *then Something good is bound to happen.*
> *For the Spirit of Jesus is in this place.*

That was Kenny's first song. *It was wonderful!* Jimmy thought to himself, just like he knew it would be! As Kenny's dad, Rev. Jennings, ascended the pulpit, taking a little sip from a small glass of water concealed within it, Kenny slipped quietly down the side isle, crossed in front of them, and sat down in the front pew, next to Mr. Thomassen. Jimmy leaned forward a bit to catch Kenny's eye, and smiled brightly.

The service continued through the usual rituals, the scripture readings, and the sermon, which began and ended with the usual short prayer. Then Kenny's dad looked up and out at the congregation to say, "Let us now render onto God a part of the bounty he has so graciously bestowed upon us."

As he said it, Kenny's mother got up from her place in the choir and seated herself at the piano, a white Steinway baby grand that had been anonymously donated (by Thomas and Susanna Thomassen.) Kenny stood up, and walked confidently up to the center of the chancel, standing attentively more or less in the cove of the piano as his mother played through the introductory passages of the piece he was about to sing.

And then Kenny began singing the Offertory ...

When I am down and, oh my soul, so weary;
When troubles come and my heart burdened be;
Then, I am still and wait here in the silence,
Until you come and sit awhile with me.

You raise me up, so I can stand on mountains;
You raise me up, to walk on stormy seas;
I am strong, when I am on your shoulders;
You raise me up ... To more than I can be.

There is no life - no life without its hunger;
Each restless heart beats so imperfectly;
But when you come and I am filled with wonder,
Sometimes, I think I glimpse eternity.

You raise me up ... To more than I can be.

Each time Kenny sang the *You raise me up ...* chorus, he began it looking directly at his Jimmy ... and then again, each time he finished it with the *"To more than I can be."* part. That was creating a lump in Jimmy's throat. He struggled to suppress the tears that he feared were soon going to follow. Tommy apparently noticed his struggle, and patted him gently on the leg with his strong left hand.

At the end of Kenny's song ... after the last *"To more than I can be."* ... the little congregation sat in perfect stillness as Mrs. Jennings quietly returned to her place in the choir, and Kenny to his seat beside Mr. Thomassen. Then all corporately relaxed their muscles and released their breath. They had not seen this boy sing before, and not many even knew who he was. But they all evidently realized they had just been blessed with one of the finest moments this small church had ever witnessed, and spontaneously broke into a vigorous round of applause – which was not their usual custom. Tommy Thomassen looked fondly down at the slight lad with the neatly combed dark hair sitting at his side, smiled, put his right arm around Kenny's shoulders and gave him a strong and affectionate hug that said ... well done! Kenny looked up at Mr. Thomassen with admiration, then straining his neck, whispered in Tommy ear ...

"See ... there wasn't any lightning."

At that moment, Rose brought her feet and fingers smartly down on the organ's pedals and keys, causing the introductory strains of the Doxology to bring everyone quickly to their feet as the ushers brought forth the platters containing that morning's take. Everybody sang the well-worn song ... even Tommy, whose arm remained admiringly around Kenny's shoulders ...

> *Praise God, from whom all blessings flow;*
> *Praise him, all creatures here below;*
> *Praise him above, ye heavenly host;*

Praise Father, Son, and Holy Ghost.
... Ahh – men

After the closing hymn, it was over. Kenny's dad said the benediction with his hands raised and his palms outstretched over his congregation ... "And now may the Grace of the Father ..." and so on. Then he hurried down the center isle to take his station at the door, ready to receive everyone's perfunctory compliments on the wonderful message he had just delivered from the pulpit.

There was, however, somewhat of a traffic jam, as a goodly number of the congregants worked their way towards the front, instead of towards the door ... to shake the hand or hug the slim young boy who had, that morning, brought the handkerchiefs out of numerous purses and pockets, and sung some life back into a tired out old church.

Jimmy was almost bubbling over with pride and admiration for his wonderful friend. His heart felt crowded in his chest, as if it wished to burst free.

He smiled at Tommy, and then quickly turned away. The darn tears had finally refused to be denied any longer.

But he had turned face to face with his grandmother. She took one look, then with her hands on either side of his face, pulled him to her breast and hugged him tight.

"I'm sorry grandma. I don't know what's the matter with me."

"There's nothing the matter with you, Jamie. Don't you ever think it!"

"I just start crying over nothing! I can't help it." he lamented, with his head still on her soft shoulder.

"It's not over nothing, Jamie. I know why, and I'm fiercely proud of you!"

"Tell me."

"There's tears of hurt, Jamie. And there's tears of sorrow. There's tears of joy, and there's tears of love. There's lots of kinds of tears. Tears shed for the love of a friend are some of the most precious of all." she told him softly, now almost in tears herself. Oh, how she loved this sensitive, tender-hearted boy she held in her arms, she thought. How proud of him indeed!

"But I feel like ... like a stupid baby!" he confided.

"Oh, yes." she scoffed "... grown men don't cry. That's never been true. Benjamin Franklin once said *Never trust a man who can't cry.*"

"Uh, I'm pretty sure that was Norman Schwarzkopf, dear." advised Lee, who had just turned towards them.

"Well, whoever." she condescended lightly.

"Anyway, Jamie, you come by it honestly. You're your grandpa's grandson; a chip off the old Smith block. He likes to pretend he's a tough old bird, but he's just as loving and chickenhearted as you ... you get it from him. It runs in his whole family."

Lee smiled sheepishly.

"Well cryin's good sometimes." he protested in his defense "... keeps you from havin' to pee so much."

Jimmy began to laugh through his tears, still hugging his grandma. With her free arm, Josie reached out and pulled her husband into the huddle. She dearly loved both of her loving, chicken-hearted boys.

———

As most of the other people retired to the church parlor for the *3C's* ritual ... coffee, cookies and conversation ... Jimmy found Kenny on the walkway in front of the church, where he had fled, having had enough handshakes, hugs and pats on the back.

"You were great, Kenny. I knew you would be."

"Thanks."

Then it was Kenny who rushed forward to hug somebody. Jimmy accepted his embrace with pats on the back, and then pushed him back to arm's length ...

"Can you work on the boat this afternoon? We can work on the mast in Tommy's yard. Then maybe go down and go swimming after?"

"I'll ask. My parents have to go into town, but maybe they'll let me stay with you while they're gone. Can my mom ask your grandma?"

"Sure ... C'mon!" And they headed for the church parlor.

* * *

<u>19</u>

That afternoon the wind was northerly, but brisk. The air was dry and clear so they thought, like it said in the book, that it was a good day for varnishing. They hadn't allowed for all the prep-work that would be involved, however. With the afternoon sun beating down intensely on Tommy's weedy lawn, Jimmy and Kenny were soon dripping sweat onto the surfaces they were trying to lightly sandpaper.

"Maybe we can move this into his garage." suggested Kenny.

Tommy's opinion was that the sanding was better done outdoors, to keep from getting dust all over everything, but that the varnishing should be done inside because it would take a long time to dry.

"Let's have a look." said Tommy, getting up from his lawn chair and walking over to the spar, which had been laid out over two low sawhorses.

"It was in pretty fair shape to begin with ... I think you've got it good enough. Rub out this here spot just a little more and that'll do. Then we'll take 'er into the garage."

With both boys applying a little elbow grease to the area Tommy had pointed out, it only took a few minutes until he was satisfied with that area too. Then he hefted the mast by himself, with Jimmy and Kenny each carrying one of the sawhorses, and the trio of shipwrights moved the project to the garage.

Looking at his watch, Tommy suggested ...

"It's almost half-past four ... why don't you two knock off and go jump in the lake. You're both all sweaty and covered with sanding dust."

They were happy to accept that idea. Kenny repeated his mock salute and said "Aye, Sir!" as he had fallen into the habit of doing with Tommy, and the two were off on the run ... down Tommy's stairway, across the beach to the water's edge, where they kicked off their sandals and flip-flops and dropped their shorts, then continued running into the lake ... Jimmy in his trim fitting light blue and white Kona Coast print, and Kenny in his little brown Speedo.

The water was not warm. It never was, but they had become overheated while working on the mast in the hot sun, and also sunburned, so were not bothered by the chill as they ran into the surf. The waves were running high, as they always did with a stiff northwesterly breeze, and it was great fun diving into them, and over them, and rolling over their crests.

While pushing tons of Lake Michigan towards the shoreline, the winds, a little more from the north than the west, created a southerly flow along the shoreline, and before they were aware of it, they found that they had drifted all the way past the little point, past Jimmy's stairway, and almost all the way down to the fence with the no trespassing sign. So, before being thrown on the rock levee that protected that side of the municipal marina, they came splashing out of the water on the run, trotted back up the beach all the way around the little point again, and fell into the warm sand in the shade, beneath their boat. Huffing and puffing a bit, Jimmy said ...

"Hey, Kenny ... look! No wet spots!"

Kenny looked around and discovered that Jimmy was right. The boat had stopped dripping. Thinking she'd lost all her water, he quickly crawled out from under, stood up and peered over her gunwales, as did Jimmy. She had not lost all her water. In fact, they had cause to celebrate, finding that she was still almost full up ... perhaps just an inch or two down from the way they had left her. Kenny turned to Jimmy with his right arm extended, and the two exaggerated a congratulatory handshake.

On closer inspection, they found about six spots along her strakes that were leaking ... but only seepage. The leaks were so slow that the heat rising from the hot sand was evaporating the water before it could accumulate into drips. Tomorrow, Tommy would probably tell them to mark those six places, then pull the plug and let her dry out.

Back under the boat in the shade again, laying in the sand with their hands used as pillows, Jimmy spoke up ...

"Hey, Kenny ... know what?"

"What?"

"I met a girl yesterday."

"You did? ... Where?"

"On the pier, with Eddie Gunderson."

"U'oh."

Kenny's *U'oh* was inflected in a way that reflected his disdain for Eddie Gunderson, and discomfort for Jimmy's involvement with him.

"What were you doing with him?"

Suddenly Jimmy realized that perhaps he shouldn't have brought this up. Were the conversation to continue in this

196

direction, he'd have to admit drinking with Eddie, and going to the pier with the idea of *scoring chicks*.

"Since you had to practice, I thought I'd just go watch the ferry's leave, and after they were gone, I bumped into him. He was cleaning up their boat."

"Oh. Then what?" asked Kenny.

"And then ... I'd rather not say what."

As soon as he'd said that, he realized it opened to door to imaginings that could easily be worse than the facts.

"Okay. I feel like I'm lying. I guess Eddie isn't a very good influence, when hanging around with him winds up with things I don't want to talk about."

"Like what?" Kenny asked, trying not to sound too curious.

"I had three bottles of beer in his boat, pissed in the river, he fed me lunch at the Bluebird to sober me up a little, and then we walked over to the pier to see if we could get screwed."

"Oh, brothers!" exclaimed Kenny. "So, did you?"

"Did I what?"

"Get screwed."

"No!!! ... of course not! But Eddie probably did."

"Good for him!" Kenny said disgustedly "I can just guess what kind of girl would have anything to do with him."

"No. You'd be guessing wrong, Kenny. There was this girl on the pier that he'd seen out there before and was all hot for. She was pretty nice. ... Looking, I mean. ... But she seemed pretty nice too. Eddie said he was going to do her."

"That doesn't mean he did. Why would any nice girl have anything to do with him?" reasoned Kenny.

"You wouldn't believe it!" explained Jimmy. "He just fell into it so easy. She'd lost her cell phone over the side just before we got there, and they were all afraid to dive for it. She begged Eddie, and he stripped off his shirt and shoes, jumped in, swam to the bottom like a big fish, and got it for her. It just happened ... like the gods were on his side, or something."

"Oh, yes. I'm sure the gods are looking out for *him*." said Kenny sarcastically.

"Well, that's the way it happened. Then after that, he just totally changed! He was very nice to her ... polite ... no dirty talk, or anything. You wouldn't believe it! It was like he was a totally different person."

"And she fell for it ... just like that?"

"Well, she'd never met him before ... why wouldn't she?"

"I guess. But he's such a creep ..."

"Now Kenny ..." Jimmy wished he could get him to soften his attitude. "Nobody's all bad, you know. Everybody has a good side ... even Eddie. He has feelings. I've seen that ... and so have you actually ... outside the church the other day."

"Okay, so *good Eddie* fools a nice girl into thinking that he's Prince Charming, then what?"

"Then they just sat down on the pier and started talking. I thought Eddie totally forgot that I was there, so I left. I don't know what happened after that. I guess you're right ... I guess I don't really know anything more than that."

"If she was nice, like you say, she wouldn't just let some strange guy she just met get in her pants, would she."

"Well, maybe ..." The imp in Jimmy suddenly woke up. "But she's a preacher's kid!" he teased, and began laughing.

198

"Yeah, I'll bet! Very funny, Jimmy. Very funny! ... and how do you know that?"

"Because the girl I met told me ... she was her cousin."

"I thought you said you left."

"I did. But she came after me on the beach."

"What for?"

"For nothing ... just to talk."

"About what?"

"About nothing ... she just felt like talking, I guess. I hadn't noticed her up on the pier. I thought she probably wanted to ask me about Eddie."

"Did she?"

"No ... she said she didn't care anything about Eddie."

"In other words, it was you she wanted to know."

"I guess."

"You guess? Are you really that slow around girls?" Kenny teased, not realizing that Jimmy was indeed slow around girls. "What was *she* like?"

"Nice." replied Jimmy.

"*Nice* ... like what? Nice body? Nice looking? Nice personality?"

"Just nice ... just average ... plain, I guess. But nice. You're right, I guess. I guess she liked me. She was easy to talk to. I don't usually find it that easy to talk to girls."

"Why?" wondered Kenny, who had never found talking to girls any different than talking to boys.

"I don't know ... I just seem to clam up. Can't think of anything to say, and when I do say something, it usually comes out sounding stupid."

"Maybe it's because you're really thinking with your balls." laughed Kenny.

"Kenny!!! Language!" Jimmy teased, and then he joined Kenny laughing. "That's what Gramps said about me when I was thinking about paying Mr. Thomassen all the money I had for the Sea Scout ... that I was thinking with my balls."

"So anyway, what happened? What's her name? How old is she? Where does she live? Did you cover any of that?"

"Yeah, her name is Jamie, just like what my grandparents call me ... isn't that funny? Eddie was wrong; they're really only from Fountain Point, not from Traverse City. That's where the other girl's dad is a minister. Her real name is Jama ... she's fifteen ... just."

"Does she have a younger sister?" Kenny asked jokingly.

"I'm sorry! I didn't think to ask. She said she wanted to see me again ... maybe we can ask her then."

"We?"

Jimmy just shrugged.

* * *

20

The following morning, the wind was still northerly, but had not yet picked up, as it would as the sun rose higher. Jimmy and Kenny were up early, and over to Mr. Thomassen's by seven thirty. They found Tommy already out in the garage, rummaging around on the shelves in the back, which held cans of all sizes, shapes and colors.

"I had some good spar varnish here somewhere." he said, having somehow noticed them without turning his head.

Finally discovering the can he was looking for, he took it down from the shelf, and over to his workbench on the side of the garage.

"Open 'er up."

After using a big screwdriver to pry off the cover, they saw that varnish was all hardened up.

"No, it's only a skin over the top." Tommy advised. "Knock that scum loose around the edges and take it out. Take care not to break it all up."

That they accomplished, without getting much varnish on their clothes.

"I hope those are your old clothes?" Tommy asked. "Now take this'ere paint stick and stir it up. And do it slow so you don't get it all full of air bubbles."

"Is that enough, do you think?" asked Jimmy after several minutes. Tommy had a look and reported ...

"Yes, that's just fine. Pour off a little in this'ere coffee can, then you can both varnish the stick." ... handing them each a two-inch varnish brush.

"Here's how you do it ... let me show you a minute. The first thing is, you work with a full brush, see? Dunk 'er in here, and only wipe the end a little on the edge of your can so it doesn't drip, then hold your brush up like this, see? Then you lay it on – from north to south, not crossways like this, but lengthwise – and then you brush it out a little and get off it. Let it settle by itself. Then it'll come out nice and smooth. Otherwise if you keep brushing away, it'll start settin' up and you'll wind up with a bunch of brush marks, and it'll look like hell ... like the work of a couple of young tyros."

And thus, the two boys varnished the mast. After they finished, he inspected their work and finding it to be quite satisfactory, introduced them to mineral spirits, teaching them all about how to clean up the brushes, and their hands.

The wind was still fairly calm, with the sun still low enough that the nearby trees still shaded the lawn, so it was a good time to start working on the boat's bottom boards.

"Before you get started on that ..." suggested Tommy, "... let's go down and have a look at the water situation."

The six leaky places were barely seeping anymore, but were still wet. Tommy took a thick round stick of blue chalk out of his pocked and circled each place.

"These are places where you're gonna have to replace nails." he told them. "There'll probably be a couple of more, maybe ... but these six for sure. Other than that, she looks like she's held up real good. I'm not surprised. Goes to show you what a good job me and your grandpa did." he bragged proudly, and then footnoted that by saying, almost to himself, "Good wood too, of course."

Kenny was standing next to the rudder at the stern of the boat. Tommy waved his arm at him and said ...

"Pull the bilge plug, boy!"

Kenny looked questioningly down at the back of the boat but couldn't see anything that looked like a plug.

"You have to do it from inside the boat, boy!" chuckled Tommy. "Climb in there and twist that brass thing down there a quarter turn, then yank 'er out."

Kenny was not wearing his swim suit, and was reluctant to get his shorts soaking wet. But otherwise all he had on was his Walmart briefs, and he didn't feel like running around undressed either. So, he shrugged, as if thinking *Oh, well ... what the heck,* kicked off his flip-flops and climbed into the water filled boat.

The drain plug came out easily, and the water began peeing a strong stream, creating a little rivulet through the sand on its way back into the lake. As the depth of the water in the boat diminished, the exiting stream slackened, and the rivulet sunk into the sand, until finally there were only drips coming from the stern.

"Leave 'er be 'til she dries out now ... it'll take a few days ... depending." advised Tommy, meaning depending on if the wind remained northerly, which generally brought dry air in the summertime, and if it remained as strong as it had been the past day or so, and if the sun still got as hot during the next few days.

"After that, you can scrub 'er up inside. She's pretty dirty, but other than that, doesn't look too bad. That probably ain't gonna take much work."

And thus, the work on the boat project continued, day after sunny June day. Mr. Thomassen predicted that towards the end of the following month, late in July, most of it would be done. In spite of the long days and hard work, the boys' interest and high hopes never waned.

————

Kenny knocked on his father's office door. The door was open and Grant was concentrating on something at his desk with red pen in hand, so he continued in, then stood and patiently waited.

"Hello, son."

"Hi, Dad."

Looking up, his father pushed his papers out of the way, put down the red pen, and folded his hands atop the desk.

"What's up?"

"Would it be alright if I went to the movie in Traverse City tonight ... with Jimmy and his grandparents?"

"What's on?"

Two For The Show ... it's Disney.

"Haven't we already seen that one?" Grant seemed to remember.

"Jimmy and them haven't." Kenny answered.

"Jimmy and they ..." corrected his father.

"Okay. So, can I?"

"What time does it get out? It'll probably be after nine. By the time you got back, it would be quite late." observed his father. "Maybe another time."

204

"Yes, since it *would* be kind of late, Jimmy thought maybe you'd let me spend the night at their place. His grandma said it would be okay with them if it was okay with you."

"There's no need for that – it's only a few blocks from here over to their cottage. You don't do sleep-overs when you live so close to your friends."

"Grant."

His mother was standing in the doorway, and had been listening to their conversation. When she said *Grant*, she was also wagging her head back and forth.

"Your mother says no, I'm afraid."

Mary corrected his misconception ...

"Oh, that's not what I meant, Grant. Boys have sleepovers just for fun. It's an adventure, not a practical thing."

"Well ..." Grant was going to debate that, but realizing that his wife wished to approve the venture, capitulated.

"Well ..." he began again "... your mother has made up our mind. So, I guess the answer is going to be yes."

"To the movie? ... and staying at Jimmy's tonight?"

"Yes, and yes." his father confirmed.

Kenny felt like jumping up and shouting *"Whoopie!"*, but always behaved reservedly in his father's office. His mother, of course, knew how excited he was, and smiled.

"He should take some money Grant." Mary suggested.

"How much?"

"Ten will be fine." and then to her son ...

"The Smith's will probably pay your way, but you should get your money out and show them that you're prepared to buy your own ticket first. Then if they insist, you offer to buy the popcorn, or whatever."

"Got it." replied Kenny as he took the ten-dollar bill his father was handing him, his excitement now showing.

————

When he arrived at Jimmy's house, Jimmy was just as happy and excited as he reported his good fortune to Lee and Josie. Josie was happy that the boys' scheme was working out. Lee was not, since he wasn't really a Disney fan, but went along with the plan good naturedly anyway, remembering how it was with him and Tommy when they were boys – always up to something, and it almost always seemed like an adventure.

The movie was not really very good, but Jimmy and Kenny enjoyed it anyway. It wasn't really about the movie. Josie seemed to enjoy it. Lee snoozed through most of it. They did, indeed, get back to the cottage quite late, but that was because they stopped at the Flap Jack Shack, up on the hill out on South Division Avenue. It was the boys' idea, of course ... not so much about a late-night snack as about not wanting the fun to end. It was after eleven as they pulled into the driveway at the cottage.

"You two better hustle off to bed." said Josie. "Did you bring anything, Kenny ... pajamas? ... toothbrush?"

"I forgot." he answered. "I'm sorry. But it's okay ... I sleep in my underwear anyway. I don't have pajamas anymore."

"I'd guess not!" supported Lee facetiously. "Real men don't get dressed up to go to bed at night!"

"Yeah, I don't." agreed Jimmy, trying to sound like he thought a *real man* might. "Besides, we forgot to buy any."

"Well, off with you then ... upstairs. You should probably have a bath first, but it's too late to go down and jump in the lake." joked Josie.

The two boys stripped to their briefs.

"Look! We match." observed Kenny.

Then they lay down on the bed together on their stomachs, side by side, looking out the window on that end of the large room at the moon and the stars. The moon was still mostly full, its reflected light brightly illuminating the earth through the cool, clear night air. It cast a silver streak across the water from out beyond the islands, which seemed to loom on the horizon out in the lake like two resting sea creatures.

"Have you ever been out there?" Kenny asked.

"Yes." answered Jimmy.

"Which one?"

"Both."

"What's it like out there? Do people live out there?"

"Nah, they belong to the park ... only park people can live there now." answered Jimmy. "There's nothing to do out there ... just camping and stuff. Gramps took me over to North once. He used to go over there with his friends and have fun back in the old days before the park came. But there's nothing left now ... it's mostly all falling down."

"Why don't they keep it up?"

"It's supposed to be wilderness."

"South Manitou too?"

"Yes, we went over there once ... Gramps, grandma and me ... just to look around."

"I mean is that all falling down too?"

"Not all of it. They keep some of it fixed up because you can go over there just for the day ... and there's three camping places on that one."

"What do you do over there."

"Nothing, much ... just walk around. It's not really worth it. For just you and me it would cost $50 for the ferry."

"Maybe when we get the boat done, we can sail over there by ourselves." dreamed Kenny.

"I guess ... maybe." Jimmy agreed tentatively, not being sure if the sailing certificate he'd earned at Culver was sufficient to handling the Sea Scout on a trip across the Passage.

The conversation continued for a while, about hopes, and dreams, and possibilities that would probably never be, until Kenny finally turned on his side with his back towards Jimmy, and sleepily said goodnight. Jimmy turned over on his back and lay there in the darkness for a while, with his hands under his head, thinking about how nice it seemed to have someone in bed beside him ... to not be alone at night. He had never had a friend over before.

———

The morning seemed to come in a flash, as if the night had been cancelled. In fact, Jimmy had drifted off to sleep so happily, and had slept so peacefully, that he was completely unaware of the night's passing, or the morning hour. He had awakened suddenly, feeling totally refreshed, and with the happy feeling still in his heart.

When he woke up, he found Kenny close by his side, facing him with his left arm draped over his chest.

208

Turning on his side towards his bed partner, he nudged him a little and Kenny turned over with his back towards him. Jimmy reached over, hugging him around his belly, to pull him closer, and Kenny responded by pushing close against him. The feel of Kenny's bare back against his chest, his legs against his legs ... skin to skin ... felt heartwarming, and once again Jimmy marveled at how wonderful it felt to not wake up in his bed alone.

He wasn't aware that Kenny had awakened, and was thinking the same thing.

* * *

21

As the summer continued to unfold June's days stealthily slipped off the calendar without notice, until there were only a couple of her days left. The days had been unusually warm, even with northerly breezes, but that had proven fortunate for the Sea Scout project, since it was good drying weather for varnish and paint.

The project had continued, with Jimmy and Kenny diligently continuing to find at least four or five hours most days to work on the boat, carefully following the instructions in Captain Kenealy's sailing book, as augmented by Mr. Thomassen's demonstrations and Lee's advice.

After the boat dried out, the boys scrubbed her inside and out, working in their swim suits, using warm, soapy water and stiff Tampico brushes. Five-gallon buckets of hot sudsy water were carried down the stairway from Tommy's house as needed. When depleted, the same buckets were used to rinse the boat off, drawing clean, cold water from the lake. The full buckets were heavy, especially for Kenny, who hung on to their bale with both hands, and waddled along with the bucket not quite between his legs. When they went to the lake for fresh water, they wound up like softball pitchers, throwing the empty buckets as far out as they could, and then ran into the water, diving after them.

After the cleaning, came the tedious job of checking her rivets, each and every one on either side, from keel to gunwale. Jimmy, being the bigger and stronger of the two, manned the heavy bucking hammer on the outside of the hull, holding it against the head of the nails as Kenny did the tapping with the ball peen hammer from the inside.

It also fell to Kenny to try each one, before and after, by attempting to wiggle the rove to make sure there was no play. When he came to a loose rivet that would not tighten up, Kenny used the nail nippers to remove it, snipping it off from the inside. Then Jimmy drove in the next larger size copper nail from the outside, Kenny slid a new rove on and tapped it down around the edges, nipped off the nail's excess length with the nippers, then peened it over with the ball end of his hammer.

When they came to one of the leaky spots they'd marked before, they replaced the rivet and added two extras, one on either side, just like Tommy had told them to do. It seemed like this part of the job was going to take forever, but the day finally came when they finished the last rivet along the top strake on her starboard side. The screws on the ends of the strakes, stem and stern, were all intact, and needed no attention, so that part was, at long last, done.

————

Eddie Gunderson was only infrequently encountered after having met the girl Keegan. He had managed to get a part-time job at a resort on Lake Leelanau, not far south of the narrows, and near Fountain Point, and that is where he spent much of his time, working or not. When he was seen around Leland, he was either cleaning up things or stretching nets at the Tarnovitch, where he was still part of the crew. He was careful not to be seen around town with Keegan.

He had changed considerably. The braggadocio and vulgarity were mostly gone, having been replaced by a new maturity, and ... perhaps ... a *gentleness*. He had always been careful about his appearance and personal hygiene, but now *careful* seemed to have turned into *impeccable* – almost always looking as if he'd just come out of the shower, even while at work. It was quite obvious to most practical people that Eddie had found a girl and was in love, even to those who had never actually seen her.

————

Jimmy had not looked up the girl Jama following their meeting on the beach south of the pier on the day that Eddie met Keegan. Their time at the rented cottage having come to an end, the girls all returned to wherever they had come from, mostly from around Fountain Point, but in Jama's case, it *was* Traverse City. He thought about her often, and was sorry that he had not gone back out to the pier again the next day. He didn't know why he hadn't, but he did regret it, assuming she had probably gotten the idea that he didn't care, or had not been favorably impressed.

That was not actually the conclusion she had come to. For her part, she was also sorry that Jimmy never showed up again. She had walked over his way one morning, ending up at the fence with the sign that said *No Trespassing*, so went no further. On inquiring about the cottages beyond it, the informant, who happened to be Harley Spence, claimed it was Leland's version of *Nob Hill*, the exclusive domain of people who were wealthy and uppity – the kind of people she probably wouldn't care to know. She didn't believe that of Jimmy, of course, but presumed it might be true of

212

his grandparents. She hadn't asked Harley Spence about the Smiths, in particular, or the Suttons. If what he said was generally true, Jimmy's grandparents would probably not approve of her, she reasoned, since she was just common, the daughter of a school teacher and a working man.

———

Lee, Josie and Jimmy had not attended services in Leland again, and would not unless it so happened that Kenny was to perform again, which he thus far had not. Rev. Jennings was of the attitude that his level of compensation was not sufficiently generous that the congregation had a right to expect anything more than his services as pastor, and not the services of his wife and son. It was enough that Mary sang in the choir. By intention, he planned the services so as to keep her away from the white baby grand, and his son off the Chancel. The Smith's and their grandson returned to their custom of attending the eleven o'clock mass at St. Francis' in Traverse City. Jimmy watched for the girl he'd seen board the Ningwis that morning, but she never appeared.

Much to the amusement of many, Tommy Thomassen, *the old Chief*, had started coming to church again, a practice he had abandoned after his late wife's funeral. He came, because Kenny asked him to come. Moreover, he came, because Kenny had made it his business to appear at his door at a quarter before nine on Sunday mornings, to accompany him on the short walk to the Congregational Church.

Tommy had grown very fond of the boy, was flattered by his faithful attention, and touched by his caring gesture. Besides that, they sat side by side in their place in the front pew, as they had on that first day, so Tommy was treated to the sound of Kenny's sweet voice whenever there was a Gloria Patri, Doxology, or hymn to be sung.

Kenny also eventually persuaded Mr. Thomassen to condescend to partake in the coffee and cookie ritual in the church parlor after the services, otherwise known as *a time of fellowship*. Tommy wasn't much on *fellowship*, but did enjoy *shooting the shit*, as he put it, with some of his former acquaintances, even some of the ladies. He also got a kick out of watching Kenny, who had taken it upon himself to help the Fellowship Committee ladies arrange and serve the donated cookies, and to some was known as *the cookie boy*. Many of those who didn't know better, of which there were few, presumed that Kenny might be Tommy's grandson.

After it was all over each Sunday morning, Kenny always walked with Mr. Thomassen back to his place. Then the two of them might look the boat over and talk in a businesslike manner about the next steps. But, more often, they just sat together in the Adirondack chairs overlooking the lake and the islands from the bluff at the edge of Mr. Thomassen's weedy lawn, with Tommy sharing the annals of his life and times, and the lessons he'd drawn therefrom. Kenny was especially keen on the stories about his Coast Guard years.

———

It was on the last Sunday of June that, through fortune, Jama reappeared. The board of Lee's foundation wanted to get together briefly to wrap up some loose ends before the end of the fiscal year on the 30th, and for most of the others, who were in the practice of attending the nine o'clock Congregational service, eleven

214

o'clock seemed like a good time to get together at Jerry Maguire's office. Thus, Lee and Josie got up early that morning, to attend the nine o'clock Mass at St. Francis of Assisi in Traverse.

They entered the church's narthex, dipped their fingers in the baptismal font and marked themselves with the sign of the cross, as was their custom, then entered the nave and found a pew, reverently genuflected – except for Jimmy, who felt awkward and did that only halfheartedly – and then took their seats.

In a moment, Jimmy felt someone tapping on his shoulder, and when he turned, discovered it was Jama. She smiled, and he smiled back. Josie turned around, looked at Jama, then at Jamie, then back at Jama and also smiled. Then the service began.

After Mass, Jimmy and Jama walked out together to the broad walkway leading into the church.

"I didn't know you were Catholic!" she began.

"I'm not really ... just my grandparents. I'm not really anything."

"Oh." she said, the tone of her acknowledgment making it clear that didn't make any difference to her.

"Well I'm glad *they* are." she added. "I wondered if I'd ever see you again."

"I'm sorry I didn't come back to the pier before you left."

"Me too!" she admitted candidly, and with mock hurt feelings.

"I don't know why I didn't. I didn't mean anything by it."

"I came over to your side one morning ... as far as the fence."

"Oh?" He was quietly pleased to know that.

"There was a park ranger there. He said I shouldn't go any further because it was private property from there on."

"A park ranger?"

"They were on one of the park boats, so I thought I'd ask."

"That was probably Harley Spence. He's sort of a jerk. Nobody likes him."

"That's what he said about the people on your side of the fence." she laughed.

"Oh; here comes my grandmother." announced Jimmy.

Jama quickly grew guarded, recalling her previous assumptions about not being considered a suitable acquaintance for this rich boy.

"Grandma, this is Jama ... the girl I met on the pier."

"I don't recall you're having mentioned that, Jamie ..." reaching out to Jama "... but I'm very glad to meet you Jama!"

"Jama's called Jamie too, grandma."

"Really! What's the matter with Jama. I think it's nice!"

"People sometimes think it's pronounced like *Jam-ma*. So, we went with *Jamie* ... it's less confusing."

"Jamie ... you, I mean." she said, pointing to Jimmy "... your grandfather has already gone for the car. I'm afraid we have to run Jamie ..." turning to the girl "... Oh, my! How very confusing this could get! ... My husband has a meeting at eleven, so we have to scoot. Might you be able to come out to the cottage?"

"Do I have time to ask my parents?"

"Of course, ... are they here?"

"Right over there ... I'll only be a minute."

Josie followed, hurrying right behind the girl to address her parents directly. They looked nice.

"We do want her to come. I'm sorry about the rush, but my husband has a meeting in Leland at eleven. Please do say yes!" she begged.

216

The immediate response was a blank, inquisitive look on the faces of both parents.

"Oh, where's my brain!" she quickly added. "I'm Joanne Smith, from Leland. This is our grandson, James Sutton, who's visiting for the summer. Father can vouch for us. We're really quite harmless."

Having not yet heard an answer, she fetched a pen from her purse and began writing in the margins of that morning's bulletin.

"Here is our street address in Leland, and our telephone number. My husband will bring her back ... when would you like her home?"

Jama's father looked at her mother and smiled, a small heave of his chest giving away a suppressed laugh. Then he looked at Father Kempinski, who had been eavesdropping on the scene while in conversation with another couple, and who now smiled and nodded.

* * *

22

"I should have brought a bathing suit." suggested Jama, as they sat atop the picnic table near the edge of the bluff, overlooking the lake. She had dressed casually, but tastefully, for Mass ... in navy blue walking shorts, an open blouse with a ribbed white cotton undershirt beneath, and leather sandals.

It then occurred to Jimmy why he hadn't returned to the pier after meeting her that first day. His fear of deep water wouldn't have permitted him to participate in what the other kids were doing, and it would have been an embarrassment. He didn't respond to her bathing suit comment.

"Me and my friend are working on a boat just around the point over there ... would you like to take a walk up the beach?"

"Will it be alright if I leave these here?" she asked, having removed her blouse and sandals.

Then they walked down the stairway to the beach, and toward the little point.

"Is your grandmother always so ... *assertive*?" she wondered. She had almost said *pushy*, but thought better of it. *Assertive* didn't seem like a good choice of words either, but she wasn't able to come up with anything else on short notice. After she'd said it, the word *exuberant* came to mind as one that would have sounded better.

"No. Actually, she's not. I think she was just a little excited."

"Oh. About what?"

"About me having a girlfriend."

"She thinks I'm your girlfriend? We're hardly even acquainted."

"I should have said ... about the *possibility* of my having a girlfriend."

"Oh, I'm pretty sure you have lots of girlfriends."

"Yes, all sorts of girlfriends! I have to beat them off with a stick." he responded sardonically.

"I'll bet you do!" she laughed pleasantly, not wishing to engage his self-critical remark.

"This is it." he said, having arrived on the scene of the boat project. "We're about ready to seal and varnish the inside. Then we'll turn her over, sand her down a little and repaint this side ... white. We've already tightened up or replaced all the rivets and fixed the leaks, so ..."

"Hi Jimmy! Is this the other Jamie?"

Kenny and Tommy had been watching from their lawn chairs at the top of the bluff when Jimmy and Jama came walking around the little point. Kenny assumed this was the girl Jimmy had told him about, since she fit the description ... and since he'd never mentioned anyone else.

"Jama, this is Kenny, my best friend ... and partner."

"I thought so! Jimmy told me all about you." claimed Kenny.

She wondered what that could have meant, since Jimmy hardly knew anything about her. But she was also pleased to hear that he had been interested enough in her to describe her in detail to this best friend.

"You're even cuter than he said." continued Kenny, to Jimmy's moderate embarrassment ... he was pretty sure he had never described her that way to Kenny. "I wondered if you might have a younger sister?"

Jama laughed. She instantly liked this younger boy, and was not surprised that Jimmy would have such a friend. He seemed so pleasantly outgoing, and was just as cute as he could be!

"No, Kenny. I'm afraid I don't." she said regretfully.

"What do you think of our boat?" said Kenny. "Isn't she a beauty?"

"Where's the rest of it?" wondered Jama.

"Up there ... in Mr. Thomassen's garage. We're working on stuff up there too." answered Kenny.

She nodded.

"I guess you figured out that this wasn't a rowboat." said Jimmy. "Do you sail."

"Yes, of course I know what it is – a little single-sticker Mackinaw. And yes, I know a little bit about sailing ... catboats, anyway, but only on the bay."

"What's a cat boat?" Kenny wondered.

"It's similar to this ... a little lower, and with a square stern though. And the mast is more forward ... about up here ..." pointing out a position just aft of the Sea Scout's bow. "The South Bay Club has regattas in the summertime for kids ... mostly sailing catboats."

"You have your own boat?" asked Kenny excitedly.

"No, it's not my boat. I sail with a friend."

Jimmy's heart sank, instantly assuming that the *friend* was a boy ... before she added ...

"It's her boat ... or, rather, her family's."

"Have you ever been in a boat like this?" Jimmy wondered.

"Only once, but I was just along for the ride. I've never helped sail one. They're supposed to be dangerous."

"Dangerous?" wondered Kenny.

"Well, maybe dangerous isn't the right word. *Unstable*, I mean. They supposedly turtle rather easily."

"Turtle?" wondered Kenny again.

"Capsize." she clarified "... all the way over; upside-down."

"Oh, like a turtle." understood Kenny. "I mean, when tipped over it's like a turtle shell floating on the water?"

"That's it ... you got it." she affirmed.

"Hmmm ... Gramps and Mr. Thomassen never said anything about that." Jimmy worried. "We'll have to check that out!"

"Yeah, that's for sure. Jimmy's not a good swimmer. He's afraid of the water." shared Kenny innocently and as a matter of fact ... and to Jimmy's embarrassment again. He was beginning to wish that Kenny would be a little less talkative.

"Is that right!" she observed. "Well he's not the only one. My dad's the same way. He never learned to swim."

"I can swim." asserted Jimmy. "It's just that I tend to panic if I get in trouble ... like if I get slapped in the face with a wave and croak, or something. So, I don't trust myself in deep water."

"When you're sailing, it doesn't matter if you can swim or not ... you wear a Mae West. We always do. Unexpected things can happen on the water ... when you're on the water, you have to realize that you're out of your element ... that's what we've been taught."

All that seemed to make perfect sense to Jimmy. The Mae West idea had, as yet, never come up, and the thought of that safety gear being able to supplant his lack of confidence in the water came as a welcomed relief. He made a mental note: at some point they would certainly have to equip the Sea Scout with Mae Wests.

"I almost forgot ... Mr. Thomassen was going to call your grandparents and my parents to see if they would like to have lunch at the Lodge." recalled Kenny.

"Gramps is in a meeting ... I don't know for how long. Do you think your parents will go?" answered Jimmy.

Kenny shrugged. "Sure. Why not?" Then he corrected that. "I mean, maybe ... I hope so."

As it turned out, Josie had already started lunch, being a little excited and pleased over Jimmy's having a girl over to visit, and therefore having decided to offer a nice lunch. When Tommy called, she promised to take a rain check on the Lodge invitation, suggested that he come there instead, and should invite the Jennings to do the same.

"Tell them that Kenny's already here ... maybe that'll help." she suggested. "He is there, isn't he?"

"He's gone down to the beach, with your boy and some girl." answered Tommy.

That's not just *some girl*, Josie thought to herself ... and then she felt somewhat meddlesome and silly ... getting the cart way ahead of the horse.

———

Josie, Lee and Tommy sat at the picnic table with Grant and Mary Jennings. Jimmy, Kenny and Jama sat on the lawn nearby, but out of hearing range.

"I feel I should apologize ..." confessed Josie. "Ham, smoked turkey, Kaiser rolls, potato salad, chips, and whatnot.

I'm afraid I've wound up with a funeral luncheon."

Everyone laughed. Then addressing Rev. Jennings ...

"I'd guess with all the funerals you've done, you're more than tired of this fare."

"No; not at all. In fact, I haven't done very many. Up to this point I've been involved mostly in the administrative end of things."

"Besides, your potato salad is perfectly lovely, as is the coleslaw." added Mary. "Will I have to twist your arm for your secrets?"

"Is this your first call then?" inquired Tommy.

"It's not really a call. The congregation didn't wish to obligate itself that way, so I'm actually just working on a temporary basis, week to week, as it were."

"That's because they foolishly let themselves get screwed by the last guy. Everybody knew he wasn't going to be a good fit, but Lucy Cooper insisted on having her way, so he wound up with an $86,000 package." reported Tommy.

"That's quite ambitious for a congregation of this size." thought Grant.

"Well that was Lucy again ..." complained Tommy "... busy spending everybody else's money! When it soon turned out that he was gonna have to go, he sued 'em."

"Yes, I heard about that part of it, of course. That's why *I'm* here," confessed Grant. "When a church gets involved in that sort of thing, the congregation gets singled out as a *troubled church* ... not officially, but in whispers and gossip. Amongst those of us in the trade, they're seen as sort of an ecclesiastical pariah."

"Oh, how unfair!" offered Josie. "Most of the people here are so nice ... no trouble at all."

"That's always the case, Joanne." admitted Mary. "It's always a matter of either a few hard heads in the congregation, or a minister whose either dishonest or has personality problems ... and most often it's a combination of both."

That seemed refreshingly candid, coming from the minister's wife.

"What was it you were doing then before you came here?" Lee asked.

"I've spent the bigger part of my career thus far working at Louisville, advising Presbyteries on the handling of just these sorts of problems. Before coming up here, I was on loan to the Presbytery at Kalamazoo, which has been going through some really tough issues with raiders from the EPC."

"What's the *EPC?*" wondered Tommy.

"They're a new evangelical faction in the Presbyterian tradition. As you probably already know, fundamentalism has been giving traditionalism a run for its money, especially among the younger members of the faith. The EPC is a group that split off from the mainline church, and caters to that movement. When troubles arise in regular congregations, they'll often appear, seemingly out of nowhere, and encourage them to jump ship ... to quit the PCUSA and affiliate under their flag, I mean."

"Mutiny!" Tommy interjected.

"More or less." continued Grant. "Unlike the situation here, Presbyterian churches are not, technically, owned by their congregations. They're held in trust by their Presbytery. Few congregants understand that, mistakenly assuming that they will be able to carry away the whole thing, lock stock and barrel, into the EPC. When they find out differently, the situation gets messy."

"You've come up here as a troubleshooter, then." supposed Lee.

"No, no." corrected Grant. "Only as an interim ... until the search committee can find someone to serve on a permanent basis. We just thought I needed some time away from the wars ... a little *R and R*, you might say." he answered with a somewhat sheepish chuckle.

"That shouldn't be hard if they're still offering eighty-six thousand." mused Lee.

"I'm afraid that's been trimmed." replied Grant. "It's a $46,000 package now. But that's still very respectable for a church of this size."

"Why don't you want the job?" asked Tommy. "But then, I suppose your GA position pays much better, doesn't it?"

"Yes, it actually does, but that's not the only consideration." answered Grant.

"I don't suppose." agreed Tommy. "You got a damned fine boy there, Reverend ..." pointing towards the three kids sitting on the lawn. "He deserves better'n Kalamazoo."

"You don't care for Kalamazoo, I take it?" asked Grant with a grin.

"Well they ain't made no national parks down there now, have they." Tommy argued. "Look around you ... you're sitting in the most beautiful corner of the State of Michigan, with all sorts of wholesome things to do ... hunting, fishing, hiking, swimming ... sailing. That's why they turned the place into a national park. Your boy would thrive up here. That's a fact!"

"You're absolutely right, Tommy." agreed Mary. "But it would be very irregular for an interim to be installed as a permanent minister. Presbyteries usually won't go for that."

"So what? This is a Congregational church ... we don't have no Presbytery or anybody else calling the shots from afar. It's up to us." asserted Tommy.

"Well, at any rate, that has never come up." said Grant, hoping to change the subject.

"What if it did?" insisted Tommy.

"We'd think about it." said Mary, answering impulsively before her husband could say anything.

* * *

23

As Josie began to pick things up at the picnic table, Jama immediately jumped to her feet to help. So did Jimmy and Kenny, but Jama raised up her hand, indicating *As you were!* ... that she and Jimmy's grandmother would take care of things. It was an opportunity for her and Josie to become better acquainted, and she discovered that Jimmy's grandmother was not at all uppity, as suggested by Harley, nor pushy, as she had too quickly, and wrongly, concluded that morning in front of the church.

Josie's opinion of Jama was merely confirmed, since she had been favorably impressed at first sight. Her grandson was very dear to her heart, and she knew him well ... well enough to know that any girl he would befriend in this way would, of course, be a quality person. After the few moments she'd spent with Jama in the kitchen, she placed her in the same category as Kenny ... she decided that she was going to like her very much, just like she had initially decided about Kenny. She prided herself as being a good judge of character, and was very rarely proven wrong. Once Josie came to such conclusions, she almost never changed her mind.

With the table cleared and the dishes washed and dried, she sent Jama back to the boys on the lawn, and she watched out her kitchen window as they disappeared down the stairs, apparently headed to the boat. Lee was still sitting at the picnic table as she returned with two tall glasses of iced tea, with a lemon wedge on the rim of each one.

"I've been thinking, Josie ... she doesn't really want him. Why don't we have him just stay up here with us?"

She was totally blindsided by that unexpected suggestion, and was immediately brought to tears ... not by Lee's wanting to have the boy come live with them permanently, but by the part about her daughter not really wanting him. She knew it was true, and her heart went out to Jamie whenever her mind exposed that truth again, which she always tried carefully to avoid. Both she and Lee loved their grandson so dearly, and he was such a fine boy! She was totally at a loss to understand how her daughter could be so ... *indifferent* ... towards him.

She was, of course, comfortable with the idea of Jamie being with them, but was not willing to abandon the hope that someday Julie would finally grow up, and realize what a precious treasure he was.

"How would that look, Lee ... him living with us in Indianapolis, with her just a couple of miles away in Speedway?"

"I wasn't talking about going back to Indianapolis."

"Lee, have you lost your senses! Of course, we have to go back home."

"No ... we don't. Maybe this is *home.* It's more home to Jamie now, than Speedway."

"Oh, Lee! I don't know. I just don't know!"

She was openly crying now, her mind in a state of confusion on being confronted with all the possibilities and ramifications arising from what her husband was suggesting.

228

He was in tears too; she knew it because Lee always turned his back on her when he couldn't hold them back. She moved to the other side of the picnic table to sit beside him, her arms wrapped around him from behind, and laid her head on his shoulder.

"How did things ever come to this Lee?" she wondered. "How could she have grown up to be so cold and self-absorbed?"

It was a conversation they'd had too many times before. Lee didn't answer. There was no use in revisiting the subject. It was what it was. Unlike Josie, he entertained no fantasies about his daughter's ever changing.

"He'll be going into high school this fall." he reminded her.

"He'll only be with us for four more years, then he'll be all grown up and off to college. It would be nice if he had at least four good years to remember."

She hugged him more tightly.

"She'll just send him off to boarding school again to get rid of him." he continued. "He'd be happier here with his friends ... with normal kids."

"Kenny probably won't be staying, Lee, you know that ... and the girl ..."

"They don't know it yet, but they might not be leaving."

"Why?"

"Because after they left this afternoon, Tommy decided they should stay."

"Tommy? That's not up to him."

"Tommy's been footing half the bills over there ... has been ever since Susie died. You know how she was about the place. He does it for her. And now the boy has come along ... I'm sure you've noticed the change."

"Yes." she agreed. Who'd have thought it ... a little boy finally being able to snap Tommy out of his long season of grief. Susie can finally go to her rest, God bless her soul."

"He's quickly taken a liking to Kenny ... like the son he and Susie were never able to have. He's a blessing, that boy."

"But how will he get them to stay here?" Josie wondered.

Lee turned around with his left palm out, pretending to be scratching it with the tips of the fingers of his other hand. "Oh, I don't think they're that kind Lee!"

"You know what Benjamin Franklin always said dear ... *money talks; bullshit walks.*"

She nodded, having not immediately caught on to his sarcasm. He continued ...

"Every man has his price. It's only a matter of figuring out what it is. And you saw *her* today, did you not? ... how she cut him off before he could say no to the possibility of accepting a call here when Tommy raised that question ... hypothetically. She would like to stay a while, I think."

"Do you think so?"

"Yes, I think so. You haven't answered my question ... what about keeping Jamie?"

———

Tommy Thomassen didn't go home immediately after leaving the Smith's cottage. Instead, he strolled back into town and knocked on the door at Lucy Cooper's place. She was quite surprised to see him standing on her doorstep. They were not friends.

"Well, this must be my lucky day!" was her icy greeting.

"Could be." mused Tommy, unperturbed by her bitter sarcasm.

"I can't imagine what you might be up to, *Mr. Thomassen*, but whatever it is, I really don't care to see you."

"Let me guess ... you're pissed off about the Gunderson boy." suggested Tommy.

"You didn't even give him a chance, you old bastard! Why do you hate him so!?!"

"That's for me to know, and you, hopefully, to never find out."

"He could have done the job ... he might have been a good fit there. People can change, you know."

"Good fit where – between some little girl's legs? Come on Lucy, get off your goddamned high horse. We both know what you were up to and why. You ought to have a swift kick in the ass ... setting up the new man like that. You know damned well that was gonna be like putting the fox in charge of the henhouse."

"You always were a pig, Tommy Thomassen!" she spewed icily again.

"Yeah, yeah ... so what about you? Getting a little old for a boy like that, aren't you?"

"Oh, I hate you ... you sonofabitch!!!"

"Better pipe down a little Lucy. Your neighbors'll hear you."

"What do you want, Tommy. Say it, and go!"

"I've got a confidential business proposition for you. Are you going to invite me in, or are we gonna fight it out right here on your damned doorstep ... in front of your neighbors?"

The operative phrase for Lucy was *business proposition*. She knew Tommy had money, probably much more than she did, and her own resources were considerable. Like most people of means, she had learned to set aside feelings when it came to money matters, and accordingly, her demeanor quickly began to change from anger and hatred, to interest ... with a healthy skepticism, of course.

"Here's the deal." began Tommy. "I mean for this preacher ... Jennings ... to stay here – at least six years."

"Impossible!" she interrupted. "He's just an interim."

"Interim, schmitterim!" sputtered Tommy. "You know damned well that doesn't mean a goddamned thing in our case, and I'm sure I can get his people down there in Kalamazoo to give him a pass."

"He's not going to stay here for a piddling forty-six thousand. He does better than that down there."

"He's getting a lot less then that now, and I happen to know he ain't getting paid much over that down south. He's just a soldier for them, you know ... the guy who does their dirty work."

"How do you know anything about that?" she asked suspecting that Tommy was just trying to bullshit her.

"I do my homework."

"So do I, mister. Make no mistake about that. Whatever you think you're up to, the day hasn't come when you'll be able to pull the wool over my eyes."

Tommy laughed. "On that we can agree, that's for sure. I do respect your deviousness."

"I'm not trying to pull anything over your eyes. I'm gonna tell 'em to have Jerry write up a six-year deal. They'll pay for their $46,000 package, and I'm gonna give them a $200,000 annuity, that will provide a matching amount for six years. So, his total compensation package will be about ninety-two thousand. And

232

considering the prospective gratuities from weddings and funerals, he'll be looking at an offer he can't refuse."

"So where do I fit in?"

"It's been mostly you and me that's been paying the bills, ain't it? So, it's gonna be our say ... it'll come down to that. The annuity's gonna be anonymous. They don't need to know where that came from ... let 'em think he has a rich uncle or something. So, you don't have to put in any money. All you have to do is sign on ... not torpedo the deal."

"Why are you doing this Tommy ... you of all people?"

"That's not important. I got my reasons."

She thought about it for a moment. He could see the wheels turning.

"It's the boy, isn't it? You've got the hots for that little boy of theirs!"

He knew Lucy Cooper well enough to know that she couldn't be fooled on this score.

She continued anyway ... "Let's see ... how old is he ... twelve? That would be what the six years is all about, wouldn't it? He'd be eighteen then, graduating from high school and going off to college."

"You hit the nail right on the head, Lucy. Yes, it's about the boy. I'm also setting up an anonymous hundred-thousand-dollar fund for him, just in case his dad is reluctant to accept our offer. He'll be able to send him to any college or university he likes."

"Umm ... I see. And what about in the meantime? Are you a closet boy lover Tommy?"

"Boy oh boy, woman! You are a special case, that's for sure. Only you would suspect something like that."

233

"Oh, get off it! What goes around, comes around. You dance in here and suggest that I'm having relations with a nineteen-year-old, and then you get all huffy when the shoe is on the other foot."

Tommy decided to keep his mouth shut. He knew that she knew that he knew she had been doing Eddie Gunderson, but he also figured that Eddie had succeeded in making her fall in love with him. That was his forte, and wealthy cougars like Lucy were easy prey. There was nothing to be gained here by his exposing her foolishness, or belittling what she hoped, and probably believed at this point, was real.

"What about Eddie?" she continued.

"What about him?"

"I think you owe him something, don't you?"

He had figured on this, and was prepared for it. He didn't owe Eddie Gunderson anything. In fact, as far as he was concerned, Eddie Gunderson was fortunate that he had chosen to ignore him, rather than destroy him, for with what he knew about him, he certainly could. Eddie knew that too, which explained why he was careful to keep away from him. But Eddie also knew why Tommy would never go after him that way.

"What do you have in mind, Lucy?"

"I was going to have the church send him to Bible College in Grand Rapids." she claimed, "... until you put the kybosh on that. I think you should undo the damage you've done, and let that proceed as planned."

"Absolutely not! I won't be a party to anything like that. Besides, that boy ain't cut out for no goddamned bible college. But I tell you what I will do ... I'll get him into the Maritime Academy in Traverse ... I'll go halfers with ya on his room 'n board and the

234

whole ball of wax. That's a four-year deal, and he'll come out of there with a certificate that'll get him aboard any merchantman as a mate. That's something he *is* cut out to do. And you can tell 'im it's you who's foot'n all his bills."

Lucy didn't need any more selling than that. She never really had been comfortable with the bible college thing, which was just her way of attempting to keep him on a leash. Now, while this old fart was talking, she envisioned Eddie rising through the ranks in the Merchant Marine, and winding up in a Master's chair. She liked it!

"You crafty old sonofabitch ... you've thought it all through, haven't you?"

She nodded her head, as if she was thinking about his propositions favorably.

"Okay." she answered too quickly. "I'm in."

* * *

24

The affair, if it could be called that, between Lucy Cooper and Eddie Gunderson was not, Lucy thought, something very many people knew anything about. She thought that, because she and the boy had always been quite discreet, and it was never spoken of – at least not within her hearing. It was, in fact, sort of a joke among the men, her having relations with a boy half her age. As for the women, most chose to keep silent, guessing that the relationship probably fulfilled certain needs on both sides that the men, because they were men, wouldn't understand.

It had begun some four years earlier, during the summer when Eddie turned fifteen, the summer after his mother had run off. Maggie had been a waitress at the Lodge, became involved in an affair with one of the bartenders that summer, and vanished, deserting her husband and her son. Nothing was heard from her until Oscar received the divorce papers. That was when his drinking began to become habitual, faltering as a father just when his son needed him the most.

Understanding the need, Lucy hired the boy to keep her expansive lawn neatly mowed, which he did diligently, using the large green John Deere riding mower from her yard barn. He was diligent about it because he enjoyed horsing around with her tractor, and because she paid very generously. She did it because

236

she was attracted to the boy ... caught up in Eddie Gunderson's way of charming the opposite sex.

At first, she watched him surreptitiously from inside the house, hiding behind the sheers in her windows. But she quickly became more overt about it, going outdoors to watch the sexy shirtless boy up close, working only in shorts and work boots, his bare muscular back glistening with perspiration.

Then she hatched a scheme that would allow her to interact more directly, deciding that the grass clippings should be composted, and lending a hand with that task, helping Eddie dump the collected clippings at a special place in the woods behind her backyard.

Lucy's growing obsession finally led her to accost the boy inside the yard barn one afternoon after the lawn mowing was finished, rushing him unexpectedly and pressing her mouth forcefully against his. He had not been surprised and, wrapping his arms tightly around her neck, pulled her to himself to prolong the deep, sensuous kiss. Whatever reservation she might have been feeling instantly turned to passion that demanded satisfaction, and her savage assault on the boy's shorts aroused his interest in providing it, right then and there in the yard barn.

Soon after that the men down at the Bird began to elbow each other, with snide comments about how Lucy Cooper's yard was suddenly being kept so neatly trimmed. Indeed, it hardly ever had a chance to grow more than a quarter-inch before she'd have Eddie Gunderson come over to *trim it up a little.*

Not too long after that first time, Lucy discovered that the boy was sometimes sneaking into her yard barn at night, to sleep in the loft, above the John Deere. She found that utterly unacceptable, announcing that she would have none of that sort of thing ... and moved him into a bedroom of his own inside her house. She was pleased that providence had apparently finally decided to smile upon her.

Lucy Cooper was the end of the line in what had turned out to be four generations of Coopers in Leland. Her ancestors, like those of the Robinsons, had originally migrated from England, initially winding up on North Manitou Island, and finally in Leland. True to their surname, they were originally barrel makers, fabricating casks for the island's farmers, and barrels for its fishermen. When the steamboats began to replace sailing vessels, the wooding business became much more lucrative, so they added that to their endeavors. When the great fires of 1871, in Chicago and elsewhere, created an insatiable demand for dimensional lumber, the Cooper operations expanded again, with logging operations and mills all along the lakeshore, from Harbor Springs to Whitehall.

Fortune had smiled on the Coopers and they had proven prodigious in the creation of wealth – but not in the production of offspring. Lucy's father had been the only son of an only son, and she was his only issue ... and, thus, the Cooper dynasty's final heir. Or, at least it looked like she was going to be its final heir.

She was not physically attractive, but was far more intelligent and well-educated than most of her male peers in Leland, so was never high on the list of any man's matrimonial prospects. She knew it, and accepted the reality of what she saw in her mirror ... a lean woman who was a little too tall, and a little to masculine-looking, and ultimately a little too close to the onset of middle-age. Moreover, she didn't care, since she considered none of them fit suitors anyway, and suspected any man who seemed so inclined as a probable gold digger.

Eddie was a different matter.

She hadn't looked upon him as anything other than an illicit lover. He was only fifteen at the time of their first *encounter* in the yard barn. She was aware of the risk, but that was part of the excitement. He had never come on to her (or so she thought) so she had envisioned herself as the predator and Eddie as the prey ... a fantasy that also enhanced her excitement and clouded her judgment. Eddie's being a mere boy; marriage had always been out of the question, so it was clear that his interest in her was not about money (or so she thought.)

Over the few years they had been engaged in what proved to be an ongoing relationship, things changed. To her, Eddie became not only a wildly passionate young lover, but the child she would probably never have. To Eddie, she became something much more than an easy, always available outlet for his rapacious teenage male urgencies – plus one who was very well healed and eager to be generous in paying for his *services*. He came to value his relationship with Lucy as a welcomed replacement for the warmth and tenderness that had been meanly torn from his life in his fourteenth year.

Now, with him at nineteen and her thirty-six, Eddie and Lucy had become solidly enmeshed in their roles within that relationship. They had remained appropriately discrete over the years, being careful never to be seen together in a posture that might suggest anything others might consider untoward. She, for the obvious reason.

In the beginning it was about guilt for Eddie, who thought of himself as a *boy whore,* since he had yet to encounter the more urbane word, *gigolo.* But as his affection for her grew, it became a protective thing. Understanding the importance to her of her reputation and social position, he was resolved to never say or do anything that might hurt her. After his night with Keegan, discretion became much more import to him, for a much different reason.

Eddie spent most nights with Lucy in her bed. The room she had provided for him was hardly ever used. He always arrived after dark, coming through the woods to her back door, which, as was the practice in Leland, was never locked. He would leave the same way, usually early in the morning, and always being careful, upon exiting the opposite side of the woods, to ensure that he would be able to do so unseen by anyone who mattered.

On the nights when the Tarnovitch made runs out into the lake to tend the Indians' nets, Lucy would sleep alone. Since the night that Eddie and the girl had spent alone together on the Tarnovitch, drifting silently under the stars far out in the Passage, it seemed to Lucy that the fishing business must be very good this year indeed, since the Indians were doing an unusual number of night runs.

She didn't know about Keegan. But she did observe Eddie's improved attitude and behavior. He was turning into the decent, sensitive young man that she had always known he eventually would ... gentler, more thoughtful, and happier.

It pleased her to think that she was the instrument of it.

Lucy understood that Eddie had come of age, and should move on – that he deserved to have a good life. She was keen on being a

240

part of making that happen, even though she knew it would probably involve his departure. The Bible College/youth director scheme had seemed like a good plan, since Grand Rapids was not *that* far away, and the church job would bring him back to Leland at least every weekend. But, in reality, she had not been comfortable with its prospects for future growth, and had begun to feel somewhat selfish in having attempted to orchestrate that.

Tommy's scheme was much better in all respects. Eddie would remain close to her for the time being, and a maritime career would ultimately provide him with unlimited opportunities for travel and advancement.

Eddie didn't show up that night ... as he usually didn't now on Sunday nights, evidently because of his job on the fish tug. So, she had plenty of time that evening, and the following day, to think about how she would announce this wonderful change of plans. She understood that Eddie had a right to his own opinions and preferences regarding the prospects for the rest of his life, so she would have to finesse the matter, not just make a pronouncement.

On Monday night, Eddie hadn't yet shown up even well after his usual arrival time. Expecting that he probably wouldn't come any more after that late hour, Lucy decided she might as well call it a day, and reluctantly went to her bed.

It wasn't but a few minutes later that Eddie turned off the road into the woods. It was a cloudy night, and without the light of the moon and stars, it was pitch black in the woods; so dark that even after his eyes became accustomed to the blackness, he still couldn't see anything. So, he walked more slowly, sensing when he strayed from the path only by the feel of the ground under his feet, and the occasional brush of a low-hanging branch on his right side or left. Eventually the dim glow of the nightlight above Lucy's kitchen window came into view.

Inside, realizing that she had already retired, he went directly to the shower, and from there, without dressing, directly to her bed. She was not sleeping. She fumbled in the dark to find his face and draw it up to hers, then let his head settle back between her breasts.

As she stroked his head, she whispered softly ...

"I love you Eddie."

He responded in kind by snuggling as close to her as he could get.

She turned on her side facing him, and with her other hand began gently stroking his back – now tracing the outlines of its muscular structure – now lightly running the tips of her fingers along his spine, down to the small of his back, and slightly, teasingly, beyond. It excited her, as she could feel it did him.

"I have a new plan, my darling boy." she whispered.

———

Lucy arose a little early in the morning. She would prepare a light breakfast so that they could sit down together and talk for a little while before Eddie left for the woods. He awoke to the unfamiliar, but delicious smells of bacon and eggs and coffee and toast. It fetched up recollections of other mornings in other places when he was little, and his mother was doing the breakfast cooking.

Eddie; rise 'n shine!' she would call out pleasantly at the bottom of the stairs in their old house. Was it when they were down at South Haven, he wondered ... he was only six then. The sounds and odors were subconsciously associated somewhere in his brain with good times, loving times, secure times ... and the resulting feelings elevated his spirits. He was in a very good mood this morning.

"What's up with all this, Luce?" he smiled.

"I thought you could stay a little while, and we could have a little talk."

"This all smells really great! Thank you, thank you!"

"I'm sorry, again, about how the church thing worked out Eddie. I know how hurt you were. I shouldn't have set you up that way. It was selfish of me; *just purely selfish!* I'm so sorry."

"Stop it. It wasn't your fault."

"Yes, it was, Eddie ... let me confess it! Now that you're out of high school, I've become scared to death of losing you. It was partly a scheme to keep you close to me."

He put his hand out, reaching for hers and holding it tight.

"Well, that would have worked for me too – I want to stay close to you."

"But I feel I was dishonest. I should have explained myself up front."

"It's okay, Lucy. Really. I've moved on. Consider it forgotten. I'm thinking about joining the Coast Guard. My dad thinks he can get me in."

"Oh, no Eddie! ... you don't want to do that!" she blurted out unintentionally.

He looked up, somewhat surprised at her sudden alarm.

"Why not? What's wrong with the Coast Guard?"

Her strategy hadn't anticipated that he might already have been considering other opportunities on his own, so his comment momentarily blew her off course. But she quickly regained her composure.

"I'm sorry ... nothing, of course. As a matter of fact, the idea I mentioned last night is probably similar in many respects to serving with the Coast Guard."

"And what would that be?" he asked with some genuine interest.

"The Merchant Marine!" she replied proudly.

"Nah, that's almost impossible to get into now unless you already have experience. And even then, it's long hours and doesn't pay very much anymore ... there are very few boats left on the lakes now, you know."

"I'm not talking about you just becoming a deck hand, you silly boy! I'm talking about you being a ship's officer – eventually probably the master of a vessel."

He knew Lucy well enough to know that she didn't engage in flights of fancy when it came to such matters ... that she must have worked out a plausible scheme of some sort ... so he did not laugh at her rather preposterous assertion.

"I'm listening."

She explained that she had connections that could get him immediately enrolled in the upcoming fall term at the Great Lakes Maritime Academy in Traverse City. He would attend for four years, with all expenses paid by herself and an interested third party. He would then graduate with a bachelor's degree, an unlimited Coast Guard license and, most likely, an appointment as a deck or engineering officer aboard a U.S. flag vessel.

He wondered about the *interested third party*.

"That person wishes to do this anonymously." she replied, being careful to say nothing that might point to Tommy Thomassen.

Eddie reasoned that it might be his mother. Lucy must have somehow tracked her down. She had the resources, and who else would want to do him any favors. And if it was his mother, she must somehow be doing very well for herself. She would be acting out of guilt, he surmised. But, so be it. There was still a spark of feeling for her; resentment had not been able to extinguish it all. He could not deny her an opportunity to try and redeem herself ... to express her sorrow in this way ... to be Lucy's silent partner.

He was on the verge of tears as he looked Lucy directly in the eyes and said ...

"I love you, Luce. I'm the luckiest boy alive. I don't deserve you, but I love you, and I always will."

She melted, as she always did when he got teary. She arose and rushed over to hold him tightly in her arms, tenderly kissing his forehead and hands.

She had won this time. Her heart was full.

* * *

25

Work on the boat continued as the summer passed its peak and the days began to grow shorter. The old Sea Scout had soaked up two coats of sealer from the inside ... a modern purchased product, rather than the concoction recommended in Captain Kenealy's book ... and after that the inside had then been varnished. Next, Tommy, Kenny, Lee and Jimmy turned the boat upside down on its cradle so the boys could paint the hull *Brilliant White* using the finest growth-resistant marine enamel the local marina had in stock.

Having finished with the sealing, varnishing and painting, she was turned right-side-up again, her newly refinished bottom boards were replaced, and there was nothing left to do but *raise the stick*, as Tommy put it.

———

Meanwhile, the two boys continued to draw closer to one another. While searching for the Sea Scout's lines and sails in Tommy's garage, they discovered an old army surplus tent that hadn't been used in years and, with Tommy's assistance, put it up on his lawn, near the bluff, overlooking their boat project. It became their base of operations, and a place where they spent many nights together, sleeping out by themselves.

Jama became a regular Sunday visitor, being picked up at St. Francis' in the morning, and driven back home in the evening by either Lee or Tommy, and the two boys. She wasn't often able to come during the week, unless Lee, Josie or Tommy could be coaxed into making a trip into Traverse for some reason or another. She grew very friendly with Josie, and when she was able to come, often spent as much time with her as she did with the boys. It turned out that Jama was much more interested in Josie's projects ... gardening, cooking and baking, and creating artistic things ... than she was in boat-building.

Eddie continued to be scarce around Leland during the daylight hours. He and Keegan were together during some part of every day – and frequently surreptitiously after dark, before he'd head back to Lucy Cooper's. He continued to be a changed and changing man, the love for his young girlfriend having given rebirth to, and serving to cultivate, his better side. He continued to grow increasingly courteous, easy-going and happy.

For her part, Keegan had at least some reason for concern. She had run full cycle once again but, so far, *the curse* seemed to have passed her over. She wasn't terribly worried yet, because she had learned from several different websites that at her age irregular periods were not to be unexpected.

Eddie never employed any sort of contraception because he was sublimely confident of his knowledge about women, and sure that all females used birth control strategies of some sort or another ... pills, patches, shots, IUD's, or whatever ... either to keep from getting *knocked up,* as he thought of it, or to regulate the intensity of their periods.

In fact, Keegan had never used any of these measures, partly because of ignorance, since at her age the issue had not yet been raised. But even if it had, her father's fundamentalist theology forbad contraception. Although not Catholic, he considered birth control as being akin to abortion, which he preached was akin to murder. She had therefore tried to learn about careful timing. But her cycle did indeed tend to be somewhat irregular, so it was difficult to employ that strategy with any sort of precision ... the only alternative being a very conservative approach which left only a very narrow window of opportunity for love making. Neither she nor Eddie could accommodate that. They were simply too much in love.

She had thought about the possibility of marriage, but had not mentioned it. The childish side of her dreamed about spending the rest of her life with Edward ... about the day he might surprise her with a ring ... and how she would throw her arms around him and accept in a heartbeat. But in her more mature moments, she knew that if it came to that at her age, her parents would never consent. They'd be more likely to have him arrested, and send her away!

Furthermore, Eddie often talked about his dreams for the future, always promising that they'd eventually marry ... never saying anything to suggest that he might be willing to take that step sooner, rather than later. And more recently, he had become exuberant about his chance to enroll in NMC's Maritime Academy, often musing about what a wonderful break that was for the both of them.

So, she kept her secret ... waiting and hoping, day by day, for the curse to return. Eddie knew nothing of her concerns. What he did know was that she seemed to be growing prettier and more desirable with each passing day.

————

Jama had gotten into the habit of attending Mass twice on Sunday's; first with her parents, and then again with Jimmy and his grandparents at the service immediately following. This morning she was a little late, squeezing past in front of Jimmy to sit between him and his grandmother.

"Are you coming over today?" Jimmy whispered. "We're putting up the mast when we get home and then we're going to finish the rigging. After that, if there's still time, Mr. Thomassen and Gramps are going to take us out for a *shakedown* cruise."

"Is there room for five?" she wondered.

"I don't know ... I guess so. Can you come?"

She did come, and helped carry the mast and the sails and the ropes down from the garage. The five of them raised the mast; reversing the procedure used to lower it, except that Jama was assigned the duty formerly handled by Josie ... sitting in front of the spar's mounting position, making sure that it was squared up and dropped properly into its shoe when lifted by Tommy and Lee, with Jimmy and Kenny holding lines to steady it on either side. It turned out to be an easy operation, and with the spar up, even with its dangling lines, the Sea Scout suddenly looked like a real sailing vessel once again.

Tommy and Lee did most of the rest of the work, showing Jimmy and Kenny how the boat was rigged. That went without a hitch also, and by late afternoon, she was ready to be launched. The two old men took the port side, with the three youngsters on the other, and the five anxious sailors picked up the old boat and carried her down to the water.

"You three get aboard." ordered Lee "... and if she doesn't sink, Tommy and I are going to take you sailing!"

The light landward wind did not seem favorable. With the two men aboard, Lee at the tiller and Tommy hoisting the mainsail, the boat began to drift rapidly back toward the beach. Lee quickly put her rudder full to starboard, which swung her sideways, almost parallel to the shore and just barely above the rocks in the shallows. Then her sail caught the wind and she took off smartly along the shoreline, with Lee skillfully guiding her out into deeper water.

"Looks like you haven't lost yer touch, Winston!" shouted Tommy.

"Quit talkin' and drop the centerboard before she goes over!" returned Lee.

Tommy motioned to Jimmy and Kenny nodding his head

...

"Do it!"

Jimmy momentarily loosed the centerboard pendant and let the heavy board drop all the way, with the line running smoothly around its cleat. Then they were off.

As the culmination of all the hard work Jimmy and Kenny had invested in making the Sea Scout seaworthy again, this initial sea trial proved more than just gratifying. It was a great thrill. Her performance was more than perfect, it was poetry in motion! Even in this light wind, she sped along swiftly and high spiritedly, as if she was overwhelmingly joyous about being on the water once more. In what seemed like only moments, Leland had been left behind, with North Manitou Island rapidly approaching.

Outward bound, Lee moved aside, permitting Jimmy to take the tiller, while Tommy directed Kenny in the handling of the lines and halyards as they tacked towards the island. They ran her all the way out to the lee side of the island, luffing just north of Dimmick's Point on the south end while Lee and Jimmy switched positions with Tommy and Kenny. Then they were off again, running her with the wind all the way back to the beach below Tommy's place.

As they sped towards the shore, Lee and Jimmy struck the sail, while Jama struggled to hoist the heavy centerboard, succeeding just in time to clear the heavy stones near the beach. The Sea Scout coasted neatly onto the little pebbles along the shore, and smoothly into the sand. All in all, the round trip had taken just a little over an hour.

After securing the sail, and cradling the boom, the five wrestled the boat back upon her cradle.

"Advanced sailing lessons begin tomorrow morning, weather permitting." said Lee.

* * *

<u>26</u>

Sailing lessons for Jimmy and Kenny began early Monday morning. The weather was somewhat threatening in the morning, with overcast skies and a northeasterly breeze that had arrived sometime during the night. But sailing wasn't on the morning's agenda anyway, so the squalls of showers that came every now and then were nothing more than a temporary nuisance.

Their training began with ground school ... learning the proper names for various parts of the boat, her lines and other components. That was followed by instruction on handling the boat, and learning the terminology associated with that aspect of sailing. After that came the rules of the road – *the law of the sea ...* all about safety and decorum out on the water. This went on for most of the first week, with Tommy and Lee serving as teaching partners, and the day's shore-school time followed by an hour or two of fun with the Sea Scout out on the water.

"How did you two learn all this, Mr. Thomassen?" wondered Kenny.

"In the school of hard knocks!" answered Tommy. "But things were much different back then. There were far fewer tourists around, and most of the locals were experienced sailors ... many of the older ones being former Mackinaw boat owners."

"So, we learned by trial and error." explained Lee. "And when we were stymied, there was always someone around who could tell us what we were doing wrong. Little by little, we picked it up."

The two boys proved to be fast learners. By the middle of the second week they were turned loose, taking the boat out by themselves to practice what they were learning, albeit not too far offshore. By the third week, it was clear to their instructors that they were capable of a more venturesome voyage, so on the first day that conditions were propitious, they were sent out on their own for a run over to the North Island and back, and they accomplished the voyage without a hitch.

Then the fun began, with Lee and Tommy eagerly watching the skies for foul weather, and taking the boys out for some rough rides whenever possible, to teach them how to handle the boat in a variety of conditions. It was essential training, because Lake Michigan was famous for its quickly changing conditions, and when the weather turned nasty, the Manitou Passage was a treacherous place to be. They learned how to watch the horizon for threatening signs, how to manage the boat in *dirty water*, as Tommy called angry seas, and how to always keep an eye out for places they could quickly scud to for shelter if need be. Everyone came back from these trips soaked to their skin.

During these outings, the two younger sailors also learned what it felt like to be terribly seasick, and how to persevere in spite of having to puke over the side every now and then. They were both *pukers*, as Tommy chided, warning them to feed the fish, and not barf in or on their boat. Kenny was always the first to succumb, but once he began tossing his cookies, it wouldn't be long before Jimmy would begin to turn ashen and start grimacing.

They were not able to get over that problem as quickly as they had learned to sail independently, but their tolerance of rolling and bumpy waters gradually began to increase. They discovered that Tommy was right when he claimed *the worse the weather, the lesser the affliction.* When busy trying to keep their boat afloat and out of trouble, they didn't have as much time to worry about how sick they were feeling.

————

With July already having dissolved into August, the Sea Scout sailed every day, rain or shine. After a midweek voyage, Kenny complained ...

"I won't be able to do anything next week."

"Why not?" wondered Jimmy.

"My dad's making me go on a Jr. High retreat all week."

"Where? Who with?"

"It's not our church. We don't have enough Jr. Highs, so they're making us go with some other church's kids ... the Lake Leelanau Bible Fellowship. They're going camping on North Manitou for a week."

"Well, shucks! I guess that means I won't be doing anything either. I can't sail the boat alone. When are you coming back?"

"We have to go Sunday morning, and can't come back until noon the next Saturday. Then I'll have to stand up in church and thank everybody and tell all about *how we found Christ out in the wilderness.* It's stupid! I hate doing that ... *witnessing.* I don't want to go. I don't know any of those other kids; I think they're all a bunch of bible-thumpers!"

"Maybe you'll get sick. We could go out and get you really seasick and pretend it was the flu!" suggested Jimmy. "Or I could break one of your arms?"

"Ugh ... I'm thinking about it. Let's see; I'm not sure which would be worse, being seasick for a week, or being out there with religious freaks for a week." replied Kenny, not really trying to be funny.

"Yeah, well ... knowing your dad, I don't suppose there's any way out of it. Besides, if his own kid won't go, why should any of the other kids have to go? You're probably being used to set an example. We're just screwed, I guess."

————

It turned out that Kenny's absence in the coming week wasn't going to be Jimmy's only problem. When he joined his grandparent for breakfast that Friday morning, Lee and Josie had bad news.

"Something's come up Jamie. Mrs. Pottier has finally passed away, and we're going to have to return to Indianapolis for the funeral. The jet is coming up Sunday to pick us up." she revealed. "She was ninety-nine; isn't that something!"

"Do I have to go?"

"Well I figured you wouldn't want to." said his grandfather. "That's mainly what we need to talk about."

"Did she ever call about me?" asked Jimmy.

Both grandparents shook their heads and frowned.

Jimmy understood their feelings.

"It isn't that she doesn't care." he assured them. "Julie does like me. It's just that she doesn't like being a mother ... being tied down with a kid all the time."

Again, both grandparents shook their heads and frowned, not saying anything in reply to Jimmy's attempt to gloss over their daughter's immaturity and selfishness.

"If I have to go back with you, will I have to stay there then?"

"I don't know, Jamie." answered his grandmother.

"I didn't know the Pottiers."

"No, we know you didn't Jamie." said his grandfather.

"Maybe I could just stay here ... at Kenny's." he suggested.

"Kenny will be gone all week." said Josie. "I thought of that and called his mother. But he has to go to bible camp, or something."

"Oh, yeah." Jimmy remembered. "What about Mr. Thomassen?"

"Tommy?" said Lee, with a sort of humorous tone of voice.

"I'm afraid not, Jamie." said Josie.

"Can I just stay here then? I'm fourteen. And I got up here all by myself. I'd be okay for a couple of days."

"It'll be more than a couple of days, Jamie." answered Lee. "In spite of her age, Charlene Pottier was still the ultimate head of the company. There'll have to be a reorganization now, according to whatever arrangements she might have made in her will, so I'll have to be there as the Board works through that. We'll be gone a week, for sure. Maybe more."

Before Jimmy had appeared that morning, Lee and Josie had agreed that it was probably a good time to tell him about the possibility of his staying in Leland permanently.

"Grandpa and I have been thinking about staying up here, instead of going back to Indianapolis for the winter. We thought you might want to stay up here with us."

Jimmy was struck with astonishment and surprise. That thought had never entered his mind.

"Really!?!" he replied, with a mixture of wonder and excitement. Then he thought about his mother.

"What about Julie?"

Something told him that his mother wasn't going to go for this idea. It was just a feeling ... he couldn't really explain it. What he couldn't explain was a subconscious cognizance of the perennial state of contention between his mother and her father, and a sense that, if she could prevent it, Julie was never going to let Gramps win in any contest of wills.

"That's the sixty-four-thousand-dollar question." said Lee with a frown, not looking forward to the unpleasantness that was sure to come.

"What about you, Jamie?" asked Josie. "How do you feel about staying?"

"Sure!" was his simple answer, given with enough exuberance that there was no need to expand upon it.

"So, if your mother will agree, you can come along with us and attend Mr. Pottier's funeral." concluded his grandfather. "After all, the Pottiers do have some significance in your life now, François having originally donated the materials for the boat you and Kenny now own."

"Then you'll also be able to go home and collect whatever you want to bring back." added Josie.

Jimmy was still skeptical.

"Umm ... I don't know." he said doubtfully. He was pretty sure that there was going to be a fight, and that if he went back to Speedway, his mother would not let him come back to Leland.

The storm came sooner than expected. The phone rang early the next morning, and Josie found Julie on the other end of the line.

"Hi, mother. I suppose you've gotten the news about grandma Charlene."

Charlene Pottier was not really Julie's grandmother, but they had been so close during her childhood that at a very early age Julie had begun calling her "Grandma." Charlene was so pleased with having been chosen by the child, she played along. As the years went by, the relationship had grown, with her becoming Julie's *de facto* grandmother.

"Yes, of course, dear. The plane is coming for us tomorrow."

"I suppose you'll be bringing Jimmy back early then?"

Josie was floored! And disgusted! All this time Julie had merely assumed that her son was in Leland with her parents. And not once had she bothered to pick up the phone and inquire. She knew full well why she hadn't ... she would have had to admit that he'd run away.

"What on earth are you talking about dear?" she asked, trying to hide her anger and sound as normal as possible.

"Please don't try to be cute with me mother. I know he's up there."

That was too, too much.

"You know nothing of the sort!!! How could you!?! You haven't once bothered to call. Do you have spies? Are you clairvoyant!?! Or what!?!

"Okay, so here we go again." uttered Julie disgustedly. "So, I take it from that outburst that he *is* there. Call me before you leave, and I'll meet you at the airport to pick him up."

"You'll do no such thing, girly-girl!!!" advised her mother.

"Why not, mother?" Julie asked in a patronizing tone.

"Because he won't be coming back just now; that's *why not.*"

"Oh, I see. Well, let's put it this way mother. *Bring him back with you ... period!*"

"I beg your pardon? When did you decide you were big enough to speak to me in that tone of voice!?!"

"Sheesh! Can we cut the bullshit mother? You have no standing in the matter, and you know it. He ran off. You and Dad kept him up there without once attempting to let me know anything about it. You're the ones who are in the wrong. Is that like kidnapping, or what! Just bring him back, life will go on, and we'll forget the whole thing."

"That would be easy for you dear, wouldn't it? That's always your answer to everything ... *life goes on ... forget the whole thing.* All you really care about is playing. That's always been your way. You were spoiled as a child, and have never grown out of it. Why do you want him to come back? Are you ready to quit playing now, and to become a mother? He needs a mother, Julie ... not just an adult companion."

"I'll meet you at the airport, mother. Call me."

"Look, Julie. Your father and I have decided to keep Jamie up here with us. We'll not be coming back to Indianapolis for the winter; we've decided to spend it up here, and he wants to stay here too."

"That didn't sound like a question, but the answer is *absolutely not!* How could you think of such a thing! It's Daddy, isn't it? He's just trying to hurt me! And he's using *my son* to do it!"

"No, he's not Julie. Your father loves that boy more than you could ever know, and ..."

She was interrupted by Julie's sudden sobbing.

"Oh, fine! Why didn't that old sonofabitch ever love me, mother? Why didn't he ever love me like that? ..." she trailed off in tears.

"Your father has always loved you Julie. It's just that you and he are too much ... Julie? ... Hello?"

———

Josie joined Lee outdoors at the picnic table.

"Who called?" Lee wondered.

"One guess."

"No kidding! Did she finally discover that her son was missing?"

"She knew we'd be coming back for Charlene's funeral, and is insisting that we bring him back with us."

"Am I going to have to go back then?"

Josie wasn't aware that Jimmy was up, had come out, and was standing right behind her with a glass of orange juice in one hand, and two pieces of toast in the other.

"No, you won't be going back right now." Josie said flatly and with finality. That matter had been settled.

* * *

27

It was arranged that Jimmy would remain at the cottage alone while his grandparents were away. Tommy Thomassen and Kenny's parents would both be available, should any problem arise. Meanwhile, he would not use the boat until Kenny got back, and after that, only with Tommy's knowledge and consent.

Lee and Josie were up early the next morning, leaving for Traverse at seven. There would be no church for Jimmy or Kenny, since Kenny would be leaving with the Ningwis at ten. Jimmy met him at the church at eight-thirty. After a brief outdoors commissioning ceremony before the regular nine o'clock service began, the two walked down to the dock together, along with the few other LCC kids.

Kenny was still reluctant, but resigned to comply with his father's wishes. After hearing Jimmy's account of what had transpired in his family the day before, he was even more unhappy about having to go, leaving Jimmy alone for a week in Leland, unable to use the boat by himself, and having nothing else to do. Jimmy tried to be encouraging and helpful, suggesting that the time would go by faster if Kenny just fell into step with whatever the program was going to be, and try to make the best of it.

Eddie was also on the dock, and Jimmy soon discovered why. Keegan was part of the group from Fountain Point, having been doomed to the same fate as Kenny by her father, the minister, and she was just as unhappy about it.

Too soon, Jake Jr. pulled the rope, the Ningwis issued the single one-second blast, and departed for North Manitou, leaving Jimmy and Eddie standing on the dock watching as she became smaller and smaller in the distance, ultimately disappearing into the morning haze.

"C'mon James ... you and me are going sailing." said Eddie.

"You're taking out the Tarnovitch?"

"No' *we're* taking out the Sea Scout."

"I can't." replied Jimmy. "My grandparents are gone for the week, and I agreed not to use the boat alone."

"You won't be alone ... I said *we*, didn't I?"

"But you don't know anything about sailing ... do you?"

Eddie lied ... "Sure I do. I used to go out with Tommy and his wife all the time when I was younger. She liked me."

"I better not. I promised I wouldn't."

"Awe c'mon. You know how your grandpa is ... *what people don't know won't hurt 'em ... boys will be boys*, and all that."

That was probably true, Jimmy thought. Gramps and Tommy gave him and Kenny credit for being a lot more grown up and capable than most others, who chose to think of them still as children.

Eddie could see that he was considering the idea, so tried to sweeten the deal ...

"Keegan didn't want to go, but didn't have a choice. Her dad made her. So, I told her we'd be following the Ningwis over today, and would land out of sight north of the Park dock, at the old

262

dock. As soon as she can sneak away, she'll be there waiting, then we'd figure out something."

"Yeah, Kenny didn't want to go either."

Eddie lied again ... "I figured that. So, I told Keegan to bring him along, if she could."

"Then what?" wondered Jimmy. "They'll probably be involved in some sort of program. They won't just be able to run off on their own."

"Then we'll see what." answered Eddie. "There're only two adults and a couple dozen kids. They can't watch them all ... at least not at night, after dark. What're ya gonna do around here for a week ... just sit around doing nothing? Wouldn't you rather be over there exploring the island with Kenny?"

Jimmy thought about it a moment more, it occurring to him that Tommy would probably still be at the church, drinking coffee and eating homemade cookies.

"Okay, let's go." he said suddenly. "We better be gone before Mr. Thomassen gets back home."

Then with another moment's thought ...

"But what about food, camping gear, and stuff?"

"Forget it." answered Eddie. "We'll make do. We'll live off the land."

They hurried off the dock, across the grass, around the fence with the *No Trespassing* sign, and around the little point to the boat. In moments they had it in the water and underway, with Jimmy at the tiller and Eddie trying to handle the halyards. It was evident immediately that he had probably lied ... that he had no experience in the Sea Scout and probably knew nothing about sailing at all.

"You lied to me." accused Jimmy.

"So? Would we be out here if I'd told you the truth? We can handle it. You just tell me what to do and everything'll be just fine."

————

The Ningwis landed at the Park dock on schedule, at eleven o'clock. A single law enforcement ranger was on the dock to meet the boat, the only Park person on the island that weekend morning. As usual, the passengers were discharged first, lined up on the dock, and then their packs and equipment were taken off and passed down the line bucket-brigade style, forming a lineup of equipment on the dock, from which each person could reclaim their own.

With the ranger leading, the group then straggled up to what served as the island's visitor center, where they were given the customary welcoming briefing, which included a review of the rules for back country camping: camping was permitted anywhere on the island, except on the beach or near landmarks or points of interest, or within sight of any other visitors' camps ... all biodegradable trash, including human wastes must be buried ... all other trash had to be packed out and properly disposed of in the nearby containers which the ranger pointed out ... no open fires, except in the fire pit at the single designated overnight camping area near the dock, and so on. Cellular service was spotty at best, and nonexistent in many island locations, especially at its lower elevations; in case of emergency, the ranger station was the place to come to for assistance. There was a single source of drinking water on the island, a nearby faucet which the ranger also pointed out ... warning that water from inland streams and lakes should

264

not be considered potable. The largest critters on the island were a few hundred deer, which none of them would be likely to see since they were nocturnal and reclusive. The same went for coyotes, of which there were also a few. Other than that, they'd see lots of snakes ... all being of the garter or ring-neck varieties, which were quite harmless ... and *micro-bears* ... as chipmunks on the island were affectionately called. Because of them, smart campers would be careful to hang anything edible in the trees and out of reach of those pesky little thieves.

After finishing his obligatory briefing and the obligatory opportunity for questions and answers ... there were no questions ... the ranger left, heading back to his office and living quarters in the old Coast Guard station. The two group leaders, a young man named Clark from the Lake Leelanau church, who looked like he was barely in his twenties, and a younger woman named Paula, who was his wife, took over.

"Okay, everyone – listen up! Gather around in a circle, join hands and we'll have an opening prayer!" Clark called.

With fifty-two hands joined and twenty-six heads bowed, Clark launched into a syrupy invocation ...

"Oh great and all-powerful Heavenly Father, hear our prayer as we embark into the wilderness to seek your Son, our Lord Jesus Christ, and to discover your plan for each of our lives ..." entreated Clark ostentatiously, and prattling on much too long.

Kenny often thought his father stretched things out, but that was nothing compared with Clark's ability to milk every scriptural allusion to what he apparently had in mind for this outing, and employing every biblical cliché he could think of. He was certainly an expert at *christianese*, as his father often called it, referring derogatorily to the blather which seemed to be a trademark of the bible thumpers. Kenny cringed when it occurred to him that this crowd would no doubt start *speaking in tongues* before this adventure was all over, which would be a real embarrassment. After what seemed like a very long time, Clark finally wound it up, saying ...

"... and now in the name of our Lord and Savior, Jesus Christ, we offer the prayer he taught us, saying ..."

Then twenty-six lips mumbled the words of the familiar prayer, Kenny singing it in his mind and entertaining himself with modifications of his own – *'Our father, who aren't in heaven – lead a snot into temptation – For thou ar't the king dumb, and the POW-er and the gory forever'*. And then the prayer circle event was finally over!

"Okay, here's the deal, folks." advised Clark. "After his baptism by his cousin John, the Holy Spirit led Jesus out into the wilderness to be tested and humbled. There he remained for forty days and forty nights, fasting to draw his attention away from matters of the flesh."

"Here in this island wilderness, deprived of all the comforts that we usually enjoy, we will follow in His footsteps, being tested in the deepest secrets and convictions of our hearts, to examine what lies in our hearts. Some of us will go through great highs in this, our walk with God. Others will find themselves in spiritual turmoil. But during these times of testing, we all need to put our complete trust in the Lord."

"All of you will be visited by Satan! The devil will come and whisper in your ears, creating doubts about God's promises: *Does your God really exist? Does He know you ... Does He really care about you? Does God really hear your prayers? Will He really be there for you in times of trouble?* When you hear the whisperings during the next several days, remember that it is written, *God has promised us, and his words are final and sufficient!*"

"When you leave this wilderness, my friends, many of you will have been born again in Christ ... a new creation! And your lives will forever be changed."

"Let us pray ..."

Then Paula began a prayer not so much different than her husband's, but thankfully much shorter. After the silly ... *'and all of God's children said ... AMEN!'* Clark took the lead again.

"Unlike Jesus' experience, in the interest of safety, we'll be teaming up in pairs, rather than wandering the island alone. I want you all to choose a partner, and not one with whom you are best friends or regular companions. If possible, choose someone who is a stranger to you today."

Keegan immediately sought out Kenny, which was a fortunate thing for him, because he hadn't met anyone among this group, most of who were from Fountain Point, with whom he would have wanted to spend a whole week searching for Jesus in the wilderness. He was surprised when Keegan immediately approached him. He didn't know her at all, and had not really noticed her in the group up to that point. But she seemed very nice, and was a very pretty girl. She didn't tell him that Eddie had pointed him out before they boarded the boat at Leland, with his instructions about meeting up at the old dock. When she introduced herself as the daughter of the minister at LLBF, Kenny thought he understood why she would have come to him ... and besides that, they *were* actually strangers.

"One last thing, people!" Clark called. "All the cell phones stay here at the ranger station. If anybody brought their cell phone, give it up now. They don't work out here anyway."

Clark then explained that they should then all go their separate ways, and began to dispatch the twelve teams in different directions, beginning with the trail that went north along the lakeshore, across the old landing strip and through the abandoned orchards.

When Keegan caught on to what Clark was about to do, she pushed a somewhat confused Kenny towards that end of the group. Perhaps because she was the minister's daughter, Clark and Paula therefore feeling comfortable using her as an ice-breaking example, she and Kenny were the first to be sent out. The others watched as the two youngsters walked away confidently along the designated two-track towards the trail that would lead them to the old dock.

"Well, what do we do now?" asked Kenny, disgustedly.

"We sojourn in the wilderness, of course." she replied derisively. "Keep your eye out for Jesus ... or the Devil." ending with a pretended scary tone of voice.

"Yeah, right!" replied Kenny.

"And speaking of the Devil ..."

They had just come around a little turn in the trail, headed for the old dock, and quite far ahead, through the tunnel framed by the trees and the canopy they created, spied what Kenny thought looked a lot like the Sea Scout!

"C'mon, Kenny." she coached, as she took off jogging toward the lake.

When they got to the ruins of the old dock, the Sea Scout was still coming towards the shore, still quite a way off, and with two people aboard. He assumed one was Jimmy.

"Who is it?" he asked Keegan, having figured out why she had pushed him through the group to the north side.

"It's Edward and your friend."

Then he could see that it was indeed Jimmy at the tiller, and Eddie standing up, hanging on to the mast and looking their way. Keegan waved eagerly from the shore with both hands over her head, and Eddie waved back. Several minutes later, the Sea Scout nosed up onto the sandy shore, several yards north of the ruins of the old dock.

As Eddie stepped over the gunwale on the port side and into the water, she ran out to greet him with a bear hug, almost lifting him up. Kenny grabbed a line at the bow and helped pull the boat further up onto the beach.

"I thought you weren't supposed to use the boat?" he inquired of Jimmy.

"Well ..." replied Jimmy, about to blame Eddie for talking him into it, but thinking that would sound rather ignoble he began again "... Well, I guess I've screwed up. But we're here now, so ..." He broke off, because he really hadn't thought about what would come next.

"So ... what?" asked Kenny, seeming to sense that his friend had been talked into doing the wrong thing by Eddie Gunderson, and feeling a little disgusted with the situation.

"So ... I don't know what." answered Jimmy, now equally disgusted with himself. "What are you supposed to be doing out here? Where's everybody else?"

Kenney explained the retreat idea, as assigned by Clark.

"Wow! Is that ever lame! ... All week?" Jimmy exclaimed.

Keegan and Eddie had walked away several yards, evidently not wanting their conversation to be overheard. There really wasn't any reason; she had been similarly filling Eddie in, and that had evidently led to the same question. As they came back towards the boat, Eddie had a suggestion.

"Let's blow this pop stand ... there's nothing going on here. It's nothing but boring trails, deerflies and sand fleas."

"*Blow this pop stand* to where?" Kenny asked mockingly.

"To South." Eddie replied, meaning South Manitou. There's at least some facilities over there ... campgrounds with out-houses and water, some old farms and other stuff."

"What about the group over here? What'll they do when they find out they're missing?" Jimmy worried.

"How will they know?" answered Eddie. "They're supposed to get lost in the wilderness and keep away from each other ... out of sight. They'll never know they're gone.

We'll come back in a few days ... by Friday at the latest ... they can join up with the group again and come back with the ferry. Nobody will ever know the difference."

That sounded plausible. Eddie continued ...

"I know a place over on South ... on the south side where there's an old house we can stay at. Nobody ever goes out there ... maybe just a few stragglers now and then. It's way out in the wilderness area."

The four of them launched the Sea Scout again, and they sailed far out into the lake to ensure that nobody would notice that they had launched from the island. With Jimmy and Kenny now

270

handling the boat, they sailed due east toward the mainland for a couple of miles, then turned to starboard, running due south. With the crib directly abaft their starboard side, Jimmy changed course to the southwest, keeping well away from the islands and the mainland. With Sleeping Bear Point directly off to port, Eddie indicated the approximate location of the place that he had mentioned, and Jimmy turned due west. Finally, with the destination dead off the starboard side, he changed course to due north, heading directly toward the beach on the south side of South Manitou Island. As they approached the island, the house came into view a few points to starboard, and the two sailors brought their boat up to the beach just below that place.

They had arrived at what had once been a wealthy landowner's farm, and then a resort, but had been abandoned for many years. It was a place the Park referred to as *the Lodge*.

* * *

28

"Welcome to South Manitou Island!" announced Eddie.

Together they pulled the boat up onto the beach as far as they could and struck the sail, intending to hide it as much as possible. It rested lengthwise along the little sand cliff at the high-water mark created by the waves lapping against the island's rising elevation. From a distance, she was not very noticeable.

"What is this place?" wondered Keegan as they climbed up the little sandy rise towards a boarded-up house.

"It was a farm until some rich guys from Detroit bought it and tried turning it into a resort." answered Eddie. "The Park owns it now, but they don't keep it up."

"Have you been here before?" Jimmy asked Eddie.

"No, we set nets around here. I saw it from out there ..." pointing out into the lake. "I wondered if anybody lived here, so I looked it up. Let's see if it's open."

"Looks like someone is trying to keep it up." noticed Jimmy as they ascended the steps at the middle of the wide front porch, which had been rather crudely patched up with new rough-cut boards.

The windows were completely boarded up, and they found padlocks on the front and back doors. But a cellar door had not been so well secured. It too was locked, but being half below ground level, the dampness had rotted the wood sufficiently that with a little encouragement, Eddie prying the hasp up lightly with his trusty boning knife, the rusted screws easily pulled out. Then he pushed the door inward, and stepped inside a dark, cobwebby cellar.

"Whoa, it's pitch black in here … anybody bring a flashlight?"

"We've got matches." Kenny offered, reaching into a side pocket on his pack.

With the aid of a few matches, he found the steps leading upstairs into the house, and motioned for the others to enter the cellar and follow. The door at the top of the steps was not locked. They entered into a room that was probably the kitchen, but with all the windows boarded up it was also totally dark inside the house, even now in mid-afternoon.

"This place is stinky and spooky." said Keegan timidly. "Can we open a window and let in some light and fresh air?"

"It just an old house." assured Eddie. "Nothing to be afraid of."

He opened one of the double-hung widows, sliding the lower pane up, surprised that it opened so easily. Then he pushed gently against the sheet of plywood used to cover the window from the outside to see if it would budge. Bracing himself on Jimmy to give it a few little sideways kicks, he found that he could detach the bottom of the sheet rather easily, and with the top still holding, it could be pushed out a bit, leaving it hanging like a long, steep awning, thereby letting a little daylight stream into the room.

"That'll work." he said in a self-congratulatory tone. "From a distance, that won't be noticed."

So, they kicked opened a couple of other windows on the first floor in the same manner. The room they had first entered was indeed originally a kitchen. The ground floor also included what had probably been a dining room, a large sitting room at the front of the house, and two smaller rooms on its west side.

"Looks like we won't be staying in here." decided Eddie.

The front room was being used for storage by whoever was working on the house. There were two stacks of lumber in the middle of the floor; one of two-by-four studs and one of the same kind of rough cut boards used outside on the porch. Two stacks of drywall leaned against the back wall and one of the side walls, with a small stack of concrete blocks in front of the latter. Among these things were various other supplies; drywall tape and mud, drywall sealer, paint, bags of ready-mix mortar, some electrical wire and wiring hardware, duct tape, and so on.

From the middle of the large front room, a narrow staircase went to the second level. Using the matches to investigate, they determined that all the upstairs rooms were probably bedrooms. They did not open any of the windows on the upper level, thinking that might attract attention from a distance. Overall, the house was filthy, with several years of accumulated dust and grim covering everything, so the upstairs part wasn't very inviting either.

They went back outside through one of the front windows that Eddie had forced open like an awning, pushing the bottom out far enough to let them through, then back into place. Sitting on the edge of the porch, Keegan wondered ...

"What are we going to do over here all week?"

"I don't know." offered Kenny. "But even with nothing to do, it'll be better than wandering around on North Manitou pretending to be Jesus in the wilderness and looking for *old*

Beelzebub." mimicking the name he'd often heard his grandmother Jennings use.

"This might help." announced Eddie, pulling a small booklet out of the back pocket of his jeans.

"*Welcome to South Manitou Island – A Pocket Guide for Visitors.* I just happened to bring this along, on the chance that we might be coming over here. It tells all about what's here, and there's this map right here in the middle." he continued, opening the booklet and unfolding the map.

"See ... we're down here, where it says *the Lodge,* and around the bend over that'a way ..." pointing eastward along the beach "... about a half mile or so is a campground ... which we *shall* steer clear of ... and out this way ..." pointing westward "... is the Morizon shipwreck ... I've been out there on the Tarnovitch ... it really stinks ... covered with cormorants. Here's also a *Valley of the Giants,* whatever that is. Up that'a way ..." pointing due north "... is a lake ... maybe we can go swimming up there. It's probably a lot warmer than the big lake, and besides all that, look at this ..." expansively gesturing towards the beach and the big lake. "Have you ever seen a more beautiful view? Is this better than North, or what! The book says this is the most beautiful view on the island."

"Yeah, I wouldn't have had anything to do in Leland anyway. At least we can explore, and find out what's up over here." added Jimmy.

"All we have to do is keep from being seen." warned Eddie. "If we keep away from everybody else out here, nobody will ever know we were here, and it'll all work out. You'll be back on North Manitou ..." indicating Keegan and Kenny "... and us two will be back in Leland to meet the ferry when you come back. Nobody will ever know about our little escapade."

During the next couple of days, the four explored the southwest end of the island, from the Lodge, way out to the high bluffs on the island's west side, and much of its interior. Keegan and Eddie frequently disappeared for a half-hour or more at a time. Jimmy and Kenny knew why. It seemed like they were intent on *doing it* at every landmark and place of interest listed in the little booklet, besides sleeping together during the night.

Having given up on the house, they had decided to use the small one-person tents that Keegan and Kenny carried on their packs. The first night they set them up behind the house, mindful of the need to conceal their presence. That had proven to be a mistake, because of the swarms of mosquitoes that came out of the dense, damp woods surrounding the back of the place. The next day they moved to the edge of the rise near the lake, just above the boat. The shoreline curved inward a little where the Lodge was, and with the tall beach grass and junipers on either side on the high ground along the ridge at the back of the beach, neither the boat nor the tents were visible from very far off down the shoreline on either side.

To make their little improvised camp site more comfortable, and to take advantage of the view across the Passage, they brought out some of the concrete blocks and four of the rough-cut planks to set up two makeshift benches, diagonally facing each other, between which they dug out a shallow fire pit. After dark they'd be able to have a small camp fire, thanks to the seclusion of the site.

276

Eddie and Jimmy had left Leland on short notice, bringing nothing with them. Eddie spent the nights snuggled up with Keegan in her sleeping bag inside her tent, and Jimmy slept with Kenny in his. Since the religious retreat was supposed to be, among other things, an exercise in fasting, Keegan and Kenny had brought only the barest of essentials ... bottled water, jerky and some trail mix. Eddie supplemented that by sneaking into the Weather Station campground in the wee hours of the morning and pilfering supplies from what the campers there had hung in the trees.

During the early morning hours, before the other three were awake, he also hiked across the island to the village area, discovering that the Park had fresh water and clean bathroom facilities over there. He also observed that there was apparently only one park ranger on the island, a small young woman who lived at the Ranger Station ... the old Coast Guard Station ... and that one of the nearby houses was occupied by a group of six volunteer workers, who always left for work around seven-thirty. On their third day, Tuesday morning, he brazenly entered the volunteers' house and helped himself to a two or three-day supply of their groceries, carrying them back to the Lodge in one of their plastic tubs, which he toted atop his right shoulder.

The other three were not very comfortable about these stolen supplies, but Eddie assured them that he'd left no shortages; that the campers and volunteers had brought over way more than they would ever need anyway, and that they might be just as happy not having to carry all the extra stuff back off the island when they left.

Keegan, in particular, was not comfortable with the absence of bathroom facilities. They had discovered that the Park maintained privies at the campgrounds and certain other points of interest, and these afforded at least some privacy. It was she, and Jimmy, who was also modest in that respect, who made quick trips to one of those locations whenever necessary.

The island's little village was mostly deserted after the ferry left at four-thirty each afternoon, at least outdoors. Nevertheless, the four always waited until after nightfall to come into the area to fill up their water bottles at the outdoors faucet, and for Keegan to use the nearby public restroom facilities, which were clean, sweet smelling, and provided with fresh hot and cold water.

They never moved around in the village area together, entering from the woods, doing what they came for, and then disappearing back into the forest, just one at a time. Had anyone ever noticed, they would probably have assumed it was just one of the volunteers or someone from one of the campgrounds. After these late-night raids on the village, instead of going back through the dark, mosquito-infested woods, they'd usually return to the Lodge by walking the beach from the lighthouse, which was just around the island's south point from the Ranger Station, sneaking very quietly past the Weather Station campground, and stealthily evading any of the campers who happened to be on the beach at that late hour.

Sometimes they'd lay on the Lodge's wide porch for a while, watching the moon and the millions of stars over Lake Michigan. Other times they'd build a small campfire with twigs and sticks gathered from the woods around the house and driftwood found on the beach, and sit on their makeshift benches; Eddie and Keegan on one side of the fire, with Jimmy and Kenny opposite.

Eventually they'd retire to their respective tents, undress down to their underwear and crawl into their sleeping bags.

Eddie and Keegan were, of course, always happy to cuddle up together in their tight sleeping quarters. But Jimmy was equally glad for the opportunity to lie close to his best friend. As the two lay there on their sides, with Kenny's back pressed against his chest, his bottom against Jimmy's middle, he thought that he had probably grown affectionately closer to Kenny than he might to his own brother, if he had one, and certainly much closer than he'd ever been to anyone outside of his family.

As they lie there, skin to skin, it felt like they were very close to being one, as if they were melting into each other. Kenny apparently felt it too, because of the way he, every now and then, attempted to nudge closer, to bring himself in tighter contact with Jimmy. In these quiet moments, Jimmy experienced what was becoming an increasingly familiar feeling ... his heart seeming to be swelling beyond the ability of his chest to constrain it, as if it might burst with joy, and at the same time feeling like crying. Within the depths of his mind, he knew that he was in love with this younger boy, just like he had come to love the boy at Culver's last summer. But he couldn't bring himself to consciously admit that, not even to himself.

Also, much as he tried to avoid it by directing his thoughts to other more mundane things, the feelings in his swollen heart at these moments aroused a corresponding response in his loins. Wrestling with ambivalence, he worried that Kenny might feel that, yet at the same time felt tremendously excited about touching him in that way.

On their third night together on the island, laying in the usual position with Kenny in his arms while thinking these things and gently massaging his friend's chest and stomach, Jimmy's fingers found their way under the elastic waistband at the front of Kenny's briefs ... his Walmart briefs with the blue and gold strips in the waistband ... ever so slowly and lightly stroking lower, towards the bottom of his belly. Again, he struggled with his feelings of arousal, not daring to go further, but not wishing to stop. But he did stop short, for fear of doing something that might prove fatal to their friendship. For many moments the two boys lay together silently, barely breathing, and motionless.

Suddenly, Kenny turned over onto his back, raised his hips, pushed his underpants down, and kicked them off with his feet. Then he turned towards Jimmy, hugging him tightly and kissing him hard on the mouth. Jimmy responded, quickly hugging him back, opening his mouth and pressing it hard against Kenny's. Kenny looked into his eyes for a moment in the dark, and then rolled back over to his original position. In the dark, Kenny couldn't have noticed the tears welling up in Jimmy's eyes.

Pressing his bare bottom hard against Jimmy's aroused middle, he took Jimmy's hand and moved it back to its former place at the bottom of his belly. A few moments later, he moved it further down, placing it over himself, while pushing his backside even tighter against his Jimmy, who had now become, in his heart, more than just a *best friend.*

That night affirmed beyond any question that Kenny's feelings for him were as deep as his were for Kenny. They were happy boys ... so full of joy and excitement that they would barely get any sleep

280

that night, until the Wednesday morning dawn was just beginning to brighten the eastern horizon.

* * *

29

"Okay, you two little lovebirds ... time to crawl out of the sack!"

It was Eddie at the front of their tent. Jimmy woke up quickly, somewhat disquieted by the *lovebirds* comment. Suddenly the loving feelings vanished, and he felt ashamed and guilty. He wondered what Eddie knew ... if he'd been spying on them. He decided it was probably just a casual remark, Eddie just teasing as he often did.

"Look what I've got!" exclaimed Eddie, holding up a bar of soap and some white bath towels.

"Eddie!" scolded Keegan. "Who'd you steal that from?"

"We're not stealing, we're just borrowing." replied Eddie.

"When we leave, she can have them back."

"She?" asked Kenny.

"The ranger." answered Eddie.

"You borrowed those from the Ranger?" asked Kenny again.

"Well, not exactly. When she left to go over to the volunteers' house for breakfast, I slipped into her place and picked them up."

"You stole that stuff out of the Ranger Station?" stammered Kenny, incredulous over Eddie's brazenness.

"Borrowed!" insisted Eddie.

"I had to do something; you two are beginning to stink the place up; you're getting a little overripe. We all need a bath. Let's go up to the little lake before the rest of the world wakes up out here."

Lake Florence was the island's inland lake, not far north of the Lodge. According to the visitors' guide booklet, it was narrow and long, about a mile long, with a little sandy beach at its southeast side. There was only one bar of soap, but four bath towels with a small *VCL* monogram stamped in blue on one end.

"Who's VCL?" wondered Jimmy.

"Veronica Lake!" joked Keegan quick-wittedly, referring to an old Hollywood sex kitten none of the others had ever heard of.

"How would you know that?" asked Eddie skeptically.

"She comes to my dad's church; she's a park ranger." she answered coyly, having decided to keep running with the gag.

"Oh." replied Eddie, still having not caught on. "Is she short ... about this tall?"

"Yes; about like me ... but not as beautiful and sexy."

Eddie whispered something in her ear. She smiled and answered with a peck on his cheek.

They entered the pleasantly warm waters of the lake from its small sandy beach, stripped to their underwear. Sharing the bar of soap one at a time, they washed up in the shallows, then went out into deeper water to strip completely, finish the job and rinse off, also using that opportunity to launder their socks and underwear. Keegan was first, and when she was ready to get out of the water and dry off, Eddie brought her one of *Veronica Lake's* towels, which she carefully used to conceal her nakedness. The other two boys politely kept their backs turned as she left the water and ran into the woods, holding the towel around herself with one hand, her dripping intimate apparel in the other.

Eddie was next and, as usual, was not the least bit modest. Tossing the soap back out to Jimmy, he walked out of the water and onto the beach, picked up one of the towels, and continued into the woods to dress.

Jimmy and Kenny washed up together, and without exposing themselves. As Kenny left the water, Jimmy respectfully kept his back turned, and Kenny rendered the same courtesy as Jimmy came in and wrapped himself in the last of the four towels. Together, they too dressed in the woods, laying their wet socks and briefs beside Keegan's and Eddie's wet things, spread atop the warming surface of an overturned aluminum boat.

They had discovered the small aluminum boat on the beach, chained to a tree at the edge of the woods alongside two aluminum canoes which were turned over and resting against it.

"Are these the Park's?" Jimmy wondered.

Eddie shrugged and wagged his head.

"Let's take these for a little spin while our undies dry." he suggested, indicating the two canoes.

"What about paddles?" Keegan wondered.

"Well, look around ... they're probably stashed out here somewhere."

Eddie was right. Not far back into the woods, and not very well concealed, Kenny found a long wooden boat box containing paddles for the canoes, oars, some life preservers, and a small outboard motor for the boat.

"Let's just use the canoes." said Eddie. "They don't make any noise."

"What about the chain?" Kenny wondered.

284

"What about it?" replied Eddie, removing his boning knife from the leather sheath on his belt.

The chains were flimsy; the double-loop wire type not really intended for security purposes. It was easy for Eddie to pry a link near the padlock open enough to uncouple it, thus freeing the canoes.

They quietly slipped out into the lake, paddling to the opposite side to distance themselves from nearby roads and hiking trails. In the event they might be caught, they'd be able to quickly ditch the boats on the far side and run off into the woods. They then began paddling leisurely towards the north end of the lake.

"Wow! Look at that." yelled Kenny, pointing skyward.

Flying northward high above the water was a huge hawkish-looking bird, dark brown and black except for its white head, neck and tail feathers.

"He's beautiful ... and huge!" cried Keegan. "What it is?"

"My God!" answered Jimmy. "I think it's an eagle ... an American bald eagle."

"Here ... on South Manitou?" doubted Kenny. "I thought they were mostly out west."

The huge bird flew a little further beyond them, then banked sharply to its left and came swooping steeply down between their boats and the shoreline, not fifty yards away. With talons extended, it suddenly flared its wings, dropping down to the surface, where it neatly snatched a fish out of the shallows. Then its wide, powerful wings lifted it gracefully back aloft, where it turned slightly towards the southeast, apparently heading back towards the place from which they'd taken the canoes.

"They must have a nest back there." yelled Kenny. "Let's go check it out."

They hurriedly paddled their canoes back towards where they'd started from, but a little to the north where the eagle seemed to have been heading. From there they began more slowly following the shoreline southward, intently scanning the treetops in search of the big bird.

"Oh my gosh!" shouted Jimmy. "Look at that!"

High above them was a huge platform at the top of one of the tallest trees. Made of a tangle of twigs and small sticks and roughly circular, it appeared to be about six feet or more in diameter. On a branch slightly above it, perched the huge eagle they'd seen fishing, or at least one like it. They were too directly below the nest to be able to see what, if anything, might be in it. But they assumed there were others ... perhaps little ones ... because the big bird on the perch seemed to have maybe dropped the fish there.

"Are we safe here? Maybe we shouldn't be so close." worried Keegan. "Do you think he might attack?"

"I don't think so." Eddie reassured. "He's just sitting there looking around ... even seems to be ignoring us."

They remained as they were, watching the eagle and the nest for several minutes. Their patience was then rewarded as a second eagle briefly appeared at the edge of the nest, dropping something overboard, and then disappeared again.

"They must be a pair." guessed Keegan. "That's too beautiful! I'm sure they have little ones up there. Oh, I wish we could see them."

"We'd better be going ..." said Eddie "... before somebody finds our stuff on the boat."

286

They paddled the canoes back to the little beach, pulled them onshore and turned them over next to the aluminum boat. Eddie chained them up as they were, hooking the links back up such that the tampering would be noticeable only on close inspection, while Jimmy and Kenny returned the paddles to the boat box in the woods. They gathered up their wet socks, underwear and towels and headed for the Lodge. The only remaining evidence of their presence at the little beach was a little soapy scum lingering along the shoreline.

Back at the Lodge they spread the towels and their wet things out on their makeshift benches, then went up and lay alongside each other on the wide porch. It was a very pleasant and peaceful time for all four; freshly bathed, free of cares, and warming in the morning sunshine. South Manitou felt very close to paradise. They were glad they'd come.

Unhappily, that was about to change.

* * *

<u>30</u>

As Keegan and Eddie crawled into their sack and cuddled up that night, Eddie vaguely sensed a cooling of the feelings between them. In fact, he had been having that feeling on and off for a while. It wasn't that Keegan was cold in any way toward him, or unresponsive to his affectionate comments and gestures, or reluctant to submit. She seemed as eager to love him and make love with him as ever, yet it seemed like there was a growing lack of earnestness, or excitement.

"Is something wrong?" he asked quietly.

"No. Why?"

"It just seems like you have something on your mind ... like you don't get as excited about sleeping together and making out ... doing it ... like you did before."

She lay there quietly beside him, saying nothing, raising no objections, offering no explanations.

"Of course, we do it all the time ... ever since I met you. I suppose the excitement is bound to wear off a little." he mused, not really to himself, but as an attempt to encourage a response.

Still she was silent. He worried that he was wrong, and had insulted her ... probably hurt her feelings. Tugging gently on her shoulder to prompt her to turn over to face him, with the intention of kissing her ... holding her tight and saying he was sorry, he felt the wetness of the tears on her face.

"I'm sorry ... I am sorry. Don't cry. I'm just a jerk. I love you!"

He kissed her forehead, and held her very tightly against himself.

"I love you too, Eddie. I always will."

Her comment had a hint of resignation in it, or so he thought. He pushed her away a little, just far enough to see her face in the moonlight, and looked into her eyes quizzically. She couldn't meet his gaze, looked away and began crying more pitifully, her body convulsing in sobs.

"What?" he asked.

"Oh, Eddie ... I'm going to have *a baby!*" she blurted out.

"You're pregnant!?! How!?!"

It seemed like a dumb question, given the realities of their relationship, he having taken her on the first day they met, and too many times to count between then and now.

"I mean, what about your birth control? How could you get pregnant!?! How do you know you are?"

"I've never used any sort of birth control, Eddie. I think it was that first time ... on the boat. I haven't had a period since then. And now I can feel it inside me ... growing."

He was shocked that she wasn't on any sort of birth control ... didn't all women use some kind of birth control? Of all the women he'd ever fucked, he'd never known one who didn't. It was an issue that never came up. This was unbelievable ... and inexcusable! He was pissed!

"Seriously! You've gotta be kidding! You're fucking the shit out of me all this time without any sort of protection!?! Are you stupid, or what!"

He had raised his voice to her for the first time ever, and was almost yelling now. Jimmy and Kenny, having not yet fallen asleep, heard the commotion, were disturbed, and got back up.

"What's wrong?" asked Jimmy.

"Nothing! Mind your own fucking business!" was Eddie's reply. "Get the hell out of here ... you fucking little faggots!"

Eddie was obviously highly agitated over something, and not in any mood to talk rationally about it. It sounded like he was almost about ready to cry. Kenny touched Jimmy's arm to get his attention, then wagged his head back towards his left shoulder, indicating that they should go, and leave Eddie and Keegan alone for now.

"Shit! Shit! Shit!" uttered Eddie as he crawled out of Keegan's sleeping bag and tent, and ran down onto the beach.

He collapsed to his hands and knees at the water's edge, repeatedly pounding his fists into the soft wet sand.

"Shit! Shit! Shit!!!"

"God dammit!" he cried out plaintively at the lake. And then more quietly and resignedly, "God dammit" ... saying it almost under his breath, as he sat down on the sand with his knees raised and hands covering his face, his body beginning to spasm as the tears came.

He cried for a long time; until it seemed like there were no more tears to cry. Looking skyward at the millions of stars above

...

"You did it to me again, you sonofabitch! Every fucking time something good happens for me, you fuck me over! Every fucking time! Why me? When do I get a break? Why do you hate me!?!"

He was thinking about Keegan ... the only girl he had ever really loved, and who had really loved him ... the one he wanted to eventually marry and make a life with. Now those dreams were destroyed ... forever! Why did it have to end this way!?!

He thought about the Maritime Academy ... seeing it all slipping away. He was sure it was Lucy Cooper who had set that up and would be paying for most of it ... and only because she was in love with him. Now that was totally fucked up too. If he had to marry Keegan Haggard, he could kiss that all goodbye. His one best chance ... gone forever ... because this stupid little bitch got herself pregnant!

No birth control!?! What the hell was she thinking! All that fucking ... it would be a wonder if she didn't drop a goddamned litter!

Then it occurred to him ... No birth control? Sonofabitch! She did it on purpose. She'd set him up!!!

"Eddie?"

Keegan had gotten up and had come down to the beach beside him.

"Eddie ... I'm sorry."

"Oh, you're sorry! You're sorry! ... Well *sorry* doesn't change anything does it?"

She was crying again now.

"Oh, Eddie ... I don't know what to do."

"Oh, Eddie ... I don't know what to do." he repeated meanly mocking her.

"You set me up, didn't you ... you sneaky little cunt!"

"Well I've got news for you, babe: there ain't gonna be any marriage. If you thought you could fuck your way into my life, and me out of my future, you were sadly mistaken, because I will never ... *NEVER* ... marry *YOU!*"

"No I didn't Eddie. I love you! ... Why would I? I couldn't marry you ... not yet. My dad would never permit it."

"Your dad? He can go fuck himself! Who cares what he thinks? If I *wanted* to marry you, he could just ..."

"Eddie ... I'm barely over fourteen." she cried as she admitted it.

"Fourteen!!! Fourteen what? Fourteen fucking years old!?! You lying little bitch!"

"I'm fifteen ... I just turned fifteen the week before we met on the pier."

"You said you were sixteen. You lied to me."

"I'm sorry, Eddie."

"Quit fucking saying you're sorry!"

"My dad is going to have a fit when he finds out."

"Yeah, I'm real sorry about that." he replied in a very surly tone of voice. "What about me ... what about the law. I'm nineteen ... you're barely over fourteen and I've been fuckin' your brains out for ..." he couldn't continue.

"I'm fucked. ... I'm going to jail!"

"No! I'll say it was all my fault ... that I went after you ... to set you up ... and ..."

"Oh, shut the fuck up. You don't know anything. It's the law. You're a child. I'm not. It's rape, period! You get to be the victim. I get life in prison! That's how it works."

She sat down beside him, in the same position with her hands at her face, weeping sorrowfully. He didn't touch her. He didn't feel sorry for her. In fact, he hated her!

292

"Keep your mouth shut, and maybe you'll luck out and have a miscarriage." he uttered meanly as he got up to leave her. Then he stopped and turned back ...

"Better yet, when we get back we can go someplace and get rid of it. I've got the money ... lots of money." Those mean comments hurt her terribly.

"How could you even say that!"

"Because I don't want it! Don't you get that? Did you ever hear me say I wanted to have any kids?"

I could never do that. My parents would never permit it ... and besides, I don't want to."

"Oh, fine. The religious shit again."

"Eddie, it's your baby too ... it's *our* baby, a part of you and a part of me ... our *love child*."

"Oh, bullshit! It's just a *fuck child.* If that's the way it's gonna be, you can have my half. I don't want it."

"I know you don't mean that Eddie. I know you love me."

"Not anymore!"

* * *

31

As the sun rose above the mainland in the east, it found a young girl lying on the beach in front of the Lodge. Keegan had not returned to her tent, having cried herself to sleep on the sand.

Jimmy and Kenny had not slept well during the night. They woke up early, just a little after sunrise, and crawled out of their tent, finding themselves alone. The other tent was empty, with neither Eddie nor Keegan seeming to be anywhere around.

"This is not good." worried Kenny.

"I wonder what was going on with them." said Jimmy.

"She's pregnant, of course ... what else." stated Kenny.

"Do you think so?"

"Of course! My dad knows her dad; they're both ministers. And I've heard my dad talking about her dad's nutty fundamentalist Bible Fellowship ... they don't believe in anything. No birth control, no abortion, no gays and lesbians, no women leaders ... no nothing."

"So?"

"So, every time they turned around, they were sneaking off to do the wild thing. He's probably been screwing her like that all along. You screw a lot without protection, and eventually somebody's gonna get knocked up."

"You don't really know that ... how do you know they weren't using birth control?"

"Because she's been taught to believe that's just like murder and because Eddie's just irresponsible and stupid!"

They were sitting on one of the makeshift benches, and as they spoke an elderly couple in ranger uniforms came around the corner from behind the Lodge.

"Oh, oh ... we're busted." whispered Jimmy.

———

"No; I know who they are ... they're not rangers."

"Well, well! ... Hello Kenny." said the woman.

"Hello Mrs. Bentson." Kenny answered. "This is my friend Jimmy ... Jimmy Sutton, from Indiana. Jimmy, this is Rev. Bentson and his wife."

"I'm Larry." said Rev. Bentson, extending his hand to Jimmy, "And this is Lillian."

Jimmy shook Lawrence Bentson's hand firmly, like a gentleman.

"Are you friends of Kenny's dad?"

"Acquaintances." answered Larry. "We're retired. As you can see ..." indicating their uniforms "... we're working for the park now ... as *VIPs* ... summer volunteers."

"Oh." acknowledged Jimmy.

Having seen only the two small tents and single sleeping bags, it did not occur to the Bentson's that Kenny and his friend might not be here alone.

Eddie had come back to the camp, but noticing the Bentsons talking to Jimmy and Kenny, ducked out of sight as he circled around and went down to the beach to warn Keegan to do the same. Peering up over the little rise at the inland edge of the beach, Keegan recognized the elderly couple.

"I know them." she warned Eddie in a whisper "... and they know me."

She then whispered a brief explanation ... that the Bentsons occasionally attended the Fellowship; that the old man was a minister, and was sometimes called upon to preach as a substitute for her father.

"You're not supposed to be camping here." said Larry to the two boys. "I suspect you already know that?"

"It's my fault ..." offered Eddie, having come up behind them. I wondered what this place was, so we came ashore here to find out ... then we saw the eagle."

"The eagle?" wondered Lillian.

"Sure, a real American bald eagle!" answered Eddie enthusiastically. They've got a humungous nest way up in a tree overlooking the little lake."

Lillian was dubious.

"I don't believe it! Here? On South Manitou? What in the world would eagles be doing here?"

"Fishing!" answered Eddie. "We saw him doing it ... peeled around and dropped down out of the sky, grabbed a fish right out of the water, and took off to the nest."

"This we've got to see!" exclaimed Larry. "I've never heard of eagles out here before."

"C'mon ... I'll be happy to show you."

Eddie began to move off toward the path to the little lake.

"Wait a minute." said Larry. "The ranger sent us out here to see what was going on. We have to tell you that you can't stay here. If you want to camp, you have to register and set up in one of the campgrounds."

296

Then motioning to the house ...

"Looks like you've also broken into the house. What about that?"

"We didn't really break in." answered Eddie. "The cellar door in back is rotted; we just pushed it open. Then we pushed open a couple of windows to let some light in so we could look around, but the place was so filthy ..."

"What about this?" Larry asked, motioning to the cement blocks and rough-cut planks ... their makeshift benches.

"Just borrowed." answered Eddie easily, without even a hint of culpability or guilt.

"We'll put them back before we leave, and then we'll close the windows back up. Maybe you can tell the ranger that the cellar door needs to be fixed?"

"We were planning on leaving right now, but I can show you the eagle's nest first if you still want to see it. While we're doing that, Kenny and Jimmy can get things picked up here."

"Yes." agreed Larry. "We have to see those eagles. Then we'll come back and help see you off."

Jimmy was always astounded at how slick Eddie was when it came to handling these sorts of situations ... how quickly he came up with the lies and how easily they slipped off his tongue. Kenny just shook his head in disgust.

————

Eddie knew he was going to have to find a way to get rid of the meddlesome preacher and his wife. If they came back, they'd see Keegan, and would probably be sure to eventually mention that to her father. Fucking meddlers, he thought. Fucking do-gooders!

They hiked to the little beach on the southeast side of Lake Florence, where Eddie went right to the canoes. He unhooked the chain again, near the padlock, first fiddling with the lock, as if he knew the combination. With his back to them, the Bentsons easily fell for it.

"These belong to the Robinsons." said Lillian. "Do you have permission?"

"Oh, sure." reassured Eddie. "I've known Jake forever. The paddles are back there in the box." pointing towards the woods. "On second thought, let me do that. It's all buggy in there ... you'll be eaten alive. Maybe you two can pull the boat down to the water?"

It had occurred to Eddie that if one of them went back to the boat box, they'd probably bring back the life preservers along with the paddles. He came back carrying only a pair of paddles.

"I'll let you two do the paddling. The nest is up that way a ways." ... pointing northward as he courteously steadied the canoe so Lillian could climb aboard. Then he climbed in himself and sat down on the bottom at its middle. With Lillian at the bow and Larry aft, they headed up the lake.

"Better keep to the middle." Eddie advised. "I'm not sure how territorial they are, but they're really big birds, and I sure wouldn't want to find out while fighting them off from a canoe."

"Oh, for goodness sake!" exclaimed Lillian, having spotted the huge nest way up in the treetops, the one eagle still on the perch just above it.

From out in the middle of the lake, the second eagle was also visible atop the nest.

"It's true ... look at that Larry! Aren't they something!"

298

With Larry and Lillian's gaze fixed on the eagles, Eddie suddenly stood up, stepped up on the side of the canoe and dove into the water. As he lunged into the dive, he upset the boat, throwing the Bentsons also into the lake. Larry immediately surfaced, looking around in search of his wife, but she was nowhere to be seen. He knew she could swim, so guessed that she was probably on the opposite side of the overturned canoe.

As he began swimming around to the other side, Eddie grabbed him by the collar from behind, pulled himself up to the old man, and with his hands on his shoulders pushed him down below the surface. The old man was surprisingly strong, and struggled like a bull. But Eddie's youthful stamina proved too much for him. He soon quit struggling, went limp and began to slowly sink into the depths.

Eddie looked around for the old woman, but didn't see her anywhere. Swimming around the boat, she was nowhere in the water so, assuming that she had already drowned, he swam slowly to the shore on the west side of the lake, opposite the eagles' nest.

————

"Where's the Bensons?" Kenny asked as Eddie walked back into the camp at the Lodge, his clothes soaking wet.

"They decided to go swimming. They won't be coming back. How come you guys haven't taken this stuff down?"

"Were you serious about leaving? We thought you were just saying that to ..."

"We're leaving. Pick up your shit and get rid of this stuff." indicating the tents, packs, and the blocks and boards from the house. Then to Jimmy ...

"You go down and get the boat ready."

"Are we in a hurry?" replied Jimmy.

"Just fucking *do it*, dip shit!"

With their tents taken down and everything properly stowed in their back packs, Kenny and Keegan began carrying the concrete blocks and boards to the house.

"You just sit here." Eddie ordered Keegan. "Me and gay boy will take care of this stuff.

With Kenny struggling with one of the heavy blocks and Eddie carrying the boards, they entered the house through the open front window. Once inside, Eddie whirled around and smacked Kenny in the side of his head with the planks he was carrying, knocking the boy to the floor, his right hand smashed by the heavy cement block. Dropping the boards and quickly grabbing a roll of duct tape, Eddie wrapped his feet together, then rolled him over and bound his hands behind his back.

"So much for you, you little smart ass." he said, as Kenny began to regain his senses.

"Keegan!" Eddie called out the window. "C'mere quick. Kenny's hurt."

As she climbed through the window, Eddie grabbed her around the neck with his forearm, forced her hands behind her back and wrapped them with the wide gray tape.

"Eddie! What are you doing?"

Then she noticed Kenny on the floor, similarly bound hand and foot.

"Why are you doing this?" she screamed.

Eddie did not reply. He pushed her down next to Kenny and bound her feet with the tape, then crawled out the window.

He returned with the four white bath towels and dragging their backpacks. Once inside the house, he began impatiently casting about for a place where he could hide them so they'd never be found. It occurred to him that there was an attic; that would be the best place, and he rushed up the stairs with the towels, the two backpacks bumping up the steps behind him up to the second floor.

Several moments later, he returned empty-handed.

* * *

<h1 style="text-align:center">32</h1>

Eddie picked up two of the remaining three cement blocks and took them to the edge where the boat had been. Jimmy had pulled it out to the water's edge by himself.

"Throw these in." ordered Eddie, tossing the blocks down onto the beach.

"What for?" challenged Jimmy.

"Ballast."

"We don't need any more ballast." argued Jimmy.

"I wasn't asking, asshole! Just put the goddamned blocks aboard your fucking sailboat!"

Returning to what had been their campsite, Eddie picked up the last block, took it over to the bank and threw it down beside the other, Jimmy having already put the first one aboard the boat.

"Where's Kenny and Keegan?" asked Jimmy as he picked up the second block.

"They're in the house. Don't worry about it." Eddie replied, jumping down off the bank to help load the last block.

"Where's their packs and stuff?"

"I said don't worry about it ... they ain't gonna need 'em."

"They're going to have to have them back on North. Otherwise somebody's gonna ask questions." warned Jimmy.

"We ain't going back to North. You're gonna scoot my ass back to Leland fast as this tub can go. Then I'm gonna get my money and hit the road. By nightfall, Leland, your pervert grandpa, you, your boy-pussy, and all the rest will be history to me."

"Gramps isn't a pervert, and Kenny isn't either!" Jimmy shot back.

"Fuck you ... you don't know the half of it, you dumb turd. It's all going on right under your noses, and you never see it. And you ... you're just like Lee ... a boy-lover."

"That's not true! I never ..."

"Save your breath. I know what you two little fudge packers were doing at night. I've got ears. And I've got eyes."

Jimmy flushed with embarrassment. Whatever Eddie thought he'd heard, he had never been physically involved in that way with Kenny. And he was sure that Eddie had never seen anything – that he was lying. Nevertheless, it was true that he and Kenny had been physically intimate during the past few nights – kissing and touching each other and stuff. Eddie was sneaky. He had to believe that he probably did know about that.

"Go out back and fix that cellar door ... close it and put the screws back in the holes, and make it look like it hasn't been tampered with." ordered Eddie. "And while your back there all by yourself, you can take a piss."

It was a ploy to get rid of Jimmy for several minutes. As soon as he was around the corner of the house and out of sight, Eddie returned through the front window, carrying out Kenny and Keegan, one at a time, and taking them down to the beach and the waiting sailboat. He laid them side by side at the middle of the boat, arranging the cement blocks at their feet; one between them, and one on either side. Tying a rope through one of the end cavities on the first block, he then tied it around Kenny's feet.

Then passing it through the middle block, looped it around Keegan's feet, and finally through an end cavity in the third block.

When Jimmy finally came back and discovered what Eddie had done, it didn't immediately register.

"What's going on?" he demanded to know.

"Nothing. Get down here and I'll help you push off."

Jimmy hesitated.

"NOW ASSHOLE!"

"No way!" objected Jimmy. "That boat isn't going anywhere ... not with them tied up like that."

"They're fine. I'm just not taking any chances with the three of you against the one of me. When we get back to the mainland, you can turn 'em loose ... after I'm long gone."

"Don't believe him Jimmy!" Kenny pleaded; his face a ghostly white. "He's gonna drown us out there."

"Oh, bullshit." objected Eddie. "Why would I want to drown you, ya' little shit-ass. You're nothing to me."

"What about her?" accused Jimmy skeptically.

"We're through ... you can have her."

Keegan said nothing. Neither was she crying or making any attempt to change the situation. She was literally paralyzed with heartbreak and fear.

"We're not going." decided Jimmy.

"The hell we're not!" demanded Eddie, drawing his boning knife out of its sheath on his belt, and then moving towards Kenny.

"You either get your shit together right now, or you're gonna be watching your little boyfriend here eat his own nuts, one by one."

304

"Don't do it Jimmy. Just run! Get help!" implored Kenny through his tears.

"You run off, you little cocksucker, and when you get back, we'll be long gone. I'll sail this sonofabitch myself, and you'll never see your little lover again ... or her. It'll be on your conscience ... your doing."

Jimmy bit his lower lip, and then decided that he was helpless to do anything about the situation. Eddie seemed to have considered all the angles, and clearly had the upper hand. The best thing seemed to be to trust that Eddie really had no intention of doing anything more than getting away before the story about him and Keegan got out.

He jumped down off the bank and onto the beach, helped Eddie push the boat off the shore, and helped him raise the sail.

"Go that way." Eddie ordered, pointing in a south-easterly direction, toward Pyramid Point.

"Leland's that way." Jimmy corrected, pointing a little north of due east.

"That way!" Eddie insisted.

From his fishing experience with the Tarnovitch brothers, he knew that there was a trench about three-and-half-miles directly southeast of the South Manitou Island light ... about half way between the island and the mainland, with a depth of over fifty fathoms ... the deepest water in the Passage.

Jimmy had no idea what Eddie was up to. He suspected that he was intending to land onshore near Port Oneida, rather than Leland, and make good his escape from there. Kenny looked at him, still ashen, and shaking his head *no*.

"I don't trust you Eddie. You've turned bad again. I'm scudding for the nearest shore."

Eddie lunged at him as he began moving the tiller to turn the boat landward, brandishing the boning knife again ... this time right in his face, the sharp point lightly touching his left eyelid.

"Listen, you little bastard! You're gonna do just exactly what I fucking tell you to do! Else I'm gonna stick this toad stabber right through this pretty blue eyeball, and fuck up your brain. I can make you half blind and half dumb just that fast!" he threatened, with a snap of his fingers. "Now do you understand me, or not!?!"

Jimmy, scared to death, merely nodded.

"You rich snots all think you're so goddamned smart." complained Eddie, taking his seat on the starboard gunwale again.

"You're really just a bunch of stupid, gutless ..."

He interrupted himself, getting up again; picking up the concrete blocks one by one and carefully hanging them over the side. Kenny screamed in terror ...

"JIMMY!!!"

"Shut the fuck up!!!" shouted Eddie. "I don't trust you, Mr. Smartass!" he muttered at Jimmy. "Any more shit out of you, and over they'll go. Now you just go where I told you."

The wind was not favorable, so progress on Eddie's ordered course was slow.

"You don't know a damned thing about your grandpa's kinky little sex habits, do you!" Eddie muttered, bringing up that subject again.

"No, and I don't want to. It's none of my business ... or yours."

"Oh well, see, that's where you're totally full of shit. It's been my business for ... um ... about eight years. That's when Lee ... good old *Gramps* ... started fucking me."

"You're lying. I don't believe anything you say anymore."

"Yeah, well good for you. But whether you like it or not, the famous Lee Smith is a *boy-lover*, and like all rich guys, he gets what he wants, when he wants it, and nothing ever happens to him."

"And guess what!" Eddie continued, laughing cynically out loud. "Like grandfather; like grandson! If it wasn't for you already fucking Kenny-boy here, Lee would have been in his pants a long time ago. I can tell by the way he looks at him that he'd love to take Kenny to bed. I've known your grandpa for a *long* time."

"Oh, stop! Nobody wants to hear it!"

"Oh, no? Well there's way more than that Jimmy, my naive young friend, and you're gonna hear it whether you like it or not. Boys who were bed partners with your grandpa and kept their mouths shut, wound up with nice fat bank accounts when they finally turned eighteen. Those who couldn't be trusted to keep their little secret didn't ... they wound up dead."

"Oh, come on! You expect anyone to believe such a dumb bunch of lies? Boy-lovers? Murders? Seriously!?!"

"They wasn't *murders* ... they was all *accidents*. One boy wandered too far out on the icebergs south of the pier on a cold February night, fell over the edge and couldn't climb back up ... drowned in the lake. Another one blew his brains out while deer hunting ... stupidly trying to climb through a barbed wire fence with his 30-30 Winchester ... it caught on the wire, went off and shot him right here." pointing to the temple on the right side of his head. "Another one was ice skating all by himself on the

Boardman River right in downtown Traverse City ... ran over a soft spot and went under. They found him trapped under the ice, looking up like this." illustrating the position by raising his arms up beside his head with a terrified look on his face.

"All *accidents*." Eddie repeated smugly.

"Even if any of that actually happened, they probably *were* accidents, and you're just shooting your mouth off about stuff you don't know anything about ... trying to make me believe that good people are like you."

"I know about Lee Smith, you fuckstick, because I've been doing your grandpa's dirty work since I became too old for him. He only likes pretty young ones, like your boyfriend here. But he's been good to me ... I've got over thirty-seven-thousand of your grandpa's dollars in the bank right now."

"He pays good when I get him what he wants ... new boys who are available and willing. And I get rid of the ones who turn into trouble-makers. I'm really good at arranging *accidents* ... there's those three of his former little boyfriends pushing up daises right now to prove it. You're right; good old *Gramps* ain't like me ... ain't like me at all. He's way worse!"

Jimmy had nothing more to say. He just raised his eyes and shook his head. The wind had picked up a little, having turned around from west to northwest. Eddie looked around, and deciding that they were approaching the half-way point, stood up and began lifting Kenny by his shoulders. Kenny cried out again ... *"JIMMEEE!!!"*

Eddie shot a threatening glance at him before turning his attention back towards Kenny. With Eddie's back turned, Jimmy quickly thrust the tiller all the way to his right, causing the boat to turn hard to port. Eddie dropped Kenny and stood back up, grabbing at his knife and turning half-way back around towards Jimmy ...

"What the hell do you think you're ...?"

The gybing mainsail boom struck him hard under the chin, carrying him overboard as it swung rapidly to starboard.

Having acted impulsively, Jimmy had not considered any consequences other than that. But as the boom continued to swing, the boat listed hard to starboard, and with the ballast of the cement blocks hanging over that side, it began taking on water and capsized. He saw the mast come crashing down on Eddie's head ... he did not see Kenny and Keegan slip over the side and quickly disappear into the depths.

Panic struck him as the boat turtled and, thrashing mindlessly in the water, he somehow reached its floating hull. Unable to pull himself up onto it, he moved hand over hand along its side, his fingers grasping the small edges between the strakes, until reaching the rudder, which he clung to for dear life.

* * *

<h1 style="text-align:center">33</h1>

At four-thirty that afternoon, the Keche-Chéemann departed the island exactly on schedule, with one long and three short blasts of its air horn. With the light northwesterly winds, it would be a very pleasant ride back to Leland, and Jake headed his boat directly east out of South Manitou's serene crescent shaped bay, on a course that passed two miles north of Jimmy Sutton and the Sea Scout.

As the sun set and the edge of dusk crept across the Manitou Passage, the winds died, and the water calmed to a very gentle roll. After several hours of clinging to the Sea Scout's rudder, Jimmy's exposed head and shoulders were severely sunburned, although he wasn't aware of it. As the moon rose in the east and stars began to appear, he was aware of how hopeless his situation was, and how tired he had become. But most of all, he was in agony over Kenny and Keegan.

Fearing that he would fall asleep, or otherwise lose consciousness, he wriggled his left hand through a narrow space between the back edge of the rudder and the boat's hull, then twisted it a quarter turn, trapping it there so that he'd stay with the boat even if unconscious, and wouldn't sink below the surface.

He remained conscious and awake throughout the night, until dawn began to brighten the eastern horizon. After that, he gradually began to succumb to exhaustion, falling asleep and fitfully drowsing until suddenly waking up, apparently without any reason, then drifting off again. By noon of that day, his second day in the water, he no longer woke up. He was unconscious.

The seas remained fairly calm again, the ferry making its scheduled runs on its normal course. With the variable winds, the position of the Sea Scout changed very little that day, and no other vessel came near. Exposure began taking its toll, with the sunburn now becoming seriously acute.

Friday came and went. The sun set and the moon rose over Jimmy's second night, floating alone and unconscious out in the middle of the Passage.

Saturday morning on North Manitou was not a good time for the group from the Bible Fellowship, and worse for its leaders, the young guy named Clark and his wife Paula. Two of the group had not yet shown up at the dock, the Ningwis was on its way from Leland, and it never waited for stragglers before departing the island.

Moreover, none of the others had seen anything of Kenny Jennings or Bethany Haggard since they'd all split up, going off on their own the previous Sunday ... six days ago. The park ranger assured them that the two were probably just late because they'd taken a wrong trail and had gotten lost ... that when they finally showed up ... probably in an hour or two ... he'd contact park headquarters in Empire and report that they were safe and sound ... they'd have to spend the night on the island, but would return on tomorrow's boat.

With no other choice, Clark, Paula and their group of religious seekers returned to Leland, minus the two missing children.

Both families were seriously upset when they met the returning ferry, only to find that their children were not aboard. Jake Jr. attempted to ease their concerns by explaining that this had happened before, that there were virtually zero hazards on North Manitou, and that the outcome in previous cases had always been happy ... no one had ever been lost out on North Manitou.

That satisfied the Jennings and the Haggards only until the sun began to go down in the west, and still with no report of anyone having as yet seen their children. At that point they drove to park headquarters in Empire to jointly and urgently request an immediate search on the island. The unhappy answer was that it was not possible ... that it would be virtually impossible to search the island effectively in the darkness.

The park Superintendent promised action first thing the next morning. The Coast Guard in Traverse City had been advised of the situation, and would be sending their helicopter out to search from the air. Meanwhile, she would be sending over a team of rangers who were well trained and highly familiar with North Manitou. They'd go at dawn on the Burton and Nahma to search the island on foot.

She promised that their kids were probably fine, and would be found.

At dawn the next morning, the Coast Guard helicopter from Traverse was on station, and began methodically crisscrossing the island, first east and west, then north and south. The park boats arrived just before seven o'clock with sixteen radio-equipped rangers, who set out in various directions on foot, according to the park's standing search plan. Grant and Mary Jennings, with

Edward Haggard and his wife, arrived on the Ningwis at exactly eleven o'clock. The word also went out to any of the campers and hikers encountered on the island to keep their eyes open for two young teenagers … a boy of twelve and a girl of fifteen … who were probably lost and in need of assistance.

The congregations at Leland and Fountain Point assembled at the usual hour that Sunday morning, minus their ministers, and prayed that the missing children would turn up safe.

In spite of it all, the children had still not been found as nightfall approached, and some began to suspect foul play. The Leelanau County Sheriff and Michigan State Police were notified, and they organized immediate assistance, coming over to the island aboard a variety of vessels of their own, and those volunteered by private parties at Leland's harbor.

Eventually hopes of finding the two kids alive faded, and the searchers began looking for criminal evidence, burials, or human remains. By the following Wednesday, absolutely nothing had turned up, even after intensively searching the island from one end to the other, and there was no point in continuing. In light of that frustrating and terrible reality, the effort was abandoned.

The Jennings and Haggards were beside themselves with worry and grief, but were told by the law enforcement professionals from the park, the sheriff's office, and the state police that the futile search might actually be good news, suggesting an abduction, rather than harm to their children; that bulletins were being distributed nationwide, and nothing more could be done now; that everyone would just have to sit tight and wait for a break in the case.

When Tommy Thomassen heard the news about Kenny, he wept. He was a realist, never having been one to cling to thin hopes. For the first time since having lost his wife, he sat all alone in his house and wept.

———

It was not at all a good week for the Lakeshore. Besides the crisis of missing children on North Manitou, one of their long-time and best-liked volunteers, Larry Bentson, had drowned in a canoeing accident on South Manitou's Lake Florence, his wife Lillian having somehow struggled to shore, but found in critical condition that Thursday, and air-evac'd to Traverse City's Munson Hospital.

The truth of that matter would never be known. It was impossible for most to believe that the Bentsons would tamper with a chain to purloin one of the Robertson's canoes, but the evidence strongly suggested that they had. Lillian had survived only by the happenstance of having come up in an air space inside the overturned canoe. She had remained there in hiding until it seemed safe to try swimming to shore. She was found later that day lying in the reeds along the shoreline, having become a helpless, but propitious host for the lake's abundant leeches. Directly overhead was the eagle's nest, so it was assumed that was the purpose of their impetuous and impromptu canoe outing. Some conjectured that the Bentsons had probably been attacked by one of the eagles after approaching too close to their nest which, the rangers discovered, did contain young.

Lillian Bentson would never be able to set the record straight. The exhaustion and exposure had been too much for her. She died ten days after having been discovered lying exhausted and unconscious on the shore of the little lake.

Her remains were returned downstate to Oakland County, where she was laid to rest next to her husband in Birmingham's Clover Hill Park Cemetery.

————

It was a fine, placid Sunday morning as the search for Kenny and Keegan had commenced in earnest on North Manitou … a clear day with calm seas. Several miles to the south, Jimmy remained adrift with the overturned Sea Scout, having been in the water for three nights, this being his fourth day as a lonely, shipwrecked sailor. But for most of this time, he had not suffered; he had been unconscious.

He was not missed by anyone.

Lee and Josie Smith were still at Indianapolis. They hadn't spoken with Jimmy, since he hadn't answered the phone at the cottage, and had left his cell phone at home in Speedway when he ran away. Neither had they been able to get in touch with the Jennings, nor heard anything from Tommy, so assumed that *no news was good news*. Leland, after all, was a quiet, peaceful place, where he would not be apt to meet with accidents or get into trouble.

As the day developed, the weather began to change. It remained sunny and warm, but the winds steadily picked up during the day to a fresh breeze out of the west-southwest. By four-thirty, the seas were running high enough in the Passage that Jake knew it was going to be a rough ride back to Leland, with lots of pukers, and that a nasty clean-up job would follow. Under these conditions, to avoid as much of that as possible, he would minimize the unpleasantness by running crosswinds, south-southwest, a little over half way to Sleeping Bear, then turn toward Leland and head home, running with the wind and a following sea. It made for a longer trip, but a more comfortable ... and less messy ... ride.

It wasn't long after making the turn towards Leland, that Jake spotted something floating on the water almost directly ahead.

* * *

34

Jake quickly switched the Keche-Chéemann's VHF radio to Channel 16 and peak power ...

"Pan-Pan, Pan-Pan, Pan-Pan ... Traverse City Coast Guard Radio ... this is Keche-Chéemann. I am ... ahh ... three miles off Sleeping Bear Point ... have encountered a small capsized vessel ... looks like maybe a Mackinaw boat ... one survivor in the water ... condition unknown at this point. Over."

"Coast Guard Radio Traverse City ... caller off Sleeping Bear Point say again your vessel. Over."

"*Keche-Chéemann* ... the island ferry out of Leland. Over."

"Coast Guard Radio Traverse ... Gitchee Geemun can you standby and assist? Over."

"Keche-Chéemann ... I am coming about and heaving to windward ... can recover the survivor ... looks like one young male hanging on to the boat's rudder – unresponsive so far ... still no others seen. Standby."

"Coast Guard Radio Traverse ... Gitchee Geemun can you say your exact coordinates? Over."

"Keche-Chéemann ... Standby ... Ahh ... forty-four, fifty-seven, eighteen point three North; eighty-six, zero one, thirty-one point four two West ... I am leaving the bridge momentarily. Standby."

Jake had pulled slowly up to the floating hull, turned the boat parallel to it and brought it to a full stop, such that the big boat was within a few feet of the overturned Sea Scout, and drifting eastward with it. Before leaving the pilot house he announced ...

"Your attention please! We have an emergency.   Passengers will please all move to the seating areas above or below and remain there until otherwise instructed. The crew will clear the front deck immediately and stand by."

The *crew* consisted of two young summer hires ... one boy and one girl, in light khaki shorts, sandals, and navy-blue tee shirts with the white MPFS logo on the breast pocket ... college students whose job ordinarily consisted of collecting tickets, arranging for island tours, selling snacks and refreshments and, on those difficult occasions, distributing vomit bags and cleaning up pukes.

Leaving the pilot house, Jake hurriedly slipped down the stairs from above, sliding on the hand rails, and donned a Mae West life preserver. After grabbing the life ring off the front of the boat's deckhouse, he quickly opened the port side gangway door and jumped overboard, safely tethered to the boat with the life ring's lanyard.

He was only a few feet from the overturned hull, and after swimming to it, worked his way back to its stern, where he saw the inverted name *Sea Scout* as the hull rose and fell with the swells. His heart sank as he recognized Jimmy Sutton, hanging from the top of the rudder; his hand somehow fouled in its hinges, his apparently lifeless body being meanly and repeatedly jerked up out of the water and then splashed back down with each passing wave.

"Oh, Jesus ... ." Jake muttered sorrowfully out loud. Then yelled up to his crew ...

"Throw down the mooring line!"

The two-inch woven nylon rope came splashing down beside him. He wrapped three turns of the line around Jimmy's torso just below his armpits and secured it with a huge rolling hitch.

"Move over to the gangway hatch and take up the slack!" he shouted up to the boy and girl in the navy-blue company tee shirts leaning over the forward deck rail.

"After I free his arm, haul him aboard fast as you can ... keep his head and shoulders above the water!"

Jake was really thinking that probably wouldn't make any difference. Jimmy did not appear to have any life left in him. His eyes were closed, his head, shoulders and shirtless upper body were severely sunburned, and he was totally unresponsive. His wrist looked like it had been crushed. It was obviously broken, since the hand was no longer properly oriented to the forearm, and the wrist had also been worn raw to the bones by the constant chafing against the boat's transom and rudder hinges.

For several moments, Jake couldn't figure out how his hand could have slipped through the small clearance, but then he discovered that as the rudder was turned to one side or the other, the clearance widened. Pushing the rudder fully away from the boy, he was able to gently twist his damaged hand as needed, permitting it to slip out of its mechanical entrapment. It looked like the hand had been yanked out of its socket, just dangling now nonsensically, but there was nothing to be done about that at the moment.

Jake raised his arm to signal the two crew members to begin hauling the boy in, then released Jimmy from his embrace. The two dragged the lifeless body rapidly across the rolling water to the gangway hatch, then struggled mightily to haul it aboard without it getting pummeled against the side of the rolling boat.

Hand over hand, using the light life ring tether, Jake pulled himself rapidly back to the Keche-Chéemann. With the help of the big mooring line and the two young crewmembers, he hauled himself back on-board the big boat.

Jimmy's body had been laid out on the carpeted forward deck, and was being attended to by one of the passengers.

"Is he a doctor?" asked Jake.

"No, but he's an EMT." the boy crewman answered.

Jake knelt down beside Jimmy's body ...

"What's the situation?" he asked the EMT guy.

"He's alive ... just barely."

Jake hurried back up to the pilot house and the VHF radio.

"Keche-Chéemann ... Traverse City Coast Guard Radio ... come back. Over."

"C G R Traverse ... go ahead Jake. Over." It was a new voice.

"I have taken aboard a single survivor ... a boy, about fourteen. He is alive, but in need of immediate ... repeat, *immediate* ... medical attention. Over."

"Standby Keche-Chéemann. C G R Traverse." Jake took notice that the new voice pronounced the name correctly.

"Jake, we have the chopper over at North Manitou. We've diverted it to your location. They'll try dropping a rescue swimmer down on your forward deck to take your survivor directly into the hospital here in Traverse. Hold your position, move the victim forward and clear your forward deck. C G R Traverse."

Jake could see the chopper already headed his way.

320

"Your attention please. We've picked up a survivor, he *is* alive. A Coast Guard chopper is on the way to pick him up. Please remain in your seating areas, and secure any loose materials topside. The chopper will be hovering above the boat for a few minutes, so there will be a blow."

The VHF radio came to life again.

"Coast Guard Rescue Tango-Charlie-Niner-Five ... Keche-Chéemann ... prepare for boarding."

"Roger Niner-Five. Keche-Chéemann." Jake replied.

"C G R Traverse ... Jake, do you have an I.D. on your survivor?"

Jake couldn't identify this voice coming from the Coast Guard's Traverse City Air Station. Obviously, it was someone who knew him fairly well.

"Yes, I have a positive identification. The boy is Jimmy Sutton from Leland ... Lee Smith's grandson. The boat is the old Sea Scout, Tommy Thomassen's Mackinaw boat replica ... also out of Leland." Jake replied.

As the chopper arrived low and overhead, the noise became deafening. The rescue basket was lowered, with a rescue swimmer riding it down. He assisted Jake and his two young crew-members as they carefully lifted Jimmy's body into the basket. He then secured it, and signaled the lift operator in the chopper to hoist away. The basket rapidly rose, twisting rapidly in the chopper's windy downwash. Meanwhile, the rescue swimmer jumped overboard, swam over to the hull of the Sea Scout, and climbed aboard to attach a lighted marker beacon.

The cable was dropped again from the chopper, this time with only a weight ball and hook. The rescue diver was picked off the floating hull and taken back aboard as the chopper quickly lifted away, veering southeastward, heading for Traverse City.

———

The Commander at the Air Station issued a *Special Notice* regarding the floating Sea Scout, now officially *an obstruction posing a hazard to navigation and transiting surface craft*. Then, being a long-time friend of the old Chief, phoned Tommy Thomassen in Leland with the bad news, and for advice about recovering his boat.

Tommy was shaken. He hadn't thought to check on the Sea Scout down on the beach just below his place, because he knew that with Kenny away, Jimmy would not be able to take the boat out.

He was also saddened and confused. Kenny was missing. Now Jimmy had been found out in the passage ... evidently having been floating out there for more than a day or two and nearly dead. He wouldn't have taken the boat out by himself, he knew him well enough to know that ... and Kenny was supposed to have been elsewhere. It didn't make any sense! Both boys in bad trouble? How could all this be happening?

He picked up the phone again and immediately called Indianapolis ...

"Winston ... I've got some bad news ..."

Within the hour, the sleek, white corporate jet was in the air with Lee and Josie Smith. They did not take time to collect their things, rushing to the airport with what they were wearing and with only what they had in their pockets and Josie's purse. Julie could not be reached. Josie left her a voicemail.

———

One of the last of the old Great Lakes ore carriers, the ancient *Perseus Intrepid* persisted in spite of the facts ... she was obsolete, too small to compete with the few remaining ships of a much larger and more modern design, and because of these realities, almost impossible to sail profitably.

Besides being worn out, she wasn't pretty anymore, having been spray painted light gray all over without much preparation, so the rust spots quickly ate through the coating and would gradually all reappear. Rusty streaks decorated the sides of her hull and superstructure, where the rains and splash drizzled down from the expanding rusty patches.

Yet, to her aging owners, and those still interested in the maritime history of the lakes, she was a thing of beauty. She was still fast, and sailed her charted courses with haste and purpose, like a man on a mission. What she lacked in mechanical efficiency was make up for in operational effectiveness. She never tarried in any port. In those special appearances in the Passage, when the old gray ship suddenly came steaming out of a fog bank into the morning sun, she seemed like an apparition ... a ghost from the past ... a vision that thrilled the hearts of those who could still remember the old days.

Her ore carrying days were long over. Now she carried bulk materials, such as gravel, lime and cement, but still sailed regularly between ports on Lakes Huron and Michigan, a familiar sight as she passed under the *Mighty Mac* – the big bridge between Michigan's Lower and Upper Peninsulas.

Because she was always on a tight schedule, she sailed the most direct route to wherever she was bound, which usually took her through the treacherous waters of the Manitou Passage. But to her, the Passage was a familiar and friendly place, whose waters she knew well, having sailed them too many times to count during her long career.

And thus, she came steaming through in the wee hours of a Monday morning, her old helmsman resting on the wheel, her equally aged first mate seated at the chart table behind, pouring over the remainder of the season's schedules. He knew his boat all too well, and would be alerted by the slightest irregular sound or vibration.

"What the hell was that?" wondered the mate, looking up to the helmsman.

There had been a dull thump, and the big boat shuddered ever so slightly.

"Haven't the foggiest." replied the helmsman, without much concern. "Maybe a deadhead."

That really wasn't likely at this place and at this time of year, and they both knew it. Neither of them was in the habit of monitoring the Coast Guard's marine broadcasts, so they were not aware of the special notice that had been published the previous afternoon. Having passed through on this downbound course so many times before, the helmsman was in the habit of paying attention to his distances from the islands to starboard and the mainland off his port side; and only occasionally looked dead ahead.

Both fell quiet, listening intently for what would probably come next. Within a matter of seconds, the ship shuddered a little more intensely as whatever it was got chopped up by her screws. They switched on the big spotlight atop the bridge and swung its beam aft, searching the wake for flotsam, but could see nothing.

Hence, they decided it must indeed have just been a floating log. The old mate went back to his schedules, and the elderly helmsman relaxed again at the wheel.

The poor Sea Scout had been run over and destroyed. When the salvage tug arrived later in the morning, they would find nothing but floating wreckage ... and the wreckage of Eddie Gunderson.

* * *

35

Jimmy remained unconscious at Munson for two days, opening his eyes for the first time the following Tuesday afternoon. He was alone; he did not know where. As his eyes began to focus, he saw it was a bright, clean place ... and then he saw the tubes connected to his forearm, and the cardiac monitor, and all the rest of it, and realized it was a hospital.

His moment of consciousness was immediately detected at the nurses' station. Two uniformed attendants hurried into the room, followed by his worried-looking grandparents.

"Welcome back." he heard one of the attendants say, seemingly from far away.

He took a little flashlight from a pocket in his smock, alternately shining it back and forth; first in one eye, then the other.

"No, don't move yet." the attendant cautioned as he attempted to avoid the bright light.

His voice had begun to sound closer now. Since he complied, the attendant decided that his hearing had not been seriously impaired by his ordeal in the lake.

"You got yourself a serious sunburn." the attendant explained. "We think it will heal without extraordinary measures ... no skin grafts or whatever ... but until that process begins, I want you to be very careful about stressing the skin in these areas, causing more damage than we already have here. Understand?"

"Yes." Jimmy whispered, trying not to move his lips.

He had tried to say it, but found that his voice didn't work. It was because they had only very recently removed the tracheal tube, permitting him to breathe naturally on his own.

The attendant, which he now assumed was a doctor, patted him on his sheet-covered thigh and turned to his grandparents.

"He's coming along very, very well, considering the circumstances. I think we're probably out of the woods now, but now that he's conscious, he'll need to be constantly watched until we can determine where he's at emotionally." Lee nodded affirmatively.

"The sheriff is also eager to see him. I'm not going to permit that just yet. We'll see how he's doing tomorrow."

Lee nodded affirmatively again, without saying anything.

"You two are welcome to stay now, but you won't be able to watch him around the clock. Are there other relatives?"

Lee wagged his head negatively ... then abruptly changed his mind. It occurred to him that Tommy would help, and the three of them could do eight-hour shifts, until Julie finally arrived. So far, they'd heard nothing from her.

"Yes, I think we can handle it ... my wife and I and a personal friend who's very close to the boy. And we expect his mother will also be here shortly."

"Okay. So, I'll leave it to you then. But *do not* leave him alone until I tell you otherwise ... not even for a minute. If it turns out you can't handle the watch, let me know and I'll arrange a security detail. That would be at your expense, of course."

Again, Lee nodded affirmatively. The doctor and the nurse then left the room.

"What day is this?" Jimmy whispered.

"It's Tuesday, dear." Josie answered.

"Is my mother here?"

Lee and Josie noticed that he had referred to their daughter as *mother*, rather than his usual *Julie*.

"Not yet, dear." answered Josie gently. "We haven't been able to find her yet. But we left her a voicemail. She'll soon be calling, I'm sure."

Jimmy's memory had not been impaired in any way by his ordeal in the lake. He felt fear grip him a little when he heard the doctor mention the *sheriff*, and *security*. At first, he assumed they probably knew everything.

"Jamie, do you remember what happened?" asked Josie.

"A little ... maybe." he whispered. Josie's question suddenly suggested that perhaps nobody else really did know everything.

"What happened?" he asked, directing the question towards either of them.

"Well, for some reason you were out in the Sea Scout with Eddie Gunderson ..." his grandfather replied "... and somehow you turtled your boat."

"Did Eddie tell you what happened." asked Jimmy, fishing for further information by pretending not to remember much.

"Eddie's gone, Jamie." answered Josie, again as gently as she could put it. "He drowned."

Lee filled in some details.

"When the boat went over, he somehow got his neck fouled in the rigging near the top of the mast. It pulled him under and

328

trapped him thirty feet under the water. It was almost like a hanging, but upside down."

"Is our boat okay?"

"The Sea Scout's gone too, Jamie." Lee answered with an expression of finality.

"How? What happened?"

"She got run over in the night by the old *Intrepid.* She was totally broken up. Eddie was too; part of him was found floating with the spar ..."

"Lee ... not now." admonished Josie.

"It's alright." Jimmy interrupted. "I'll be alright with it. What happened."

"Well, Eddie and the boat went through the Intrepid's screws, got chopped up and spit out. It wasn't pretty." answered his grandfather. "And that's the whole long and short of it."

"We're going to have Tommy come down here and sit with you. That'll be three of us. But before he comes, you should know that ..."

"Why do I have to be watched?" interrupted Jimmy. "Are they worried that I'll try to escape or something?"

Josie looked at Lee, meeting his surprised expression with her own. Then they both smiled softly, presuming that Jamie was being facetious ... a good sign. His sense of humor apparently coming back quickly.

"No, Jamie." Josie responded. "They're concerned about your emotional condition. After all, you've been through a very harrowing ordeal."

"A suicide watch!" Jimmy exclaimed in a louder hoarse whisper.

Josie smiled lovingly, indicating that she understood.

"Anyway ..." Lee continued "... we'll have Tommy share the watch. He'll be happy to sit with you, but you need to know that there's more bad news – Kenny isn't back yet from the North Manitou thing. He and a girl are missing."

Jimmy turned his head away from them as the tears began streaming down the sides of his temples. Josie went to him, hugging him around the waist, avoiding his sunburned upper body.

"I'm so sorry Jamie. We know how upsetting that news must be for you too. Tommy is also very upset ... he was almost beside himself."

"What happened?" Jimmy whispered through his tears.

"Nobody knows yet, dear. They've searched all over the island, but haven't been able to come up with anything. They just somehow vanished. But something will turn up ... you'll see. We're all praying that they'll be found safe and sound somewhere."

Jimmy now understood that little was apparently known about what had happened ... only what they'd seen; that he and Eddie had gone out for a boat ride, it had somehow capsized ... not unexpected for a damned Mackinaw boat ... his arm somehow got caught in the rudder, miraculously saving his life, while Eddie had not been so lucky. Apparently, that accident had not been connected with the disappearance of Kenny and Keegan. He was extremely upset inside, knowing what he knew, but not knowing how much of it to reveal, or to whom

"If you want to stay here, I'll go up and get Tommy, and we'll see if we can get into the Park Place." Lee suggested to Josie.

She nodded, and he left. The Park Place Hotel had been a landmark in Traverse for many years, and Lee Smith was a favored client. They would have no trouble being accommodated there for as long as it might take to get Jimmy well and back to Leland. Josie took to a chair beside the bed, opened her purse, retrieved a small paperback book, and, greatly relieved now that Jimmy was safe and on the mend, quietly resumed her reading.

Continuing with his thoughts, Jimmy remembered Kenny's parents ... his poor, poor parents ... and Keegan's ... and even Eddie's father Oscar ... probably crying their eyes out ... hoping against hope for an outcome that could never be. At least in Oscar's case, he knew the awful truth ... that his only son was gone ... and he at least had a body to bury. Kenny and Keegan might never be found if he kept his mouth shut about what they had done, and what had happened out in the lake. Their parents would never know what had happened to their child.

And it was he who had killed them ... he, himself. With his stupidly careless attempt to stop Eddie from harming Kenny, he had killed them himself. And maybe Eddie wasn't even actually going to throw them overboard anyway ... maybe he was just trying to be hateful and mean ... to scare the daylights out of them. He felt like a murderer. He had killed his best friend. It was too much to bear. He turned his head away from his grandmother, letting the tears silently soak into the pillow.

———

It was after dark when Tommy came to relieve Josie. Jimmy did not know exactly when he had arrived. He had fallen asleep sometime after Lee left. He didn't know when, or for how long, but could see it was now dark outside.

Turning his head towards his grandmother's replacement ...

"Hello Mr. Thomassen." he rasped.

"Hi Jimmy. You look like hell; how are you feeling."

"Okay, I guess. The skin on my face and shoulders feels really tight. But it doesn't hurt much."

"Yeah, you got burnt to a crisp, that's for sure. How long were you out in the water?"

Jimmy gave that some thought. He had decided to be guarded about answering questions ... about getting himself in trouble by giving incriminating answers, or tripping himself up by lying. Kenny and Keegan were gone, and he had decided to leave well enough alone. Their parents might be better off never knowing what happened to them ... that their children were tortured by Eddie and drowned by him ... Keegan with Eddie's baby in her belly. Destroying himself would not bring them back, or make things any better. For the time being, at least, he would answer what he could answer factually, else claim he didn't know, or couldn't remember.

"I guess since last Thursday afternoon." he answered in a carefully measured way.

"Four days and nights! Jesus Christ, boy, you're lucky to be alive after that much time in the lake ... lucky your hand got caught in the rudder ... and most of all, lucky that Jake got you out of there before Sunday night."

"What happened Sunday night?" wondered Jimmy.

"That's when the lake boat ran over your boat, chopping her to pieces. Her mate logged that for 02:23 hours Monday morning. They knew they'd hit something and run it over, but weren't able to see what. When the Rowan Brothers showed up later that morning to right her and bring 'er in, there wasn't much left but kindling wood."

He felt like telling Mr. Thomassen that he had jammed his hand between the rudder and the transom on purpose, but decided not to say it ... that it would probably not be wise to volunteer any information that he didn't have to.

Tommy went back to his evening newspaper, which he had been reading before Jimmy awoke.

"That was a helluva week for the park!" he uttered, shaking his head.

"One boy drowned off South, one almost, two kids lost on North, one old volunteer drowned on South, his old lady here in critical condition ... probably also done for ..."

"What?" Jimmy asked, suddenly alerted.

"Oh, I thought they already told you about Kenny." he apologized in a strangely weak voice.

"No, I mean about the volunteers."

Tommy passed him the newspaper. On page two of the Record-Eagle, the headline of a small article said ...

Mrs. Bentson Still Critical

Reading on, he learned that the two were thought to have taken a canoe out on Lake Florence last Thursday, were probably attacked by an eagle, and tipped over. Rev. Lawrence Bentson, a long-time park volunteer had drowned. Mrs. Bentson had somehow made it to shore, but was found unconscious and was rushed to Munson Medical Center in Traverse. Her condition remained critical, but stabile. Rev. Bentson's body was recovered by a Coast Guard team the following day near the middle of the lake.

He realized at once that Eddie was, without doubt, the culprit ... that he had murdered the old man, his wife having somehow survived. He remembered Eddie having returned soaking wet and saying ... *They decided to go swimming. They won't be coming back.* He also realized that he was hopelessly implicated in this mess too ... that when Mrs. Bentson recovered, she'd have a story to tell. Then it would all come out.

As he folded the paper and handed it back to Tommy, he didn't know that he had just shared time and space with Lillian Bentson in intensive care, where she still remained, just down the hall, and just barely clinging to life.

* * *

36

The next day, Jama came to see him, and she came the following day too. Jimmy was glad to see her. He felt comfortable with her, and closer than ever before. She was all that remained of his summertime friendships now.

She arrived during his grandmother's shifts. Josie liked her, and trusted her. After exchanging a bit of pleasant conversation, she would thoughtfully excuse herself, retiring to the hospital's cafeteria, leaving them alone.

Jimmy expected that Jama would have questions, but she never asked anything about the boating accident, or their missing friend Kenny. Jimmy wasn't comfortable with that ... not knowing what she might actually be thinking. When he finally tried to bring those things up, she stopped him immediately.

"I don't need to know anything more about that, Jamie." she said. "All I need to know is what I see ... that you're safe, and are getting well again."

He was relieved and touched by the kindly way she said it, understanding now that he meant a lot to her ... that somehow, they were quickly becoming more than just friends. As in his mind he pictured better days ... himself, Jama and Kenny laying on the beach in the shade of the Sea Scout so many weeks ago, the familiar lump in his chest began to grow again, and he could feel his eyes moistening.

He didn't want to be such a wimp! ... always in tears! He tried to fight it, but it was no use. Tears came anyway.

So did hers. She got up from her chair, sat beside his legs on the edge of the bed, laid her head in his lap ... and cried with him. He gently stroked her soft hair with is good hand, and for a long time they were quiet.

Nothing more was said of it.

————

The Leelanau County Sheriff arrived on Friday morning. It was a meeting that Jimmy had been foreboding since hearing of it two days before. He arrived with Lee, in plain clothes, and with a woman, also in plain clothes, who he introduced as a detective. Josie had been *on watch*, as it were, and after having introduced the detective, she, Lee and the Sheriff left the room.

"How's the wrist?" the detective began.

"It's fine ... sore. I guess it looked a lot worse than it really was." he answered, wiggling his fingers, which protruded from the top of the bandaging, to demonstrate that the hand was already partially functional again.

"I suppose you know why I'm here?" the detective began.

"I guess." answered Jimmy, with a shrug ... then grimacing from the pain of the sunburn on his neck and shoulders. "Well, not exactly. Is it about the accident?"

"We can start there. How did it happen?"

"I'm not sure. I was steering and Eddie stood up to do something on the starboard side. I guess we screwed up. I should have yelled *"Gybing!"* to warn him, but I didn't ... so I guess it's mainly my fault. The boom hit him, and he got knocked overboard. Then the boat flipped over, the mast hit him, and he went under."

As he said that, in his mind he was picturing the actual events of that moment, with Kenny and Keegan bound and laden with the concrete blocks ... Kenny screaming *JIMMEEE!* ... and then the two of them going overboard and disappearing without a sound as the boat capsized. It was too much for him again, and he began crying softly.

"I'm really sorry, Jimmy." offered the detective. "I'm sure that's a terrible thing to remember. Would you like a moment?"

"No, it's alright. I always do this ... I'm a wimp!"

"I doubt it." she objected. "You were able to stay with the boat?"

She was taking notes on everything he said. He wondered why she didn't have a voice recorder. She just kept asking questions with her head down, busily scribbling on a yellow legal pad.

"It was just luck. I don't swim very good ... I panic. But I somehow managed to struggle back to the hull, and then work my way back to the stern."

"How did your arm get caught in the rudder."

"It didn't ... I put my hand through the gap so in case I passed out or something, the boat would keep my head and shoulders out of the water."

"Eddie never reappeared?"

"I never saw him again after he went under."

"You weren't supposed to take the boat out?"

"No."

"Then why did you?"

"Eddie wanted to go out ... he said he knew how to sail it ... that he'd been out in it before with Mr. and Mrs. Thomassen ..."

"What day was that?"

"Sunday, after the ferries left."

She stopped writing, and looked up.

"Sunday?"

Jimmy began to get uncomfortable. The questions were heading into difficult areas and he was trying to answer everything very carefully, without having to lie about any of it.

"It was probably about ten-thirty. I didn't want to go, but got coaxed into it ... he said he knew how to sail the Sea Scout."

"Did he?"

"Did he what?"

"Know how to handle the boat?"

"No. He was lying."

"Where did you go that morning?"

"We ran over to North Manitou, like we did on our first trip with Mr. Thomassen and Gramps after we fixed the boat."

"The accident was on the following Thursday." she stated factually, looking up to prompt an answer.

"We took the boat out again and sailed over to South. It happened on the way back."

That answer called for a lot of assumptions on her part.

Jimmy was praying that she would not go for details.

"Kenneth Jennings and you were best friends?" she asked.

Jimmy felt a tinge of relief as the subject seemed to have abruptly changed.

"Yes."

"And the Haggard girl? ... you knew her also?"

"Who?"

"Bethany Haggard ... Eddie's girlfriend."

"Oh, I didn't know that was her name."

"Then I assume you didn't know her."

Jimmy understood that was a question, but didn't answer.

He merely shrugged his shoulders, and then winced again.

"You did, or you didn't?"

"I knew he had a girlfriend. She was called Keegan. She's my girlfrien... er, *my friend's* ... cousin."

"Your girlfriend?" asked the detective, with a coy smile.

"Well, she's a girl, and we're friends."

"Name?"

"Jama Kelly"

"Is she friends with Kenny too?"

"Yes."

"What were you and Eddie doing on the dock Sunday morning, the week before last?"

"I helped Kenny carry his things down there. I guess Eddie was doing the same ... for his girlfriend."

"And you stayed to see them off?"

"Yes."

"Why didn't you go with that group?"

"I wasn't invited ... we're Catholic."

"Did you ask?"

"No. Kenny didn't want to go either."

"Then why did he?"

"His dad's the minister; he made him ... to set an example for the other kids, I guess."

"Did Kenny have any enemies that you know of ... anyone who would want to hurt him?"

"He doesn't like Eddie, and Eddie didn't like him."

He was framing his answers cautiously, being careful to refer to Kenny and Keegan in the present tense.

"Was there a problem between them?"

"They were just different. Eddie was crude and vulgar; Kenny is polite and decent. I think Eddie wanted to be liked ... like Kenny is. He was probably mostly just jealous."

"That's all?"

"That's all I know of. Kenny is really nice ..." then the tears came rushing back "... nobody would want to hurt him."

She continued writing on the yellow legal pad, waiting for him to compose himself again.

"You and Kenny were very close?" she asked quietly.

He noticed that she had been just as careful to refer to Kenny and Keegan in the past tense ... perhaps she was trying to trip him up.

"I love him ... like a brother I mean. He's the best friend I've ever had."

"Uh-huh." she acknowledged, and wrote something more down ... a lengthy notation.

"Can you tell me if there was any reason why Kenny and Bethany might want to run off together?"

"No." Jimmy answered emphatically. "Kenny's only twelve!"

He was going to add that Keegan was fifteen ... too old for a twelve-year-old boy, but stopped himself. No need to revisit the detective's assumption that he didn't know much about Keegan.

"And she was ...?"

340

Jimmy just shrugged again, and wagged his head a little.

"Eddie was nineteen." he volunteered, as a more complete response to her question, suggesting that he understood that the girl was older than Kenny.

"Bethany Haggard was only fifteen ... just fifteen." she told him.

"Oh."

"Is there anything more you want to tell me, Jimmy?"

"I don't know ... I don't think so."

"Well, we're done here, then. We appreciate your help, and I'm very sorry for your situation. I hope you'll be feeling better soon ... time heals, you know."

"Thanks."

"Here's my card. If you think of anything that might help us find your friend and Bethany, call me ... any time, day or night. Okay?"

"Okay."

As the detective left, Josie and Jama came in immediately. Jimmy was a little edgy. He was relieved that the interrogation was over, and thought that he had probably done a good job of answering the questions without raising more questions or incriminating himself, but she had been a little cagey and probing, so he couldn't be sure.

For her part, the detective met up with her boss and Lee Smith at a table in the hospital's cafeteria. Over coffee, she reported to the Sheriff that Jimmy had been pleasant, relaxed and cooperative, but evidently didn't have much to offer that they didn't already know ... that he was apparently really broken up by what he'd been through, and even more by the news that his friend was missing.

As they parted, she complimented Lee on his cute grandson ... such a nice boy, and a fine young man.

The doctor had approved the Sheriff's visit that day, because he had decided to discharge his patient that afternoon, and he decided it would be better to be done with that before Jimmy left the hospital. He still had lingering doubts about the boy's emotional situation ... he seemed to be adjusting too early and too easily from what, all things considered, should have been a severe emotional trauma.

He was not comfortable with the situation, but it was only a hunch. There was, clinically, no reason to keep him. With his grandparents, old Mr. Thomassen, and the girlfriend, he seemed to have a capable support group.

On the other hand, his mother had still not surfaced, and the boy had never commented on her absence.

That was not a positive indication.

* * *

37

Leland did not seem the same anymore. The scenery had not changed, of course, nor its people or the summer crowd. The days were still pleasant, and the sunsets were still beautiful. But he didn't feel like a part of it now. He felt more like a visitor, or perhaps not even that ... maybe like a ghost who roamed all the familiar places, but invisible to everyone, and not belonging with anyone.

Jama came every day now. They'd usually just sit at the picnic table at the end of the lawn, overlooking the lake. Sometimes they'd go down the steps and walk the beach, but only once did they go past the little point, towards Mr. Thomassen's place. The sight of that spot, and the missing Sea Scout, stirred up memories that were, as yet, too painful to revisit. So, they'd usually walk the other way, shinny around the fence with the *No Trespassing* sign, then sometimes sit on the Fishtown dock and watch the water falling over the Leland River damn.

Jama understood that he was rapidly healing physically, but not at all emotionally. He often seemed detached and disinterested. Sometimes when sitting quietly at the picnic table, across from each other and holding hands, or while watching the water, he'd suddenly begin to cry. He was jumpy, and complained of sleeplessness and dreaming. She guessed that he was suffering from *post-traumatic stress,* thinking it would be totally understandable under the circumstances, so she read up on that to learn how she might be able to help him. Everything she read suggested that she should encourage him to talk about the traumatic event and the things he was feeling. But Jimmy wouldn't talk. He just looked down and shook his head *no* ... as though he couldn't.

If Eddie had actually just been trying to destroy his close, companionate relationship with his grandfather, he had succeeded. At the time, Jimmy rejected his nasty comments and accusations, yet some of what Eddie said seemed to have a spark of credibility in it.

He already knew that his grandfather had an eye for boys the ages Eddie had mentioned ... he'd often seen an attractive looking boy catch his eye when they were out and about. He also came to realize that he really didn't know much about his grandfather ... what he did on all the trips he made up here and elsewhere ... what he did at night, in the wee hours ... why he kept permanent accommodations at the Leland Lodge and the Park Place. He was rich enough to be able to do whatever he wanted, and pretty much whenever and wherever he wanted.

Since they had returned to Leland, he had begun to watch his grandfather more closely, and listen to the things he said more carefully. At odd moments he began musing through his memory, searching his recollections for similar evidence. Some of the vaguely understood things that Gramps had said in the past now seemed clear, and damning. He gradually began to suspect that Eddie had been telling the truth ... that his grandfather was a homosexual pedophile ... a boy lover.

That, no doubt, was why Gramps and Julie had never gotten along ... she had made the mistake of being born a girl.

Besides, as Eddie said, *like grandfather, like grandson*. He knew it was true; he, too, was queer ... and a boy lover. He had loved the younger kid at the Culver camps, and he had loved Kenny. And he had molested them both. He liked Jama, but the same kinds of feelings didn't arise when he was with her. He was not interested in touching her, like he was with Kenny.

The suspicions and the bad feelings metastasized in his poisoned mind like a cancer, until the thought of being like Lee Smith eventually disgusted and sickened him. Would he too turn out to be a murderer, like his grandfather? He couldn't call him *Gramps* anymore. If he had to call him anything, he began to call him Lee. But most of the time he just avoided him.

He wondered about his grandmother now too ... and Tommy Thomassen. How could they not know about Lee Smith and his little boyfriends? Maybe Tommy was in on it ... maybe he was one too. He doubted that Josie was, but resented her being so ignorant about what had been going on right under her nose all those years. Yet maybe she was; perhaps to selfishly preserve her life of leisure, affluence and influence, she had intentionally chosen denial while her meal ticket molested and murdered young boys.

Julie had finally called, the Sunday after he was discharged from Munson. She had been away with a friend, on a fourteen-day Royal Caribbean excursion to *the land of the midnight sun*. After learning that he had passed the crisis, was out of the hospital and was apparently doing well, she decided to come up the following Saturday to set Lee and Josie straight once and for all on the custody thing, and take her son back home to Speedway.

So, she had been on an excursion with *a friend*. What friend? Knowing what he now knew about himself and her father, he suspected that Julie was probably queer too. That would explain why she had never loved him, never hit it off with guys, and usually did things, like this so-called *excursion*, with a *girlfriend*. His mother was a lesbian!

As his attitude became increasing dark, Jama had become increasingly distant. Ultimately, the only bright spot left in his life was Jake Robinson. Jake seemed to understand his crappy situation, and was interested in helping him cope with it. As the days went by, he grew closer and closer to Jake, almost like he used to feel about Gramps, but more so … like Jake really cared and could be trusted. Almost like the father he'd never had.

Understanding that the boy needed to have his mind diverted from his troubles, Jake took him on as a crewmember. Not a real part of the crew, of course, because he was underage and could not be legally employed. But he was outfitted in the light khaki shorts and navy-blue tee shirt with the white MPFS logo on the breast pocket, and invited to ride the Keche-Chéemann and help out whenever he felt up to it. Jake paid him the same as the college kids … under the table, of course.

* * *

38

As the last week of August had arrived. most of the summer people left to spend Labor Day at home with their extended families ... a last summer celebration as the days grew shorter and cooler, and the sun's shadows lengthened.

Already, there were lots of empty seats on Jake's big boat; it was probably not really even worth making the trip. After Labor Day, the ferries would begin sailing a limited schedule, no longer leaving every day at ten. After Labor Day the streets of Leland would, once again, become deserted and quiet.

Jimmy stood in the port side door of the pilot house, half in and half out as the Keche-Chéemann pulled away from the South Manitou dock. It was exactly four thirty. Her horn had announced her departure ... the familiar one long; three shorts. The ranger and a couple of volunteers, the only people left on the dock, waved farewell as they always did, to nobody in particular. He did not wave back.

Running her in reverse with rudders hard to port, Jake skillfully backed her diagonally away from the dock and into deeper water, until he was far enough out to swing her around, and then she headed due east out of the bay. Jimmy came in and sat next to him, looking out over the bow and the passengers on the forward deck. He no longer felt special about being up top in this privileged seat.

It was a fine, calm late afternoon, which promised an especially smooth and relaxing cruise back to the Leland harbor for the few who were aboard. When the weather was good, return trips were always much more settled and quiet than trips to the island, with the excitement of the day trippers having abated, returning volunteers tuckered out, and returning campers snoozing in their seats above and below, or seated on the floor of the forward deck, quietly recounting the memories they'd be taking back home.

After well underway, Jake climbed down off his captain's chair at the helm, and motioned for Jimmy to take his place.

"How about you taking over for a moment, while I go below and relieve myself." he offered.

In times past, he would have been excited and eager for such an opportunity to, frankly, show off. Jake had never done this before, so he was pretty sure it was another attempt to get his mind off the bad things, and to cheer him up. It was thoughtful of Jake to try, and taking him under his wing, as it were, was indeed an unusually kind gesture from this man whom many thought of as being rather self-centered and difficult. He knew that.

But he also knew that Jake didn't know the truth of all that had happened at South Manitou, and that made him feel guilty about accepting his kindnesses.

"Just keep her on her present course ..." instructed Jake, pointing to a faint bright landmark just south of the Leland harbor "... just make for the whaleback out there. I'll be back up in a minute or two."

It turned out to be much more than a minute or two, of course, and when Jake did come back up, he gave no indication that he

348

wanted to take back the helm. When Jimmy moved to get up, he put a hand on his shoulder, indicating that he could stay put. Except for an occasional correction for her slight northward drift, the Keche-Chéemann didn't need much steering. She seemed to know where she was going. So, Jimmy sat back, as he'd often seen her other helmsmen do, and relaxed. He was quiet, mostly because he was absorbed in thoughts of his own, and also because he was not able to think of anything to say.

"When will you be leaving?" asked Jake, attempting to make conversation.

"This weekend, I guess. My mother's supposed to be coming up today. Lee and grandma will be here for a while yet."

"I heard they were thinking about staying up here permanently."

"It didn't work out." answered Jimmy, offering no further detail.

"What about you ... wouldn't you like to stay up here? It's really not so bad in the winter, you know. You might like it."

"Nah, I don't ..."

He stopped himself. He was going to say that he didn't feel like he belonged here anymore ... like he didn't know how he could stay here where everything seemed to remind him of the better days; recollections which always dredged up his feelings of guilt and remorse. He didn't see how he could continue living with Lee, after all the things Eddie had revealed about him, while always wondering if it was true, and if it was still going on. He suspected it was, largely because of what Eddie had so often also said about him ... that he was just like his grandpa. Indeed, the reality seemed to be that he, himself, was *queer* for young boys. Where else would it have come from?

"I'd like to get some air." he said, getting up to give the helm back to Jake.

Jake took over again, comically saying "I have the con."

"Aye. You have the con Captain." Jimmy replied, attempting a smile as he left the cabin.

He walked back to the rear of the top deck passenger area and leaned against the rail looking forward, with the breeze in his face. There were only a small number of people up top, most apparently preferring the more restful seats in the lower cabin. He thought about his mother flying up in the jet to take him home, and thought that Speedway never really felt like *home*, the way Leland always had. But then his next thought was that, for him, Leland would never feel that way again ... that he had succeeded in ruining everything that had made this place so dear to his heart. He wondered if he would ever again have any place to go where he would feel welcomed, loved and safe.

Through the small windows in the back side of the pilot house he could see that Jake had assumed his regular relaxed posture, behind the helm, looking forward across the bow to the distant mainland. Off to port they were just passing by *the crib*, the offshore lighthouse on the end of the North Manitou Shoal. They were much further out in deep water now than during the morning trip.

Many of the passengers in front of him were leaning on each other, else sitting alone with heads down, resting or asleep; a few were reading; two small boys were sitting on the painted steel deck near the front, facing each other and playing with something together.

With nobody noticing, he lifted his right leg over the rail he had been leaning on, and having gained an outboard foothold, his left. Nobody noticed as he let himself slide down over the large Lexan windows on the back of the lower passenger cabin, onto the small ledge atop the Keche-Chéemann's wide transom. The few people inside the lower cabin were also mostly snoozing or reading, so none of them noticed him either.

With that, he leaned back and let go, falling into the backwash of the boat's powerful propellers, and thus being quickly pushed under the water and out several yards.

When he surfaced, the Keche-Chéemann was well ahead of him, still making towards Leland. Nobody had noticed him leaving the boat. No alarm had been raised.

He lay in the water on his back; flipping his hands back and forth much like a fish's fins and frog-kicking lightly, watching the distance stretch between himself and the back of the boat. A man came to the rail on the top deck, peering out in his direction with a hand to his forehead as a visor, as if he might have thought he'd seen something out in the ferry's rolling backwash and spreading wake. But with the setting sun casting a golden path across the water, from the horizon, over the boy, and right up to the back of the boat, he could not be seen, and the man eventually dropped his gaze and returned to his seat.

Laying on his back in the water, he looked up to the sky, where the setting sun was just beginning to paint the edges and bottoms of what had been the day's beautifully fluffy clouds. He stopped his hands and his feet, and for a moment continued to float on the surface without any effort.

As he very slowly began to sink, with his eyes still open, the clouds began to blur, and the little wind ripples on the surface of the gently rolling water now above him sparkled in gold and silver as they randomly caught reflections of the setting sun. Under the water it was suddenly silent, except for the sound of the boat, ever so far off now; a faint and unfamiliar humming-swishing sound. He let go his instinctually held breath, and as he breathed the clean, clear water into his lungs, it felt cool and soft inside his chest ... and friendly ... not choking.

Continuing downward, the golden and silver sparkles became smaller and dimmer until they had mostly disappeared, as had the sounds of the Keche-Chéemann. The water was beginning to feel warmer now, he thought. That, and the silence of the increasingly darkening depths, seemed to take his sorrows and fears away, leaving in their place a cozy, welcoming feeling, much like what he always felt upon crawling into his bed upstairs at the cottage ... a feeling of coming home again ... of being in a place where he was loved and safe as evening fell.

As the depths continued to darken, his body began a backward roll, sending him more rapidly towards the bottom, where a brightening now seemed to appear far below, like the afternoon sun shining on a clean, sandy bottom. Feeling increasingly euphoric, it seemed as if that was where he must go. From somewhere down there he heard a sweet treble voice singing. He grew frantically eager to reach the brightness and the song ... to get to that place so far below where peace and joy awaited!

Spreading his arms and his legs, now swimming with all the elegance and beauty of form as his poor lost friend, he felt like a bird of the sea ... like an eagle, gracefully and joyously soaring into the depths.

He did not panic – he was not afraid.

* * *

BoysMind Books

Grand Haven, Michigan USA